The Tribe: (R)Evolution

A.J. PENN

CUMULUS PUBLISHING LIMITED

Copyright

Published in 2019 by Cumulus Publishing Limited

Visit The Tribe's website at **www.tribeworld.com**

Contact addresses for Cumulus Publishing Limited
and companies within the Cloud 9 Screen Entertainment group
can be found at www.entercloud9.com

Dedication

Dedicated to all fans of The Tribe, both young and old,
along with all those who have the courage to dream -
and the resolve to always keep that dream alive.

PREFACE

It was the sound that woke her. A piercing cry of a bird calling out. Tai San's eyes flicked open, startled by what she was hearing. The harsh screech of a gull, wings fluttering, joined quickly by that of several more - a cacophony of noise growing in intensity, curious at this newcomer in their midst.

Tai San quickly leapt off her bed, moving to the window in her cabin to try and gauge her surroundings. With the seagulls darting around, it could only mean one thing – they must be approaching land. Their destination. Wherever that destination might be.

Opening the window, Tai San breathed in a welcome intake of fresh air, the sea breeze rustling her hair as it rushed into the cabin.

More seagulls raced past her window, squawking in anticipation as they clustered around the back of the ship, joining in a feeding frenzy as the powerful engines churned up frothy waters, bringing fish to the surface in their wake.

Angling her head to the side to get a better look at the front, she could see the bow of the ship ploughing through the waters, throwing up mists of spray – but it was clear to her from sensing the movement of the vessel that they were gradually slowing down, the ship on a slight angle as it altered course, heading towards the large landmass before them.

The land itself seemed hostile, unwelcoming, a stark series of jagged cliff faces towering above the waters, their rocky silhouettes under the shadow of bleak ominous clouds, the sun yet to pierce through the dark morning skies, the only life outside being the seagulls greeting the ship.

Tai San felt a sense of foreboding, nervous in anticipation of where they were going, why they were going there – and what it all meant for her.

The ship had been travelling for many days and nights and Tai San herself felt further away than ever before from the city that had once been her home.

She missed the Mall Rats greatly. They were not only her tribe but her closest friends and allies. Since the demise of the adults they had become more like her new family.

Her heart ached with the pain of being so far away from them. Especially Lex. He was more than just her lover. The only true one for her. She missed his voice, his very presence, the tenderness of his touch. His spirit, his lively personality that was always so full of surprises, brightening each of Tai San's days with his life force, as it used to do. Thinking of Lex and the many times he made her laugh, the wonderful moments they had shared made Tai San smile. But each recollection also stabbed at her heart with the ache that she was no longer with him.

Now more than ever before, she felt truly alone – as if the unknown land before her was another world and that the life she once knew and the people she cared for was in another lifetime. When she had once been free, an independent spirit.

2

For too long Tai San had been a captive. This voyage was the latest in a number of journeys she had been forced to take since losing her freedom.

She had lived the life of a slave, passed from owner to owner, bought and sold like an inanimate object, treated like a possession, stripped away of her very humanity. But never her self-respect. She held onto that with every ounce of her fibre and being, determined that no matter the adversities inflicted upon her by her captors, she would never forget where she had come from or who she was. She wouldn't lose her sense of identity, her dignity. If she ever did, she knew in her heart she would only lose herself forever. By retaining her spirit she somehow would always remain free.

Her current 'master' called himself The Broker. He had bought Tai San at a slave auction many months earlier. Prior to that she had lived an arduous existence performing manual slave labour in the fields, an agonizing routine filled with back-breaking work, day after day, with no respite.

The Broker, by contrast, for some reason put Tai San in a state of material comfort prior to embarking upon this latest voyage. And she could never understand why. For many months she had lived in *The Gardens of The East*, a once luxury hotel from the adult era. She had been given her own room, was always well fed, but had spent most of her days alone in confinement. The only times she had human contact was when the guards brought her meals, a fresh change of clothes – or when she was taken for questioning, 'meetings' as he liked to call them, with The Broker, the master of her enslavement.

The Broker had asked her many times about her experiences at Eagle Mountain, the mysterious, abandoned scientific base in an apparent observatory not far from Tai San's own city. She had gone there with the Mall Rats not long after the virus and they had discovered equipment, cryptic messages the adults had put in place for the surviving younger generation to inherit and use in the aftermath of the adults' own extinction.

The Broker had wanted to know everything, in fine detail, and had interrogated Tai San repeatedly about what she had seen, double-checking facts, information, meticulous in his research and line of questions.

But it was his interest in the lives of the members of the Mall Rats – as well as Tai San's own life story – that had initially bewildered and then caused Tai San concern.

She had been reluctant to tell him anything – her life was private, what she had done, where she had been, her thoughts on her tribe. These were all cherished memories, precious, for only herself to know. Even had she chosen to co-operate, Eagle Mountain was in fact a complete mystery and clearly whatever the reasons behind the interrogation, The Broker was as intrigued about the existence of Eagle Mountain as she and the Mall Rats had been.

But Tai San was wise enough to realize that her very survival was very much dependent upon The Broker believing she had information which could be useful, so she played along. It was her only hope of fighting back. Drip-feeding details which were sometimes fabricated.

She had felt she had no other option. Silence on her part would come at a price that was too high to pay.

The Broker was the one in the position of power and had used it ruthlessly, relentlessly, trying to break down Tai San's barriers of resistance. She had allowed him to believe she had been broken. Perhaps that is why he called himself 'The Broker', Tai San rued at the time. But unknown to him, her spirit remained strong and this fuelled her stoic resolve – aware that she was the real one in power.

Then unexpectedly Tai San had been taken from the hotel by The Broker and brought aboard a cargo ship, *The Leviathan*.

She didn't know what or who else was on board besides herself, The Broker, and a number of guards who periodically checked in on her, making sure she remained in her cabin – perhaps that she was still alive.

Now Tai San's mind raced with the uncertainty of what this journey all meant and what lay ahead for her as the approaching landmass loomed closer and closer.

The sun's rays started to peek through the clouds, flowing through the window causing Tai San to see her reflection in the glass pane, staring back at her.

"Don't forget who you are," Tai San urged herself in a whisper. Clenching her fist, she summoned the vestiges of her inner strength, vowing to stay strong, to somehow stay true to who she was, when all else was so uncertain around her.

Staring out at the land, she knew that whatever was going to happen, she would find the answer soon – and she promised herself The Broker would never crush her spirit, that she would be ready for whatever the future would bring.

* * *

The Leviathan was a large cargo ship, the biggest Tai San had ever been on in her many travels since becoming a slave and being transported from one place to another – but the ship was dwarfed by the size of the port it had docked in.

In the time of the adults this must have been a very busy shipping route, Tai San judged, imagining the hustle and bustle of international trade in its heyday. Her eyes scanned the vicinity, seeing if she could recognize any signs or landmarks, something to show which port in the world they might be in.

Around them stood row upon row of cargo containers, stacked high in uneven lines of walls, imprecisely placed like a child's building blocks, as if they might tumble over.

Giant cranes towered higher still, immobile, frozen in time, rusting hulks of junk but also monuments to the old days that had once been, a past civilization that was no more.

They were standing on the large concrete pad of the dockside, like ants beside the ship that had carried them there. Nature seemed to be reclaiming the land with plant life forcing its way through the various cracks in the foundations.

Tai San was beside The Broker, the two of them surrounded protectively by his forces. The guards had weapons poised, primed for action, as they scanned the periphery of the port in a state of alert.

For all the time they had spent together over many months Tai San had never truly gotten to 'know' The Broker. Where he had tried to find out everything about her, she had been unable to find out anything about him apart from his blatant cruel streak and matter-of-fact ruthless efficiency in carrying out his actions.

But to her surprise Tai San could now sense a vulnerability in The Broker. Or more precisely – fear. His eyes darted furtively back and forth, surveying the scene. Beads of sweat were on his brow and he cleared his throat from time to time to relieve the tension within.

Tai San wondered what it could be that was making him and his forces so on edge – and how whatever – or whoever - was affecting them so much could impact her.

Perhaps it was the fact that the only cargo that had been onboard appeared to be Tai San, The Broker and his guards. *The Leviathan*'s cargo doors were open and its enormous hold revealed nothing but a cavernous emptiness, echoing the footsteps of some of The Broker's forces who moved around inside the ship.

Had there been a mistake in the delivery? Had the entire voyage been to no avail? Was this the karma that The Broker deserved? Had he somehow failed? Had someone double-crossed him?

Tai San was surprised to hear another sound further away, the sound of distant laughter, childish giggling.

The Broker's guards defensively aimed their weapons at the source of the sound.

A group of very young children were scampering in the waters lapping into the harbour, searching through flotsam and jetsam that had washed ashore. It was like a sea of debris from the adult times, the banks of the harbour awash in a tide of rubbish, plastic bottles, garbage bags. Rotten fish decayed at the surface, the waters filthy, thick with mud, grime.

The children looked feral in their barely-fitting, ragged clothes, were covered in sores, flies buzzing around them, and had visible cuts and bruises.

Tai San was shocked, repulsed, by the sight. Whatever land she was now in she quickly realized that there were 'strays' just as there were in her own land. Those not members or under the protection of any tribe. It was pitiful.

Suddenly the loud sound of engines rumbled into the port, the weight of the vehicles vibrating and almost shaking the very ground itself.

"Finally," The Broker exhaled nervously to himself as he gazed ahead at a fleet of long-haul transport trucks approaching, followed by a convoy of other vehicles which looked strangely futuristic to Tai San.

The impoverished young children stopped their playing and instead ran for cover, nervously ducking behind the debris washed up around them. They appeared to be panic-stricken.

From The Broker and guards' uneasy demeanour, Tai San wondered what was about to occur. But it was soon clear that the newcomers who had driven into the port weren't there for a fight – but were there to trade.

The Leviathan was quickly loaded with all manner of goods, the delivery trucks driving right up to the cargo hold so that the items they had carried could be placed inside. There were domestic household appliances, a sports car from the adult days - its polished chrome glistening in the sun. But of little value in the new world with clean water more of a sought-after commodity. As evidenced now with several containers being loaded, along with cattle being led inside the hold.

But mostly there was agricultural food – a mountain of grain was accumulating in the vessel as workers carried buckets full to the brim, dumping out the contents, piling it further, higher. A smaller heap of rice was growing in size in the middle of the ship as it, too, was unloaded from the trucks.

All of this produce and selection of goods were being exchanged for the one thing that The Broker had brought to these shores after the long voyage of many miles.

It was Tai San herself.

To her shock, *she* was being traded – again – and couldn't believe her 'worth' or value was ever measured in so much food. It could feed so many people for so long. What had she ever done to become such a commodity of equal value? Who were these people – the ones giving so much so they could take possession of her? What did they want from her?

While the workers continued loading the ship, an advanced party from the futuristic vehicles arrived. They were dressed in protective decontamination suits. Some of the entourage wore strange medical masks and plastic gloves, and they were being very careful of Tai San, treating her gently, like a prize possession, as they started to examine her, monitoring different aspects, determining her status. None of them had asked permission, even spoken to Tai San to enquire how she might feel about proceedings. She had got accustomed to being treated as an 'object' rather than a person in her many dealings as a slave but still felt a sense of shame, indignity, in the way in which she was being examined like a laboratory specimen without having any say in the matter. There was nothing she could do to stop them though, she realized, and all she could do was try and keep her integrity intact as best as she could. Not show emotion, any sign of weakness, that her new 'masters' could exploit. She wouldn't give them that.

It was a humiliating ordeal, inhuman. Invasive. Taking away her rights, they - whoever 'they' were - seemingly had control of even her own body but she would never allow them to possess her spirit.

Her height and weight were recorded, her temperature taken, pulse, some blood tests conducted, her body measurements taken. Her oral hygiene was checked, teeth probed one by one, details recorded in a tablet computer. Her hair and scalp were painstakingly examined, presumably for lice or some other form of infestation, perhaps disease of some kind.

A piece of equipment Tai San never even knew existed was put against her eyes and a wisp of cloud squirted closely onto the surface, making her eyes water, as the machine somehow 'read' her retina, making a recording of the details of her very eyes.

And through her haze Tai San couldn't help but notice an image of herself appearing on all of the tablet screens. Matching the very same photograph The Broker had in his possession when she first encountered him and she surmised that this exercise was probably some official confirmation of not only facial recognition but identity.

Tai San closed her eyes, slowed her breath, deep in meditation in an effort to stay calm, imagining she was in another place, back at her home in the mall with her beloved tribe as the medical scientific unit performed more sets of blood tests, finally injecting needles painfully into Tai San's arms, forced outstretched by some of The Broker's guards. Tai

San wondered if she was being somehow immunized against something. The only question was – what?

The unit examined the monitors of their machines and tablet computers, punched in data and left, passing a stranger who emerged from a vehicle at the head of the convoy.

Tai San was quickly aware that whoever this person was, he was clearly powerful and she could tell from the respect given in his demeanour by The Broker that this new figure had to be of high authority in this land.

He was about Tai San's age, tall, exuded confidence. Almost bordering on arrogance as he signed a bill of goods and said somewhat cynically, "It would appear our transaction is complete. I just hope the enormous value I paid is worth it."

Tai San could sense that there was more than a sexual inference as he cast a glance down her body, looking over her appreciatively - Tai San detecting some lasciviousness in his gaze as well as pride at having secured her.

"Who are you?" Tai San asked cautiously.

"Life. And death," the stranger replied, amidst a charming smile. "Do you have her data?" he asked The Broker.

The Broker nodded and handed over a hard drive.

"You'll find all the information and detail on these drives, Selector," The Broker said.

Tai San listened and watched in growing unease as the apparent 'Selector' signed more documents, handing them back to The Broker before indicating to the paramilitary guards surrounding him.

"Place the cargo in the vehicle. We need to keep on schedule," The Selector stated, eagerly.

"Where are you taking me?" Tai San interrupted.

"To the future. And The Creator."

He smiled at some unknown irony in his own comment and responded with more than a hint of menace and veiled threat. "We all have a long journey ahead."

CHAPTER ONE

The motorcade made its way through a range of winding roads across a seemingly endless barren land.

In the front and rear of the convoy were military vehicles carrying the militia who had been at the docks. Around Tai San's vehicle she was flanked by several more on each side.

Her vehicle was armour plated, driverless and she was its only occupant. With no means of escape. The doors were locked from the outside, it was clearly automated without even a steering wheel or pedals, no driving seat or dashboard, controlled and moving as if by an unseen force.

The barren landscape looked almost primitive with no signs of life, as if from the beginning of time. And yet this vehicle was futuristic and whoever was controlling it had access to advanced technology.

Before the darkness descended and in the times of the old world, artificial intelligence had become more prominent. But this vehicle seemed to be so very far advanced and Tai San wondered if someone was controlling it remotely from another location. Or perhaps from one of the other vehicles in the long convoy. Or if her course had already been preordained and planned, programmed by a computer system somewhere, somehow.

She had cuts on her hands from the efforts she had initially made to get out of the vehicle. Unable to open the doors, she had bashed her fists against the thick glass of the windows in an attempt to break out in some way, even kicked from her seat, striving to prise a way through.

But it was no use – she was being taken somewhere and could do nothing to influence matters.

She wouldn't give up though. If there was a way to escape or alter her fate, she was determined to find it. Or at the very least – to try.

The Selector was transported in a vehicle of the militia at the head of the convoy and throughout the journey Tai San felt a continual sense of foreboding as she wondered why he had gone to such efforts to take her into his custody. And above all, who or what was 'The Creator' The Selector had referred to.

Tai San tried to assess how many miles they had travelled. But it was difficult to ascertain. All the terrain looked the same. Desolate, barren. Harsh. Lifeless, apart from their own convoy. She hadn't even seen any wildlife of any kind, not even a single solitary bird since leaving the port, let alone any landmarks.

The earth was mostly coloured red, making Tai San feel as if she was on a different planet. The wind gusts threw up clouds of dust like red snow, covering the vehicles, the windshield wipers working back and forth rhythmically to keep the front screen clear.

Some of the ground seemed blackened, charred in places, with potholes on the road, its tarmac melted, crumbling. And judging by some mammoth craters which Tai San noticed, there had been some explosions at some point in time. Huge explosions.

Tai San tried somehow to put any notion of a post-apocalyptic event out of her mind but the thought continued to prevail, especially as she became aware of acres and acres of large animal bones, carcasses of cattle, looking like fossils of dinosaurs. Had there been a drought? A famine? A war? Some accident? Was it the result of the virus somehow? Or something more ominous? Sinister?

As the journey continued, Tai San spotted sudden warning bio-hazard signs on the roadside, alerting their viewer to not pass any further. Warning of extreme danger. With any presence being strictly prohibited.

Yet the convoy continued, relentlessly, paying no heed or notice to whatever threat there had once been. Or still could be, Tai San contemplated.

A mile or so later, Tai San spotted the first grave.

An unmarked grave, the first of many, stood in the emptiness around, quickly becoming row upon row of graves as far as the eye could see, on both sides of the road. Endless, long lines of gravestones indicating the extreme loss of life that had befallen the region.

It was overwhelming. And very moving. Tai San could hardly contain her emotions, so upset was she at the suffering and waste. Bringing back memories of what had occurred in her own land, which sent a shiver down her spine, recalling the sheer scale of loss. Parents, friends, family - with the very real threat that the human race would become extinct.

Tai San had at least one connection with the occupants of this strange and desolate land. The experience of suffering, loss, the memorials to so many who had gone before. It made Tai San angry at the senselessness of it. The virus – or whatever caused these people to die – was something that *had* to be beaten, Tai San vowed. Somehow, life just had to go on. Not only her own life but the lives of others. Humanity had to endure, not become extinct. The graves marked a sad tribute

– and also a stark reminder that everyone's time was limited, that life was precious. Tai San would never forget that. No matter how dire her own situation could be – she was still alive and determined to make her own life count. To honour herself along with all those who perished. To give justice to the gift that life was so it could reach its full potential.

Her feelings of fighting back against death itself or those who stood in the way of life surged when the graves receded and finally signs of life began to show in what had been so far an otherwise lifeless land.

Grass sprouted up around the roads, becoming fields, rolling hills. A gradual change was taking shape with every passing mile that unfolded. There WAS life after all. And hope.

As the journey continued, the fields evolved into agricultural pastures, plains, cultivated, worked upon by farm workers, probably slaves Tai San reasoned, tirelessly toiling in the soil, raising crops. Some ploughed fields, others sowed seeds, more still harvested, some watered crops.

The workers didn't even cast a glance at the passing convoy and seemed almost robotized, paying more attention to images projected on some outbuildings as if advertising some forthcoming event – '*THE CUBE – COMING SOON*'.

Tai San noticed that some of the pastures the convoy passed were full of sheep, cattle, supervised by their herders who once again paid no attention to the vehicles in the convoy that sped past, which Tai San found strange and unnerving, fuelling her uncertainty of what might lay ahead.

What was certain though was that the area was teeming with life - plant, animal and human.

Such a contrast to what had been, the barren landscape, the rows upon rows of graves.

She was in a society rebuilding, growing and organized too. Compared to whatever destruction had occurred.

Now her vehicle made a notification pinging sound from within which signalled, unbeknownst to Tai San, she had arrived at her next destination. Her journey was over. But in reality had only just begun.

* * *

Tai San had arrived at the *Lakeside Resort* – so named because it was precisely that, an alpine resort complex that overlooked a large body of water. And clearly at one time would have been luxurious but was now decaying and in decline, being reclaimed by nature with plant life sprouting throughout the walls, even branches of trees puncturing the infrastructure.

The view though was beautiful, a spectacular location with the hotel facilities placed so its occupants would have had the best view on offer of nature's wonders.

The lake's waters looked clean, shimmering in the sun, inviting anyone who viewed them to go in for a swim.

Around the lake were snow-capped mountains, rolling hills, covered in all manner of trees, a forested area. Birds and insects flew around, the lake clearly the heart of an eco-system supporting so much life. Perhaps even the humans who lived here, Tai San reasoned.

The Selector personally escorted her to the entrance of the resort – advising that this was to be her temporary home, that she would find everything she needed to make her stay comfortable. The Selector explained that although she would be welcome to live in the resort on a temporary basis – she couldn't leave. Ever. He warned her this was for her own protection – that it wasn't safe in any event for her to be in the outside environs. Or for her to be on her own. Even if she was able to escape.

Around the perimeter of the resort Tai San noted what she perceived were surveillance cameras and also guards had been established in their positions on watch.

The Selector soon left after leading Tai San into the main lobby. He told her that he had other business to attend to for The Creator – and hoped that she would enjoy her stay and that he would be in touch very soon.

Tai San wandered out of the lobby and decided to explore the resort. Apart from the guards on the outside perimeters – she appeared to be the only 'guest'. She wondered if perhaps there were other staff there. Security? Anyone?

It became apparent though that she was indeed alone as she walked through the long, empty corridors. It was like being among the ghosts of the past. The resort providing an eerie connection to the old days. She could easily imagine the sound of children, happy families spending time there on holiday, enjoying the facilities and all that the lake complex had to offer.

The restaurant was empty, tables abandoned, gathering dust.

A children's play centre stood idle, toys littering the room, unused any more. Tai San thought of the poor children she had seen at the docks – why weren't *they* the ones here? They should be living in such a place with its comfort and resources, not her. The world was truly crazy, as it was unpredictable. And confusing.

Did she have an assigned room? Where was she meant to go? What was she meant to do?

She couldn't see any evidence of security cameras but considered that there could be some hidden somewhere. And she wondered if she was being watched by someone. And if so – who? And why?

Exploring the resort, Tai San was getting lost in a maze of corridors, eventually arriving in a kitchen area by accident that must have once serviced the bars and restaurants.

To her surprise she could smell traces of food. The kitchen must have been used recently. Had to have been. There was no way that the residue of meals could have been left over from the adult times. Or were her senses so heightened that her mind was fuelling her natural expectation?

After examining further, she realized that there was indeed no one else around. She was well and truly alone.

Or so she thought.

Tai San's expression clouded in a mixture of concern and confusion as she suddenly heard what she perceived to be splashing when she passed a different part of the resort where signs indicated there was a pool. Someone else WAS there. There was no doubt about it.

Confirmed especially when Tai San heard *laughter* emanating from the pool area.

Tentatively approaching the entrance to the pool, she grasped the handle on the doorway – and taking a deep breath, bracing herself for whoever could be there – she opened the door and stepped inside.

Tai San quickly became aware of a large swimming pool – but it was the people in the water that so astonished her. She felt like she truly was seeing ghosts. Faces she only knew all too well. Was this for real? Or just a dream?

"Watch this," the young man shouted as he ran, diving from the side of the pool into the water with a mighty splash.

"Not bad," the young lady replied. She was lounging in a sun bed and added with a mischievous grin, "But I can do better. Stand back, amateur."

The young lady got to her feet, preparing to jump, to water bomb – and it was then that Tai San just knew that it really was who she thought it was.

"Alice?" Tai San's voice called out, almost in disbelief. "Is that really you?"

Alice's mouth gaped open. She was frozen in astonishment, dumbstruck at seeing Tai San standing before her. She tried to reply – but simply couldn't.

The young man turned from the pool he had dived into and exchanged long glances with Tai San, who questioned in utter amazement – "Ryan!?"

"Tai San? It is you!" Ryan replied, equally amazed and in delight, drowned out by Alice, who exuberantly tried somehow to contain her emotion and joy at seeing Tai San.

"What are *you* doing here?" Alice called out in pure disbelief.

CHAPTER TWO

"Go to sleep, little man," Amber whispered, gazing down lovingly at her son as she rocked the cradle gently back and forth, hushing him - the combination of the motion and the soothing warmth of her voice sending the baby into his slumber – and dreams.

Amber still couldn't believe that she was a mother. She felt so young herself and the responsibilities of parenting were complex - even overwhelming at times, bringing sleepless nights, worry and stress – but fundamentally her son brought unrequited joy, total happiness and above all, a sense of a greater purpose and meaning to her life.

Another dimension which was extra special was the fact that she was sharing her parenting experiences and responsibilities with the baby's father – and her soulmate – Bray. He had finally returned to her, after so much time spent apart when the Technos invaded their city, with destiny reuniting them a few months earlier. Amber was elated to have two special 'men' in her life in Bray and their new born son.

Though once, there had been a third. Jay. When Bray and Amber had been separated shortly after the invasion that had torn them apart, she had struggled to cope with the notion that she might never see him again. It wasn't just a question that he seemed to have disappeared off the face of the Earth but painfully Amber had to face the very real prospect that he might not be alive.

Over time she had found solace - and love – in Jay, one of the Techno commanders who had turned on his leader, Ram, and helped put an end to the authoritarian regime who had invaded the city, finally joining Amber and the Mall Rats.

Jay was kind, principled, selfless, had a sense of duty to the vulnerable members of their tribe and behind his militaristic bearing and fondness for efficiency and order, there lay a caring and sensitive heart. And she had loved him for it, the two enjoying a strong relationship which evolved into them becoming a unit.

Though in the end Amber had come to realize that although she loved Jay, she wasn't IN love with him. For all that it was possible, she pondered, for people to love and perceive that they might be able to find other soulmates – ultimately it was impossible to connect with another kindred spirit. And this was Bray. It had always been him, since they were first thrown together by fate when the pandemic wreaked its havoc across the world. Bray and Amber's lives were intertwined.

Whether or not it was a matter of opposites attracting or if they recognized similar qualities and traits signifying that perhaps in reality true love emanates from recognizing similar aspirations in one's partner – they were the quintessential star-crossed lovers, almost made for each other.

Bray 'understood' Amber in a way that nobody else did – and she had the same effect on him. They almost had an invisible language where they knew how the other one was feeling without a single word being said. And she was looking forward to building their future life together with their son.

Both Bray and Amber though regretted that Jay could not be with them on this journey as the new generation tried to build a new world from the ashes of the old.

Jay had been killed defending the mall, paying the ultimate price, and in so doing had saved many innocent lives.

His efforts would not be in vain, Amber promised, leaning down to kiss her child, who was now fast asleep. She and Bray had named their son Jay, in honour of the former Jay, a fitting tribute so that his name would live on, a reminder that life would endure and hope prevail.

Amber was determined to grasp all the opportunities that now lay ahead for her tribe and felt a renewed surge of energy, purpose.

It wouldn't be easy – there would be many difficulties and challenges to confront and overcome.

But she was ready.

Smiling lovingly at her son, gently sucking his thumb in his slumber, she left her quarters quietly so as not to disturb him.

Heading along the upper concourse of the mall, she motioned to Sammy, who was playing basketball with some of the other younger members of the tribe.

"Try and keep the noise down. And keep an eye on baby Jay for me, will you please, Sammy?"

Sammy sighed. "But what if there are any nappies or diapers or whatever you call them to change?"

"Oh, and I suppose you have better things to do – like playing basketball."

"I could have gone with Bray and Lex, checking out the city and different sectors."

"I think you'll be able to 'protect' Bray and Lex at some point in time, Sammy."

"Really?" he questioned excitedly.

"When they become elders," Amber replied, sensing a way in which to motivate Sammy. "And when you're an elder yourself, who knows, maybe you can teach young Jay to protect you as well? Not that you might need it. I'm sure you will grow into a mighty warrior."

"Got it!" Sammy replied. "Oh, and don't worry about the baby being changed – I'm sure I'll find someone who can do it."

Amber smiled, despite herself. "It might be useful for you to learn too, Sammy. Because we all have to depend – and look out for each other. That's what being a part of our tribe is all about."

Sammy nodded and moved away to the other players, cautioning them to keep the noise down and move away further from Amber and Bray's quarters because Jay was fast asleep and he didn't want the baby to be disturbed.

Amber thought there was hope. And this incident punctuated that she needed to look for it in any way that she could, however seemingly trivial.

* * *

The Guardian locked his eyes with Amber as she approached, a hateful expression on his face, full of spite, simmering anger and vengeance.

He was being held in isolation in a makeshift cell, a caged area in the basement of the mall, originally used by the adults to keep various supplies and goods in the cavernous shopping complex of the old world.

He had to be kept alone, the Mall Rats felt, because of the extreme danger he presented to others, let alone even to himself. He was unpredictable and had tried on many occasions to attack those guarding him whenever they got near to him. His face was covered in scratches and cuts. He had also injured himself in the past, using any implements he had access to in the cell in order to 'punish' himself, some bizarre form of self-flagellation to ritualistically appease his 'divine master', Zoot.

The Mall Rats had learned to not let anyone get too close to him – and to not leave any items in his possession that he could otherwise use to cause harm.

"Traitorous witch!" The Guardian hissed venomously, his arms stretching through the bars, reaching out intensely as if he was trying to seize Amber, who was standing some metres away, keeping her distance the other side of the cell.

"How is he doing?" Amber asked Salene. It was Salene's turn monitoring the prisoner, with each member of the Mall Rats taking shifts on the rota.

"Much about the same."

Salene indicated her clothes which were covered in freshly made stains of still warm soup resulting from an incident minutes before Amber's arrival when The Guardian had flung the meal that Salene had brought him, the plastic bowl zinging through the bars and spilling its contents all over her.

"Are *you* okay?" Amber asked, hoping Salene wasn't hurt, let alone finding her time guarding the cell too distressing.

"I'll be fine," Salene smiled, putting on a brave face. "Good thing we've all had so many meals with Lex. I'm used to bad table manners."

Amber couldn't help but smile slightly too. As well as feel enormous pity for The Guardian, sympathy. He wasn't well. Of sound mind. She reasoned that whatever it was, he clearly had some severe difficulties, a mental illness, without access to the care, maybe even medication, that he so obviously and desperately needed.

The Guardian began to manically laugh at Salene's remark. "Lex... Lex, Lex, Lex," he whispered repeatedly, faster and faster, getting into a fervor of excitement, building himself into a frenzy, saying Lex's name over and over again, multiple times – before he stopped suddenly, thrusting his gaze upwards to the ceiling.

"L-E-X!" The Guardian shouted one final time, his arms reaching out to the Heavens as if in worship, a serene countenance on his face. He stared, looking up, in a deep sense of inner reverence. "Some thought you should return to the jaws of your foul, slavering master of Lucifer in Hell! But had you not released the Mighty one, Zoot, then there would be no God in the heavens to lead us all into the salvation of Power and Chaos!"

Amber and Salene exchanged a sad glance while they watched The Guardian cautiously. Amber so wanted to help. As did Salene. To do something, anything, to ease The Guardian's inner turmoil, bring peace somehow to his deeply troubled mind. And soul.

The tribe had no idea what they were going to do with him. Let alone some of the others who were also being kept prisoner in the aftermath of the recent battle.

At an initial meeting Lex had stated he was in favour of putting The Guardian on trial so he could serve justice for the many war crimes and wrongs he had committed. But would it be a fair trial? That was Amber's concern. Would The Guardian even be in an emotionally fit state to stand trial? Or was it too late, was he lost forever in the grip of some form of madness?

Lex scoffed at Amber's stance, believing that the only people suffering any form of madness would be the tribe themselves if they gave any sympathy to The Guardian.

Fortunately, when it was put to a vote, Amber was supported by other members of the tribe who agreed that The Guardian was fragile, a victim of his own mind, and needed care. If they were to have any hope in rebuilding a better world and creating the type of just society Amber and the Mall Rats so wished for, then they had to find some way of rehabilitating The Guardian, along with any others who faced great difficulties and needed extra care. They couldn't just cast them away – or keep them locked up for eternity. Or even release them into the dangers and challenges they would find in this God-forsaken world in which everyone was not only struggling to exist – but survive.

The Guardian was just one of many issues with which the tribe had to contend. Amber was looked to as the de facto leader, because although she had not been recently elected as such, everyone always came to her with their problems, hoping she would have some advice or find a way to help. And characteristically, she possessed a seemingly natural ability to provide sound and unsentimental advice – and to lead in a fair and just way.

Amber's next task was to visit a separate area in the mall where The Guardian's former allies – and more opponents of the Mall Rats – were being kept.

"Good luck," Salene wished as Amber started to leave.

"You're going to need it!" The Guardian yelled menacingly, watching Amber go, a manic glint in his eyes, prior to erupting into a fit of hysterical and vengeful laughter.

Amber didn't look back, ignoring his goading.

"It won't be long now!" The Guardian shouted out as she went. "And you don't even know! Lex thought it was The Technos I was warning him about! But you haven't seen anything yet! Just wait until you meet the *true* bringers of Power and Chaos!!"

Though she was resolute and didn't engage The Guardian further – or even know what he was referring to – The Guardian's words and demeanour did unsettle Amber, along with Salene.

And The Guardian's reference played on her mind as she arrived where Eloise and the warriors of the Legion tribe were being kept – the members of The Collective.

"Amber! How lovely of you to visit," Eloise said, her words dripping with sarcasm, the malice on her face all too plain to see as Amber approached the cell where Eloise was housed.

"Is this a social call?" Eloise continued, "Or have you just come to check in on the baby? It could be yours if you're 'nice' and wanted to adopt another one."

Eloise gently patted her swollen stomach, indicating the baby she was carrying inside. She was several months pregnant and had originally claimed Bray had been the father, an accusation Bray had strongly denied – and one Amber knew could never be true. Eloise had just been using Bray, her captive at the time, as a puppet figure, trying to manipulate him so she could position herself as the mother of his child – and therefore occupy a place among her followers, the 'Zootists', who were part of The Collective. Eloise was well aware of the power, let alone the exalted status she would have being the one to carry a child in whom the 'blood of Zoot' flowed due to the family connection with Zoot being Bray's younger brother.

Whoever the baby's father was, Amber dreaded to think of how life would be having Eloise as a mother. She seemed devoid of any compassion, with a penchant for cruelty – indeed she seemed to enjoy inflicting it upon others, judging by what Bray had recounted to Amber when he revealed all the indignities he had witnessed and pain he had even suffered himself during his imprisonment under Eloise and her Zootist forces.

"Are you ready to talk?" Amber asked.

Eloise leaned her head back in her chair, luxuriating in the relaxing feeling as one of her warriors, also imprisoned, brushed her long dark hair, pampering their leader as best as they could. Closing her eyes, it was as if Eloise was starting to go to sleep, deliberately ignoring that Amber was even there.

Since the battle when the Mall Rats became victorious, Amber had been trying to find out information from Eloise and the other prisoners which could reveal more about The Collective. In addition to the Zootists, they were apparently a powerful coalition of other tribes from a faraway land who had joined forces under the supreme leader, known as Kami, and had expanded, invading other cities, sectors and lands, creating a growing empire for themselves.

Ram had first alerted the Mall Rats to the existence of The Collective, saying that he had been in contact with Kami online in the past around the time of the demise of the old world, the Collective leader trying to recruit Ram and his Technos to join them.

Ram had supposedly refused and instead invaded the city where Amber and her tribe lived. Ram and The Technos had subsequently been defeated and although he was not a member of the Mall Rats, Ram had aligned with them and was being co-operative. Amber felt at times that Ram was being overly co-operative, a sentiment shared by other members of the Mall Rats, and no one could shake their suspicions about Ram's true intentions or how far they could trust him.

According to Ram, The Collective presented a dire threat. To the very future and existence of humanity. He claimed that in addition to invading other lands, they were specifically interested in Eagle Mountain, a facility that housed an otherwise hidden underground military base left over from the adults who had seemingly been using it somehow during the height of the pandemic, leaving behind all kinds of sophisticated technology, including a massive supercomputer, the *K.A.M.I* system.

The system was almost mythological and the source of many theories, ranging from it being part of an infrastructure to facilitate evacuation to not only foreign lands but other planets. Even that the system was controlled by an unseen military force in the old world who had inflicted the virus as a form of bacterial warfare.

In truth, no one, including even Ram, really knew the answer to all the mysteries and whether or not any conspiracy theories were valid and true.

They were all aware, however, that it hadn't been that long since Amber and the Mall Rats, along with Ram, had been inside the vast complex of Eagle Mountain and they had been amazed by what they had discovered there. Including a selection of adults, who were neither dead nor alive, but 'frozen' in strange cryogenic hibernation chambers, perhaps, Amber reasoned, awaiting the day the younger survivors of the virus would maybe be able to revive them.

* * *

"Quiet!" Sammy whispered in growing unease. "Or you'll get us all in trouble."

He had managed to persuade the younger ones to forget about their basketball game for fear of it wakening baby Jay. Now, though he realized the suggestion of a different game seemed like a good idea at the time - it was becoming a nightmare for him to control as Brady exuberantly raced through the main concourse of the mall with an excited squeal, followed by Tiffany, the two girls trying to keep away from Shannon, the children engaged in a high-energy game of hide and seek, each participant counting to ten but resisting every urge to peek through their fingers to see where others were choosing to hide.

"This'll have to be your last game," Trudy called out to the kids, "Your lunch is almost ready."

Sammy breathed a sigh of relief as he noticed Trudy signaling to the younger ensemble from the food hall.

Trudy had been helping May prepare a meal, some large cooking pots of stew simmering on the stove in the food court, and it was a delight to see Brady so happy while she played. They had been through so much together, such drama already in Brady's young life and Trudy hoped that finally they, as well as the tribe as a whole, had a chance to start afresh and build something new. A better and secure future for successive generations.

"It actually tastes pretty good," May said, surprising herself as she tasted a spoonful to make sure it was finished.

It was the best she and Trudy could come up with given the scarcity of ingredients. They had thrown together an assortment of tinned food and almost hoped for the best – and somehow, they had delivered an appetizing stew.

The children certainly seemed to enjoy it – but suddenly all let out a wailing scream, along with Trudy and Salene, as they noticed Lex swagger through the food hall carrying a mammoth carcass of a wild boar over his shoulders.

"What on earth is that?" Trudy asked, trying to put on a brave face to calm the distraught children while Lex casually flung the carcass on a counter.

"What do you think it is? – dinner, for the next week hopefully," Lex replied, while washing his blood-soaked face and hands in a nearby sink.

"I'm exhausted. Can someone fix me something to eat? That smells pretty good," he added, glancing at the stew in a saucepan as he slumped in a chair.

"I'm sure you're quite capable of serving yourself, Lex," Trudy said, while exchanging an indignant glance with May.

"We're not your servants, you know," May added.

"And I'm not going to bring home the bacon and be expected to cook it. That's woman's work!" Lex sneered disdainfully.

"I hope you're joking, Lex," Trudy said.

"Of course. Well, maybe a bit," Lex replied, enigmatically.

"Calm down, kids," May appealed. "There's no need to be afraid of that pig Lex brought. Because he's the biggest threat until he learns the true meaning of equality."

The children were still distraught, gazing clearly repulsed by the sight of the dead animal on the counter, its eyes staring, opaque at the moment of death with an expression as equal to the fear the children clearly had.

"Charming," Lex scoffed to himself.

"I mean it, Lex," May continued in her disdain. "You're the biggest pig I know. A chauvinist pig."

She smiled proudly at her own wit and Trudy couldn't but help smile too.

"Here. I'll fix something for you to eat but just don't make it a habit," said Trudy, while ladling up a bowl of the stew and passing it to Lex, who lifted the bowl and slurped on the contents without using a spoon.

"How did you kill it, Lex?" Sammy probed, in a mixture of intrigue and excitement.

"It probably fainted when it saw another pig," May continued, mocking Lex. "I mean one who's such an amazingly strong alpha male."

"Give it up, May. I'm not in any mood," Lex snapped, prior to shrugging modestly to Sammy. "It was no big deal. I used a couple of large stones to drop it and then speared it with a branch."

"Can you teach me to hunt one day?" Sammy pleaded.

"If you get me another bowl of this stuff, then I might consider it," Lex replied, sliding the bowl to Sammy who crossed to the stove and served up another portion.

"You're something else, Lex. You really are," May sighed.

"Thanks," Lex replied, shrugging again modestly.

"It wasn't meant to be a compliment," Trudy added.

"Well it should be," Lex replied. "Especially after what I've gone through all morning trying to keep this tribe safe, as well as fed."

Few could have foreseen – let alone Lex – the irony in the comment and how the lives of the Mall Rats were destined to be changed, forever.

CHAPTER THREE

Over the past few days Lex and Bray had been deployed to search the city and environs to make sure the region was fully deserted as they believed to be the case. But all agreed that it would be wise to scout all the sectors just to make sure.

Bray and Lex planned their routes on a grid with each searching various sections of the city and the outlying suburbs.

The only sign of life Lex had found was the wild boar. And during Bray's scouting he found no evidence of life either. The city and environs seemed to be well and truly deserted. At least in their searches so far.

Later that evening when Bray returned, he compared his findings with Lex which brought a degree of relief to all in the Mall Rats, realizing that at least there were no other dangers they might have to contend with. At least so far.

All concluded that the previous inhabitants of the city and suburbs must have also evacuated as the Mall Rats had once done prior to returning to the city, to escape the ominous threat posed by a supposed new 'virus' released by the renegade Techno Commander, Mega, hoping to use a chemical weapon for leverage over the population. But in reality, perhaps Ram had been right and it had been nothing but bluster, a ruse, or that some other force, perhaps even The Collective, had somehow managed to sabotage the plans with the 'virus' which was released to be nothing but a dark cloud of smoke. But whatever had truly happened, it was enough for the population, including the Mall Rats at the time, to flee.

The only people who remained in the region, now it seemed, were the Mall Rats and their prisoners in the mall, as well as the other former captives who had once been under Eloise's sway.

She had brought with her a group of expectant mothers in various stages of pregnancy, all of them teenagers, first time mothers, frightened, worried about their own futures as well as those of the babies they were carrying inside them. It was all part of some repopulation programme on the island she once lived where the Zootist tribe were based.

They would soon have many more mouths to feed. Particularly when the maternity unit gave birth, which would only add to those who had already been born. The mall was already ringing out with the sound of crying babies, hungry, demanding their mother's attention and to be fed.

To Lex's relief, let alone some of the others in the tribe, the maternity unit was housed on the ground floor, inhabiting various areas of a disused department store on the north side of the mall.

Lex liked Amber's suggestion of segregation, viewing it as empathy given the disruptive noise the babies made round the clock. Amber hadn't actually brought this into consideration. It was more due to the fact that Lex, as well as some of the other male members living in the abandoned shopping mall, might have also been distracted by so many breast-feeding females and she wanted them to have the dignity of privacy.

As mothers themselves, Trudy and Amber had also taken on a lot of extra responsibility - 'mentoring' the new mothers how they might expect things to be on the pathway of motherhood.

Eloise's group were all single mothers, as was Trudy, and Amber was especially grateful that she had the luxury of having her baby's father, Bray, by her side. All in the tribe, even Lex, were determined that the mothers would get the support they needed as best as they were able to give it to them and most of the tribe had also become makeshift midwives, childcarers, offering tips, practical assistance. Though Sammy and some of the little ones didn't exactly respond favourably to any babysitting.

As well as a rota for guarding the prisoners, the Mall Rats had also organized at various times for meal breaks which were staggered and the maternity delegation usually gathered in the food court for a communal meal whereas others in the tribe ate at different times.

Ebony joined the group who had once been under Eloise and The Guardian's control. They were all ex-Zootists, vulnerable young people who had been manipulated, 'brainwashed' into believing in the cult of Zoot, previously devoting themselves with some fanaticism to the cause in service of their former leaders, The Guardian and Eloise.

The Mall Rats and Ebony had spent some time 'de-radicalizing the group, telling them the truth about what had really happened in those dark, early days of the city when the legend of Zoot began. Zoot – or Martin as he used to be known – was no God, unlike what they had been told, and was a troubled young soul who had badly lost his way.

Ebony had been there then in those early days, by his side, as his lover – and the Queen of Zoot's tribe, The Locos. She had been instrumental in re-converting the Zootists away from the bonds that connected them to The Guardian and through him, to Eloise. Due to her history with Zoot, she was looked upon with a mixture of some awe, respect – but the days of Zoot were long ago. She wasn't a Loco anymore.

Life had moved on for Ebony. For everyone. But Amber especially recognized that Ebony still commanded a degree of loyalty from the Zootists who almost still viewed her as their Queen.

So, Ebony agreed that she should try and spend time with them to bond – for all that Sammy and some of the younger ones thought simply that her motive was getting 'two meals'. One with the Zootists under her so-called control. And the other meal with the senior members of the Mall Rats – though in reality meal times were also a forum for discussions and planning.

Including the best way to de-radicalize the ex-Zootists who walked freely among them and how they might be given some meaning and purpose in their lives.

The best way to do that, Ebony believed, was to use the 'muscle' that the former Zootists provided to form a new militia under the influence of the Mall Rats and Ebony, in particular. The ex-Zootist members would be free to join but could refuse if they preferred. Eventually perhaps even being able to be released into the city or environs to live free and pursue their own aspiration as a tribe.

Lex and Bray strongly disagreed with this notion. It wasn't only a question of being able to trust the Zootists but also Ebony, who hadn't exactly shown herself to be totally loyal in the past and seemed to characteristically place her own aspirations ahead of everyone else, which usually coincided with her desire for power.

Amber and the other Mall Rats in secret meetings fully understood the concerns of Lex and Bray and indeed shared them. Where Ebony was concerned. But taking a more pragmatic approach, Amber believed there was merit in what Ebony was suggesting where the Zootists were concerned, believing that once de-radicalized that they might well wish to live together in their own base in peace and harmony.

They could certainly add weight to a potential militia which the Mall Rats would need to enhance their capability of defending themselves as they built their future and grew in population.

All had resolved, however, to let matters unfold and assess the results. And especially to keep a watchful eye on Ebony.

Not all Zootists were allocated to be trained for potential work in the militia. Some of the group preferred to be integrated into other areas of routine. Working with Amber, Trudy and Salene on the maternity unit. Others researching with May the possibilities of building a medical capability not solely confined to the care of those who might become sick but also concerning matters of nutrition. Even a potential education system for some of the younger ones – for all the notion of any schooling was met with utter disdain from Lex who viewed teachers and schools with cynicism and contempt from his experiences in the old world.

Now though, Lex was more in his element working often with Bray, as well as Ebony, putting the potential militia through their paces, giving them some physical exercises, playing 'wargames' in the deserted streets bordering the mall.

Ebony also seemed to relish the challenge but she was aware that there was a degree of mistrust throughout the process.

She had never truly fitted in, she felt. She was never going to really be a Mall Rat, no matter how hard she tried. There was always a degree of tension, disagreement, between Amber, Bray and Ebony especially. Due in part to a long and complicated history going back to the days when Zoot remained as leader of the Locos controlling the city streets.

Amber's vision of the future had clashed many times with Ebony's and her methods of surviving the world the adults had left them.

Moreover, there had also been some romantic conflict between Amber and Ebony in the past. In what now felt like a lifetime ago, even occurring in another world, Ebony had once harboured hopes of being able to build a relationship with Bray. In their school days. But he flatly rejected her approaches.

Ebony had even for a time found happiness in Jay before he, too, flung her away, preferring Amber over herself. Ebony had never forgiven Amber for twice getting what she, despite her independent spirit, still so truly wanted. Amber, with Bray, had a strong loving relationship – Ebony had no one but herself.

With the militia seemingly so loyal to her, Ebony certainly had the signs of having everything she needed to put herself in a strong position moving forward. And was shrewd enough to recognize several options. She could continue to co-operate with Amber and the Mall Rats to safeguard the mall and provide a defensive force in case another enemy manifested or more of The Collective's forces ever did appear. Or, she could leave the mall entirely and start anew, maybe returning to her old base at the Horton Bailey Hotel with the militia as her own personal tribe.

Perhaps she could even turn once again and use the militia to free the imprisoned Guardian, Eloise and their warriors. She wondered if Eloise was the type to strike up a deal in which The Collective might reward Ebony handsomely for allowing Eloise to leave and return to them. She was uncertain if Eloise could be trusted, however, or if she would even honour any bargain they struck. It took one to know one and Ebony could recognize a master manipulator when she saw it.

Ebony was keeping her options open and in so doing confirmed and validated the Mall Rats' concern. That she had the potential of reverting to type and doing what she did best – surviving.

In the ever-changing game of life Ebony found herself once more as being of influence as a potential 'kingmaker' – and she promised herself that this time around she would be the one to end up in charge. Not as 'king' of course. But as a 'queen'. And not the queen to a leader such as Zoot. But a potentially powerful leader in her own right. Whatever choices she was going to make in future, she would be sure to be on the winning side. Even if that included liaising with the Mall Rats which was certainly a possible option if they evolved into a more powerful force. But in whatever event, Ebony resolved that she also required power to place herself in a strong negotiating position.

* * *

The frenzied sound of finger-tapping on computer keyboards greeted Amber and Bray as they visited Jack, Ellie and Ram to see how the trio were getting on.

They had been working late into the evening and mostly around the clock and Amber and Bray were keen to check on whether or not there was any progress.

During their last visit to Eagle Mountain, the Mall Rats had taken possession of a small, golden hard drive that had been located in one of the cryogenic chambers belonging to one of the adults in suspended animation in the military compound.

No matter how hard Ram, Jack and Ellie tried, they were unable to 'read' whatever data might be on the drive.

"The problem still seems to be in the binomial area which should be linked to a possible hardware system – with its own software, possibly incorporating trinomial antipods," Ram pondered.

"I agree," Jack said, as he turned it all over in his mind.

"In English – please?" Amber said as she and Bray smiled slightly to themselves.

"What – you think we're just 'geeking out'?" Jack added, slightly offended.

"Well, that's one way of putting it," Bray confirmed.

It was true that Jack had a love of computers – rivalling, or exceeding his feelings for Ellie, she had often joked – and was well versed in all manner of systems and their software. Ellie herself was also quite knowledgeable in computers, having studied them at school before the demise of the adults.

Ram, conversely, was on a totally different plane – more like another planet. Eccentric, gifted – he possessed incredible skills that he had so often in the past used but put to ill-use when leading the technology-driven society he had tried to establish when he founded The Technos tribe, who had originally invaded the Mall Rats' home city.

That was long ago, however, and for some time Ram had claimed to be on-side – not a Mall Rat, but no longer was he an enemy of them. He had joined their side in taking down the authoritarian regime put in place after he was usurped as leader of The Technos. Ram had also been important in subsequently defeating Eloise's Collective forces.

Most in the Mall Rats, including Amber, although she still reserved her right to have doubts, believed that Ram had truly changed and could be trusted to lend his considerable talents and abilities to a more noble purpose in rebuilding a new and better world. And there was no one better to interweave the elements of technology which would certainly be required and which seemed to occupy every fibre of Ram's body - but also his brilliant mind.

Nothing else seemed to matter.

"If you want it in plain English, then cutting to the chase – I'm a genius and I'm still struggling to understand the codes of the software which still seems to be encrypted," Ram said.

"You're also quite modest," Bray said wryly.

"I don't know about modest – but he's really good," Jack added.

"And so are you, Jack," Ellie said proudly.

"You're not so bad yourself," Jack replied, shrugging modestly.

"If you could all forgive the intrusion of your mutual admiration society and tell us what you have planned, then we'd be very grateful," Amber added.

"In fact, there's several equations which we've still got left to try. And it's all going to take time," Ram stated.

"So, in a nutshell – you're still unable to access whatever is on the drive?" Amber queried.

"Simply put – yes," Ram responded. "Whoever wrote this software and put it into place certainly wanted to give whoever might wish to access it - a challenge, to say the least," Ram advised.

"That's for sure," Jack added. "They didn't want anyone to find whatever information is on this thing – if they did, they would have made it a heck of a lot easier."

Amber and Bray, of course, totally believed Jack. And Amber wanted and hoped she could believe Ram. But she had a nagging doubt, wondering if he was being straight with her.

The biggest concern though was what other 'secrets' the adults might have left behind. What it all meant. Were there other military bases like Eagle Mountain waiting to be discovered? Did the complex have any more things inside to reveal? And what of Ram? Did he know more than he was revealing?

Was this even all some game for him? Did The Collective represent the magnitude of threat that Ram had warned?

"Well, if we haven't given up trying to use this drive, do you think anyone else will? Like The Collective?" Amber probed.

"Once we find out all the data that's on this drive, I might be able to answer that question," Ram replied. "But one thing's for sure. If there is something on this – someone, somewhere, at some time made every measure to protect and keep it all hidden in Eagle Mountain for whatever purpose – then, yeah.

Certainly someone like Kami's not the type to give up on this kind of thing."

Ram had said he had never spoken directly with 'Kami' and didn't in truth know exactly who, or what, they were. If it was 'they'. It could have even been an 'it'. Kami was just the name that had popped up online when Ram had communicated with them in the final days of the adults, in the gaming world, when he was number one on the leaderboards. Soon thereafter, the whole world seemed to have come to an end and a new generation was left to try somehow to survive and ensure the human race would not become extinct.

Whoever 'Kami' was, or whatever 'it' was, Ram knew the power behind the mega computer systems would be relentless, very capable themselves – and had been the only ones to ever truly challenge Ram. Kami, in whatever incarnation, was a genius - which was worthy praise coming from someone like Ram. Indeed, Ram couldn't deny that Kami was even on another level to him. So much so that Ram had chosen to run, withdraw his mighty Technos from any association with The Collective, than face being controlled by them and their unknown leader - which heralded the Technos' invasion of the city the Mall Rats inhabited in the first place.

Jack suggested that maybe they had all been going about this all wrong. Maybe the reason they hadn't been able to make any inroads yet was that they had been so focused on trying to uncover what was on the hard drive - that they had forgotten one obvious and important thing: "That we need a different type of computer. One with the capability and power and grunt to handle the complexities of the software," he recommended.

And there was one place where there was a computer unlike anyone had ever seen. And that was housed in Eagle Mountain.

For all the unease anyone might have in returning – they painfully realized that there was no other option but to yet again return to Eagle Mountain and examine all the contents held within the ominous and mysterious facility.

CHAPTER FOUR

Tai San still felt as if she was dreaming. There, sitting opposite her, were Alice and Ryan, looking back at her with equal surprise and delight that she had been reconnected with them in their lives, appearing as if from nowhere.

Ryan had grown a short beard since the last time Tai San had seen him and it suited him. He looked well and still seemed the same old Ryan - kind, gentle, placid, physically strong, though Tai San could tell from his countenance and spirit that he had been through a lot since being separated from the Mall Rats. They all had. It had somehow manifested with a sense of weariness and strangely a resolve.

"I still can't believe it," Ryan said.

"Neither can I," Tai San agreed, almost speechless, overcome at their reunion with joy, emotion.

"That makes three of us," Alice chimed in. "And I need another drink."

Alice went over to the bar area and began pouring herself a glass of whisky, exchanging glances and smiles with Tai San as she filled up her glass, thrilled to be in the company of her friend once more. She had always had a close bond with Tai

San and for a time had even been her personal bodyguard, in a different life that had felt so long ago.

Ryan was particularly interested in any news of Salene. Alice was eager to discover anything of her younger sister, Ellie.

Tai San had told them everything that she knew. She had last seen Ellie and Salene, along with the rest of the Mall Rats, albeit briefly, at the mall when she had helped Mega overthrow Ram. However, Mega had his own agenda and had double-crossed Tai San, using her, as he had ironically Ram. She had been 'played' and regretted how trusting she had been, falling for Mega's clever machinations in his quest to depose Ram and become the new leader of The Technos, prior to being transported to other lands.

She began her long period of enslavement from one owner to another, being moved around before ending up in the 'possession' of The Broker, then eventually The Selector.

This news gave Alice and Ryan renewed hope that somewhere, out there in the world, the rest of the Mall Rats may be still alive. Alice and Ryan only hoped that their paths might cross again one day, as they had with Tai San.

They were sitting in the main lounge area of the *Lakeside Resort*. Alice and Ryan had arranged some food for Tai San from the well-stocked kitchen. She had been hungry after her long journey and Tai San's now empty plate rested beside her on the large couch that she was sitting on.

Information on their captures was still very much a mystery but Tai San had quickly become aware that whoever The Selector was and whoever he was working with – they seemed to be in tune with the natural world on some level given the organic produce that stocked the kitchen, along with various herbs and spices.

This kind of diet had always appealed to Tai San who preferred a more plant-based approach, aligning with her being very much in tune with Mother Earth and the environment.

Whereas Ryan and especially Alice didn't find the produce available so appetizing.

"I am a meat and two potatoes gal," Alice had stated while she was preparing the food. "But at least this stuff might help me lose a bit more weight."

"How?" Ryan asked.

He was certainly a gentle giant, Tai San thought affectionately, and she often wondered if Ryan had some kind of special need. He was always a little slower than the others intellectually in the tribe but through his simplicity always seemed to hold an inner wisdom, even peace, as if he in reality knew all the secrets to life.

Tai San explained about the produce and how a plant-based diet was becoming more of an importance even way back in the old world, with people becoming more and more concerned about global warming and climate change.

A tragic irony considering what actually took place with the pandemic bringing about the very real threat of human extinction.

"At least we might have a chance to escape if we're being held by vegans," Alice grinned, during the meal. "Most of the guards I've seen around this place seem to be a bunch of wimps and me and Ryan could easily take them."

Tai San was aware that both Alice and Ryan were mighty adversaries and could take care of themselves as well as others under their protection. So escape could be an option. At the right time.

"Fancy one yourself?" Alice offered, holding up an empty glass and waving it at Tai San, having downed the shot of whiskey.

"I'm fine, thank you anyway."

"How about some of this other stuff?" Alice continued, while examining the shelves and bottles containing a range of non-alcoholic drinks and juices and an abundance of fresh bottled water.

"Hey, they've even got green tea. That was always one of your favourites," Alice explained, while finding a range of teas in a display cabinet.

"Maybe later," Tai San responded.

"Then that just leaves more of the hard stuff for me and Ryan," Alice said, pouring a glass for him.

"We've got so much to celebrate!" Ryan grinned. "The old team – three of us, anyway. Back together again."

"Well, let's enjoy the moment while we can," Alice suggested, raising her glass to make a toast. "To Tai San. Ryan. Myself. And the rest of the Mall Rats, wherever they might be."

As the night went on, the initial surprise at their unexpected coming together – that though it felt like it, it wasn't some dream but was very much happening - was replaced by the reality of coming to terms with their situation.

Alice and Ryan explained to Tai San that they had both been living at the resort for what felt like an eternity but was only a few days since they, too, had been brought there individually by The Selector, who had advised that they were honoured 'guests' of The Creator.

Ryan had arrived first before being joined by Alice. He was naturally thrilled and surprised to see Alice, but also have some company, as well as her assurances that The Selector's references to The Creator was not that he or she was some kind of god. And Tai San agreed with Alice and Ryan that although the resort was luxurious compared to what the three of them had recently experienced – they were certainly not in heaven.

Ryan relayed to Tai San – as he had done to Alice when they were first reunited - what had happened to him when he had been sent away by The Chosen who had invaded the city and home of the Mall Rats.

Initially, Ryan had faced severe punishment. He was brutally beaten by The Chosen, getting revenge on him for daring to attack their leader and for being a 'non-believer' of their God, Zoot. He was denied food, water, kept in squalid, terrible conditions. He thought that would be the end of him, that his days were numbered.

And in a way they were as since that time he had existed rather than lived, having been traded, eventually ending up in the mines in a faraway land performing hard manual labour. And as bleak as that was, it was a far greater improvement on what he first thought his fate would be.

Soon after that he was traded again. His captors travelled to the coast so that they could continue their journey by ship to another destination. Ryan had managed to break free of his shackles and get away, finally escaping to a forested area, where he spent several days by himself, lost, surviving off berries and anything he could eat.

He stumbled upon a tribe of nomads and was given temporary shelter but rather than allies, the nomadic tribe yet again traded Ryan, who eventually found himself in yet another different land where he ended up as a type of gladiator, forced to take part in different combat spectacles to entertain the spectators eager for action, baying for blood. It was horrific, Ryan recalled, dreading to even discuss the awful memories.

"They treated us like animals," he told Tai San, listening attentively to his tale, as did Alice, who was as gripped hearing it second time around as she was when Ryan revealed the details to her.

He literally had to fight for his very life but always refused to kill his opponents, to the disappointment of the crowds, instead using his strength and prowess to render them harmless, never more than unconscious. He may have had no choice but to fight – but it was his choice, he felt, how to deal with those he was fighting. They were unwilling participants. Slaves, just like him.

There was one other thing that Ryan was fighting for, in addition to self-preservation and the hope his destiny would change. One reason, above all the others, that kept him going during his darkest times when it was all so unbearable and it would have been easy to have given up. It was the vision of him being reunited one day with Salene.

He loved her so much, so deeply, with all his heart. Their relationship had always been complicated, fractious at times. Salene had her difficult moments with many personal struggles, anxieties. But Ryan gave her the support she needed, respected her, showing her kindness. Dignity. And above all understanding. He felt that underneath her sometimes troubled moments, at her essence she was always nurturing, caring, possessing a similar compassion much like his own.

Alice had already told Ryan the sad news that Salene had tragically lost their baby - she had been there when it happened and blamed herself for the accident that caused it. Ryan had been devastated to hear the truth, that in addition to having lost his freedom and Salene – he had lost the son or daughter they had been expecting and his dream of becoming a father at that time.

Tai San was relieved that she didn't have to break this news to Ryan and as she continued listening to what had happened to him, Tai San said a silent inner prayer hoping that Ryan's spirit might find some peace so that he could come to terms with the loss.

Ryan, the 'reluctant gladiator' as the crowds had dubbed him, had been put up for sale at a major slave auction – and it was from there that he ended up in the hands of forces under the control of The Selector, who had brought him to the *Lakeside Resort*.

Following Ryan's revelation - Alice told Tai San what she had gone through since they had last been together in their home city.

On the fateful day The Technos invaded, changing their lives forever, Alice had been in mourning over the death of Ned, her lover.

Ellie had been a source of great comfort to her big sister throughout her grieving period. Until one day needing some space, Alice went outside for some air to take a walk. And it was the last time she would see her little sister. As well as the other members of her tribe, the Mall Rats. Due to The Technos' invasion.

Hearing the aircraft, the explosions rocking the city, Alice had at first tried to get back to the mall but was quickly overpowered by an advanced guard of Techno warriors and was dragged away, literally kicking and screaming, placed into a vehicle along with some other recently captured prisoners and taken to the airport.

The military style planes that had been used to transport the conquering Techno forces waited like massive mechanical birds of prey, their cargo doors open, as if to gobble up Alice and the other captives who were ushered inside against their will.

In the days before the virus, the airport had been a place of joy where Alice, with Ellie and their family, had embarked upon many memorable adventures growing up, flying away to various destinations on holiday. This time around, it had felt to Alice that she was being taken on a voyage of the damned. When the Techno aircraft was full of prisoners, the cargo door closed off Alice's view of the city she had called home.

The flight took about two or three hours. Upon arrival, its human cargo was emptied onto the tarmac. They had been sorted into groups, separated by age, by gender, and Alice's group of older girls around the same age as her were exchanged, traded, for all manner of goods. Computer equipment, medicines, food supplies, had been unloaded and given over to their new possessors.

Alice's group of slaves was soon put to work, she recalled to Tai San, and it was arduous. Reminiscent of what Tai San had also experienced. A terrible routine, every day.

They were a chain gang, mostly growing wheat and corn, which was itself then presumably being sold off to other buyers elsewhere, Alice thought. The slaves who did all the hard work to cultivate the fields in the first place certainly didn't receive the bulk of the bounties they produced from their crops and were poorly fed, malnourished. Many of the slaves became ill due to the extreme conditions and didn't survive.

Having grown up on her parents' farm, Alice understood agriculture and was very good at it. She knew how to live off the land, to care for and nurture living things among the soil. As a young girl, she had actually hated farm work and had daydreamed of far off adventures in exotic lands. This was quite contrary to anything she could have ever imagined, however. She was far from home but in a living hell. Being so close to the earth again, out in the fields, was the one thing that ironically helped her to keep going. It was a link to the past for her.

Unlike many of the slave workers around her, she had a connection to the land and though she despised her plight as a slave, feeling the fresh air and the soil beneath her feet kept her grounded, helped somehow to absorb the tumult and emotional pains she experienced as not only being a slave but being such a distance from her loved ones. From the Mall Rats. And her sister, Ellie.

Having experienced the near extinction of the human race with the demise of the adults, Alice thought she had a pretty high threshold when it came to hurt and distress. All of the young survivors who had inherited the world in the wake of the virus had been through it all, seen things, felt things, that no one should ever have to suffer, let alone teenagers, children.

Being apart from her little sister though had ripped a hole in Alice's heart.

Ever since Ellie's birth, a day she could recall vividly, one of the happiest in her life, she had taken on the role of 'big sister'. It was a position she relished, cherished, being the one to look after Ellie as she herself grew up. They had played together, went to the same school, enjoyed many happy moments on the farm. Alice had always been there for Ellie – ready to give sisterly advice, to give any assistance, to share a laugh, to just enjoy the close bond she had developed with her sibling over the years.

Following their parents' passing, along with the rest of the adults, Alice was even more aware of her responsibility to Ellie and did everything in her power to make sure that they both survived the advent of their new world. Ellie was quite capable herself of course, resourceful and independent, but Alice would always be 'watching out' for her, forever being Ellie's big sister. Alice had even saved Ellie's life when she had fallen ill, which brought the Mall Rats into their lives in the first place when she went to the city in search of medicine.

After leaving the city, Alice was traded again at a slave market and was 'bought' by a sea-faring tribe who lived further up on the coast – The Orcas. They were based in a remote fishing facility, feeding off a diet of seafood harvested from the waters, which they also traded upon with other tribes in the region.

It was a far cry from the privations Alice had endured previously as a slave worker on land. Especially when it became clear that the reason Alice had been brought to their shores was the amorous intention of the leader of The Orcas, who called himself The Captain, to woo Alice and make her his bride.

Alice was at first baffled and amused why 'The Captain' would wish to marry her. Not that she thought herself unworthy of romance. It was more that The Captain was a complete stranger and knew nothing about her personally.

But The Captain revealed that he had 'a thing' for oversized women, which was hardly surprising because he was very large in stature and overweight himself. And she couldn't help but feel a little flattered by his attentions and the fact that she had experienced something alien in her life to date – being perceived as a 'sex object'.

Rebuffing the advances of The Captain, Alice soon wore out her welcome among The Orcas and she was brought to 'Labour Island', a place where tribes in the region gathered to meet, to trade with each other, reminiscent of the Mall Rats' tribal gatherings in her homeland.

For some reason she had been singled out by a mysterious unit of militia who didn't seem to belong to this region and definitely weren't interested in any other produce which was available.

She was seized and taken to a waiting ship and after a long journey was placed into the custody of The Selector.

Upon her initial arrival at the *Lakeside Resort*, from where she met Ryan once more, she had hoped fate might take a better turn, that her period of enslavement had finally come to an end. But as she quickly discovered, in a way it had only just begun - and had taken on a different dimension to anything she had experienced before.

As with Ryan, her captors seemed to be more hospitable and again as with Tai San, Alice was advised that she could stay at the resort as a 'guest' of The Creator, under The Selector's 'supervision' and 'protection' as he called it.

There was still so much that Alice and Ryan didn't know about the ones who were responsible for their plight and what exactly it was that they wanted with them. So they couldn't shed much light on Tai San's questioning – and they were just about as confused by it all as Tai San was herself.

The one thing they did know, however, was that The Selector certainly knew a lot about Alice and Ryan. More than they did about him. He had visited over the past few days to question them. But it felt more like being interrogated, Alice explained to Tai San. The Selector – who was always apparently there on the instructions of The Creator, was meticulous in his research, a fine eye for detail and possessed a keen, Alice felt more like a calculating, mind. With an insatiable appetite for detail he was overly pedantic, intent on gathering all kinds of information about her life, as well as Ryan's, to date.

It was all a little reminiscent of the techniques The Broker had used on Tai San herself during her time in his captivity, constant probing and questioning for detail, any detail, of not just Tai San but the other Mall Rats.

Neither Alice or Ryan had ever encountered 'The Broker' who had kept Tai San prisoner or heard anything about him.

Cooped up in the resort, they had never met 'The Creator' – whoever and wherever they were - and apart from The Selector's references to carrying out The Creator's bidding, they wondered if The Creator was even a real person. Alice had thought perhaps The Selector had invented the supposed existence of The Creator as another form of influence or leverage over them, The Selector promising that 'The Creator' would reward all those who joined in the new world they were 'creating'. Alice assumed this was some form of incentive, a type of 'bribe' given by The Selector to motivate and encourage their co-operation with him, to extract information, detail.

The Selector had assured them The Creator was very much real and that when The Creator deemed it necessary, Alice and Ryan would find out their true purpose and 'destiny' which formed part of The Creator's overall plans.

In his interrogations, The Selector had often been focused on Eagle Mountain.

Ryan had been there before, along with Tai San, during the fateful visit of the Mall Rats long ago, the tribe discovering the top level of the secret military-scientific base the adults had left behind. Alice hadn't been a part of the Mall Rats then but had heard what they had been through and relayed what she knew to The Selector.

The Mall Rats themselves were always the main subject of great enquiry by The Selector. He had asked Ryan and Alice everything they knew about the tribe. Their lives before the virus, their hopes, fears, personality types, romantic connections, their friends, their enemies, the challenges they had faced, what type of society that they themselves had been trying to build. Their diet. Awareness of technology. Their source of food, water. Their dealings with other tribes in the city. How they had felt about The Chosen, Zoot and the Locos. Ebony even. What it was like when The Technos invaded, what they thought of Ram, how life had been under the reign of The Technos, the strategies they used to defeat first Ram and then his successor, Mega. Their opinions on Ram's technology, their firsthand experiences of the virtual reality Ram had been implementing.

The Selector was also curious about how the Mall Rats got on with each other in the tribe – who was closest to who, their personal chemistry with one another, every aspect of their otherwise private lives.

It struck Tai San as odd, not just a coincidence, that she herself had faced many questions during her time as a prisoner of The Broker, who had also asked her about Eagle Mountain and the Mall Rats.

Now that Tai San had arrived, Alice and Ryan speculated that she would probably be in for more questioning herself. And the three of them pondered what might lay in store for them. Would they be safe? Continue staying at the resort? Would they all be set free to carry out whatever purpose the so-called Creator had for them?

Maybe, Alice reasoned, The Selector was nothing more than a powerful trader – gaining knowledge and information, even on other individuals who may have some value for him, in much the same way that The Broker had operated in selling Tai San to The Selector in the first place. It was possible, Tai San and Ryan agreed, that after some time being held in the resort that The Selector might 'sell' them on again via an auction to another buyer, exacting a good return in the process. The Creator could be a client of The Selector's, Tai San suggested. None of them knew for sure.

"I know one thing," Alice said to Tai San. "The Selector gives me the creeps. He's strange. And I thought I'd seen it all with The Guardian."

Alice described how The Selector sometimes came across in his manner as being overtly friendly – but it was too friendly. It was a guise, Alice was certain, an ingratiating mask of good manners which hid an otherwise insincere personality who seemed to have ulterior motives that neither Ryan nor Alice could fathom. Other times The Selector seemed cold, unfriendly, hostile even, alternating between subtle, passive aggressive outbursts to more blatant threats he would pose at Alice and Ryan if he felt he wasn't getting his way. Whenever he talked about The Creator, The Selector spoke with reverence, complete respect and adoration. It was like there were different 'versions' of The Selector who would show up at the resort and it did Alice's head in, she said, never knowing how The Selector might behave from one day to the next.

There was one final thing, Ryan emphasized. It was difficult to explain but The Selector seemed to be always 'testing' them somehow. He was constantly monitoring their reactions to his behaviour, to the things he would say, to the answers they were giving him themselves during his talks with them. And he seemed to enjoy their obvious discomfort in not knowing the reasoning for their continual captivity. Sometimes he wouldn't say anything at all, Alice said. There would be long gaps of silence on his visits where he would just stare at them – gauging their reaction to him, seeing if they would maintain eye contact or look away.

Other times he would be the one to avoid eye contact with them and instead keep his face down, busy typing into the laptop that he brought with him for his interrogations. The Selector was an enigma and whether his inconsistencies were on purpose, for effect, or just the result of a complicated soul, Ryan and Alice both felt that somehow they were forever being examined in some way when they interacted with him.

What he was the 'Selector' of was a mystery.

Tai San was determined not to stick around and find out, however. She agreed with Ryan and Alice that when the time was right, they should try and make plans to escape.

* * *

Several miles away in his dwelling, taking a sip from his chamomile tea, The Selector's eyes remained focused on the image of Tai San in front of him, engaged in conversation with Alice and Ryan.

The Selector sat at a bank of screens, flickering in the otherwise pitch-black room, the light of the monitor nearest him glowing on his face, just inches away from it. The other screens showed different perspectives of areas in and around the resort from the cameras that had been securely placed long ago. Showing various angles of even the perimeter guards on watch.

Leaning forward in his chair for an even closer look, The Selector focused his intense gaze on Tai San, studying her mannerisms, her every move.

On one monitor there were waveforms gauging Tai San, Alice and Ryan, the noise level of their voices, every inflection, similar technology although more advanced to lie detector tests in the old world.

The Selector had heard every word of the discussions Tai San had been having with her two Mall Rat friends and smiled, pleased with how things were progressing. Tai San's reunion with Ryan and Alice was not only informative, The Selector had also found it entertaining. Their views and speculations on him had especially been most intriguing.

It was so good to have the three of them there, The Selector considered. Everything was going well and truly according to plan.

CHAPTER FIVE

With a goodbye kiss to Amber and their sleeping baby, Bray had gotten up just before sunrise, and after a quick breakfast set out on his task of scouting the area to ensure that there were indeed no other inhabitants in the city and environs.

The previous night the Mall Rats had decided that a separate expedition was due to leave later that morning with Ram, Jack and some of the others heading on a mission to investigate Eagle Mountain.

Initially Bray was going to accompany them but decided that he would be best served staying behind to work with Amber on all that needed to be done – but at the heart of it, Bray felt uneasy at the prospect of leaving Amber and the Mall Rats alone, along with his baby son, given that Lex would be joining the Eagle Mountain expedition.

Maybe they could even gain further understanding on what the adults themselves had been doing at the mysterious underground facility, Bray thought, as he set out from the mall. The Mall Rats on their last visit had been astonished to discover the size of the complex, split across multiple levels, the advanced technology left behind – and even adults, apparently of some prominence, who had gone into cryogenic hibernation seemingly in an effort to escape the virus that was ravaging the world.

The fate of the Mall Rats seemed intertwined with Eagle Mountain, Bray considered, thinking back to their first visit long ago, when Zandra, Lex's lover at the time, had been killed in an explosion which had rocked the top level of the observatory. Amber had also almost lost her life in the blast.

Bray could only hope that this time around, no such tragedies would befall the Mall Rats. His main task today though was to check out the forest that bordered the city to establish if the Eco Tribe had returned to their camp.

Amber had once lived among them, and the Ecos, led by Hawk, were more than allies of the Mall Rats. They were close friends who shared the Mall Rats' quest to live in peace and harmony – the only difference being that the Ecos preferred to live closer to the land and Mother Nature.

Upon arriving at the location where they had once lived, Bray found the camp was abandoned, however, and there was no sign of the Ecos, who the Mall Rats believed must have fled the environs of the city, along with the rest of its population, to escape what was then feared to be the new 'virus' released by Mega and his Technos. It was an assumption, of course, and no one knew for sure but whatever fate had in store for the Ecos, their destiny certainly wasn't here.

After checking out the abandoned Eco camp, Bray scouted the far north end of the city. It was eerie to walk the deserted streets entirely alone, Bray thought, the sound of his boots from every step being the only noise he could hear, apart from that of his own breathing, as he made his way past some stores, long since looted. At that moment, it felt to Bray like he was the only person left in the world.

The streets were paved with memories, Bray thinking back to his life in the days of the adults and all the times since. The many events that had occurred to him and the other Mall Rats. There were reminders around almost every corner. One of the graffiti-covered empty stores he had passed had once been a favourite toy shop of his younger brother, Martin, which he used to visit when they were growing up. The windows now smashed, the building a burnt, derelict shell of what it once was.

It felt symptomatic of what fate had befallen Martin himself, Bray having watched helplessly as Martin's world crumbled around with him re-inventing himself eventually as Zoot, before his own young life was tragically cut short after becoming the leader of the Locos. His reputation was that of a tyrant. And although Bray couldn't deny that the Locos' ideology of Power and Chaos and anarchy was totally alien to everything Bray stood for, as well as the ideology of the Mall Rats – he could never fully reconcile the transformation of his young brother.

Martin had always been rebellious since the day he was born but it tore deep into his soul the prospects of his late parents ever conceiving what had occurred to their second son. And Bray himself remained torn apart also from the same conflict.

He was looking forward to getting back to the mall later on. He hadn't seen that much of Amber recently, only at night, the two of them so preoccupied by what they were doing each day and all their responsibilities. There were so many issues to work out – what to do with The Guardian, Eloise, her dangerous warriors imprisoned in the mall. The group of young mothers in their care. The mystery of Eagle Mountain, The Collective and any threat they might pose.

Bray had suggested that he and Amber place aside a part of that afternoon for themselves, even an hour or two, so they could enjoy some quality time together. It had been too long since they had last done that and Bray longed for a precious, fleeting moment with Amber where they could, somehow, put away all their other cares and responsibilities - and simply enjoy being with each other.

Making his way from the north end of the city, Bray arrived in Sectors 8 and 9 which were once under the control of the Locos and his late brother, Zoot.

Seeing the graffiti in the decaying streets was a stark reminder not only of what occurred before but the fact that Ebony had been involved as the girlfriend of Zoot and Queen of the Locos.

For all that Ebony had seemingly changed, Bray never fully trusted her and resolved that she really must be watched closely – especially with the imprisoned Zootists who could influence her, or worse still, she might influence them to instigate an uprising.

The jury was still out where Bray was concerned though, and to be fair to Ebony, he decided to keep an open mind given that she seemed to take threats seriously if the forces of The Collective made their presence felt. Bray recognized it was important to ensure the Mall Rats were as prepared as much as they could be in case they ever came under attack from The Collective or any unseen force.

Since they were so few of number, the Mall Rats certainly needed allies and Ebony seemed the best candidate to help drive their defence efforts. After all, the ex-Zootists were a highly trained militia and Ebony herself was a very capable commander – tough and street-smart. She had a lot of combat experience and was very much a strategic thinker.

And that was the prime thing that concerned Bray. He *knew* Ebony. And had known her for a very long time, going back to the adult days. She was too smart. Cunning. Despite her claims of wanting to do what was best for the Mall Rats, Bray remembered the many times Ebony had put her own personal interests above all others. He wondered if she had some ulterior motives – a card, if not a deck's worth, up her sleeve. Some other plan she was seeking to carry out that might end up in the Mall Rats being betrayed.

* * *

They looked so peaceful, Amber thought, from the doorway, peering in at what had once been a furniture shop in the mall.

Sitting on one of the beds inside was Emma, a girl in her mid-teens who had been telling a bedtime story to Trudy's daughter, Brady, who she was babysitting, as well as her own little brother and sister, Shannon and Tiffany. The three younger children were nestled, snuggled up, beside Emma – and each was drifting off in slumber as she finished off the story she was making up about a magical dog who could speak to humans.

Her own baby fast asleep in her arms, Amber couldn't help but smile in appreciation of not only Emma's story and her child caring skills – getting three, often hyper, kids to sleep for their daytime rest was no easy feat - but in admiration of Emma's many inspiring qualities. She couldn't see the warmth of Amber's expression because Emma in fact was blind. Yet she continued to live her life as best as she could with courage, perseverance and great kindness to others, especially the younger more vulnerable ones. Almost ignoring the fact that Emma, given her disability, was vulnerable herself. If only others were like her, Amber mused, the world would be a far better place.

After stopping to check in on Emma and the little ones, Amber was on her way to the food court to prepare a special surprise for the 'date night' she had planned to have later on with Bray when he got back. The other Mall Rats had supported the idea fully, recognizing that Amber and Bray did so much for everyone else and it was only fair they tried to do the same for them.

Trudy, confronting the ghosts of her past, had insisted that she be the one to take over Amber's watch of The Guardian in his cell so that Amber didn't have to complete her rota that day. Similarly, Ebony had volunteered to oversee Eloise and the Legion warriors in their custody, being assisted on guard duty by some of the Zootist militia.

Lia, who was Lex's new romantic flame, was in turn staying by Ebony's side – ostensibly to help her keep watch over the prisoners but it was also, Amber was aware, to make sure Ebony herself didn't get up to any subterfuge or wrongdoing with her former allies behind bars - Ebony having once been on their side. Lex had asked Lia to stick around Ebony like glue and be vigilant of her every move.

Ram, Jack and Ellie were no longer at the mall, having already set out with Lex for Eagle Mountain, Lex accompanying them to provide protection in the event they encountered any unexpected dangers. But also, to ensure that Jack and Ellie weren't vulnerable if Ram had ulterior motives.

It was a sensible precaution, Amber had resolved.

There was so much to explore of the vast underground complex at Eagle Mountain and Amber, like Bray, had partly wished she could have gone along with the others to assist, or that they could have sent a larger expedition. But it wasn't possible. There were so few Mall Rats in number and Amber and Bray needed as much help as they could get while Lex, Ram, Jack and Ellie would be away.

With every passing hour Amber just hoped they were safe, and looked forward to their return, as well as any news they might bring back with them.

Life had to go on at the mall in the meantime. Emma's story was interrupted suddenly when Sammy arrived.

"Amber! Come quick!" he cried out.

"What is it?" Amber replied in growing concern.

"It's Salene! And May! They're crying, big time!"

Rushing to their living quarters, Amber found Salene and May sitting side by side on the bed, hugging, comforting each other. May was emotional, tears streaming from her eyes. Salene was also upset, her shoulders heaving as she, too, sobbed.

"Is everything okay?" Amber asked, going over to sit by them to lend her support. "What on Earth is going on?"

"It's Salene..." May explained through her tears. She seemed that she wanted to say more but was finding it hard to get any words out of her mouth.

"You can tell me, whatever it is," Amber encouraged. "You'll feel better if you talk about it. A problem shared is a problem not only halved – but solved."

"It's nothing bad, Amber..." Salene spoke up, trying to regain her own composure, taking in a deep breath, "It's May... She said..."

"She said what?" Amber wondered.

"She said - yes!" Salene explained with a sudden grin, and she started to laugh – and then cry at the same time, totally overwhelmed by her feelings, May doing the same.

It was then that Amber quickly realized Salene and May were so emotional because they had been crying tears of joy.

"May and I – we're going to get married!" Salene blurted out elatedly.

"That's – that's amazing! Congratulations!" Amber exclaimed, wrapping her arms around them to give a big hug.

* * *

The vehicle skidded to a halt, kicking up a shower of gravel, as its occupants surveyed the observatory building in front of them atop Eagle Mountain.

"Well, we made it," Lex said, turning off the engine and jumping out from the driver's side. He was concerned that there would be enough gasoline in the tank, especially given that there were no tribes around to trade in the deserted city and environs.

Jack and Ellie exited from the back seats and gazed ahead uneasily.

"There doesn't seem to be anyone else around from the looks of it," Jack pondered.

"Hopefully," Ellie said, in mounting anxiety at the thought of what they might encounter inside.

"If they were, you probably scared them away by your driving," Ram sighed, clambering slowly out of the front passenger seat. He looked like he was going to be sick and felt Lex had driven far too quickly – and erratically – for his liking. "Remind me to never hire you as a chauffeur!"

It was a long journey from the mall to Eagle Mountain and throughout, they hadn't seen signs of anyone else. The entire region was deserted apart from a few wild stray dogs, probably former pets from the adult times and now feral, and all had commented that they hoped they wouldn't encounter any wild animals who previously inhabited the city's local zoo.

Now, it was as if they were up on top of the world, the air cold and fresh due to their altitude, strong winds all around, pushing the clouds just above at some speed, which were so close that they felt they could almost reach out and touch them.

"I don't know what's more beautiful," Jack said loudly over a gust, "the view down there – or the sight of you."

He was speaking to Ellie, the two of them hand in hand as they started walking towards the observatory entrance. The view across the rolling hills looking down below was certainly breathtaking, panoramic. As was Ellie, to Jack, her hair billowing in the wind.

"Such a charmer," she said coyly. "Maybe I'll use some of this wind to blow you a kiss."

"Just the one?"

"Alright, lots. Maybe one of them will even be a real kiss."

Jack beamed at the idea of that. But Ram and Lex looked plainly sick.

"Will you two give it a break? I'm not entirely into this lovey-dovey stuff," Ram sighed. "What about you, Lexey-boy?"

"In case you hadn't noticed, Ram, I'm what is known as a lover, as well as a fighter," Lex winked in an attempt at macho camaraderie.

Ellie ignored their mocking remarks, giving Jack a loving smile, and it helped keep him calm and ease the anxieties he otherwise felt swirling inside – the prospect of going back inside Eagle Mountain gave Jack a feeling of trepidation. It was a vast, intimidating place.

"Give me a moment," Lex suddenly said. And the others realized the significance while they watched Lex cross to Zandra's grave, which he had dug himself at the time of her demise. It brought back painful memories of her passing at Eagle Mountain. In the explosion which claimed her life, the baby she had been carrying in her early pregnancy was also lost. Lex wasn't just paying respects to his lost love but to the son or daughter that could have been theirs. As a tribute, he placed some wild flowers he had taken from the hillside beside the grave, putting some rocks on top to make sure they didn't get disturbed by the wind.

Ram watched Lex by the grave – and knew that shortly there would be more graves to dig. After all, they couldn't leave the adults entombed in Eagle Mountain forever.

They had discovered the adults in the depths of the Eagle Mountain complex on their last visit, 'frozen' as if in a deep sleep in their cryogenic hibernation chambers. It had been an incredible and eerie sight – mind-blowing to Jack, Amber and the others to see adults from the days before the virus once more, the like of whom they thought they would never look upon again.

Jack had initially hoped it would be possible to even revive the adults somehow from their chambers. And if so, there would be so many questions to ask them - but Eloise, in a fit of rage, had disconnected the units from their power sources.

Ram had some knowledge of the cryogenic units the adults had been stored in. He had been to Eagle Mountain himself many times during his reign over the city when he had been the leader of The Technos.

Discovering the hibernating adults, he had studied and reverse engineered some of their chambers to gain an understanding of their workings, hoping to use one of the units himself so he could 'escape' the real world and live forever, in a perpetual state of sleep, inside his own virtual reality paradise. His dreams. To hopefully waken at some point in time in the future. Even a thousand years when hopefully the world might be filled with technology on a level that even someone like Ram, who was obsessed with it, could not even conceive, let alone understand.

Without power, Ram had told Amber, he thought the adults would stay 'on ice', in some manner of preservation, for a couple of months. Though there were no longer any life-support systems connected in the aftermath of Eloise's actions, their chambers were hermetically sealed and intact. Eagle Mountain, where they must have hoped to outlive the virus, would become instead a tomb, Ram had advised, the adults remaining undisturbed in their chambers. They still had some time, Ram speculated, otherwise they would have to dispose of the bodies. Amber and the Mall Rats felt it was only right to pay their respects, to give the adults, whoever they were, the dignity of a proper burial and send-off if the adults couldn't be revived.

"Are you ready?" Lex asked, returning to Jack, Ellie and Ram at the observatory entrance.

"As ready as we'll ever be," Ram said.

Due to his many visits in the past, Ram led the way as he knew the interior of Eagle Mountain well. It was good to have him guiding their group because without him, Lex imagined, they could have easily gotten very lost inside the labyrinthine tunnels inside the vast complex.

Ram had brought a supply of flashlights along and they certainly needed them, the spotlight of his beam cutting a pathway through the darkness, illuminating the walls.

On their last visit to Eagle Mountain, then as prisoners of Eloise and her Collective forces, Ram had instructed the *K.A.M.I* computer to shut down all systems, plunging the facility into darkness. His improvised move had enabled the Mall Rats to escape from the Legion warriors and to then subdue Eloise herself, their commander.

The massive compound had been left in the dark and Ram said he had planned to try and restart the core systems, bringing back the artificial light, when they got down to Level 3, the area where the *K.A.M.I* computer was based, which he hoped to reboot.

Standing for *Knowledge Artificial Machine Intelligence*, *K.A.M.I* was a sophisticated, next generation colossus possessing artificial intelligence – even its own 'voice' that it had used to communicate with Ram and the others on their previous visit – and it seemed to have been tasked and programmed by the adults with running all the various systems inside Eagle Mountain, including monitoring the cryogenic units that the hibernating adults had been inside.

"How much further, Ram?" Jack asked, his voice echoing down the long passageway.

"Not long now," Ram replied. "At least, I hope."

"Are you sure you know the way?" Jack probed, casting a look behind him into the darkness. His mind had started to play tricks and he felt like he was exploring some sort of haunted, nightmarish castle, imagining ghosts around every corner.

"We'll be fine," Ellie said, giving Jack's hand a supportive squeeze. But she sounded more convinced than she looked. She too was clearly on edge.

Even Lex was bracing himself, ready for action.

The air was getting more stale the further down they went into the cavernous structure, the atmosphere claustrophobic, and Jack dreaded to think of all the layers of mountain up above them.

Ram reassured everyone, as well as himself, that it wouldn't be long before they could get to the *K.A.M.I* computer and be able to instruct it to restart the absent air-conditioning, bringing in a flow of fresh air to breathe in, as well as proper lighting back to the complex.

Then they could try and connect the hard drive that Jack had been carrying in his backpack to the *K.A.M.I* machine, in an effort to make some progress in deciphering its contents.

A few minutes later they finally approached their destination, the massive *K.A.M.I* supercomputer looming up ahead – and that's when Ram was first concerned by what he was seeing – and hearing.

"INTRUDER ALERT. INTRUDER ALERT. INTRUDER ALERT," the *K.A.M.I* system repeated, over and over again in its monotone voice which reverberated and echoed in the chamber and far beyond.

The area was bathed in artificial pulsing light, the multitude of tiny lights on the *K.A.M.I* computer blinking away, while red lights flashed from alarms in the ceiling, lighting up the faces of Ram, Jack, Ellie and Lex as the alarms wailed unbearably.

"What the hell is it?" Lex asked in mounting panic.

"Something's not right," Ram replied.

Suddenly twin piercing beams of green laser light shot out from a sensor in the *K.A.M.I* system, sweeping over the contours of Ram's face, scanning his features, in recognition, examining Lex, who froze in the glare, uncertain what to do.

"WELCOME BACK, RAM," the machine greeted him. He had spent much time down there in the past during his Techno days, examining the sophisticated technology the adults had left behind, the machine recognizing his return.

"Good to see you, old friend," Ram responded.

The beam of light moved from Ram's face, switching *K.A.M.I's* attention to Ellie, Jack and Lex, who stood frozen in fear.

"AND THESE ITEMS?"

"This is Jack, Ellie and Lex," Ram advised.

"HUMAN OR ROBOTIC?" *K.A.M.I* asked.

"Human," Ram replied.

"HAVE WE MET BEFORE, LEX, ELLIE AND JACK?" *K.A.M.I* asked, with a degree of distrust in the tone.

"I don't think we have… er… had that pleasure," Jack said politely, clearly trying to ingratiate himself.

"WRONG!" *K.A.M.I* exploded in sudden disdain. "YOU HAVE VISITED HERE PREVIOUSLY ACCORDING TO MY MEMORY BANKS AND THE DATA I HAVE ON FILE."

Lex, Ellie and Jack recoiled in mounting fear while Ram tried to calm the colossus machine.

"You didn't ask if they had visited, *K.A.M.I.*"

"YOU ARE VERY LITERAL, RAM," *K.A.M.I* said, more friendly now.

"And so are you, *K.A.M.I*, my friend," Ram said, reassuringly. "Now why don't you restart all core systems?" Ram instructed the computer. "And turn off those alarms."

The alarms stopped flashing, the 'INTRUDER ALERT' audible warnings ceased – and they could hear the sound of equipment, machinery whirring and reactivating, Eagle Mountain coming back to life – and all the other lights inside the complex switched on in an instant at the same time. Jack, Ellie, Ram and Lex breathed in deeply the welcome rush of fresh air that was flowing in from powerful fans in the ceiling.

"That feels so good," Ellie said, gasping the new air.

With the lights back on in the complex, it was then that Jack was the first to be able to see clearly. The area where the adults had been, inside their cryogenic hibernation chambers, was now completely empty. All of the rows of units that Jack vividly remembered seeing before, their image imprinted on his mind, were missing and no longer there.

"Where – where are they?" Jack cried out, stunned by their absence.

"They couldn't have just walked outta here," Lex said. "Have you got anything to do with this, Ram?"

"Nothing, nothing at all!" Ram said, running his fingers through his hair, mystified and stressed by the development. "For once I know about as much as you do, Lexy-boy."

"But they were here," Ellie said, almost refusing to believe what her own eyes were telling her. "They were right here," she said again, pointing to the spot where the hibernation units had been. All that was left were a series of complex wires and cables sticking out from the floor in each spot, disconnected from the units that had once been there.

"*K.A.M.I* – where are the adults that were here?" Ram asked, looking up at the huge mainframe towering above him.

"UNKNOWN. UNITS 1 THROUGH 38 HAVE BEEN TAKEN AWAY BY INTRUDERS. DEFENCE SYSTEMS COMPROMISED. MANUAL OVERRIDE. UNAUTHORISED VIOLATION OF PROGRAMME 1, SUB-SECTIONS 3 THROUGH 35."

"Intruders?" Lex said, taking it in.

"What 'intruders'? Who are the intruders?" Ram questioned the computer again.

"UNKNOWN. IDENTITY RECOGNITION UNSUCCESSFUL."

"So, what do we do now?" Jack wondered. He felt the hard drive safely in his backpack, its contents seemed the least of their worries at the moment.

"What does it all mean?" Ellie said.

"It means we've gotta get back to the mall and tell the others," Lex suggested, with a sense of urgency.

"You're right about that," Ram agreed. "One thing's for sure. It means that someone else has been to Eagle Mountain. Recently. The only question is – who!?"

CHAPTER SIX

Tai San was in the middle of a deep dream. She was on the beach, walking arm in arm with Lex. It was a beautiful day, the sun shining in a crystal-clear blue sky. The two of them on the sands, the waves gently lapping over their feet. They had been swimming just before and Lex was making Tai San laugh by 'drawing' two strange-looking faces in the wet sands with his big toe – one, a stick-figure of Tai San, the other a self-portrait of himself. The tide coming in and out kept making the figures get washed away, Lex digging in his toe to redraw the lines of the stick figures in the sand between each incoming wave, Tai San finding it amusing.

"Wake up, Tai San," a voice said.

"Lex?" Tai San said seductively, kissing the hand on her shoulder. "Kiss me. I want you."

As the dream faded, Tai San quickly gained consciousness, awakening with a start - and felt someone's hand pressing on her shoulder, shaking her gently to rouse her from her slumbers. And it certainly wasn't Lex.

She had stayed up late into the night sitting in the lounge of the *Lakeside Resort*, reminiscing with Alice and Ryan about old

75

times, as well as speculating about their current situation and what it might all signify for the future.

When they could keep awake no longer, their minds full and having gone through a range of emotions at their reunion, exhausted, Tai San had gone to the room she had chosen in the vacant hotel. It was next to Alice's, who was in turn next door to Ryan's room.

Being the only ones there in the large and luxurious resort made it all a strange and surreal experience for Tai San, as did the uncertainty of not knowing the intentions of their 'hosts', The Selector and 'The Creator' he referred to. Overwhelmed, Tai San had quickly fallen asleep the moment she had gotten under the covers of her comfortable bed and had slept soundly – until now.

"Don't touch me!" Tai San cried out, recoiling and looking up from her bed at who it was who had woken her, and whose hand had just been on her shoulder.

It was The Selector.

"Good morning, Tai San," he greeted her amiably, as if he had done nothing untoward or out of the ordinary. "Did you sleep well?"

Tai San noticed the door to the bedroom was wide open. She had locked it the night before from the inside. The Selector must have had a master key and had let himself in.

"Why are you so agitated, Tai San?" The Selector asked.

"Why do you think!?" Tai San snapped.

"That you might have something to hide? Tell me about this person - Lex."

"I don't know what you're talking about," Tai San lied, unwilling to give out any information.

The Selector was standing alone in the room and for a moment just watched her – as if studying Tai San and her reactions. She recalled Alice and Ryan's observation that The Selector often seemed to be 'testing' them in some way.

Tai San could also detect a slight shift in his gaze, that he was subtly eyeing her up provocatively and she quickly pulled the sheets over her to cover herself up.

"Are you feeling – 'embarrassed' – Tai San? If so, you have no reason to be. Because I do understand," The Selector said.

"Understand – just exactly what?"

"That you are developing into a very beautiful young woman. Nature has been kind to have given you physical qualities that many would wish they had. You must have excellent DNA and come from a good line. What about your family – can you tell me about your parents?"

"That's none of your concern," Tai San said, confused by The Selector's questions – and her intuition firing, feeling increasingly threatened by his presence.

"Everything about you is my concern, Tai San. Including even your genetics. Which I am sure The Creator will be very interested in. Now, I suggest that you shower and I'll meet you in the lobby in precisely thirty minutes."

Tai San didn't move.

"Interesting," The Selector remarked. "You clearly need to learn how to follow instructions. For your own sake." There was more than a hint of threat as he picked up a ripe peach from a bowl on a side table and started taking mouthfuls, the juice dripping down his chin.

"They're really quite delicious. You should try them. Millions of years of change have given us this," he indicated the half-eaten peach. "One of nature's gifts. As are you."

He put the peach down and turned his back, Tai San watching as he left the room – without a word – and shut the door behind him. Tai San could hear the door being locked from the outside.

On her own again, Tai San tried to gather her thoughts. She couldn't understand The Selector or the strange experience she had found herself in. It was like being in another dream, surreal, nightmarish.

There was a sudden knock, a tap-tap, from outside the door.

"Alice? Is that you?" Tai San called out warily.

"No, it's me," The Selector responded from the other side of the doorway. "Alice and Ryan will join you in the lobby in precisely twenty-seven minutes. You are losing time, Tai San. And that is not a wise thing to do. So, get yourself ready."

"Ready for what?"

There was no reply.

Tai San was totally perplexed by what was going on.

Even more so when a few seconds passed – and then a few minutes – and still, The Selector had not given her an answer. Or even said anything further. There was only silence.

Tai San climbed out of bed, crossed to the door, unlocked it and opened it, peering carefully outside - where The Selector stood and sighed impatiently while glancing at a digital device on his wrist.

"You now only have seventeen minutes. And you won't want to suffer the penalty of being late!"

He glared at Tai San, then walked down the corridor.

Tai San thought it would be wise to go along with matters for the time being. She took a quick shower, dressed, all the while wondering what The Selector was up to, why he was playing all these mind games with her.

She had never been through anything like it before. Even with The Broker. And hoped that she would soon have an answer as to what were The Selector and The Creator's plans for her. As well as Alice and Ryan.

Tai San arrived in the main lobby where she saw Alice and Ryan waiting for her. They were sitting in armchairs but were surrounded by guards, along with the same group of medical-scientists Tai San had encountered at the dock - all wearing decontamination suits with medical surgery masks covering their faces.

"Ah, you made it, Tai San," The Selector said, with a benevolent smile. "With eighteen seconds to spare. Please, take a seat. We need to remain on schedule."

He glanced at the digital device on his wrist and indicated another chair. Tai San sat, where she was strapped, along with Ryan and Alice in their own chairs, so the medics or scientists or whoever they were could go about their tests.

"Get your hands off me!" Ryan bellowed, struggling to free himself.

Like Ryan, Alice was also squirming in her seat as the guards continued strapping her down, tying her arms to those of the chair.

'Relax. All of you. You have nothing to fear," The Selector said reassuringly. "For your own safety, we just need to carry out some more tests and then you will be free to enjoy the rest of the day."

As soon as Tai San was secure, the masked medical team began feverishly working on the three Mall Rats, taking readings of their vital signs.

"Why are you doing this?" Tai San demanded, flinching as one of the medics performed a blood test on her exposed arm.

"It will soon be over," The Selector reassured her, walking over to Tai San's chair. "Sssshh, hush now, everything will be okay," he said, stroking her hair with his fingers as if to relax her. But it only made the situation worse for Tai San, detesting the violation of her freedom, her body even, as the medics, with machine-like efficiency, carried out more tests, taking swabs of her saliva. There was something so inhuman about it all.

The Selector snapped his fingers, indicating a guard to pour three glasses of juice. Tomato juice. Which three guards placed at the mouths of Tai San, Alice and Ryan. "Drink. It's fresh. You'll love it."

Tai San, Alice and Ryan considered the glasses of juice in front of them cautiously and The Selector smiled. "It's not poison, if that's what you're concerned about. Here, I'll show you."

He crossed to the counter and poured himself a glass and sipped on it, savouring the taste. "Delicious. Now drink – all of you!"

Tai San, Alice and Ryan sipped on the glasses which were held to their mouths and as they swallowed, all gagged as if they were about to vomit.

"That's not tomato juice!" Ryan yelled. "It's blood!"

"Why does it revolt you so, Ryan? Tell me," The Selector urged him to reveal.

"You're crazy!" Alice gasped, trying to gain her composure and wash her mouth out with her own saliva to get rid of the taste.

"Why do you think that, Alice?" The Selector asked, intrigued. "What if the drink was in reality tomato juice? Would we be crazy offering you that to drink? Whereas blood is so very important. After all, you'd be desperate to receive it if you had an accident and had to receive a transfusion."

"That's a little different," Tai San said. "What you're doing is absolutely disgusting. Inhumane. Have you no mercy? Compassion?"

"I have an abundance of compassion, Tai San, you can be sure. As well as blood. And you've just drunk some. So now we are interconnected. The three of you, with me."

Tai San, Alice and Ryan gazed unbelievingly as The Selector started to pace, gathering his thoughts, deep in contemplation, while the medics began unpacking other equipment from boxes they had brought with them.

"The Creator informs me that as well as our spiritual needs, we are a tool-making species," The Selector suddenly spoke, addressing the Mall Rats before him. "Ever since our ancestors learned to make fire, to hunt, to cook, to co-operate with each other – it is our ability to make tools that has propelled us along every evolutionary step, advancing our society, our humanity. We have expanded over every land on this Earth, learned to fly, conquered the seas, we're soon to explore the heavens, set out for the stars. Tried to control nature itself. We have even become so proficient at making things, we have upset the balance and threatened our very world we depend upon."

"What is this – some kind of history lesson?" Alice blurted sarcastically, interrupting The Selector, who did indeed sound like an absent-minded professor giving an impassioned lecture. And he certainly possessed the skills of an orator.

"It's a reminder of where we have come from. Of who we are," The Selector continued. "Despite all of our great accomplishments, as well as our faults, and the many incredible, miraculous things that humanity has brought into being – underneath it all, as The Creator has revealed – you and me, all of us, are organic creatures ourselves. Made of flesh and bone. Also, blood. Our time on this Earth is short and each of us is nothing more than a candle in the dark, waiting for our flame to one day go out."

"What are you talking about?" Ryan said, totally confused, struggling to get out of his bonds.

"We think and act like we are immortal but we are quite the reverse. All it takes is a pathogen. An accident. Maybe a wicked act committed by one of our own kind. A natural disaster. Perhaps an illness brought on ourselves by our own life choices. A virus even. The adults learned the hard way - in the end, we have to do everything we can to look after our flesh and bones. Our blood. Every fibre of our health. All of our future achievements, all of our dreams, after millions of years of life still depend on the functions of our organic parts. On a spiritual level, however, one can't live without love. But there can be no life without blood."

"Poetic," Alice scoffed. "Who was your inspiration? Vampires and Dracula?"

"Not exactly. I would suspect bats had something to do with those kinds of tales. An interesting species – bats. We have been studying them in some of our breeding programmes. All manner of species. Amazing creatures. It's absolutely fascinating when one takes into account the properties of sound and how radar evolved, heralding the most extraordinary technology."

The Selector thought about his comments introspectively.

If Tai San, Alice and Ryan had any doubts about The Selector's sanity, these quickly evaporated, and they realized that he was either totally mad – or possessed a zealot conviction to all he referred to in his impassioned lecture.

After addressing the Mall Rats, he crossed to the counter, poured himself a glass of his blood and drank it while the medics unpacked strange looking capsules of some kind from sealed foil bags that they were then inserting inside large, hypodermic needles.

"You Mall Rats may think you understand the sanctity of life," The Selector continued addressing his prisoners. "But I wonder if you truly respect it, treasure it. As does The Creator. Life is precious, to be valued. It is the foundation of our society. Our very existence. Let alone the future. And that is why we are here today."

"We're ready, Selector" one of the medics said, certain that the hypodermic needle they were handling was loaded properly.

"As our most recent arrival, Tai San," The Selector informed her, "You will have the honour of being the first recipient of one of the adults' last technological breakthroughs which, thanks to the infrastructure The Creator has put in place, we have refined and adapted."

The medic holding the large needle stood beside Tai San, positioning it carefully over her arm, choosing the appropriate spot.

"No!" Tai San cried out, terrified at what was happening. She shifted in her seat, willing her bound arm to be free, but it was no use, the guards holding her down, under pressure, keeping the arm tied to the chair, the tip of the huge needle getting ever closer, just millimeters over her right hand.

"You're hurting her!" Ryan yelled, enraged by the treatment of Tai San.

"Sometimes the thing that causes the most pain, can also bring the most pleasure. And end up being the best thing that ever happened to us," The Selector said, watching developments with a macabre fascination.

Tai San knew the needle was going to hurt, big time. It was wide and the longest needle she had ever seen and she dreaded whatever they were going to inject into her. "I haven't given you my permission to do this!" she screamed angrily.

"But they have *my* permission," The Selector insisted. "Don't worry, it's quite safe. Each of you are about to have an advanced microchip injected into your body tissue. It will ache at first, but it is for your own good. And after this, you will wish this day had happened sooner."

"Don't bet on it!" Alice roared.

Tears began to stream from Tai San's eyes, due to the intense pain she felt as the needle was inserted, going deeper into her hand, deeper still, her arm cramping painfully.

She wanted to stifle the pain, to not show any weakness or vulnerability, to resist The Selector to her last breath. But the pain was too great and she screamed out, in agony, unable to fathom the insensitive cruelty, let alone the hurt she was suffering.

The Selector looked on sadistically, studying Tai San as she writhed in her seat. He wiped away the trace of a tear from her cheek with his little finger, which he then placed in his mouth, sucking on his finger. Then bizarrely, he began to copy her facial mannerisms, wincing in his own mock pain, as if he was going through the same, in a type of phantom ordeal.

And then it was over, the needle was slowly extracted from Tai San's hand, leaving a red welt on her skin from where it had gone in.

Tai San felt angry, humiliated, her hand throbbed, and that she might pass out at any moment.

She sobbed uncontrollably, tears running down her face.

"It's all for the best, Tai San," The Selector assured her, wiping away another tear from her cheek with his fingers.

Holding his hand to the light, he stared at the tear droplet, reflecting under the glare.

"What makes us all who we are?" he mused to himself, studying the tear.

"Untie me from this chair and I'll show you!" Alice threatened.

"Oh, you'll be untied, Alice. As well as Ryan. After your own injections."

The medics injected the biochips into Alice and Ryan, who gritted their teeth and cried out in as much pain as Tai San had experienced. During the process, The Selector watched eagerly.

"Don't forget to take any tears away for analysis," The Selector instructed his medics, who complied, beginning to scoop up fresh tears from Tai San's face, putting them into containers, along with some tears from Alice – but so far, Ryan hadn't produced any, although his face was writhed in agony.

A medic examined various screens. "We're getting readings starting to come through, Selector. The biochips appear to be functional. Everything's operational. They're in the system now. Data's being sent through to the base. Adrenalin and pulse rate's a little high though," the medic added.

"As it should be," The Selector concurred. "The *fight or flight* response. You can't get away from millions of years of evolution – we're all still just animals, in the end."

"Some, more than others," Ryan snapped angrily.

"Indeed," The Selector replied calmly as he crossed to Tai San and removed a small vial from one of the medic's trays. "Open wide," The Selector instructed. "Don't be afraid. I just require another swab," The Selector reassured.

He took the swab, then crossed to the entrance.

"I'll go and personally inform The Creator that preparations are in order. And do some of my own tests on the genetics," he stated.

As he left, he was slightly preoccupied by the device strapped to his wrist which wasn't solely a digital watch but displayed a screen which The Selector gazed at intently.

As he walked, he inserted the swab he had taken from Tai San, then studied DNA readings on his wrist monitor

He had found the Mall Rats' ordeal most interesting. And slightly melodramatic. Even naïve. Unbeknownst to them, he had been injected with a similar biochip at the very beginning when he first met The Creator. He knew the pain they were going through. But it was necessary to connect them to not only The Selector but The Creator as well in ways that Tai San, Alice and Ryan were yet to realize. But they would, soon.

Arriving outside, the doors of a futuristic looking pod - a vehicle - opened automatically, The Selector took his seat, the doors swung shut and the driverless vehicle sped away.

CHAPTER SEVEN

Bray took cover in the street in the suburbs behind some abandoned, burned-out wrecks of vehicles, ensuring he remained unseen as he cautiously watched a party of ex-Zootists who were gathering produce from a park.

The Mall Rats had once planted potatoes and Amber and Bray thought it would be an interesting exercise for the ex-Zootists to make themselves useful by doing some manual work. But it would also give them a chance to check out if the ex-Zootists could indeed be trusted while working alone. Bray agreed with Amber that it would be wise for him to discreetly check on them at the conclusion of his scouting. He had more or less completed checking out the city and environs which were well and truly deserted.

Absent from any contact with Ebony who had stayed back at the mall, the Zootists seemed to be dutifully carrying out their tasks, harvesting the potatoes, placing them in an abundance of rusty shopping carts.

It filled Bray with some reassurance that perhaps the Zootist militia could be an asset to the Mall Rats after all, rather than representing some form of threat, since they had seemingly done nothing more untoward than carry out all that had been asked of them.

Maybe Ebony herself *had* changed, as she kept insisting she had to Bray and Amber in recent weeks, and Bray considered he had possibly been overly cautious of Ebony and should give her more benefit of his doubt.

His optimism was short-lived though when he overheard one of the Zootists suggesting that the group make a trip to Sector 6 before they got back to the mall, reinforcing the need that *none* in the group could tell Ebony of their secret detour, however.

This gave Bray another dimension of concern. They clearly were not totally de-radicalized because Sector 6 was a legendary area of the suburbs where Zoot had gone to school and had become not only a mythological but a revered and hallowed place for those with the original Locos' ideology, let alone the derivative Zootists.

No matter how disciplined and well trained the militia were and the progress the Mall Rats believed was being made during the de-radicalization process, this particular group Bray was furtively following clearly had their own sense of independent spirit.

Now Bray was filled with dread as he kept out of sight but watched the Zootists arrive at the old school which Bray himself had once attended. Ebony had also gone there, as had Trudy, Bray meeting them both in the last days of the virus. Bray's younger brother, Martin, had also been a student there. The school itself was where he had one day brazenly rebelled against not only the teachers, but all forms of authority, everything that the adult world represented – re-inventing himself as Zoot, the leader of The Locos. The school was the place where the legend had begun.

It was now in a state of decay, ruins, its windows all broken, the walls covered in graffiti – including many tags portraying

The Locos scrawled in paint on its peeling exterior – the school had visitors once more.

Bray was aghast, stupefied, as the Zootists knelt down, bowing before the building at the entrance by the school gates.

"Zoot lives! Zoot lives!" they began to chant, their voices echoing around the deserted suburbs as the cry repeated, each mention of his brother's alter ego causing Bray nothing but emotional pain at the memory of what was and anxiety at the thought of what could be.

Shocked by the apparent 'pilgrimage' the Zootists were making, Bray realized he would have to get back to the mall quickly to let Amber and the others know of his discovery. Bray hoped Ebony would be surprised to learn that those who they thought were ex-Zootists were still very much under the thrall of the zealous beliefs instilled in them of late by The Guardian and Eloise.

Suddenly, a high-pitched noise whined above as the shadow of something soared over the school, passing by at high speed.

Bray was so lost in his own concern at what he had discovered with the Zootists that at first he almost didn't register it – and thought that he might have imagined what he had just heard and seen, a strange, unexpected blur in his peripheral vision.

Looking up, he was astonished to see a drone, making fast, zig-zagging movements high above the streets in the sector.

"What the hell is that?" Bray said to himself, stunned.

Another drone flew overhead – and then another – the air whistling with the sibilant sound of their engines. It was like a plague of machines had just flocked into the skies, some drones making rapid movements, altering their course and direction as they sped by, other drones hovering for a few seconds in mid-air before continuing on their journey.

Bray had a fleeting thought of UFOs and the notion that what he was viewing was actually from another planet, let alone world. As did the Zootists.

"Power and chaos!" they yelled in reverence, gazing up at the drones that hovered directly above the school.

One Zootist yelled with utter joy, thrusting his arms into the air. "Oh, Mighty Zoot. Thank you for connecting with us and sending these signs from the Heavens!"

The Zootist suddenly cried out in pain as he was hit by a targeting laser light which shot out from a drone, striking him. And he slumped to the ground, writhing in agony.

Panic-struck, the other Zootists began to scatter, dispersing in all directions, terrified by the unknown machines and what they were capable of, flying high above them.

And Bray himself was equally concerned, having no idea where the drones were coming from and whose control they were under. He knew, however, he had to immediately return to the mall and warn Amber and the others of the extreme danger all were in.

Adrenalin and fear coursing through his veins, he took off running as fast as he could through the suburbs, trying somehow to keep obscured in an effort to stay out of sight from the drones.

* * *

Lex drove the vehicle at extreme high speed, running off the road for a few seconds, the vehicle's tyres grinding in the muddy grass, skidding, before he was able to turn the wheel and regain control. Back on the road Lex floored the accelerator, picking up even greater speed.

"Can't you please SLOWDOWN!" Ram cried out, gripping the front passenger seat, the dashboard, anything he could to hold on.

"Zip it!" Lex shouted, keeping his eyes on the road. "I know what I'm doing!"

"I hope so. For all our sakes!" Ram yelled, closing his eyes tightly so he didn't have to watch, panicked. But he was frightened more than by what he thought of Lex's driving like a madman – his suspicions on what they might encounter when – and if - they arrived at the city filled him with dread.

Jack and Ellie, in the back of the vehicle, were literally thrown out of their seats throughout the journey, often getting airtime, the seat belts holding them down as the vehicle hurled down the twisting road, Ellie giving off a nervous shriek in fright, Jack one of his own, as the vehicle skidded precariously.

The sense of urgency at that time had nothing to do with the drones Bray had noticed. The source of their panic was to warn the others of their discovery that *someone* else had been at Eagle Mountain, the adults housed in the cryogenic hibernation chambers had seemingly gone missing.

Lex was doing his best to get them back to the mall as quickly as possible – and he was succeeding as the panoramic views of the city appeared in the distance as they rounded another corner on the road leading back down from Eagle Mountain.

Suddenly he slammed on the brakes, the vehicle skidding to a halt. He was stunned at what he could see. They all were.

A fleet of ships, in the distance, was visible.

"Is that what I think it is?" Jack muttered in surprise, disbelief.

He wasn't just referring to the ships out in the open sea heading for the harbour but was watching a military type of aircraft making its descent, soon to land where the airport was located, many miles away.

"It can't be!" Ram said to himself. He looked like he was staring into the abyss, his worst nightmares. "They're finally here…"

"Who?!" Ellie demanded, in mounting panic.

"Who'd you think?! The Easter bunny??" Ram shouted. "I'm getting outta here!"

He began unbuckling his seat belt and opened the passenger door – before being yanked back into the vehicle by Lex's strong grip.

"You're not going anywhere. Sit down!" Lex roared, leaning over and shutting Ram's door shut. "What do you know about this!?"

Ram clutched the sides of his face with his hands, trying to calm his rising tensions and fear, to stave off a panic attack.

"Who are they, Ram!?" Lex asked.

"Who?! Don't you get it!? It's gotta be The Collective! That's who!"

"The Collective?" Jack wondered, considering the notion of what Ram was suggesting.

"They'll be here for me! And for you! Eagle Mountain – the whole city! Turn this thing around, Lex – we got to get away, as far away as we can! We're all in danger!"

"Possibly not," Ellie said, trying to convince herself as much as the others. "They might not be The Collective. But could be friendly."

"Somehow, I very much doubt it," Jack said, gently.

"Well, whoever they are – we just can't leave!" Ellie insisted. "We've got to get back to the mall and warn the others."

"Exactly!" Lex bellowed, slamming his foot on the accelerator, the vehicle hurling forward at high speed once more, Lex driving towards the city, peering through the windscreen as he noticed the drones flying in the far distance.

"What are those things?" Ellie cried out.

"They look like drones to me!" Ram said, totally panic-stricken while trying to open the passenger door again but Lex had locked all the doors from the main control by the driver's seat.

* * *

The Mall Rats were gathered in the food court, standing together, huddled in a group - but they were now prisoners of the invaders, having surrendered the mall moments before. Not without putting up a brave fight, however.

Amber couldn't believe what they had been through. It had all been over in a matter of minutes. From the moment the first stun grenade had gone off, the blinding light and smoke had disorientated everyone from its shockwave. And with other stun grenades exploding all around them – they had never really stood a chance.

The Mall Rats had been swiftly and totally overpowered in a clinical, efficient and devastatingly effective display of force. They had tried to fight back as best as they could. Trudy had gone into a fit of rage when the attack commenced, her love and motherly instincts driving her to defend her daughter, who had been sleeping under Emma's care while Trudy had been overseeing The Guardian. She was only able to hold off the warriors for a few seconds before she, as well as Brady, had been captured.

Amber had been in the food court earlier at the time with Salene and May where she had been trying to make a wedding cake. But those plans were now dashed, all their lives turned upside down from the first second the invaders rushed into the mall in a clearly well co-ordinated assault.

Salene and May had resisted, throwing pots and pans at the intruders, as did Amber before resorting to using her bare hands. She had been utterly desperate to get to her baby, then in Lottie and Sammy's care, to stave off the attack. All her efforts were in vain. For all the skill in hand to hand combat, none of the Mall Rats were any match for the disciplined fighting units that had so unexpectedly descended among them.

Now Amber knelt down beside Bray, who was crouched on the floor, cradling his ribs.

He had raced into the mall soon after the attack had begun and had fought well, taking out some of the invaders, knocking them unconscious, before another warrior had blasted him with a stun gun device, similar to the type of weapons used by The Technos when they themselves had invaded in the past.

But now there was also advanced weaponry deployed, seemingly laser-orientated, much like the drones had deployed at the school when the Zootists had been struck.

"Are you okay?" Amber asked Bray, gently helping him climb to his feet and he nodded reassuringly.

"He'll be fine," stated the imposing figure beside them. "As will you and everyone else, if you co-operate with us and follow instruction!"

He was tall, stocky and had a commanding aura which was hardly surprising given that although his subordinates even referred to him as Commander or 'Sir' - his name was Snake. He had personally led the raid on the mall, as well as the entire city, from what Amber could understand, other units having contacted him on occasion via his security earpiece to give updates on their progress.

'Snake' was aptly named – with his intimidating physique and combat prowess, he had crushed those in the mall and all who encountered him couldn't help but be slightly repelled by the unsightly tattoos he had of reptile scales on the side of his face, running down his shaven head. It was like he was some strange combination between man and reptile.

"*All areas secure so far, Commander,*" Amber could overhear a voice communicating via Snake's earpiece. "*No opposition to report.*"

"Have the units double-check the entire region and report back to me as soon as possible if you find any sign of inhabitants," Snake ordered whoever he was talking to.

Towering above her, Snake looked down at Amber, who he was aware had been listening to his exchange, while others under his command were checking data on tablet computers and scanning the various faces of their prisoners to try and identify all who were under their control.

"Any sign of Ram?" Snake asked one of this militia.

"Nothing so far, Sir," his subordinate replied, while checking various images of the prisoners on his tablet. "And there seems to be three Mall Rats missing. Lex. Jack. Ellie," he added.

"Where are they?" Snake demanded as he crossed back to Amber and Bray.

"We have no idea what you're talking about," Bray lied. "And even if we did, there's no way any of us would tell you."

"My team have ways to get you 'Rats' to talk. And believe me - they'd enjoy what I'd order them to do. But you wouldn't!"

"Lex, Jack and Ellie are no longer members of the Mall Rats," Amber lied, trying to sound as convincing as she could while meeting Snake's threatening steely gaze with her own defiant one.

"Are you sure about that? Because I'm not. Wherever Ram is and the rest of your tribe – they can't hide forever. We will find them!"

Snake turned and strode abruptly, briskly, out of the food hall and towards the lower concourse to where a group of Legion warriors were who had been held under guard by the Mall Rats until Snake's forces had released them all – along with Eloise and The Guardian, who were standing, now free, beside the Legion members and Zootists.

"Oh, mighty Zoot – you have blessed us with this divine victory on this day!" The Guardian shouted, raising his arms aloft in triumph, in praise to the Heavens. "This mall – this city – this very world! – will be yours, from this day onwards! And we will deliver you not only revenge but salvation to all who follow!"

Snake ignored The Guardian's rambling and approached Eloise.

"Your orders, Commander Eloise," Snake advised, handing her a tablet computer with a set of instructions which she began to attentively read. "The Guardian and the Zootist followers will remain under your control."

"I understand and will of course obey," she responded.

"Wise," Snake informed her, with a slight smile.

Snake commanded his forces to separate all the prisoners into different groups. With the Mall Rats being isolated in the food court.

The expectant mothers in various stages of pregnancy were assembled in the lower concourse. All were terrified of Snake and his fearsome warriors, carrying out their task with relentless efficiency, herding the girls together like they were animals.

In the food court where the Mall Rats were being held – the core members of the tribe were separated into one area being Amber, holding her baby Jay, along with Bray, Trudy, Brady, Salene, May, Lottie and Sammy.

Lia, who had originally been present, was taken to another area along with Emma, unable to see but hearing everything. She was in great distress, bravely doing her best to contain her emotions and control her tears so as not to in turn upset further her already scared younger brother and sister, Shannon and Tiffany, who nestled in as close to their big sister as possible.

Bray and Amber, along with some of the others, warned of the consequences if any Mall Rats or those under their supervision would be hurt and implored them all to be treated with decency and respect. But the warnings were of course impotent and Bray especially realized that there was little he could do at this point in time to assist. But he resolved that he would come up with a plan to at least try.

Ebony was with a group of captives being held in another area of the lower concourse with the remnants of the few loyal remaining members of the ex-Zootist militia. An irony which was not lost on Ebony herself, who couldn't believe she now found the situation reversed - with herself a prisoner, her former prisoners now seemingly set free. She decided she would have to play this one carefully, unsure if her survival might be contingent upon her supposed allegiance to either the Zootists. Or Mall Rats.

"Name!?" Snake asked when he arrived, noticing Ebony standing apart from the other Zootists.

"Ebony," she replied cautiously.

"Are you a Mall Rat?" Snake probed.

"I could be," Ebony replied, trying to gauge his reaction. 'There again, I was once Queen of the Locos and 'mistress' to the leader, Zoot. And that group of Zootists you are setting free simply adore me, if I do say so myself. As did Zoot. And for good reason. He was an amazing lover. But nothing compared to me. Oh, how I miss him. Pity I couldn't find a good man who might be interested in all I have to offer," she said, seductively, while running her tongue over her lips suggestively.

"Interesting," Snake replied, considering Ebony before checking data and images on his tablet screen, one of which was a photograph of Ebony along with lines of text. Ebony noticed the photograph but couldn't read details of the text.

"I hope you'll agree that the photograph you have there isn't the best one of me. And that I'm hopefully a little more attractive in real life. I'm very experienced in all areas of combat and can be really useful if you're looking for recruits."

"I know all about you," Snake answered. "You're not a Mall Rat. You never have been."

"Is that a good thing or a bad thing?"

"Oh, you'll soon find out!"

"Find out what!?" Ebony responded despondently, aware that her strategies for survival were seemingly to no avail.

"Prepare her!" Snake barked out an order. "And the others! We need to leave and stay on schedule!'"

Ebony started to back away as a unit of Snake's militia descended upon her. She was quickly overwhelmed, warriors gagging her, binding her arms behind her back, her legs together, rendering her totally immobile, unable to utter even a single word no matter how hard she tried.

"Power and Chaos! Power and Chaos!" The Guardian cried out, in mounting intensity.

As she strained to be free of her binds, Ebony saw Eloise, who had walked over to Bray and the rest of the Mall Rats who were now shackled and were being led down the staircase to the ground level from the upper concourse.

Amber watched intently, as did all the other Mall Rats, as Eloise gave Bray a kiss on one cheek.

He recoiled in disgust. Eloise dug her long fingernails into his cheeks as she clutched his face and hissed venomously. "You're never ever going to forget me, Bray." She pressed her lips on his own, forcing a kiss, taking passion from his incapacitation, along with his groans as she dug her nails in deeper and scratched each cheek.

But she enjoyed Amber's horrified expression more as she stepped back and smiled sweetly to Amber and the other Mall Rats.

"I hope you all have fun," she sneered, while watching them being led to the exit of the mall.

Ebony watched them leave as well as she was dragged towards the centre of the ground level.

She was completely powerless, humiliated, and now extremely frightened – she had no idea what was intended for the Mall Rats, let alone herself.

The last thing she felt was the sharp sting of a needle being inserted into her arm – causing her to pass out, slipping into an unconsciousness state and had freedom only in her dreams.

CHAPTER EIGHT

Lex had a terrible feeling that he was walking into a trap. But given the situation they found themselves in, there was no other option, he felt, than to keep going. There was no turning back.

He carefully, cautiously, made his way across the second level of the derelict multistorey car park, heading towards one of the entrances to the mall. He listened for the sounds of anyone, his eyes scanning the rows of abandoned vehicles, long ago vandalized and looted, as he slowly advanced, attentive to any signs of movement.

So far there was nothing to indicate any presence of the mysterious invaders.

He turned to give a thumbs up and a quick wave to Ellie, who signalled back in return from the driver's seat of their vehicle.

They had driven to the multistorey car park hoping the building would give them some form of cover to keep out of sight of the occupation force, Ram convinced they had to be The Collective - much to his grave concern.

Ellie was slouched at the wheel, keeping her head low in case anyone *did* notice the vehicle had occupants. She had left the keys in the ignition and was in a state of alert herself, peering around the car park, ready to switch on the engine to get away as fast as she could in the event they needed to make their escape.

Jack was in the back keeping watch on Ram, in the front passenger seat, who was still in a condition of absolute panic. The former leader of The Technos claiming that he was a wanted man.

Throughout the drive back into the city, most of the drones that had been visible from afar at the initial onset of the invasion were no longer flying in the sky. Only a few drones remained, gliding overhead in a circuit, as if in a routine pattern of aerial patrols over the different sectors. Ram speculated that the bulk of the drones would have been busy assisting the occupiers in some other way elsewhere - perhaps unloading or transporting cargo from the invaders' ships in the harbour, doing reconnaissance in the suburbs, with the city centre already scouted and secured.

Lex detected a strange 'smell' in the air, not realizing that it had emanated from the stun grenades which had been deployed in the attack in the mall.

So far as he could gather, the invaders were nowhere to be seen.

Ram was also aware of this fact and hoped it would stay that way. It was possible, he thought, that the main attack force was at the docks, unloading equipment, possibly other vehicles, from their ships. Or loading the vessels with whatever it was The Collective or whoever was responsible, had taken from the city – including the uncomfortable notion that this could include some human 'cargo' in the form of those who had been in the city at the moment of its invasion, the Mall Rats among them.

"Not much fun being on the receiving end, is it?" Ellie said quietly in the vehicle, remembering the day Ram and his Technos conquered the city themselves.

"You should have told that to Lex," Ram sneered.

"I think Lex is very brave," Ellie continued.

"All we got to do is sit here and wait. And we'll probably end up being captured," Ram responded, despondently.

"Lex is putting his neck on the line," Jack added.

"For all of us," Ellie agreed. "Even you, Ram. And let's just hope that The Collective or whoever it is hasn't arrived at the mall as yet."

Jack peered from his crouching position, watching out the window as in the distance Lex slowly opened the door leading into the mall.

Lex moved cautiously, furtively, entering into the upper concourse levels which looked to be an absolute mess. Some of the shop windows had been smashed, their contents strewn out all over the place causing Lex to step over the debris. The mall appearing like it had been totally ransacked.

He remained alert, making sure there was no one in sight lying in wait to ambush him, and felt his anger levels rising, outraged at the thought of what had obviously gone on.

Arriving at the food court, usually the focus of the mall's daily life, Lex found it totally abandoned. He could smell the scent of food still in the air from a lunch that had clearly been interrupted and there were more remnants of smoke from the stun grenades which had been unleashed.

Tables had been knocked over, chairs were on their sides, littering the floor.

It must have been one hell of a commotion, Lex could tell. He was sure the Mall Rats would have put up a good fight, defending themselves and the others in their care. If only he could have been there. To get his hands on the attackers, to make them pay for what they had done.

Suddenly Lex heard voices approaching and ducked for cover behind one of the fallen over tables in the food court – before carefully peering out to see who was getting near.

Two invaders were going through the mall, loading up supplies, and were unknowingly closing in on the part of the food court where Lex was in hiding. He wondered if there could be others from whatever attacking force.

Assessing his options, Lex felt he didn't have long before the invaders would discover him – so there was only one thing he could do.

Bursting out from behind the table, Lex charged at the warriors, taking them completely by surprise, crashing into one of them, sending him flying, collapsing into a heap.

The other warrior pressed the headpiece in his ear and barked out an update.

"We've found Lex! Repeat, the Mall Rat 'Lex' has been found-"

He was unable to finish his sentence, however, Lex striking him flush on the jaw, the warrior going unconscious before he even hit the floor.

Lex took the headpiece from the warrior's ear and held it up to his own, listening in to see what he could hear as he ran, as fast as he could, back the way he came.

"*Transport Lex to the airport immediately for evacuation with the others. Do you copy?*"

Lex stopped and remained frozen for a moment before the voice repeated.

"*Confirm instructions. Did you copy?*"

"Got it," Lex finally replied into the mouthpiece, hoping that his disguised voice sounded convincing. But his biggest concern was to get out of there fast to warn Jack, Ellie and Ram.

* * *

The vehicle burst through a hedge, tearing an uneven hole in it, sending twigs and leaves flying, scattering all over the windscreen as Ellie drove into a field, adjusting the wheel slightly to correct the onset of a skid from the back wheels as they dug into the muddy terrain.

"Goddammit! – and I thought Lex was a bad driver!" Ram grumbled, the movement shaking him around in the back-passenger area.

"You haven't seen nothing yet!" Ellie promised, flooring the accelerator as far as it would go.

Ellie had grown up on her parents' farm and she had driven a car around the property, as well as tractors, and used other machinery.

It was strictly illegal at the time, Ellie not old enough to hold a license - but her parents didn't mind, encouraging the independent spirit they saw in their youngest daughter and thought it useful she learn some 'real life' practical skills that would hold her in good stead in her future. Especially when her parents had become sick during the virus. Ellie, with her sister Alice, had been increasingly left on their own and she had often driven the old family car in places never intended for it, to get quickly around their property. She was at home in the outdoors and knew how to 'read' the contours and lay of the land.

Even Lex was now holding on, one arm steadying himself in his seat as Ellie sped along the countryside. Jack was in the front passenger seat, also gripping the front dashboard as they hurtled along.

"They'd need a fighter jet to catch us," Jack said, pleased with how fast Ellie was going – and how far they had left the city in such a short time. He kept turning around from time to time, looking behind to make sure they weren't being followed.

When Lex had returned to the vehicle after his clash with the invaders, he had urged Ellie to drive away as quickly as she could while he leapt in the back, joining Ram, with Jack occupying the passenger seat next to Ellie. And she had done well, exceeding even Lex's own expectations at how fast the vehicle could go.

Ellie had suggested they avoid the main roads in and out of the city in case the drones that were on patrol flying above spotted them – even better, Ellie thought, they even avoid any roads altogether.

She had driven the vehicle literally across the countryside, travelling in parallel to the main highway about a mile to their south, and was barreling through overgrown field after field, the vehicle taking a battering, its tyres likely damaged. Time was running out, the fuel gauge showing signs that it would soon go into the empty reserves zone.

They were headed for the airport where the Mall Rats were apparently being taken, according to the communiques Lex had eavesdropped on.

In the old days, before the virus of course, they had all been there many times, going on family holidays or to meet arriving visitors, but Ellie had never thought she would ever make a trip like the one she was currently doing.

Ram had even landed his Techno planes there when he had carried out his own invasion and reasoned there could probably be a prominent force in place.

Their plan, as desperate and crazy as it sounded to the four occupants, was to get as far away from the city as they could – and as close to the Mall Rats as possible, maybe even to rescue them somehow from their abductors. There seemed to be no other option open. At least to Ellie, Jack and Lex. Ram thought it was a ridiculous idea predictably and had suggested, in vain, that they try to get away from the entire city area, including the airport. And as far away as they could from the impending danger and doom he knew was in store. Lex, Ellie and Jack refused to even consider what he was suggesting, believing they couldn't just leave the Mall Rats to face whatever their fate was at the airport.

"You might need to come up with another option, guys," Ram sighed, concerned as he noticed a drone approaching through the back window.

Lex turned to peer for a better look himself and sighed. "That's all we need."

"What do I do!?" Ellie yelled in growing tension.

"Just keep going," Lex responded. "Let's try and lose it."

"I think you might be a little optimistic," Jack stated, unnerved at the entire event unfolding as he craned his head, squeezing his face to the window to gaze up for a better look and noticing that the drone was now flying above them and following their course.

"Try and get back on the highway, Ellie," Lex shouted, in mounting panic. "I've got an idea on how we might shake them!"

"Glad you do," Ram responded. "Because I don't. And we're not exactly on the same wave intellectually. If I'm a genius and I can't come up with something, how the hell will you?"

"We've got to try something!" Lex said in desperation.

The vehicle hurled through other fields and then suburbs. All the time the drone followed, speeding high above.

Before long, Ellie sped onto an exit ramp leading to the main highway.

"Good girl," Lex said, encouragingly.

"Yeah – good girl," Jack repeated, slightly jealous even in this moment of danger that Lex might be getting too personal and overly friendly.

"Now, when we get to one of those flyovers ahead, I want you to stop," Lex instructed.

The vehicle screeched, skidding to a stop when they arrived at the flyover – but the drone kept going before stopping itself and then flying in a zigzagged formation, as if still searching.

Inside the vehicle, Ellie and Jack exchanged a high-five and even Ram was euphoric. "Nice one, Lex. I like it! But I don't know how long it'll be before that drone finds us."

Ellie screamed hysterically as she suddenly noticed the drone appearing through the driver's side window, hovering at low level, as if watching all the occupants inside.

"Hit it!" Lex yelled.

Grinding the vehicle in gear, Ellie sped away with the drone following and all realized that they had no hope of shaking their technological pursuer.

They reached the perimeter of the airport before very long, Ellie urging the vehicle to go even faster as she rammed it, at high speed, into the wire mesh fence surrounding the airport grounds. This demolished the fence easily, Ellie nearly losing control in the process, a large dent appearing in the front of the vehicle from the collision. The engine also appeared to be damaged after the beating it had taken, thick smoke beginning to erupt from inside.

Still, the drone hovered overhead, slowing its pace as the vehicle was slowing to what would clearly be an eventual stop.

"Well – I'm sure we're going to have a welcome party very soon," Lex relayed.

"Great!" Ram shouted, slamming his fists on the side of the vehicle in frustration. "We're doomed! And that means I'm going to be dead! Thank you very much! If only you'd listened to me!"

"Shut it!" Lex bellowed. "They haven't caught us yet!"

Lex had another idea as the vehicle was soon to arrive at the derelict ruins of a passenger plane from the adult times that had been left to decay, straddling the side of the runway, the vehicle scraping the exterior of the aircraft as it ground to a halt.

And still, the drone followed and hovered above.

"Get out!" Lex instructed.

"Are you crazy, Lex!?" Ram replied.

"Maybe I am – which means that this might actually work! No one in their right mind would try and do this!"

"Do what!?" Jack asked.

"Giving the three of you at least a chance. If I act as a decoy. It might also give me a chance as well if I operate on my own without having you lot to worry about!"

Finding no other option than to agree to Lex's idea, Ellie, Jack and Ram quickly crawled out of the doors of the vehicle and after shutting the door, the three of them crossed furtively and ducked underneath the plane, dropping to the tarmac, scrambling under the shadows of the fuselage, taking cover behind its large wheels.

Lex's plan seemed to have worked. He had leapt into the front seat and driven off, with the drone following. Jack and Ellie loved him for it, realizing that his chances were very slim but at least he had given them both a chance. And even Ram was relieved at the respite, for the moment at least, to immediate danger.

Lex sped away from where he had dropped off the others and could see up ahead large grey military style cargo planes, with United Nations insignia visible on their sides, which had been used in the adult days but now had clearly been used for this invasion. Strange looking drones of different sizes, some as big as buses, were also grounded beside the planes.

Lex's vehicle sped past the terminal at fast as it could but smoke poured out from its damaged and overheating engine.

He caught a quick glimpse of some other vehicles parked around the aircraft – and noticed some were approaching at speed.

And it wasn't long before Lex's luck ran out. His own vehicle slowed down rapidly, before crawling to a complete stop, its engine finally surrendering in a waft of thick, black smoke.

Lex bailed, leaping out the driver's door, and started racing towards the main terminal building. But he was no match for the vehicles of the invaders, which converged on him at pace, moving in like the well trained predators that they were, their leader, Snake, among them – and Lex was swiftly overpowered, the warriors picking him up by his limbs, dragging him, helplessly, into the back of a military vehicle of their own.

"Nice of you to join us, Lex!" Snake sneered, as the vehicle door was slammed shut behind him.

At the airport perimeter, Ellie, Jack and Ram poked their heads up and peered out from behind the wheels of the plane underbelly they were seeking cover under, watching the figure of Lex in the distance, being driven towards the military cargo aircraft.

The vehicles stopped. Lex continued to resist as he was led towards one of the aircraft.

"You got a lot of fight in you, I'll give you that," Snake said, as he personally manhandled him, carrying Lex by his arms, two other warriors the other side lifting their prisoner by his feet.

"I'll give you 'what' - lizard boy!" Lex yelled at Snake, noticing his reptile-like tattoos. And he kicked out, shaking his legs in an effort to get free, the warriors keeping him in their vice-like grip.

They were clambering up the open cargo bay door, angling down from the aircraft onto the ground, Lex being hauled into its maws.

"Lex!" he heard Trudy cry out at seeing him.

As he was carried inside the cargo hold, Lex could see Trudy, Brady by her side, along with Amber and Bray, their baby in Amber's arms, Salene and May, as well as Lottie and Sammy, surrounded by more of the invasion force.

Ebony was there too, though she was being kept apart, sitting on the opposite side from the Mall Rats. She was the only one gagged, Lex noticed, while the Mall Rats were bound, Amber being the only one whose hands remained untied so she could cradle her son.

Placed down onto the metallic floor of the aircraft, Snake towering over him, Lex was bound like the other prisoners.

"Where's Ram?!" Snake demanded of him.

"How the hell should I know?" Lex lied. "Who'd you think I am – his mother?"

Snake cast Lex a wicked smile, grudging respect at Lex's bravado. "You'll talk eventually, Mall Rat. Just like you all will. You just wait."

"Let's get this bird up in the air!" Snake barked out an order over the communication headpiece in his ear. "We've got all our cargo, we're ready to go!"

The door to the cargo hold started to close, the interior of the hold getting darker as it gradually shut, the daylight receding, sealing the Mall Rats inside.

The engines of the plane began whirring to life as the military aircraft started to taxi for take-off.

"You should've stayed away while you still could," Bray said, commiserating at Lex's joining them as prisoners. "Why'd you come back to the city?"

"To warn you guys there were others around."

Bray nodded gratefully and both he and Lex exchanged glances, communicating something unsaid, well aware that they had a duty that went far beyond protection with their fellow members of The Tribe. And both clearly realized it as Bray noticed Lex giving a slight wave to baby Jay, as well as little Brady, who clung to her mother and waved back coyly.

"What's going on?" Trudy asked. "I wonder where 'they' are taking us?"

"I don't know. But if we can just all try and remain calm – I'm sure we'll be alright," Amber said, her expression giving away her obvious concern, the worry and fear showing in her eyes, mirroring the unease of all at what might lay ahead.

The plane barreled down the runway, its engines roaring, the noise thundering as if shaking the very ground as the aircraft quickly screamed past the derelict plane under which Jack, Ellie and Ram were hiding.

They watched, ducking their heads instinctively for cover, the sound deafening, as the military aircraft passed by overhead and receded into the distance, eventually disappearing from sight into the darkening, early evening sky.

CHAPTER NINE

"That's it!" Alice muttered, turning the taps on in the bathroom as far as they would go. "I've had enough of this place!"

She had gone to Tai San's room at the *Lakeside Resort*, Ryan accompanying her, where they found Tai San in a state of distress, so much so that when Ryan and Alice had initially knocked on the door, Tai San had refused to answer for several minutes, fearing that it could be The Selector paying her another unwelcome visit.

The initial joy at her reunion with Alice and Ryan had given way to feelings of helplessness. Tai San had always thought she was a strong-willed person, that few things would ever break her.

Her spirituality and ability to get in tune with what she perceived destiny had in store had also given her not only an inner strength but peace during the demise of the adults when the pandemic had struck.

Yet the ordeal she was now going through and the strange world of The Selector she had been thrust into had rattled Tai San to her core. The Selector was so unpredictable. And she couldn't instinctively 'read' him.

In addition, the injection of the biochip against her will felt like such a violation of Tai San's very essence, her living energy. And she had always felt a connection with all things living and the miracles of Mother Nature which surrounded her. Nature was what sustained Tai San. The biochip now inside her body was something she objected to on so many levels. It was polluting her being, what made her who she was. The way it had been injected into her was inhuman, against her fundamental rights. As long as it stayed in her body, she felt she was no longer the same person that she had naturally been before. Her chakras were well and truly out of alignment.

Alice and Ryan had comforted Tai San from the moment she had let them into her room – both sharing similar sentiments. And they found sharing their predicament helped give a degree of relief.

"There – that ought to do it!" Alice said, the taps loudly spraying water into the sink in Tai San's en suite bathroom.

The three of them had gone into the bathroom for another impromptu private meeting. Alice suggested they couldn't take any chances. For all they knew, the resort could be bugged or monitored somehow – and they didn't want anyone to listen in on the conversation they were planning to have with Tai San next, the sound of the water hopefully would drown out the whispered words of their discussions. Which mainly centred about a plan to escape.

* * *

It really was such a beautiful view, Tai San thought, appreciating the sight of the lake in front of them, flanked by rolling hills all around, covered in trees. It was like looking out on a real-life painting that had been brought to life, the reflection of the trees and hills shimmering on the water from the afternoon sun. No wonder the adults had built the *Lakeside Resort* in such a perfect location.

Tai San, walking side by side with Alice and Ryan, were making their way at a gentle pace over the lawns at the rear of the resort towards the lakeside. A few ducks flew towards them, quacking in anticipation of perhaps receiving a few crumbs – Ryan was eating some freshly-made bread and threw a few pieces into the water for the ducks to share.

Alice turned around to discreetly survey the view behind them. Several of the perimeter guards were in position at various points around the resort. They were intently watching the three prisoners standing by the side of the lake, Ryan continuing to casually rip off tiny mouthfuls of bread for the ducks.

"Everyone ready?" Alice whispered to Ryan and Tai San.

"Yep," Ryan said, wiping his hands, shaking the last of the crumbs over the feeding ducks.

"Let's do it," Tai San agreed.

The three of them suddenly took off in different directions, taking the guards by surprise as they noticed.

Ryan raced across the lawn to the left side of the resort, running by the water's edge, a small boathouse ahead of him with the forest visible over the other side.

Tai San sped off as quickly as she could to the right side of the resort, running towards the tall trees lining the lake as if her life depended on it, which of course it did.

Alice, who was aware she was never the fastest of sprinters, nevertheless set off as fast as she was able to the resort car park, around the corner of the main building, where she thought she might commandeer a vehicle perhaps.

Initially caught unawares by their unexpected moves, the guards quickly set off after their prisoners, splitting into three different groups.

It wasn't long before the guards began rapidly closing in on Alice and she knew she wouldn't be able to outrun them – but she felt confident that she could take out one, possibly two guards approaching, with her combat ability, let alone strength of her bulk. And her strategy was correct. She knocked one out with a single punch, the other needed two blows.

Alice hadn't counted on confronting other guards who were now closing in and soon caught up with her as she ran through the car park.

She gazed around at the vehicles and leapt in one. But there was no engine to hot wire, no steering wheel. Just a voice coming from the dashboard. *"STATE DESTINATION."*

Alice had no idea how to reply but had to try something as the guards were almost on her now. "Home!" she said, unable to think of anything else.

A ping sounded as the voice announced. *"FACIAL RECOGNITION IMPLEMENTED. YOU HAVE ARRIVED AT YOUR DESTINATION."*

Alice slammed her fist down on the control panel in utter frustration, which seemed to activate the system somewhere and the driverless pod vehicle took off at high-speed, with Alice gripping to her seat and gazing behind her at the guards in pursuit.

With his powerful build and sporting prowess, Ryan was also making good progress, running flat out, losing several guards trailing after him. And, like Alice, was able to cause a diversion that might assist Tai San in her efforts to get away. Tai San was more than capable of defending herself, having been trained in mixed martial arts. But her combat capabilities paled in comparison to the sheer muscle and brawn of both Ryan and Alice.

So far at least, the perimeter guards had focused their attentions on pursuing Ryan and Alice, which left Tai San to make it into the woods unencumbered. She hoped that all three would be able to rendezvous as they had planned, meeting up at an intersection they had all noticed on their journey to the *Lakeside Resort*, leading into the forest region.

* * *

Tai San was exhausted but urged herself to keep going, pushing herself to her absolute physical limits.

She was now some distance away from the *Lakeside Resort* and had made it far deeper from the wooded area into the depths of the forest bordering the lake, which was now completely out of view.

She continued to run at a high pace. It was unrelenting and she had been ignoring for some time the feelings in her body demanding her to stop for a moment's rest.

The tall trees in the ancient forest were all around her now, looming above, their thick canopy of branches and leaves casting the area of the forest in shade, a welcome feeling of slightly cooler air flowing on Tai San's face as she ran through the forest, sweat pouring from her. The surrounding nature seemed almost to give her strength beyond her body's natural stamina.

Leaping over a tangled knot of roots on the ground, Tai San's foot slipped and she nearly fell over, only just managing to keep her balance. She yelped in pain as she twisted her ankle in the process – and despite her desire to keep moving on, Tai San seized up, with no option but to now slow down.

Panting breathlessly, Tai San doubled up, bending over to catch her breath. She looked down at her ankle and rubbed it, the side of her leg burning in agony, her muscles in her body aching in a state of protest at what she had put them through. It felt like she was about to start cramping in her leg and she slowly moved it up and down, gently wiggling her foot, trying to stretch her leg muscles, struggling at the growing pain that was spreading from around her ankle.

She took a moment to examine her surroundings, now she had stopped fleeing – and determined she was well and truly clear of the *Lakeside Resort*. She had run in a diagonal direction from the resort and estimated she had to be several miles away by now. The only living things in the area, apart from the trees and Tai San herself, were the insects buzzing in the air, the fluttering and calling of the bird life up high in the branches of the trees.

In another time, Tai San would have luxuriated in it all. But now, she began to feel dizzy, her head spinning in a swirl. She was so tired – and with the extreme discomfort of her sprained ankle, she had nothing more to give and couldn't go on any further.

Tai San slumped to the forest floor, lying on her back, stretching her legs out in front of her in an attempt to relieve the cramps and the pressure she had been putting on her ankle when she had been standing up.

Though every part of her body was sore, her ankle especially, with her head leaning against the fallen leaves on the ground she looked up to the skies, peeking through the branches above – and she breathed out a grateful sigh, smiling in relief at what she had achieved, thanks also to Alice and Ryan's help.

Despite all the odds, Tai San had managed to escape.

* * *

The sensation of a light breeze on the side of her face woke Tai San from the sleep she had unintentionally been in. She had fallen unconscious, overwhelmed by all she had gone through, her body shutting down - and she was startled, awakening with a fright, when she realized it was no ordinary wind – but it had been coming straight from the mouth of The Selector himself, who was peering over Tai San, gently blowing on her face to waken her.

Around The Selector were some guards. Somehow, to Tai San's alarm, they had found her.

Tai San immediately and instinctively started backing away from them – but the pain in her ankle bit at her as soon as she moved and she clenched her teeth, trying to resist the stabbing feeling in her leg, desperate to get away from The Selector.

"Where did you think you were going?" The Selector calmly asked, walking towards her, watching intrigued as Tai San slowly shuffled away from him on her hands and knees, fighting the obvious discomfort she was going through. "Don't you know that continuing in this direction there's nothing but forest for the next few hundred miles?"

"Keep away from me!" Tai San called out.

"Now now, don't be so emotional," The Selector chided her, taking another step closer. "I gave you a very warm welcome. And is this how you repay me - by running away from what I have to offer?!"

The Selector seemed to be irritated now, in growing anger, Tai San could see it in his expression – and he presented an intimidating sight, his guards following as he slowly got even closer to her. Tai San, still on the ground and unable to stand up, retreating backwards, struggling to open up some distance between them.

The Selector suddenly lunged forward at Tai San – who held up her arms to protect herself, thinking The Selector might even strike her, in her vulnerable position.

Tai San was astonished when The Selector instead planted a gentle kiss on the side of her face – before stepping back, giving her a warm, manifestly caring smile.

"What do you think you're doing!?" Tai San said, almost speechless, outraged, wiping her hand on her face to remove any trace of the kiss she had just been given.

"I'm just happy to see you," he said softly, any tension he had been showing previously having dissipated. "Everything will be okay," he insisted, his demeanour overtly sensitive, but overly friendly.

"Help her up – but be gentle," The Selector instructed the guards – and they moved in as ordered, carefully lifting Tai San from under her arms to a standing position but making sure she didn't have to put any of her body weight on her legs.

"We'll get that leg of yours seen to straight away. I'll have my medics take a look and make sure you get everything you need."

"I doubt you have enough Chamomile, Garlic, Ginger and Turmeric," Tai San said wryly, almost to herself.

"Don't forget ice. Mixed together with what you suggest will be just fine, but we'll need to keep an eye on this graze and ensure it doesn't become infected, in which case you might need some Goldenrod, which we have in abundance," The Selector said.

He was certainly playing mind games with Tai San but also had a clear knowledge of alternative medicine.

As far as the graze he was referring to, he indicated the scratches on Tai San's leg which was bleeding slightly from her fall. He touched a trickle of the blood, gently with his small finger and dabbed it in his mouth.

"You're still B-negative, it would seem, Tai San. I think you need a little more Iron in your diet," The Selector advised.

Tai San felt from The Selector's gazing at her ankle and leg that he was interested in more than just her health, stealing a lustful glance at her figure.

"Leave me alone!" Tai San demanded – angered and frightened to be in the company of The Selector once more, as well as repulsed by what she felt was his false sense of concern and creepy physical attraction for her.

Tai San dreaded the prospect of returning to the *Lakeside Resort* and had hoped that Ryan and Alice had managed to escape.

"Alice and Ryan are waiting for you back in their rooms, Tai San. So, I suggest we head back so you can join them!" The Selector snapped, impatiently. And for a split second, Tai San wondered irrationally if he even had the ability to read her mind. Either from natural forces or more likely the biochip which had been inserted into her body. But she quickly dismissed any notions, believing that The Selector at least looked to other areas of not only knowledge but beliefs as he gazed around appreciatively at the forest.

"The Creator is all around us, Tai San. In every tree, in every bird – and in every one of us. Thanks to The Creator's vision – I will be able to know every place that you go from now on, everything that you do, everything that you think, everything that you feel, right down to even the beating of your heart."

His anger had subsided once more and he gave Tai San a warm smile – this time, she sensed it was not insincere but was genuine.

"The Creator's vision is taking another step closer to being achieved with every step we take, Tai San," The Selector said, as they made their way through the forest back to the resort, the guards steadying and assisting Tai San as she limped. "We really need to get you rested up and your ankle better. Alice and Ryan will be interested to hear of your adventures in the forest today. And you don't know how it makes me feel to know that we're together again. I'm beyond thrilled."

"Not for long. I'll leave here one day. That's a promise," said Tai San.

"That's where you're wrong. According to The Creator, you and me, and your Mall Rat friends, are going to be spending the rest of our lives together!"

CHAPTER TEN

With his baby in his arms, Bray carefully made his way through the semi-darkness past the guards and his fellow prisoners sitting on the floor of the aircraft's cavernous cargo hold.

All the Mall Rats sat in silence, lost in their own private reveries induced by the long journey so far and speculation of their fate.

Lottie and Sammy were asleep as was May, who leaned her head on Salene's shoulder. Throughout the journey Lex carefully checked out the guards for future reference. They were certainly well-disciplined and capable warriors, he could tell. Ebony's attention was more on Snake, assessing any potential weakness she might exploit. Not solely regarding his physical prowess but in his personality.

Bray held his son tightly, fighting the shift in gravity, altering his stance, trying to keep his balance as the aircraft took on an angle for a moment, altering its course.

"Don't try anything," Snake urged, giving Bray a glare. He was standing by the doorway leading from the cargo hold to the other interior parts of the plane, blocking it with his large frame, his arms crossed, an unpassable barrier.

121

"As if I'm going to step into the cockpit and land this aircraft," Bray scoffed. "My son's just restless," he added – and it was true enough, baby Jay was crying incessantly.

Snake nodded, glancing at the baby, which registered with Ebony and she wondered if he might have children of his own, given his sympathy. A chink, perhaps, in his armour. Ebony realized that Snake wasn't without feeling.

In addition to calming the baby by going for a walk and giving Amber a chance to sleep, Bray wanted to walk around the limited part of the aircraft as Amber had whispered that she had noticed windows on her previous stroll. And Bray hoped he could have another look out the windows in an effort to gain any further understanding on where they were being taken.

Snake had given permission for Amber to stretch her legs earlier in the flight, as well as Trudy, so she could in turn give comfort to her daughter, Brady, getting upset several times, terrified at the ordeal of their captivity – and Snake in particular, who, with his frightening tattoos, seemed like something from one of her nightmares.

Amber had walked down the metallic corridor to the end, gently cradling her baby, soothing his tears.

Through a small, smoked-glass window in the door, leading to another compartment, Amber noticed windows on the outer walls in the side of the aircraft, along with other compartments, rooms or cabins of some kind, their doors sealed. Amber wondered what was inside – or who – but there was no way of finding out. If she tried the door handle at the end of the metallic corridor, Snake would be bound to come charging after her to reprimand her. There was certainly no sound coming from inside what was behind the doors, nothing Amber could hear over the drone of the engines.

The aircraft reminded Amber of the military planes The Technos had used when they had invaded the city under Ram in what now felt like an eternity ago. Ram had told Amber that he had found a lot of 'hardware', various equipment, technology and vehicles that the adults had left behind in some military bases in the land of The Technos and had adapted them for their own use.

Amber wondered if Ram could somehow be involved in the Mall Rats' latest plight or whether their captors were in fact connected to The Collective, which seemed to continually cause Ram unease.

Ram had explained that he was aware that The Collective had discovered several otherwise hidden adult military complexes, similar to the one that was at Eagle Mountain, where the adults had attempted to survive the pandemic. Under their enigmatic leader, 'Kami', whose exact identity Ram claimed to have not known, The Collective had used the resources they had plundered from the adult compounds to help build and expand an empire for themselves after the virus.

Where The Technos, at the height of their power, had a few planes and vehicles – The Collective likely had their own fleet, as well as several ships in their possession and much more advanced technology - while the rest of the world around them descended into an almost primitive, anarchic way of life. A new Dark Ages.

It certainly appeared that Ram had been telling the truth about that, Amber reflected, recalling the ships she had seen in the harbour on the journey from the mall to the airport which, in turn, brought back memories of the massive cargo ship, the *Jzhao Li*, that the Mall Rats had themselves once encountered.

The invaders' military cargo planes, with their United Nations regalia, were reminiscent not only of the *Jzhao Li*, a UN ship itself and apparently part of a United Nations fleet, but of other aircraft the Mall Rats had once seen at Arthurs Air Force base, which had at one time had a United Nations presence, from the evidence of what they had left behind.

Including cryogenic hibernation chambers, like the ones they later had discovered in Eagle Mountain.

But it was still an entire mystery regarding what it all meant. Clearly whoever was responsible for it all in the old world had plans around the time of the pandemic, which was the source of many conspiracy theories. With some believing that there was something more sinister responsible for the demise of the adult population resulting in so many children and teenagers being evacuated.

Amber had briefly peered out of the window on her earlier walk with the baby and had seen they had been flying over water at the time, crossing a vast ocean.

She was then stunned, during a subsequent stroll to see the aircraft travelling over land. The terrain was strange, lifeless, desolate – a barren world.

There had even been a large mound that had caught Amber's eye that the plane flew over, seemingly in the middle of nowhere. She only saw it for a few seconds but the image of it was imprinted on her mind.

The mound hadn't looked like a natural formation, a hill or ridge. It reminded Amber of a Neolithic burial mound, something she had seen in a history documentary before the virus, a place where primitive generations had buried their dead. The massive mound of earth had filled Amber with dread and she wondered if it could be a mass grave, potentially filled with thousands of fatalities. If this was the case, she wondered whether they were adult casualties of the 'virus' buried within – or perhaps victims of something yet unexplained and the notion had sent a chill down Amber's spine.

Her thoughts had drifted to where they were headed to – and what the purpose was for the invaders in holding the Mall Rats captive – something that eluded Amber, neither Snake or his warriors giving any answers to the questions Amber and the others had asked them.

The invaders hadn't caught all of the Mall Rats though, Amber knew. When Lex was unexpectedly thrust into their midst, she had been grateful that Jack and Ellie, also Ram, had not been among their number. Wherever they were now, she wished them well and hoped that they were safe. She would ask Lex, when they could talk out of earshot from the guards, for an update to explain what had happened to him and the others who had gone with him to Eagle Mountain that day.

Now, it was Bray's turn to sway his son gently in his arms as he approached the smoke-glassed window in the corridor door for a quick glance of the outer windows on the walls of the aircraft and he was aware that darkness had fallen. He surmised that they must have been flying for perhaps five hours.

He noticed some lights shining in the distance, twinkling on the far horizon – signs of life out there, through the dark night sky.

"You'd better sit," Snake called out to Bray, before addressing all the others in the cargo hold. "We'll be coming in to land in a few minutes."

* * *

After the aircraft landed and taxied to a control tower, finally stopping near a bordering hanger, the cargo bay doors opened. Snake and his guards escorted Ebony and the Mall Rats, who were now not bound, leading them across the tarmac, their breath vapours visible in the cold night air.

They had arrived at what appeared to be a remote airstrip. Not a main airport, as such, like the one they had departed from in the Mall Rats' home city – there were no large terminal structures or restaurants left over from the adult era, no car park buildings.

Around the control tower was a series of other hangars and small prefabricated units, seemingly temporary buildings. A few dormant digger machines sat idle, beside a couple of cranes. A mesh fence ran along one side of the landing strip. Beyond that, a thick forest of tall trees was visible, stretching across rolling hills, towards the silhouette of a mountain range in the far distance.

The air was so fresh Amber began to shiver, aware looking around their surroundings it seemed that they were high up in altitude.

A few artificial floodlights were spaced out at even points around the airstrip, illuminating pockets of light on the ground in the otherwise dark night. It felt very eerie, the light casting long, distorted shadows over the tarmac.

This was not the source of the unease, however. When the passengers disembarked the aircraft, Ebony and the Mall Rats were stunned to find a small crowd of onlookers lined up on each side of barriers which had been put in place to hold back the spectators.

And the crowd on both sides began clapping, breaking out into enthusiastic applause, cheering Snake and his guards, welcoming their arrival – but above all, shouting out in utter joy and celebration at the procession passing by them – calling out in reverence and recognition the names of the Mall Rats themselves.

Some of the onlookers were clutching flaming torches reminiscent of a primitive time which was punctuated by the way in which they were dressed. Most of the crowd were tattooed and had body piercing visible, especially on the males, all of whom looked as if they had stepped out of a gym with their bare, muscular physiques visible under furs. Some even had elements of flaxen plants adorned to their furs. Particularly the females who wore skirts of flaxen and had hair extensions adorned with feathers and plants.

Most of the crowd were around the same age as the Mall Rats and without exception, the one thing all the Mall Rats were aware of was that all the onlookers were enormously physically attractive, every one blessed with good looks. And seemed to exemplify the personification of excellent health. Their teeth were white, their complexions flawless. All were suntanned.

"Amber!" one of the males yelled as she was escorted past. He was incredibly handsome, his body honed, his muscles and face chiseled, clearly in a condition of great fitness, a perfect specimen of a human being. "Amber!" he called out to her again, reaching out across the barrier, stretching his arms desperately, hoping to make contact somehow, to touch her shoulder with his fingers, even fleetingly, for a moment.

"Keep away from her!" Bray said, struggling to be free from the grip of the guards flanked either side of him, so he could protect Amber and their baby from the frenzied spectators all around.

"Bray!" a voice shouted out. "You look so awesome in real life. Much better than the photographs!"

Lottie and Sammy were as equally confused as the other Mall Rats and clung to May and Salene, who were puzzled as they heard a cacophony of overlapping voices shouting out in excitement.

"Hey, Sammy – Lottie - give us a wave!" some children among the spectators asked desperately. While others' attentions were focused on May and Salene who were passing by. "You look like a perfect couple!" one spectator said enthusiastically, wiping a tear from her eye. "I'm so glad that you both have found each other and someone to love!" the spectator continued.

"Stay back!" Snake threatened to another male, who was reaching out to try and touch Amber's arm at the front of the procession.

"Who *are* these people?" Amber asked, unable to comprehend the rapturous reception. And especially that they knew her by name.

"Some of The Privileged," Snake explained, matter-of-factly. "It's a reward for them to see you first."

"Is that – *Lex*?" one of the female spectators cried out in utter disbelief as he was led past. "Did you do it? Did you really kill Zoot!?" Lex heard her ask, the tone of her voice impassioned, hysterical – unstable even, he felt.

"No," Lex called back to wherever the female was in the sea of faces. He was avoiding eye contact, looking away from the crowd, trying to be inconspicuous. "You must have got me mixed up with someone else."

From his many experiences with the Zootists, he had always been concerned what they might eventually do if some of the most zealous followers ever got their hands on him. He was responsible, after all, for Zoot's death.

It hadn't been intentional on Lex's part, he had been trying to defend the Mall Rats at the time on that fateful night Zoot wandered into the mall to meet up with his brother, Bray, who had, unbeknownst to most of the tribe at the time, encouraged Zoot to meet Trudy and their then baby daughter, Brady. In a resulting scuffle with Lex, Zoot had accidentally fallen from the upper level of the mall to his death. Ever since, Lex had wondered if any of the Zootists would ever come after him in reprisal, getting revenge on the one who had killed their God.

Further down the line of prisoners, Brady started to cry and cling to her mother, overcome by the noise of the crowd and faces illuminated by the flaming torches, which took on an almost nightmarish element.

"It's alright, Brady, it's alright," Trudy said, doing her best to calm her daughter as much as she could, both of them unsettled by the welcome they were receiving from the strangers. Trudy was keeping Brady close by, two guards also assisting, making sure the onlookers didn't get too near.

One of the younger males in the crowd suddenly rushed forward, breaking through the guards, over the mesh railing, to Trudy and Brady – and prostrated himself before Trudy, who recoiled and forced the male's hand back as he tried to clutch desperately at Brady, in a state of awe that he was within touching distance of the actual child of Zoot – and her mother.

"Take me with you – *please*!" he begged them. "Would you give me a blessing? Show me a miracle, Supreme Mother!?"

A guard swooped up the male in his burly arms and hurled him back over the barrier to the crowd of onlookers.

At the very back of the procession, Ebony heard the commotion up ahead of her – the joyful cries and cheers, the enthusiastic welcome the Mall Rats were receiving. And was just as confused as they were.

As the guards escorted the new visitors past the crowd, however, the mood among the spectators quickly changed. The euphoria replaced by an increasing hatred, which was spreading through the onlookers as Ebony herself was marched past.

Ebony wondered how this group – whoever they were exactly – in a land so far from her own, would even know who she was, as well as the Mall Rats. But somehow they seemed to know of her, and she clearly had some sort of reputation or standing among them – one which gave her concern as the crowd started to boo and catcall a range of bitter insults. For all their seeming reverence to Zoot, they clearly didn't seem like normal Zootists.

"Traitor!" some yelled. Others were more intent on some kind of revenge. And began chanting in unison, "Stone her! Stone her! Stone her!"

Up ahead, the Mall Rats had arrived at a convoy of vehicles which were waiting. Military trucks, surrounding driverless pod-type futuristic vehicles, similar to the type used to transport Tai San from the docks earlier. Without exception, as the Mall Rats were put inside the pods, each couldn't help but feel a degree of sympathy for Ebony, the victim of so many insults and the baying crowd.

With the Mall Rats inside the driverless vehicles, the guards got in the military trucks and the convoy sped away.

The booing and insults continued from the onlookers as they glared in disdain, watching Ebony being placed in a single driverless pod vehicle which was accompanied by military trucks either side. The onlookers started to shriek and chant a rhythmic intonation as both convoys transporting the Mall Rats, and separately Ebony, receded in the distance up a mountainous road.

CHAPTER ELEVEN

They had been hiding underneath the belly of the derelict plane for several hours and Jack was amazed, as well as relieved, that they were still unnoticed, though for how much longer none of them could tell.

It was late into the night, the darkness all-encompassing, and with the temperature dropping it had gotten very cold.

Ram's teeth were 'chattering', his arms folded across his chest as he crouched behind the wheel under the fuselage in an effort to retain as much of his body heat as he could.

Jack and Ellie were huddled together, their arms wrapped around each other trying to keep warm, taking cover by one of the other wheels of the aircraft.

They were all tired, thirsty and hungry and had long ago eaten the few consumables - some raw vegetables that Jack had brought with them on their original journey to Eagle Mountain with Lex the day before. He still had his backpack on, yet now, devoid of its provisions, the only thing it contained was the hard drive they had taken to Eagle Mountain with the objective to try and decipher its contents. Jack had joked that he wished it was edible in an attempt to lighten the mood, as well as satisfy his hunger cravings.

Now, their chief concern, as it had been for many hours, was to keep out of sight of the ominous presence that remained at the airport, indeed, over the city following its conquest by the invaders. Ram still convinced that they were the infamous Collective.

There were still guards in proximity, hundreds of metres away at the main terminal buildings, their vehicles driving around the airport frequently, making some sort of patrol, Ram presumed, the vehicles' headlights casting their beams into the dark emptiness of the night.

Whenever an invader vehicle had driven past the runway by their own location, Ellie, Jack and Ram had literally frozen, not making a sound, not daring to even breathe in case they gave away some indication of their own presence there, beneath the rusty aircraft.

There had been a particularly close incident a couple of hours earlier when one of the patrols had stopped on the tarmac beside the abandoned plane, one of the warriors getting out. Jack, Ellie and Ram were sure their hearts would beat out of their chests, so anxious and full of adrenalin they were at that time.

Jack had been prepared to even run out from behind the wheel where he had been hiding, beside Ellie, to confront the tall, well-built warrior who had gotten out of the van. And so it was to Jack's surprise, albeit mixed with revulsion, when it became clear why the vehicle had stopped, the guard simply deciding to casually relieve himself on the front wheel of the plane, which he must have viewed as nothing more than a giant piece of scrap metal.

Ellie had found it especially disgusting and she had breathed out a sigh of relief, along with Ram and Jack, as soon as the warrior had finished going about his business, before resuming his patrol.

At least it had shown that they were well and truly hidden, but it was only a matter of time they all dreaded before they would have another close encounter with the invaders.

Their potential sources of danger were not only from the invaders' forces on the ground who seemed to be working around the clock transporting supplies and equipment by military helicopters, which they suspected must have been deployed from the ships moored in the harbour further away, deep in the city. And all had speculated what equipment might be dangling by the long strops underneath the bellies of each helicopter. It was certainly heavy-duty equipment and was being loaded into one of the military cargo aircraft. They assumed that there must have been a larger force of warriors disembarking from the ships and wondered why they might be wishing to inhabit the city and environs. Clearly, the invaders weren't just an advanced party searching for the Mall Rats, along with especially Ram, as he was convinced.

"It's strange really. When I was there, I wanted to be here. Now I'm here, I want to be there," Ram sighed, reflectively.

Jack and Ellie exchanged a confused glance and considered Ram, who was deep in thought.

"What are you talking about?" Jack asked.

"A plan," Ram replied. "I'll give you more detail once I've figured it out."

Some of the drones had continued to operate throughout the night, taking off and then returning later to the airport, their lights blinking, engines audible as they whirred. Some drones looking quite futuristic, of different sizes and many alien to what they had ever seen before.

Certainly, many were small reconnaissance types, Ram believed, probably using a type of night-vision, infrared camera to scout different areas in and beyond the city, perhaps looking out for heat signatures in case there were any other inhabitants in the city. The drones could even be 'hunters', roaming around from the air in an effort to find Ram, Ellie and Jack - and the hard drive that was in their possession. Ram thought it was likely the invaders would expect the three of them to still be in the city, sure that Lex would have stubbornly not revealed anything to his abductors that might give away their true location. But all realized that they couldn't exactly stay hidden forever.

It was a stroke of good fortune, if not a miracle, that none of the spy drones had flown over the exact place where Jack, Ellie and Ram had been hiding, or Ram was certain they would have picked up their heat patterns. It was possible, Jack had suggested or hoped to be the case, that the metallic hulk of the plane they were beneath might be shielding them from the prying cameras of the drones or causing interference somehow which had enabled them to go undetected so far.

The largest drones they had noticed coming to and from the airport appeared to be as big as a light aircraft. They were likely used, along with the helicopters, for ferrying more cargo, Ram assumed, transporting equipment from the ships in the harbour to various key points around the city, in addition to couriering supplies from the airport that the large military cargo planes might have brought with them in the initial stages of the invasion. The large drones could even be shuttling around human cargo, in the form of warriors from the invasion force, to different sectors of the city.

Ram expressed his jealousy to Ellie and Jack at never having possessed such high-tech drones for himself during his days in charge of The Technos. The invaders must have plundered the drones from the adult military bases they had discovered, he speculated. Ram had been aware of the existence of such technology but in the few hidden underground compounds

The Technos had been to, Eagle Mountain among them, none of them had any drones.

Once again, Ram was convinced the invaders were in reality The Collective, given what he knew of their methods of operation. They had the capability to examine far more complexes, from what Ram recalled of his discussions online with their leader, Kami. They certainly had a lot more 'toys' and resources than The Technos ever did, Ram observed, including the advanced drones they had seen flying around.

Ellie, Jack and Ram watched as the latest vehicle drove down the far end of the runway on patrol, its headlights arcing, casting their glow as it moved around the airport.

"I don't know about you, but I don't fancy spending the rest of my life hiding underneath this thing with the two of you," Ram said, in a whispered undertone, keeping his voice quiet in case it attracted any attention, drone or human.

"Well, that's something we can agree with you on," Ellie whispered.

"I've been thinking," Ram remarked.

"Meaning?" Jack enquired.

"I know a place where we could go."

"And where would that be?" Ellie questioned.

"As far away from here as possible," Ram said, with a smirk, amusing himself by what he was about to suggest.

Ellie gave him a disdainful look – she was never sure if Ram was 'trolling', winding them up, and wasn't in the mood for any of his antics.

"And how are we meant to do that exactly?" Jack asked.

"I've got an idea – but it's one you're probably not going to like to hear."

Ram explained his plan, Ellie and Jack listening intently. He was right, they didn't like what he was proposing.

"You've got to be crazy," Ellie commented, when Ram had finished.

"Don't knock it. This mind of mine has kept me alive," Ram said, indicating his forehead with one finger. "So – what do you reckon?"

Jack and Ellie exchanged quizzical looks with each other – and they could tell what the other was thinking. No matter their reservations and reluctance - given their dire situation, there didn't seem to be any other alternatives. Ram's idea seemed the best chance, if not the only one they might have, to alter their fate.

* * *

Ram was either a genius or a madman – perhaps both - Jack and Ellie thought, as they continued to follow him away from the plane they had been hiding under into the darkness of the night, down the side of the runway. They were furtively keeping to the grassy verge beside the tarmac, believing it would help muffle any sounds they were making as they crept along stealthily towards the main terminal buildings.

It wasn't just Ram. The three of them had to be out of their minds to be taking such a risk, Jack felt, but he resolved they really had no other choice.

He just hoped Ram's gamble would pay off, the airport terminal slowly getting closer with every step they were taking. They kept peering around in all directions, looking behind them, anxious that the patrol they had last seen might now be making its way back, or that a passing drone would suddenly fly overhead and spot them. They were out in the open, exposed, and feeling very vulnerable.

Ram's mind was like clockwork. Prior to emerging from the aircraft, Ram had timed the duration of the patrols, how long it took each to complete their circuit.

It seemed to occur approximately every hour. With the patrols taking about twenty minutes.

Ram's expression was a picture of concentration, though neither Jack nor Ellie could see it well in the night. They could just hear him, almost a whisper, quietly counting the seconds to himself as they made their way down the side of the runway. There were a lot of moving parts for him to keep track of and remember, concurrent timings requiring some complex mathematics which Ram was constantly running over in his mind.

"We have to speed up," Ram urged quietly, and he picked up the pace, heading towards the airport terminal, Jack and Ellie in his trail.

They would only have a narrow window of opportunity, Ram had explained before they set out on his plan. He had worked out they would have about a ten-minute period where there should be no ground patrols and no drones flying overhead – that is, assuming there was nothing unpredictable occurring.

And they had to use every second they had available to get to the main terminal in time to have even a chance of Ram's idea succeeding. They were closing in, just a little further to go, the airport buildings looming ahead. Jack and Ellie were in an increasing state of nervousness, their adrenalin rising, feeling like they were walking straight into the lion's den and could be discovered at any moment.

They had made it to the airport terminal. Crouching down, so as to keep out of sight from within the partial cover of some cargo containers, they could see before them several drones on the tarmac, seemingly being recharged, Ram suspected, the air humming with electricity, connected to large generators.

Several crates of supplies were also visible in the shadows, stacked in piles. It was difficult to know what all their different contents were in the dark but Jack could see some of the crates appeared to contain some sort of grain, others were full of rice. The invaders must have been obviously planning to feed a large group of people, from the amount of food they had transported, Jack realized, and he wondered how many of their number were now in the city – or if the provisions were awaiting future invader forces who were yet to arrive.

The drones being recharged looked like a flock of metallic flying creatures, as if they were in a state of rest, with various wingspans and shapes – some were the smaller surveillance types, others the larger drones designed for carrying freight – and they were the ones Ram was focusing upon.

"There – that's the one," Ram whispered, indicating the largest drone in view. It was as long as a bus and three times as wide, thick cables plugged into it from the power generators.

"Are you sure?" Ellie whispered back – but she didn't get an answer.

Ram, eyes fixed intently on the large drone, went towards it, fleet of foot, and without hesitation he quickly began detaching the cables from the generators, looking around agitatedly to make sure no one had spotted him.

Jack and Ellie raced over, as quietly as they could, helping Ram pull the remaining cables out – before following him in through the door in the side of the drone.

It was dark inside and the cargo hold was empty, apart from the three of them, their feet scrunching on some bits of grain that must have spilled on the floor during earlier shuttling trips made by the drone.

Ram had an excited look on his face as he surveyed the cockpit, loving the technology before him, as well as being thrilled, on the edge, at the audacity of what they were attempting to achieve.

"Are you sure you know how to fly this thing?" Jack asked, in growing panic.

"No," Ram said, slightly preoccupied as he surveyed the console before him.

"Great! Now you tell us!" Ellie said.

"Relax. No need for me to pilot this thing. Not with computer systems. These things should be mostly automated," Ram said, running his fingers over the various electronic controls, getting a 'feel' of the different buttons, hoping to sense what their function was.

"The onboard computer does all the work. We just gotta find the main switch," Ram continued, having difficulty locating it. "It should be around here somewhere."

"I think I found it," Ellie said, suddenly reaching forward to push a small red button she had noticed.

Lights immediately flicked on, slightly illuminating all in the cockpit in a green and red glow, reflected by the touch sensitive display which appeared in the centre of the main panel, the drone wakening, its systems powering up.

"That's my girl," Jack beamed with pride.

"Not just a pretty face," Ram said, impressed by her technical skills, and he gave Jack a subtle wink of approval at having Ellie as his partner.

Ram started punching data on the touch display which was showing their current location blinking on a map. With his other finger he moved an arrow across the map, entering the destination co-ordinates into the drone's navigational system.

"And now, the moment of truth," Ram said, hoping that his plan was going to work. By his reckoning, they only had a couple of minutes left before the invaders' patrol made its way back to the airport terminal.

For all of Ram's intellect, and his photographic memory, his calculations were out and the patrol had arrived back at this area of the terminal slightly early. Ram, Ellie and Jack swallowed nervously, noticing a vehicle approaching and picking up speed.

"Great!" Ellie screamed in panic. "What do we do now!?"

"*START JOURNEY?*" a voice replied – but it wasn't Jack or Ram's, even Ellie's. It was the computer giving instructions, advising to confirm co-ordinates.

Ram quickly scanned the display panel and pressed buttons on the screen to confirm the co-ordinates as the patrol vehicle was closing in and picking up speed.

The engines of the drone suddenly burst into life, whirring at increasing intensity, their blades spinning at incredible speeds, preparing for flight.

Seconds later, the drone lifted off the ground, rising up into the dark sky vertically, just above the patrol vehicle beneath. The guards visible, gazing up in concern at the drone.

The blades of the drone angled slightly as the drone rose higher into the air then set off horizontally, speeding away.

Ram, Jack and Ellie breathed a sigh of relief.

"What did I tell you?" Ram grinned, thrilled they had pulled it off. "I hope you enjoy your flight with Genius Airways."

"Let's just wait till we get away first," Jack said, peering out the window, feeling a sense of elation at seeing the airport receding into the distance, illuminated by the headlights of several other vehicles which seemed to spring into life, realizing that one of the drones of the invaders had taken an unscheduled departure.

"Relax, Jack. There's no way they'll be able to come after us," Ram said, watching out of the window, the drone picking up speed, its electric engines humming at high pitch as it broke through some night clouds, the ground beneath zooming by under them.

"What makes you so sure?" Ellie enquired.

"Exactly," Jack agreed. "I mean it isn't as if we're travelling in the only drone. There's dozens which might come after us."

"Not a problem," Ram replied confidently. "I doubt they'd have much success if they tried to pursue us. And even if they did – don't forget, these things are automated. And I'm the only one who knows our destination co-ordinates."

Jack and Ellie were relieved, comforted by Ram's reassurances.

"You're something else, Ram, you really are," Jack said in admiration.

Although Ellie was as equally relieved, she just hoped that she and Jack could fully trust Ram – and asked carefully, "You mentioned about trying to use one of these drones to get away, but you didn't say anything about an exact destination," Ellie enquired. "Those co-ordinates you programmed into the navigation - do you mind sharing with us just exactly where we're going?"

"Home," Ram replied, whooping it up excitedly.

CHAPTER TWELVE

Tai San heard the familiar sound of the door to her room at the *Lakeside Resort* being unlocked from the other side – and as she woke up that morning, she braced herself for another encounter with The Selector.

She hadn't seen him since he had visited with the medical team who treated her sprained ankle with ice to reduce the swelling, before wrapping it in a compression dressing.

The medics were among the very best The Selector had to offer, he had proudly stated to her, and he claimed he would do everything in his power to ensure she got the highest level of care. They, like The Selector, were well versed in all manner of medicines, including homeopathic, herbal, as well as a more conventional approach and certainly seemed to know what they were doing. The ankle was less swollen than when the initial injury occurred, though Tai San was still sore and in discomfort.

Her greatest concern remained The Selector himself. He observed all the treatments and seemed fascinated more by Tai San's emotional state and her reactions to his presence, as well as to the medical procedures she was experiencing.

Tai San had writhed in pain on occasion when the medics had been directly examining her ankle – suspecting at one point that she might have broken it but thankfully it was just a bad sprain.

She did sense, however, that The Selector was deriving some sort of sadistic pleasure from her condition and seemed quite aroused even, staring intently when the medics had applied ice on her exposed ankle before helping himself to some of the ice from the pack and sucking on the cube fervently, savouring the taste as the cube melted in his mouth.

His odd behaviour and apparent enamoured interest in Tai San personally had disturbed her greatly.

Lying on her bed, her legs raised up on a stack of pillows, Tai San tensed as the door opened. And the medical team entered again, thankfully without any sign of The Selector, to her relief.

"It's a beautiful morning," the main medic said, a young female around Tai San's age. "What a day to be alive."

"Is it?"

Tai San regarded the medic with suspicion. Though she had treated Tai San's ankle when she arrived at the resort after her attempted escape and had regularly visited to monitor her progress, she had been the same medic who had injected the biochip into Tai San's hand the day before.

"Where is *he*?" Tai San asked warily.

"The Selector's got something special arranged," the medic advised while she and her team gently began their work on Tai San's ankle, carefully unwrapping the compress dressing. "At least the swelling seems to have reduced. But there's still signs of some synovial fluid around the bruising. So you'll need this compress dressing for another day or two. Now - we'll need to get you up and about. The Selector has brought somebody important to visit."

"Who? The Creator?" Tai San enquired carefully.

"It's not my place to say," the medic replied.

While the main medics wrapped Tai San's ankle in a fresh compression bandage, other medics in the team began applying make-up to her, forcibly holding Tai San's face firmly in place so she couldn't turn away, adding a little blush on her cheeks, putting some lipstick on her lips, brushing her hair, neatly styling it, others gently sprayed sweet perfume.

"What are you doing!?" Tai San asked, mystified.

"The Selector wants us to get you looking your very best," the main medic said, before stopping to admire the work of her fellow medics. With the exaggerated make up, Tai San looked almost like a doll. "There – that's a lot better. What a pretty picture. You look – perfect."

Tai San caught a glimpse of herself in the mirror and didn't agree, aghast at the exaggerated blush and especially the eye make-up, while being lifted to a standing position, where the medics began dressing her, leaving her feeling utterly confused and humiliated by their actions, especially concerned about what The Selector might have planned.

There was only one possible explanation for all the fuss they were making over her and her presentation, Tai San thought. The 'important somebody' she was going to be shown to had to be the one who The Selector always referred to in respectful, reverential terms. Tai San believed that she was indeed finally going to meet The Creator.

Tai San was escorted by the medics down the corridors of the *Lakeside Resort*, making her way on some crutches.

They were headed to the main lounge area, where she had been told she would be joining Alice and Ryan.

It was slow progress down the long corridors.

She finally rounded one corner, leading into the lounge – and dropped both crutches, almost falling over, stunned at the sight of the group standing before her. She could hardly believe what or more importantly who she was seeing.

"Tai San!" Amber cried out, racing over to embrace her.

Amber was accompanied by Bray, a baby in his arms, Trudy, with Brady by her side, Salene and May. They, too, rushed to embrace her, thrilled to be reunited.

A younger girl and boy were with them who Tai San didn't recognize, being Lottie and Sammy, the two of them watching the delirious delight as Tai San hugged her fellow Mall Rats.

Above all though, Tai San's gaze fell upon Lex – standing rooted momentarily in his place, dazed, like he was seeing a vision, a ghost from his past.

"Tai San?" Lex said, absolutely overcome that Tai San was there, almost questioning what was before his very eyes.

He tried but didn't say another word, tearing up slightly, and rushed to her, wrapping his arms around her tightly, clinging as if by releasing his grip she might somehow disappear from his life again.

Tai San responded, hugging with everything she had.

They would need to talk, to reconnect, to find out what had happened since they had last been in each other's company. There was so much they both had to say to each other. For now, they were just enjoying the feeling of being in each other's arms, amazed to be reunited.

"I don't believe it!" Trudy said, happy to see Lex and Tai San so overjoyed. "I never thought we'd ever see you again, Tai San."

"Who would have ever thought?" Amber agreed.

It had all felt like a strange dream, but compared to the nightmare that had descended on their lives from the invasion, their reunion with Tai San was the only positive thing in what had been utter chaos and uncertainty.

Throughout their journey in the driverless pods, none of the Mall Rats had gotten much sleep. Amber had discussed their plight with Bray in the pod they were travelling in. It was hard to come to terms with what they had all been through – the invasion of the city, their captivity, the subsequent transport by air to a faraway land, and especially the strange welcome by the tribe at the airstrip who seemed to know everything about the arriving Mall Rats.

May, Salene and Trudy, in another pod, had also discussed this and were as equally confused and concerned by the reception the Mall Rats had encountered from the waiting crowd, who Snake had referred to as part of The Privileged.

Their fervor and focus on Brady and Trudy in particular evoked the fanaticism of The Guardian and his Chosen.

May, Salene and Trudy were also unsettled, disturbed at the possibility of Ebony's fate, having seen how she had been treated and segregated and wondered where she had been taken to.

Their convoy had driven all night, passing through various types of industrial, military facilities en route to a mountainous forested area, finally arriving as the dawn broke at the *Lakeside Resort.*

Commander Snake explained that they were free to roam the resort but there would be severe penalties if they tried to escape. Which would be pointless as they would be tracked down – eventually.

Bray and Amber, along with other members of the Mall Rats, pressed him for more detail, questioning what was going on, why they were being held. But Snake didn't provide any information, advising that The Selector would brief them when the time was right. And Snake and his guards' instructions were simply to deliver the prisoners to the resort.

Amber demanded Snake tell them what had happened to Ebony. She and Ebony had never been close, far from it, but she wished Ebony no ill will or harm.

Snake explained that Ebony would be quite safe as long as she co-operated in her tasks but didn't provide any insight into what those tasks might be, any detail whatsoever. Except that the resort was to be the exclusive living quarters for the Mall Rats only for the time being and Ebony, who was not a Mall Rat, was apparently being kept somewhere else.

The Mall Rats were also troubled by what fate had befallen Emma, her younger brother and sister, as well as Lia and the group of pregnant young mothers who they had last seen in the custody of The Guardian, Eloise and their warriors.

But Snake didn't provide any insight other than advising that they were all on a journey of their own, taking the next steps in their lives that would lead them to a new purpose. It was all so vague with Snake either refusing or not knowing some of the greater detail.

Bray and Lex quickly noted that for all the Mall Rats were apparently free to live temporarily in the resort, there were perimeter guards patrolling and both felt a little more optimistic, viewing that there may well be some options in store for escape.

The reunion continued when Alice and Ryan, escorted by the guards, arrived in the lounge area – both of them stunned to see the other Mall Rats gathered around Tai San.

"Oh my God!" Alice blared out, and she ran towards them, her arms outstretched, wrapping Trudy, Brady, and Lex in an enormous hug.

"Salene?" Ryan said, ecstatically. He looked like he was going to faint – incredulous to see so many of his former Mall Rat friends who had been separated for so long – but especially Salene. He had been dreaming of this moment and the realization quickly dawned on him that she actually *was* there, just a few feet away, after too much time being kept apart.

"Ryan – it really is you, isn't it?" Salene wondered, feeling in a daze herself, stupefied – and she soon got her answer when Ryan excitedly bounded across the lounge heading straight for her.

"Of course it's me!" Ryan said, giving Salene a hug he had been saving up and playing out in his mind for many months, thrilled to be with her once more, literally sweeping her off her feet in his arms.

"You're still alive!" Salene said, overwhelmed to see him again, feeling a sense of protection in her current predicament by Ryan's loving, strong embrace, during which she cast an uncertain glance at May, who was standing watching them. May was equally overjoyed to see Ryan alive and seemingly well but it was difficult for her to watch the former lovers embracing.

"I've got so much I want to tell you!" Ryan said, squeezing Salene tightly out of affection.

"Me too, Ryan. Me too," Salene said, looking at May once more, almost wishing May could give her some guidance. Instead, May shrugged and smiled. She was genuinely happy but knew, however, that Salene would have to break it to Ryan that though they had once been married, Salene had moved on from him – with her partner now being May herself. And judging from Ryan's delight at seeing Salene, he clearly hadn't seemed to have moved on from her.

"This is incredible!" Alice beamed, hugging each of the Mall Rats in turn again. "Tell me everything – *everything* – you know about Ellie!" Alice asked them, desperate to hear news of her younger sister.

"We were with her only yesterday," Bray revealed, Alice relieved and delighted to hear it. But she shook her head slightly, indicating discreetly with a wave of her hand not to reveal any other information.

"Well, you'll have to tell me about it. Later. In private." Alice added.

Lex and Ryan, best friends since the evacuation boot camp around the time of the demise of the adults, gave each other a warm bear hug, casting aside any machismo, and displayed genuine affection.

Lottie and Sammy gave all the assembly hugs as well. Tai San, Alice and Ryan were delighted to give Brady a hug. She was growing so fast. And were thrilled to be introduced to baby Jay.

Alice, in an extreme undertone, had mentioned to the recently arrived Mall Rats they needed to be careful of what they might say as she, Ryan and Tai San were concerned that the resort might be bugged. All understood and spoke mainly superficially with no great detail, unwilling to provide any deeper information which might be used against them and resolved that they would need to have a check if there were any hidden cameras or monitoring devices which might pick up their voices.

* * *

The Selector gazed intently at various monitors displaying different angles of the reunion and was indeed listening to most of what had been said.

His prime focus though was on Lex hugging Tai San, the two of them obviously close, having a strong connection and personal chemistry as well as history, which he was obsessively keen to find out more detail on.

The Selector felt pangs of jealousy at the attention Tai San was giving Lex. He had many matters to attend to, especially now that the Mall Rats and Ebony were in his domain and he was due to visit The Creator later that day to give an update on the success of this phase of their plan.

But as well as dutifully working to achieve The Creator's goals, watching Tai San give Lex a warm smile and long lingering kiss, The Selector already had some ideas forming in his mind about how he might deal with Lex - so that The Selector could continue with his own personal agenda, which very much included Tai San, viewing her as an objective which he needed to achieve.

CHAPTER THIRTEEN

Throughout the long journey Ebony was unable to catch any sleep. All night her mind was racing, speculating in her innermost thoughts what might happen to her - if her captors were going to keep her alive. But she reasoned that if they had wished to kill her, they probably would have done so by now.

This didn't exactly give her much reassurance though. She simply had no idea what lay in store for her. She literally was in the dark and gazed out the windows of the driverless pod futuristic vehicle at the passing scenery. It was difficult to see much though given that it was night, but Ebony was aware that she was part of a motorcade with military trucks accompanying her vehicle on the journey.

Ebony was disturbed, confused, let alone angry at how she had been treated by her captors and one thing for sure, was that if she ever had an opportunity to seek revenge, then she would gleefully take it.

She wondered what had happened to the other Mall Rats. Their arrival had been met with a rapturous reception. Whereas she had received nothing but scorn, resentment, suspicion, from the onlookers whom she had encountered briefly.

For whatever their reasons, it was clear to Ebony that she didn't exactly have a good reputation – and she wondered if there might even be some bounty placed on her head.

She eventually managed to fall asleep briefly and woke up as the dawn broke, the horizon ablaze as the sun rose slowly, enabling Ebony to more clearly see the landscape.

They were passing fields and what appeared to be farm workers toiling the land and she wondered if her fate might be to join them because no doubt they were slaves, given their early start.

Her expression clouded in a mixture of confusion and growing concern when she noticed images on some outlying agricultural buildings which seemed to be displaying information – specifically advertising an event. Then she stared open-mouthed as she noticed a huge blown-up photograph of herself on the side of the building with text illustrating *'EBONY. A CONTESTANT OF THE CUBE. COMING SOON'.*

Ebony decided that she must try and live in the moment otherwise she simply couldn't handle her plight with any more speculation and would take it all one step at a time and adapt accordingly to whatever she might encounter.

After so much time living in the concrete jungle of the city, Ebony couldn't help but appreciate the stunning views outside the windows, the spectacle of nature in the raw, without any graffiti or debris in sight.

The convoy now seemed to be ascending a winding road and soon a large, beautiful lake came into view, bordered by forest, with snow-capped mountains beyond.

Shortly thereafter, the convoy arrived at its destination – a rustic lodge overlooking the waters.

Ebony was ushered inside by the guards from the military vehicles, who then left while she gazed at the opulent splendor of the lodge's décor and luxurious furnishings, the lodge clearly belonging to someone of prominence. It was a refuge of peace and quiet and must have been a fishing or hunting lodge in the adult times, Ebony thought.

There were several different varieties of fish mounted on the walls. Stuffed animals of various kinds, ranging from small birds to some large wild boars, preserved by taxidermy in their frozen poses, stood lifeless in the hallway of the lodge.

Perhaps her luck was about to change, Ebony considered. She hadn't been bound and was being allowed to walk freely around the lodge, wondering who she would be about to meet, clearly someone of very high status.

Ebony was determined to make a good first impression. She started running her fingers through her hair, styling it in an impromptu manner, and wiped herself down, rubbing off any dirt she could see on her clothing from her captivity, adjusting her appearance so she could look the best she was able to in her current state.

She wandered into a large study, bristling with books on its many layers of shelves. Its windows had an outlook over the lake. On the walls were glass cases and display frames filled with a multitude of preserved insect species inside.

In one corner of the room Ebony was stunned to see a cryogenic hibernation chamber, similar to the type Ram had used in the city, long ago, when he had tried to escape into his virtual reality paradise.

It reminded Ebony of the units that Amber and the Mall Rats had described seeing at Eagle Mountain and she wondered what it was doing here – disturbed by the thought if there could even be an adult or someone inside the chamber, its darkened glass surface concealing its contents and whatever, or whoever, could be lurking within.

Her attention was mostly drawn, however, to the unusual-looking figure sitting behind a large wooden desk. He was intently staring at her, tapping his fingers together rhythmically,

155

as if in a ritualistic obsessional manner, in deep contemplation of her.

"Hi," Ebony said, smiling politely to break the unbearable silence.

"Hi," her host replied, with a smile that was ice cold.

"You wouldn't be *Kami*, by any chance?" Ebony ventured, aware that if her abductors were The Collective, then her host might be the enigmatic leader Ram had often spoken of.

"You may call me The Selector," her host answered.

"Appreciate it. It's a pleasure to meet you," Ebony said, trying to ingratiate herself.

"Is it?"

Ebony smiled again but still felt great unease at the cold tone of The Selector. "Well, it's certainly a pleasure for me. And I just hoped that you might be the kind of man who enjoyed some pleasure, too," Ebony added, slightly seductively.

The Selector didn't say anything in return and just watched Ebony, studying her reactions, her behaviour. She felt like she was on display, like one of the stuffed animals she had seen, his intense observation of her and odd behaviour making her feel uncomfortable.

She stood in silence, her heart beating almost in time to the old grandfather clock which ticked rhythmically, and she couldn't help but watch the pendulum almost as if she was being hypnotized - which registered with The Selector.

"Are you nervous, Ebony?" he enquired. "If so, just keep staring at the pendulum. It might relax you. So, breathe deeply and relax. Breathe slowly."

The Selector's voice was soft, soothing. Ebony found it difficult to avert her gaze from the swinging pendulum of the grandfather clock. But she eventually forced herself to look away and glanced at The Selector again, who himself was breathing in through his nose and exhaling slowly as if somehow to calm himself.

"There is so much pressure in this world, Ebony, one needs to take some time out and slow our biorhythms."

"I quite agree," Ebony replied, becoming more reassured by The Selector's friendly demeanour. And she mimicked his breathing, slowly in her nose and exhaling out through her mouth, shaking her arms slightly, twitching her neck as if to de-stress.

"Feel better?" The Selector asked.

"Absolutely."

"What kind of animal would you say that you are, Ebony?"

"What type of question is that?"

"One that needs an answer."

"I dunno," Ebony said. "Maybe a unicorn. Something special."

"I don't know about a unicorn. But I think I know exactly who you are. You're a fox."

"Is that what you say to all the ladies?"

The Selector grinned, amused by her remark. "You're cunning, Ebony. Resourceful. You possess great survival instincts, from what I can gather. You're adaptable. But you're also dangerous. You put your own needs and interests ahead of others. Your track record shows you are not to be trusted. With your guile and slyness, you're as wily and capable as the fox."

"I take that as a compliment. The thing is – are you the type of man who can appreciate what a fox might do for you, if she was by your side? You see, I'm more than just a fox. But also, a woman, with strong desires."

"Interesting," The Selector replied.

"If you don't mind my asking – what kind of animal are you?" Ebony probed carefully.

"A chameleon, I would say. But I'm of course not an animal. But am of the human species. Though we can certainly learn a lot from our spirit animal, whatever that might be."

"The only thing I've learned, Selector, is how to survive," Ebony said.

"Presumably you didn't learn that from the fox? Pretty soon that species sadly might become extinct. Thankfully we'll do all we can to assist with our breeding programmes."

"Do you have a breeding programme?" Ebony enquired. "For yourself?"

"Of course," The Selector responded. "If it is the will of The Creator."

Ebony wondered who The Creator was – as well as who The Selector was, and how he fit into the structure of The Collective. If indeed they were the ones holding her.

She felt she was being judged somehow, like it was an interview, The Selector deciding what to do with her. She didn't want to end up imprisoned again or to spend the rest of her days as a slave or even worse, recalling the hostility the crowd at the airstrip had shown to her. She sensed she had to make good of this chance to impress The Selector and try and establish some influence over him, for her own sake.

So she decided to change tack.

"I was Zoot's woman," Ebony said, proudly. "I take it you know of him?"

"I do. And you abandoned his legacy to carry out your own agenda."

"I don't know where you got that kind of information but believe me, it's all wrong."

"How dare you question my sources and insult The Creator!" The Selector erupted in fury, slamming his fist on his desk.

Ebony was taken aback at the sudden outburst and swallowed nervously. "Sorry... I didn't mean any offence."

The Selector considered her, then smiled. "Apology accepted."

Unnerved by the unpredictability of The Selector, Ebony thought that she needed to quickly change tack again and try something, anything, to alter the course of the meeting. She started to unbutton her blouse, deliberately revealing some cleavage.

"What are you doing?" The Selector said, quickly diverting his gaze as if embarrassed, which was encouraging to Ebony, believing the power balances were shifting slightly.

"I just thought you might find it personally interesting to know that I'm very attracted to men in positions of power. And you certainly seem to be a very powerful man," Ebony smouldered.

"And why would I find that interesting?"

Ebony was always aware that she had been the object of desire by many males in the past and had used her sexuality to her advantage. Despite his odd qualities, The Selector had to be like any other man, Ebony thought. She had nothing to lose and so much to possibly gain, even if it meant sharing The Selector's bed for a while. It was a small price to pay to gain advantage.

"Would you like me to show you more of what kind of fox I can be?" Ebony drawled seductively, unbuttoning more of her top.

"Please don't," The Selector asked, seemingly disturbed by what she was suggesting as Ebony approached the desk, sure she had finally gotten to him, her good looks and sexuality to the rescue once more.

"How about I do some things you might have never imagined?"

"Would you stand on one leg?" The Selector suddenly asked, intrigued.

"Sure. Whatever turns you on," Ebony replied – and she did what she was asked, standing on her right leg, thinking it was a strange request.

"Would you – do a little dance for me?" The Selector asked. He wasn't flirtatious at all but was enquiring in all seriousness.

"A dance? Yeah, I'll dance for you. We could be doing a lot more than dancing though."

Ebony was finding The Selector's questions bizarre, to say the least. Maybe he had a few odd fetishes, she thought. She wouldn't put it past him, he seemed the type. Nonetheless, it was evident he was in a position of power and she was determined to bond with him, to make the best out of any opportunity to enhance her position.

No matter how foolish she felt, without any music, Ebony began to dance rhythmically, and was deliberately making sure she was doing so in an alluring way, that all her curves were showing and on display to this most unusual male.

"Are you going to join me?" she enquired.

"No. You can stop now."

She stopped dancing and gave him uncertain, wary looks, confused by his increasingly unpredictable behaviour.

"Stick your tongue out."

Slowly, she did so, before pulling it back in. "You know what we can use our tongues for?" Ebony tried again, suggestively.

"Lick the lid on the chamber."

"What is this!?" Ebony said, having had enough, refusing to do so. Partly thinking that The Selector was just playing games with her but also uneasy at the thought of something possibly living under the smoke-glass canopy.

"So, even you have your limits," The Selector observed.

"Think again," Ebony said, determined to make an impression. She ambled over to the cryogenic unit and started to lick the glass cover. It might turn The Selector on, Ebony thought initially, but that feeling faded as he gazed intently, absently, and then excitedly started typing in data on the console of his computer.

"It's yummy," Ebony said. "You should try it," relieved that she hadn't noticed anything living in the chamber. At least as far as she could see.

"I now know your profile, Ebony," The Selector advised, getting to his feet. "You will clearly do anything you have to, to make sure you will survive. Your traits are very strong. And admirable. Rather than a fox, you might even be a wolf."

"So, what does that mean for me?"

"Guards!" The Selector shouted.

Two guards burst into the room, ignoring Ebony's state of undress, focusing their attentions on The Selector.

"I want you to take Ebony immediately to The Cube for induction."

"The Cube?" Ebony wondered, buttoning up her blouse, recalling the strange images she had noticed on her journey earlier that morning.

"If you do well and prove you have the right qualities and characteristics, there is a chance you can redeem yourself and fulfil a more noble purpose in life in service of The Creator."

"And how do I know what I need to do in order to 'do well'?" Ebony asked, struggling as the guards began to lead her to the door.

"That's one of the first things you will need to find out. I'm sure the audience will *love* you," The Selector advised.

"Audience? What are you talking about? Where are you taking me!?" Ebony cried out, as the guards dragged her away.

The Selector followed excitedly.

"It's time to put a fox in with the chickens and discover if the fox is really a fox or a wolf!" The Selector said, prior to slamming the door shut with force as Ebony and the guards left.

He turned from the door and breathed in deeply through his nose and exhaled through his mouth, trying to calm himself from his excitement, aware that Ebony would be a worthy addition to The Cube.

CHAPTER FOURTEEN

"Useless – heap of – junk!" Ram yelled, kicking the drone in contempt and in the process hurting his foot which left him hopping on one leg and groaning in utter frustration.

They were back on the ground once more, the drone having crash-landed in a forested area.

"So much for 'Genius Airways'," Jack sighed despondently as he and Ellie watched Ram slump to the ground and massage his foot.

Jack and Ellie were in discomfort themselves, feeling the intense afternoon sun bearing down on them. They were all hungry and Ellie had resourcefully found some raspberries in one of the bushes to keep them going but they would need to eat something proper soon.

Even the grass, the leaves of the trees, were starting to look appetizing, Jack thought – and he exchanged a look with Ellie, the two of them wondering how much longer Ram would keep going in his efforts to find out what was wrong with the drone – as well as marvelling at his endless bad temper and foul language.

He was now back in the cockpit checking a console and had earlier used all of his considerable technological knowledge to attempt to diagnose what the problem was with the drone. Jack had assisted, even Ellie, adding what expertise they had checking if it could be an engineering or mechanical issue, a software glitch or a bug in the navigation computer.

So far though it was to no avail. Ellie and Jack accepted that it was all out of their expertise. But Ram refused and they watched him trying all manner of possible solutions to discover what was plaguing the machine. Ram had become obsessed with his quest to figure out what had caused their difficulties.

"Don't you know who I am!" Ram said, glaring accusingly at the control panel. "You'll never beat me," he continued, while slamming his hand on the console as if punishing it.

"I don't think that's going to help do anything, Ram," Jack said. "Except maybe give you a sore hand in addition to your foot."

"Well, that might be the least of our problems," Ellie said, gazing around uneasily. "Don't you think we should maybe head off?"

"Where?" Ram snapped.

"You're the 'genius'," Ellie scoffed.

"Calm down, guys," Jack interrupted. "It won't help us by arguing. Maybe Ellie's right and we should try and rely more on human co-ordinates, rather than whatever you programmed in that computer."

Ram ignored Jack and continued punching in data on the console. But from his frustrated demeanour, he too was clearly losing hope - in ironic contrast to him being so euphoric with his idea, which he himself admitted was ingenious, even for him – to steal the drone and use it to make good their escape. And for the majority of the journey, it seemed as if it was working. But before long, as the flight went on, however, it had become clear that all was not well with the drone.

It had started behaving like it was possessed, as Ram had described it, altering its course in midair. He, along with Ellie and Jack, had been concerned that the drone might even crash, so erratic had its changes in direction been at times. Ram had corrected its bearings as they flew, re-entering the destination co-ordinates he intended them to reach - yet the drone would continually veer off the path Ram had set it, eventually clipping the top of a tree and descending, crash-landing to the ground.

Now, after so much effort troubleshooting what could be wrong with the drone, Ram climbed out of the cockpit and advised Ellie and Jack that he was beginning to suspect more and more that the dilemma was not the result of an accident. He believed that the drone had to have been hacked, that someone from the outside had been interfering, countering Ram's own many attempts to manually override the drone during the flight. It was the only explanation left to explain what had happened – the drone had to have been taken over and forced to land there by a third party.

"Like who?" Jack wondered.

"Do you think it could be The Collective?" Ellie speculated.

"I'm not sure," Ram replied. "But we better not stick around, to try and find out."

They set off on foot, Ram leading the way through the forested area, eventually arriving at an overgrown botanical gardens which gave Ram some comfort that his plan had almost worked, realizing that they were close to the town where Ram had grown up.

The house that had once been his home was perhaps twenty miles away, he estimated, out in the suburbs.

In taking the drone, Ram's original plan was to travel to his former home town and stay in the house he was raised in. It seemed like the safest place he could think of to go at the time. He had hoped that they could use it as a literal safehouse, and from there, regroup and work out a way forward.

If they felt it was safe to do so, the next step, after some initial time, would be to return to the place that had once been the main base of The Technos.

Ram explained to Ellie and Jack that after he founded his tribe, The Technos were once located at an abandoned factory on the outskirts of the town in an industrial complex. It had its own power source, excellent infrastructure and the Internet speeds were out of this world.

When The Technos had permanently moved out so they could take over the Mall Rats' city and Ram could claim Eagle Mountain for himself, they had relocated all their personnel and most of their equipment. They had gone as far as to purposefully sabotage the base they were leaving behind, blowing parts of it up, gutting it, making sure they left no trace.

Ram didn't think there would be any Collective presence in the area because his former base would be the last place on Earth The Collective would ever go to because there was nothing there anymore – no Ram, no Technos, nothing of value. Even if any of The Collective's forces had ever been there in the past, they would have had no reason to have stayed behind.

"That's what I wanted Kami to think anyway," Ram said, a mischievous smile of delight on his face. "Let's just say I didn't take everything with me when The Technos moved out. As a contingency in case I ever wanted to return. I just hope there's some toys and hardware left behind, hidden away where I put them."

Jack and Ellie knew that Ram had taken refuge in the community of Liberty outside of their home city, believing he had a bounty on his head and living in total paranoia that the mysterious Kami would try and seek him out as a result of him usurping supposed plans Kami and The Collective had in place to invade the city - by doing it himself. But as always with

Ram, he played his cards more than close to his chest and it was difficult to know the exact situation.

"What if The Collective were able to see through your ruse?" Ellie wondered. "If Kami's as smart as you say, maybe they figured out your old base could still be of some use to them. For all we know, maybe there's some there right now."

"In which case we'd be truly out of the frying pan and into the fire," Ram said, dreading the prospect. "But I don't think The Collective will be around. To anyone who wouldn't know otherwise, there's nothing there anymore. Including me. As far as they would believe, that is."

"Then who do you think might have brought the drone down?" Jack asked.

"They probably tried to override it back in the city," Ram surmised.

As they proceeded furtively through the botanical gardens, Ram recalled going there with his parents as a young child. He was re-treading some old memories, not all of them fond ones. His parents had been harsh, his father a strict disciplinarian. Although they had given him an excellent education, recognizing the precocious gifts and intellect of their only child, Ram's was a house and a childhood often filled with anger and fear, rather than love. At least that's how Ram perceived it at the time. There were no incidents of domestic violence but his parents were not tactile, attentive.

Ram always felt that they were somehow disappointed in him, that he could never meet their high expectations, even if he did achieve the highest of grades at school.

His father was once in the military and expected Ram's room to be tidy, for him never to be late for even a meal. Everything had to always be so exact. A keen sportsman, Ram's father was always disappointed that Ram seemed to have no interest, aptitude or ability in any kind of sport, preferring to gain knowledge of anything and everything which impressed his mother.

She was once a supply teacher and sanctioned Ram's obsession with any studying – until his focus became on computers and on information technology. This provided some respite and he eventually escaped from the real world by entering the digital fantasy world offered by computer systems. Both software and hardware had been his companions, the only friends he had ever really known growing up.

Ram's former town seemed lifeless now. There was no trace of anybody, just the three of them, making their way down the street that bordered the botanical gardens which gave them all a degree of hope that they were well and truly alone.

They took a moment to rummage through a decaying and looted convenience store, its contents strewn all over the floor. There wasn't much left of any value but they were relieved when Jack found an old box of cereal bars under a pile of rubbish, long past its sell by date. They were stale and tasteless but in their sealed foil wrappings, it was the only choice of food they had on offer to try and quell their ravenous appetites.

Returning to the street, they still had about another hour's walk ahead of them, Ram felt.

Ellie and Jack were missing the other Mall Rats and were concerned about what had happened to them and where they had been taken on the military cargo planes they saw leaving the airport of their home city. Both pressed Ram for more information - if the invaders were indeed The Collective.

Ram wasn't sure where The Collective were located exactly. So, he couldn't provide any detail as far as that was concerned. All of his communication with Kami in the past had been done online. He didn't know who Kami was – if his online, supposed friend was male, female. Sometimes Ram wondered if Kami could even be an adult, judging by the mature and knowledgeable manner displayed when Ram had liaised and communicated online.

Ram had even wondered if Kami could be a computer, a form of artificial intelligence programme that was still hooked up online, speculating if there was some connection with the *Knowledge Artificial Machine Intelligence* super mega computer at Eagle Mountain, or if there were others like it, the machine having the acronym *K.A.M.I*, which he suspected couldn't be entirely coincidental.

Ram said he wished he could shed more light on matters but he genuinely could not, including where the Mall Rats might have been taken.

Now, the Mall Rat's home city – and Eagle Mountain – could be under the occupation and control of The Collective, Ram, Ellie and Jack speculated.

"It's the classic paradigm of conquest," Ram reflected, as they walked down the street. "To the victors go the spoils. Including some pretty awesome equipment the invaders seem to be stripping out of the military facility at Eagle Mountain."

"Ssshh! Get down!" Jack urged, suddenly ducking for cover the other side of an overturned rubbish bin, Ellie following quickly behind.

Ram looked terrified as he noticed what had come to Jack and Ellie's attention.

He could hear the sound of engines, vehicles, approaching at high speed.

Ram rushed, leaping over the rubbish bin, to join Ellie and Jack in hiding.

It was just in time, Ram finding cover as a vehicle approached around the corner and passed by at high speed.

"I thought you said nobody else would be here!" Ellie whispered in an urgent, hushed undertone.

"They shouldn't be!" Ram shrugged anxiously, nervous at who it could be and if they would return.

The vehicle slammed on its brakes at the end of the street and turned 180 degrees, speeding back towards the rubbish bin.

Jack, Ellie and Ram remained motionless, trying to not even breathe for fear of making any sound.

Through a crack in the bin, Jack noticed the doors of the vehicle, which had skidded to a stop, opening. And he could see four pairs of legs getting out. There was no indication of identity – except for an impatient voice.

"Come on out! We know you're there!"

Ram flinched. He couldn't believe it. Jack and Ellie exchanged incredulous looks. They recognized the voice too. Surely, it couldn't be?

"We found your drone and followed your trail. I won't ask you again. Come out if you know what's good for you!"

Slowly, Jack, Ellie and Ram got to their feet, emerged from behind the rubbish bin – and were astonished to see who was standing before them.

"Well, well – now *this* I would have never expected," Ved said, amazed in turn to observe his former Techno leader and master, Ram, as well as the two Mall Rats.

Ved was accompanied by three guards, all about the same age as him. One was carrying a device which was bleeping. Ram wondered exactly what it did but he was sure they must have used it to track them down somehow.

"Ved?" Ellie said, stunned to see him. But more wary if he was currently a friend. Or foe.

Ved had been Ram's talented and devoted apprentice at The Technos, a computer prodigy who had helped Ram try to achieve his vision of creating a perfect, virtual reality world. Temperamental and rebellious at times, he had disappeared in the last days of Ram's regime, with the rumours being that Ram had played a part in Ved's initial removal from The Technos. Nobody knew what had happened to him. They all believed he was missing and gone forever, 'deleted' by Ram's successor as Techno leader, Mega.

"You're alive! We thought you might be dead," Jack said, unable to comprehend the sight of Ved in front of him.

"For a time – so did I," Ved stated.

He gave Ram a fixed stare laced with anger.

"So. You're back on your own two feet again."

The last time Ved had seen him, Ram had been unable to walk and was confined to a wheelchair due to a serious accident he had suffered in his past.

"A lot of things are different since we last met," Ram remarked. "I'm glad to see you're alive and well."

"Yeah? Well, I can't say I feel the same about you! I never wanted to see your face again. What are you doing here, Ram!?"

"I was about to ask you the same question," Ram replied – looking in concern at the stun blaster Ved was now levelling in his direction.

"Take this as a hint," Ved said. Jack and Ellie instinctively cried out as Ved fired the stun gun, hitting Ram's mid-rift, Ram collapsing to the ground.

CHAPTER FIFTEEN

After their initial surprise and elation at being reunited with Tai San, Alice and Ryan - the Mall Rats had spent several hours with them outside in the grounds of the *Lakeside Resort*, catching up on all that had happened in their lives since they had last seen each other. They believed that at least they could talk more freely in case the inside of the resort was bugged for sound and they didn't want to give away any information – though all were aware that whoever was holding them seemed to know a lot about the Mall Rats already.

Alice was overjoyed to find out Ellie was alive and well, or at least she certainly was when the Mall Rats had been with her at the mall before the invasion. It was such good news for her to hear that Ellie had found happiness in her continued relationship with Jack, Amber relaying how they seemed such a good fit for each other and were so content together.

That Jack, Ellie and Ram hadn't been brought to the resort so far filled the Mall Rats with hope that they were somehow still safe from the occupation forces. Lex tried to keep what he knew of what had happened to them vague, telling Alice he had last seen them 'around' and thought they were still somewhere in the heart of the city.

Alice suspected that Lex was choosing his words carefully, not giving away everything that he knew – for all that he denied it.

There was so much to bring each other up to date on. Bray explained what had occurred to him after The Techno's invasion. Amber described Ram's Techno regime and his fall from power, leading on to how they had worked with Ram to bring about Mega's defeat when he had, in turn, ruled over their city.

Trudy told of their re-encounter with The Guardian, the ordeal they had been through with Eloise and her forces. Lex spoke of their revisit to Eagle Mountain where they had discovered more secrets and tantalizing clues about what the adults had been doing before their extinction by the 'virus' – and their surprise encounters with remnants of the adults themselves, locked away, as if in a perpetual deep sleep inside their cryogenic hibernation chambers.

Alice and Ryan reported what they had endured during their lengthy period as captives – but also the detailed questioning they had been put through by The Selector about Eagle Mountain and worryingly, the Mall Rats themselves.

Amber was outraged to learn of the biochips that had been forcibly injected into Tai San, Ryan and Alice – and she dreaded if she and the other Mall Rats would be subject to the same experience.

Following Tai San, Alice and Ryan's recent attempts, escape didn't seem to be an option, especially given the security presence all around the resort and the possibility that the biochips could be trackable.

Tai San, Alice and Ryan were made aware of the strange and euphoric welcome their fellow Mall Rats had received at the airstrip upon landing and were disturbed at the apparent reach and influence in these lands of what felt, at first impression, like a mythology around Zoot and those who were most connected to him. Trudy recalled with utter anguish the male who prostrated himself before her and Brady after they landed, asking them for a blessing, a miracle.

Tai San, Alice and Ryan described The Selector, who the rest of the party hadn't met as yet. And all speculated why they had been brought together and why they were being held prisoner in such a way.

The Selector had mentioned, Tai San, Alice and Ryan informed them, that all that was apparently happening to them was due to 'The Creator''s vision and plan, even though none of them knew what that entailed or who The Creator was, let alone if they even existed, whatever or whoever The Creator was meant to be. Was The Creator the same as Kami? Or had The Creator displaced Kami and was now the ruler of this group? Or was The Creator the alter ego of The Selector?

There were so many questions, so much that they didn't understand, even if the group holding them were indeed in reality The Collective. Or, some other regime.

After all they had been through, they were overwhelmed, exhausted, and in need of rest and recovery. The newcomers had their pick of empty rooms to choose from and they went their separate ways, Trudy and Brady going in one room, Amber, Bray and baby Jay in another. Lottie and Sammy were to stay with Alice as the two younger children especially felt frightened at what might occur but were reassured by Alice's obvious prowess as a warrior and bodyguard.

May would wait a little bit before picking her room, she advised. She would be sharing with Salene but was aware Salene would need to talk in private with Ryan first to let him know of their status.

* * *

Ryan gave Salene his own guided tour of the *Lakeside Resort*, showing her around the scenic grounds outside by the lake, the pool and gym where he spent some of his spare time keeping fit – but Salene could tell Ryan just wanted to be with her, the tour a pretense to spend some time together alone. Which suited Salene as well.

Salene knew in her heart she would have to let Ryan know the truth about her relationship status with May. She had to be honest, she owed him that much. He was a special guy, uncomplicated, slow at times intellectually, but his heart was pure and true.

Salene didn't feel clean inside. In the past she had 'led' Ryan on, she shamefully admitted to herself. She liked him, she thought she genuinely loved him at one stage. But despite their history and all they had been through together, in truth Salene was aware that deep down she had never had the same feelings for Ryan that he had openly expressed he had to her. And the same applied to any other male Salene had been involved with. Even Pride.

Ryan was more of a very close friend. And not the soulmate he had been so keen to be. Certainly not for Salene. She hoped he would find romance elsewhere in his life. He deserved it and she wanted him to live a happy life. But it couldn't be with her. The love of her life was May.

Salene dreaded relaying this situation to Ryan, which felt like a truth that was too great to tell. She would try though. He deserved and needed to know.

"Ryan, we need to talk," Salene said gently, leading Ryan to a bench overlooking the scenic lake.

"We are talking," Ryan replied, slightly confused.

"You don't understand, Ryan. There are some things I need to tell you. And I just hope you can accept everything I say."

Ryan knew Salene enough to know that there was something of great importance bothering her and he encouraged her to open up and to tell him what was troubling her so.

Salene began by explaining to Ryan that after he had been sent away by The Guardian and The Chosen, she thought he had initially been killed. And that perhaps she might never see him ever again.

She recounted how she had gradually fallen in love with Pride, or so she thought at the time, entering into a relationship after Ram and The Technos had invaded the city. Ryan appreciated her transparency and Salene was surprised when he told her he already knew all about it. Tai San had revealed details to him of the Eco tribe shortly after she arrived at the resort and that she thought Salene had been in some kind of relationship with Pride, though she didn't know the full extent of it or how serious it was, having only encountered the Mall Rats briefly the last time she saw them in the city.

Ryan put his hand gently on Salene's. "Maybe you and Pride just weren't meant to be. Like what happened with our baby. It wasn't the right time. No matter how much either of us wanted it."

Salene began to cry, remembering the tragic loss of their unborn baby soon after she had last seen Ryan, when he had been forced to work in the mines by The Chosen. Their final days spent together as a couple were marked by so much tragedy and heartbreak, painful memories.

"Maybe you and I have been brought back together for a reason," Ryan suggested, confirming Salene's suspicions about where he was hoping things might be headed. "It might not be too late to turn the clock back. Me and you..."

"Ryan, it's different now. What we had was a long time ago."

"What we had was something special, Sal. So why don't we try again? I know we can make it work. We could even try for another baby."

"You're not listening to what I'm saying," Salene said, struggling to get the words out. "It's different now."

"How? What do you mean?"

"It's not you, Ryan. It's me."

"I know it's you. And you're what I want. It's always been you."

"No – there's someone else," Salene admitted painfully.

"Who?" Ryan said, confused and feeling like his whole world was starting to crumble. "Who is he?"

"It's not a *he*," Salene said, aware that this was becoming far more awkward than she could ever have imagined.

"What are you talking about?"

"It's a *she*. The someone else - is a she."

Ryan took a moment for it to all sink in. "Are you telling me you're - gay?"

Salene nodded.

"Is this some kind of joke? Did Lex put you up to this?"

"It's not a joke, Ryan... I'm being completely serious," Salene insisted. She was now feeling overwhelmed. A part of her wanted to flee, to become invisible, to disappear. It wasn't because of any shame about her feelings for May – there weren't any. It was more due to Ryan's reaction. She didn't want to hurt him. She cared enough that she wanted to do what was in his best interests and she worried how he would be when he found out the truth. But she couldn't live a lie and pretend her life was unreal, to herself or to Ryan.

"Who – who is she then?" Ryan asked. "This person you're meant to be so in love with?"

"Promise me you won't do anything."

"Who do you think I am?! What do you think I'd do?"

"Promise me, Ryan. When I tell you, you won't do anything to her – or to yourself. You're one of the most important people in my life – and I care about you. I want you to be okay. For us to always be friends, forever."

"Then as a 'friend' of yours – would you tell me who it is?" Ryan said, trying to contain his emotions.

"It's May," Salene revealed it. "I'm in love with May and we're together."

Ryan sat in silence, trying somehow to assimilate it all before taking Salene's hand and gently squeezing it. "Just as long as you're happy, then I'll be happy too, Sal. That's all I've ever wanted – is your happiness."

"Ryan – please don't. You're making it so difficult for me." She raised his clasped hand and kissed it. "You really are special, you know."

"If you don't mind, Sal, I'd like to spend a bit of time alone. I've got some laundry to do. So, I'll catch up with you later."

He walked away to the resort entrance and Salene knew it was just some kind of excuse.

She felt heartbroken, torn by guilt. She realized Ryan would need some time to come to terms with it. But what they had was in the past. Her future life was one she wanted to spend with May. Whatever lay in store for them in their current predicament.

* * *

The Selector gazed contemptuously at an image on the monitor of Tai San in her room, sitting up on her bed, leaning against her fluffy pillows, her ankle raised on some cushions at the other end. She couldn't stop herself smiling. And didn't want to. She was thrilled to be reunited with Lex, who was sitting next to her, equally enraptured to be around her again. Then Lex disappeared from frame and suddenly the image also disappeared from the screen, replaced with static, electronic snow.

Inside Tai San's room back at the *Lakeside Resort*, Lex had found a small device in the corner of the ceiling and had disabled it. It was small and crushed easily when he dropped it to the floor and ground it into pieces under his boot. "I wonder if that 'thing' only picked up sound?"

"Hopefully not vision," Tai San said, with a shiver running down her spine at the prospect of being observed, especially by the creepy Selector.

"I don't know," Lex replied. "But it sure as hell won't be working now. How's that ankle feeling?"

"Much better – now that you're here."

Tai San proceeded then to tell Lex an overview of what she had been through since they had last seen each other, so long ago. He had been shocked to hear of her experiences as a slave, her captivity under The Broker, and lately the ordeals she had suffered, as well as Ryan and Alice, as 'guests' of The Selector.

She had refrained from telling Lex the entire situation, however, worrying that if she mentioned the full extent of The Selector's creepy behaviour and blatant physical attraction to her - that Lex might angrily react and do something impulsive in an effort to protect her, even attack The Selector at the first chance. He would inevitably only endanger himself in the process, Tai San felt, and no doubt be harshly punished by The Selector and his warriors.

The Selector had a cruel, sadistic streak in him, Tai San knew that all too well by now, and she had to spare Lex from it. She would tell Lex everything that had happened to her when she felt it was right to do so but she wouldn't allow Lex to risk himself for her. He had only just unexpectedly returned into her life and she didn't want to suddenly lose him.

Lex had wondered why Tai San, during her time as a spy in The Technos in league with Mega to bring down Ram, hadn't tried to go back to him then. She explained that she had wanted to – and was indeed desperate to - but things had quickly developed out of control and she had gotten in too deep. She was trying to save the city, many innocent lives, Lex's included, and had got caught up in the echelons of The Technos, living a false life as one of their own and had been unable to return to Lex and the life they had once had.

It was always her goal to do so once The Technos were defeated. But Tai San had been taken away from the city, ending up in faraway lands, enslaved, never to see Lex again, she thought.

She asked what had happened in Lex's own life since their separation. He told her how devastated he was when she had first disappeared after The Technos invaded - and he had done everything he could to try to find her. As time unfolded, he believed she had been tragically killed, or was 'deleted' by The Technos, as they referred to it. Lex revealed he had gotten involved with a few other girls since her, including Ebony's sister, Siva, as well as later a brief dalliance with Gel. Tai San was aware of Lex's relationship with Siva, who had been a prominent Techno herself.

"And there's one more confession," Lex admitted to her.

"Just the one?"

He described how he had only recently had a fling with Lia. She was not a Mall Rat, of course, and he met her on the island where The Mall Rats had their initial encounter with forces of The Collective, under their commander, Blake. Lia was pretty and enjoyable to be around but they still didn't know each other that well, it was nothing too serious. They weren't a proper couple.

And he hoped that Lia would be safe, along with the others who had been seized by the invaders. Lex and Tai San speculated on what might have happened to them, both, of course, not having any clear idea other than the Mall Rats seemed to be segregated for some reason from the other prisoners.

Tai San appreciated Lex's honesty and openness about his 'love life' and let him know that since Lex, there hadn't been anyone special in her life.

"So - where does that leave us?" Lex wondered, inching across the covers, towards Tai San.

"I don't know what you mean," Tai San said, coyly.

"Maybe I can remind you exactly what I mean," Lex said. "I reckon this bed's big enough for two."

"Hmmm. You're probably right." Tai San teased. "But who could I possibly get to keep me company at night?"

"How about me?" Lex replied.

"Oh, I think that might be a good idea," Tai San said.

"But first, I'll go and tell the others about the monitoring device I found in that corner."

Lex met Bray in the corridor when he left Tai San's room and accompanied him to his and Amber's room where they discovered another device in the same area, Lex ripping it from the corner and hurling it to the floor, Bray then grinding it into pieces with his boot.

"I still think we'd better be careful about what we say," Bray cautioned. "I'm pretty sure that device is probably totally disabled but it's better to not take any chances."

"Agreed," Lex replied, eager to return to Tai San. And he left, as quickly as he arrived, giving a wave to Amber, who was sitting on the bed holding baby Jay, lulling him to sleep with a soft song.

Bray had gone to get Amber a hot chocolate from the automatic vending machine in the kitchen area and watched as Amber gently placed their sleeping baby in the second bed in the room.

"Are you okay?" Bray asked, handing Amber the cup of hot chocolate. She nodded but was clearly distressed by the latest events and explained that being reunited with other members of their tribe - it had all suddenly hit her. She had just felt so aware of her responsibility and what the people around her meant to her. They had become more than just a family. She cared enormously for them, loved them dearly and had always tried to do everything she could to look out for their interests.

But she was not just uneasy about whatever was planned but was scared and tried to hide her fear from the others, wishing not to fuel their own. In addition to feeling concerned about what future their baby might have in this unpredictable world.

"Everything will be okay," Bray reassured her, placing his arms around her to give her a comforting hug. "I promise you, somehow we'll all be okay. And don't forget, you're not on your own, you know. I've got some pretty broad shoulders – at least, I thought so, last time I checked," Bray smiled.

It made Amber smile too. He gave her a long, loving kiss. Amber clung to him, holding him tightly like she had never done before. She needed him by her side, to feel his strength and loving support, to face whatever the future might have in store for not only them and their son but all of their tribe, the Mall Rats.

CHAPTER SIXTEEN

Following her encounter with The Selector in his lodge by the lakeside, Ebony was taken on a journey by boat, Snake and his warriors transporting her across the water to The Cube. Snake refused to answer any of Ebony's questions about what would happen to her when they arrived at The Cube – and even what, or where exactly, it was.

She initially wondered if they meant to perhaps punish her in some way, if The Cube was a form of detention centre or worse, a place where she might be tortured, perhaps dealt with permanently. She remembered the cold and resentful atmosphere of her welcome when she first arrived at the airstrip compared to the adulation Amber and the Mall Rats had received ahead of her. She also remembered The Selector's mention of something about there being an 'audience' of some kind.

The boat arrived at a large island located further down the lake in an otherwise remote area – it was like they were in the middle of nowhere, the lake enveloped by nothing but forest and mountains all around.

The island itself was a few kilometres from the distant shoreline in all directions, Ebony reckoned, observing the lay of the land as the boat drew up by an old rotting pontoon. The water looked cold and uninviting and had to be deep that far out from the shore, Ebony believed. The island was well guarded, warriors lining its perimeter and saluting Snake in acknowledgement when the boat pulled in. The island was completely cut off and seemed like it was a world of its own.

The archaic pontoon was the first proof that there had clearly been some developments and a human presence on the island in the past and that the island wasn't an untouched wilderness.

Ebony was marched on foot along some narrow pathways which seemed like former cycling or walking treks in the woods during the adult era, branches protruding as the trees began to encroach on the old routes. A few benches, most of them in disrepair or broken, were scattered along the way.

They walked past some signposts lining the paths, the information on them fading but Ebony could still discern the text was describing the flora and fauna of the region. It must have been a nature reserve, Ebony assumed. It was certainly a place adults had visited, maybe even a holiday destination.

There were a few abandoned buildings, slowly being reclaimed by the natural world, the panes of glass of what had been windows cracked or missing as plants and trees grew, uncontrollably, slowly covering the human traces of what had once been. One of the ruins was an old boathouse. There were the remnants of an old wedding chapel, scarred by charred fire marks.

They finally arrived at The Cube. It was aptly named due to it being a perfectly square-shaped construction. Unlike the other buildings she had walked by, The Cube was in good order, the trees around it had been routinely cut back, keeping the forest at bay. All of its windows were intact and it was a large, rustic building, made of logs, located in a clearing, a barbeque area at the front.

Snake told Ebony to wait outside by the entrance. After a few minutes, the doors opened and a group emerged from within, being ushered out by several other guards. They seemed to be prisoners of some kind, mostly around Ebony's age. They followed each other in a line, stepping out from The Cube, deferentially proceeding behind another male, who, from his demeanour, carried some authority.

Ebony did a double-take. She recognized one who had been escorted outside.

"Hawk?"

It *was* him.

"Ebony?" Hawk replied, stunned to see her there.

Hawk had been the leader of The Eco Tribe, who had lived in the forest outside the city that had been the home to Ebony and the Mall Rats. He was an ally and good friend of the Mall Rats. Amber had once found sanctuary in the Eco camp. Even Ebony, on a temporary occasion. But she wouldn't have ever claimed Hawk was a friend – and was sure he wouldn't say the same of her. But Hawk was a familiar face, someone Ebony knew and respected as a survivor and leader of his tribe. Hawk meant well. He was sincere in his beliefs and desire to live peacefully with nature and by doing so, to make the world a better place. Ebony, otherwise alone and feeling threatened and uncertain of her fate, was pleased to see him.

"What are you doing here?" Ebony called out.

"The question is – what are *you* doing here?" a voice replied. And it didn't belong to Hawk but the male who had led Hawk and the prisoners.

He announced that he was known as The Gamesmaster and he was in charge of The Cube and everything that took place on the island.

He mentioned that some of the other contestants were gathered from the furthest reaches of the lands, as was Ebony, who had travelled some distance from her home to where they were. In case any of them were not fully aware of who she was, The Gamesmaster revealed Ebony had been chosen by The Selector himself to take part in The Cube.

In her city, her reputation spoke for herself. She was not only once a tribe leader but had been the leader of the entire city. And as some of them may have heard, it was true that she had even been connected with the legendary god Zoot and his Locos tribe for a time before choosing to follow her own path in life.

The other contestants would have to be careful of Ebony, The Gamesmaster warned them. She was cunning, ruthless, manipulative, devious, dishonest, untrustworthy, selfish and dangerous.

Ebony listened, in dismay at the character portrait The Gamesmaster was presenting of her, more like a character assassination, she felt.

"That's not all," Ebony added. "You forgot to mention that I'm actually a pretty nice person, once people get to know me."

"You will all decide for yourselves, and make of Ebony what you will," The Gamesmaster insisted to the other prisoners. Then he indicated to the guards. "She needs to be chipped and prepared for the next trial."

Ebony was injected with a biochip by a medic who had emerged from The Cube so that she could be tracked and her health monitored. The injection was painful and Ebony would have fought back had she not been held firmly in place by Snake and some of The Gamesmaster's guards.

She was then fitted with a chest harness, as were the other prisoners, including Hawk. Each harness contained miniature cameras, pointing outwards, to apparently record the viewpoint and activity of each of the competitors.

"Remember the rules of The Cube," The Gamesmaster addressed the assembly of contestants. "If you remove the camera or your harness, you are disqualified from the game. If you try to leave the island and escape, you are disqualified from the game. If you damage The Cube or any equipment, you will be disqualified from the game. If you disobey me or any of my staff, then you will automatically forfeit the game. And if you remove your biochip or try to take it out, you will immediately lose your place in the game."

"What happens - if we get disqualified?" Ebony asked, carefully. Perhaps that was something she might intentionally want to do, she was considering, if it meant she could leave the island and get out of whatever she was otherwise getting into.

Hawk and the other contestants were clearly exhausted, had cuts and bruises on their faces and by all accounts had been through some difficult experiences. Maybe no longer being in The Cube wouldn't be such a bad thing compared to the prospect of being here.

"Disqualification means you come last in the round. And whoever comes last is immediately Discarded," The Gamesmaster answered.

"Discarded? What does that mean?" Ebony asked, confused.

"It means that you would be cast away – and that your life would effectively be over. To be Discarded means to be permanently ejected. But if you are unworthy of The Creator, it would be a fate that is deserved. You would be expelled, extradited, exiled – and extremely unfortunate to ever be disqualified."

"What happens if I win?" Ebony enquired.

The Gamesmaster advised that she would be given one 'point' and at least be able to remain a contestant. Until the time she received ten points, in which case she would enter an initiation phase to eventually be brought in front of The Creator for further assessment.

"And if I lose?" Ebony asked.

"Then you might even remain a contestant for the rest of your life," The Gamesmaster smiled, but it was ice cold.

Ebony glanced again at her fellow contestants, the prisoners, and suspected that they had participated for some time given the state of them.

"You mean that we might have to hang around this place – forever?" Ebony asked.

"Until you die – yes," The Gamesmaster replied, indicating an area littered with crosses nearby, no doubt housing some of the past contestants.

Ebony wondered what the 'trials' were and how she would be competing against Hawk and the other contestants. She had found the notion of finishing last and being Discarded no longer held any appeal. She had to understand what was going on, find some way to ensure she wasn't the one who ended up being Discarded. Or staying in the game forever.

She liked the sound of achieving ten points and being brought in front of The Creator, which seemed like Ebony's only chance to truly survive, and determined to encounter whatever that might entail at that time.

The Gamesmaster revealed more rules. That they were all taking part in the 'trials of life' that The Creator had helped design. On the island, those who stayed at The Cube were simulating life, taking part in a living experiment. They had each been selected by The Selector because they possessed distinct traits and characteristics.

The Cube was a microcosm of society, life. A study of the interactions of people and an examination of the human species. The contestants would be exposed to a series of challenges, pushed to their limits. Each feat would bring out and show the best – and worst – of human nature. And humanity's interaction with nature itself. Those who would be watching the trials would be learning about adaptability, resourcefulness, the ability to improvise and inventiveness.

The contestants would be tested not only physically but mentally, morally, spiritually. And it would inspire the audience who would be watching. No doubt, to ensure they didn't become participants, Ebony speculated.

And she was partially right. The Cube also was a form of entertainment. As the sun set across the lands, farm workers and slaves toiling in the multitude of fields watched images being transmitted onto agricultural buildings and heard The Gamesmaster's voice blaring through speakers which reverberated around the lands and far beyond as if from the heavens above.

"Welcome, friends! To another episode of The Cube! Brought to you courtesy of The Creator. This evening we welcome a new contestant. Will she live? Or will she die? Will she stay in The Cube forever? Or will she be brought before The Creator? Only time will tell. So, don't miss a single episode. And don't forget you will be questioned by your protectors and masters in whatever region you might be located. So it's in your interests to pay attention to all the action you are about to witness unfold."

The vast crowds across the lands sat gazing almost hypnotically at the various images transmitted on the buildings as if they had long since become fully brainwashed and were now almost robotized. Without doubt though, each were gripped by the images they were watching and fascinated by The Gamesmaster's rhetoric booming through the speakers.

"Can we change who we are? Can we adapt? What does it say about our lives as individuals? And who we are as a society? A species?"

The Gamesmaster added that The Creator would be often observing and monitoring what went on in The Cube. The contestants should therefore feel honoured to have been selected and by their actions would deepen an understanding of what it meant to be human.

"Now, all of you watching in your home sectors will be well and truly aware of the nine contestants who you have seen each and every week. But sadly, Kala won't be joining us or indeed anyone else. He'll be staying on the island for all eternity. Why don't you join me now in welcoming Kala's replacement and our newest contestant – the one, the only, Ebony!"

The audience around the lands didn't applaud in any way whatsoever but just stared transfixed at the images showing Ebony faking a smile into the cameras.

Back on the island, Ebony braced herself as she watched a guard bring out ten knives from inside The Cube and placed them on top of a counter at the old barbeque area outside.

In the upper level of the building, a technician called out from the windows that all perimeter areas were standing by for streaming feeds from all the cameras.

"Then let the trial begin!" The Gamesmaster shouted into his headpiece microphone, occasionally glancing into the camera which followed him as he paced before the assembled contestants.

He urged each to take a knife from the counter, which they proceeded to do.

For a moment, Ebony instinctively felt that she would like to plunge the knife into The Gamesmaster's throat to give his intended audience an unexpected thrill. But for the time being at least, she realized that her own survival very much depended upon her playing along.

She clutched the handle of her knife tightly, her adrenalin racing. She was on edge and wondered if the ten of them were meant to fight each other and be forced to take part in some macabre contest, played out on camera.

Ebony started readying herself for imminent battle and was sizing up the other contestants, trying to gauge from their body language and attitude the type of people they might be, looking out for any weaknesses or vulnerabilities. She thought she might suggest to Hawk that the two of them team up against the others.

"Each of us and every living thing has but one life," The Gamesmaster began, commentating into his microphone. "We can only use our life once – and when it is over, it is gone forever. There is no backup. No safety net. The most important resource any being or species has is the fact that it is alive."

Ebony breathed out a nervous sigh, firing herself up, determined that she would preserve her life for at least another day, at whatever the cost. Which meant receiving one of the ten points The Gamesmaster had referred to earlier.

"Our new contestant, Ebony, had consciously forsaken the god Zoot and his teachings in her life. Will he now forsake her in return? In today's trial, our contestants must decide how they use the gift of life and choose well what they do with the limited time life provides. On the island, we have placed a food source. The winner is the one who finds it and knows how to use it best. The last-placed will be Discarded, unworthy of continuing in The Cube. You have one hour. Starting exactly from – now!"

The blare of a hooter emitted a deafening sound which reverberated through the darkness.

Ebony hesitated, wondering if The Gamesmaster would say anything more about what they had to do while Hawk and the other contestants raced away from the immediate area of The Cube, heading off in search of the food source they had been instructed to find.

"Is that it?" Ebony asked The Gamesmaster. "How do we know what it means to 'do well' in the trial?"

"Isn't that the same as in life?" The Gamesmaster replied. "How do you ever know who wins? There are no set rules in our day to day lives… But some people clearly emerge as the winners. Others, losers. And I'm sure our audience would agree that you're running out of valuable time, Ebony. So, I suggest you join your other contestants."

He indicated and Ebony rushed off in the direction Hawk and the others had taken. If anyone knew how to survive in the wilderness, apart from herself, it would be him, she reckoned. And since he had been in The Cube longer than she had, he might know more about precisely what was required of them in the trial.

The ten contestants were soon spread out and ran through the forested island, looking around for the goal of the trial.

Ebony soon caught up with Hawk, who had run towards the lake edge.

"Where are you going?" Ebony called out after him, breathlessly, as she struggled to keep up with his pace.

"The one place I'd hide something if I was them," Hawk called back.

"Them? Who?" Ebony enquired.

"Just follow me and you'll see," Hawk said, leading Ebony to the lakeside where the abandoned boat house was. And for a moment, Ebony was tempted to try and make good her escape by diving into the water. She was sure there was a good chance she could reach the other side of the lake. The presence of The Cube's guards by the lake, however, with broadcasting crews aiming their cameras from various vantage points, deterred her from making such an effort.

She followed Hawk into the boat house instead. He was searching through the canoes inside, looking under the tarpaulins that covered them.

"What exactly's going on here?" Ebony asked him, joining him in rummaging around the boat house.

"We'll talk later!" Hawk said urgently, focusing instead on the task at hand. "First, we've got to get through this trial!"

After a few minutes, it was clear that there was no food source placed in the boat house and time was running out – they were worried one of the other contestants might have found it by now and won the race.

Ebony suddenly had another idea. "If we're looking for a food source – what about the lake? I mean, unless the fish wanted to get out of here just as much as I do."

"No, that would be too obvious," Hawk said. "It's not the way these people think. I reckon we should head back to the barbeque area?"

Hawk ran off, with Ebony in pursuit, as fast as they could across the island towards the barbeque area. Ebony realized what he had in mind when she heard the sound of clucking nearby inside a small chicken coop made of wood and wired together. A rooster within called loudly to try and defend the two chickens that were inside it.

The Gamesmaster arrived, yelling into his headset microphone and smiling occasionally into the camera being held by a crew member of The Cube who joined him. "You're getting closer! Exciting! But you'd better hurry! Others, as in life, always seem to want what you might have. And the question is – will they get it!?"

He was referring to other contestants who had arrived, breathless from their journey so far, and they closed in towards the chicken coop. But Ebony waved her knife at them, yelling for them to back off.

"They're mine!" one contestant screamed out, struggling to get past Hawk and Ebony.

"We got here first!" Ebony shouted, lashing out with her knife and striking the contestant across the face. "These chickens are ours!"

"Oh, vicious!" The Gamesmaster screamed into his headset, casting a wink at the cameras. "I'm sure our audience are loving it!"

Hawk suggested Ebony take one end of the chicken coop and Hawk would grab hold of the other and that they bring the chickens back to The Cube.

Ebony had other ideas, however, and reached inside the coop, grabbing one of the chickens from inside, the chickens squawking under protest.

"What are you doing!?" Hawk implored, stunned by Ebony's actions.

But she knew exactly what she was doing. She remembered The Selector referring to her as putting a 'fox in with the chickens' – and if it was a case of kill or be killed, Ebony was willing to do whatever was required to be the one who survived.

"I know the best way to use this food source," Ebony said, preparing to deliver a blow with her knife to the chicken. "We cook it!"

"No!" Hawk bellowed, reaching out. "Do not take another life!"

"What are you Hawk? A hawk? Or a chicken?" Ebony yelled, slightly playing up to the surrounding cameras and The Gamesmaster watching intently.

In one swift motion, Ebony disposed of the chicken, decapitating its head while it squawked and flapped its wings, blood pouring from the carcass and over Ebony as she reached in the coop for the others. She was certain she had made a good impression and was intending to be the winner of the very first trial she had experienced in The Cube.

Hawk was joined though by another contestant who yanked Ebony away and accompanied Hawk, each side carrying the chicken coop towards the main Cube building, followed by the camera crew and Gamesmaster, as well as other contestants, including Ebony.

The hooter emitted a sustained blare again. Audiences across the lands watched their screens, entranced, while The Gamesmaster's voice boomed through all the various speakers.

"And we have a winner!" The Gamesmaster announced. "Today's trial is won by Hawk, with Nova in second place and our recent contestant, Ebony, in third."

Ebony couldn't believe that Hawk had supposedly won and wondered why Nova was in second place and she had only come in third. She, after all, had killed the chicken. But she then slowly realized the reasons as The Gamesmaster addressed the cameras.

"It's so interesting, the human species. We can certainly kill. Or we can end up being killed. In the chickens' case, Ebony was correct that she was providing a food source. But in so doing, she was denying an ongoing source of food. Being – eggs. If we feed the chicken, the chicken can feed us. Possibly forever. But if we kill the chicken, then we might eat just for one night."

Ebony had been given credit for the chicken but the contestant who assisted Hawk was awarded second place, with Hawk coming in first, given that he had tried to prevent Ebony from killing the chicken. And he therefore was declared the overall winner.

Ebony hadn't made the impression she had hoped on The Gamesmaster, and presumably the audience, whoever they were. She knew she would have to learn to adapt – and quickly – if she was to have any hope of doing well on the island. Her mind began to race, calculating her best option, to make sure she survived and made it through the next episode of The Cube, which she knew would be advertised, judging by the images she noticed on the screens on her initial journey. No doubt, she would have other challenges coming very soon.

CHAPTER SEVENTEEN

"I would say, welcome home. Except you're not welcome. And this isn't your home anymore," Ved said, watching as Ram slowly came to, waking from the stun gun blast Ved had given him earlier.

Ellie and Jack were sitting at a table, Ram beside them, nearly falling off his chair as he regained consciousness, becoming aware of his surroundings just in time and stopping himself from crashing to the ground.

They were inside the factory that had once been the prime base of The Technos before Ram had vacated it, relocating their operations when he had originally conquered the city where Jack, Ellie and the rest of the Mall Rats had lived.

Ram shook his head, trying to rouse himself out of his dazed state – and he was slowly taking it all in, recognizing where he was again, a place full of many memories - as well as feeling concerned at being a prisoner, alongside Ellie and Jack, of his former protégé.

The room they were in was once an administrative office on the upper level of the factory. Looking around, Ram could see the guards who had accompanied Ved previously in their vehicle, now standing at the other end of the office, guarding the door from the inside, making sure it remained shut – and keeping Ram, Jack and Ellie in.

Ved was casually and adroitly spinning the stun gun in his hand like something out of the wild west days – and watching Ram intensely, in deliberation.

"I've been thinking what to do with the three of you," Ved commented.

"You could – just let us go?" Ellie mentioned hopefully.

"Why'd you blast me before?" Ram asked, rubbing his head in an attempt to ease the pounding sensation inside.

"Why'd you think?" Ved answered. "You've had it coming for a long time. And besides, you looked tired. I figured I'd give you a couple of hours of rest because you didn't seem that 'stunned' to see me. So, I thought I'd stun you myself," he added sarcastically. Coldly.

Ved felt he had every reason to be aggrieved. When he had been the Techno leader, Ram had become increasingly extreme in his behaviour, having been obsessed with realizing his creation of a virtual world, a 'paradise' that he could be connected to, living in it forever in an adapted cryogenic hibernation chamber he had recovered from Eagle Mountain. Several of those who had lived in the city had been sent away for daring to oppose Ram and his controlling regime – including Cloe, a Mall Rat who Ved had fallen in love with. Ram disapproved of Ved's relationship with Cloe, who was removed from the city, ending up in slave labour elsewhere.

Ved had done everything he could, while he was still a Techno, to try and find out exactly where. But he, too, eventually disappeared - Ram, becoming more unstable and paranoid, apparently instructing that Ved also be traded, exiled from The Technos.

"I'm different now. These two'll vouch for me. I've changed from who I was," Ram insisted.

"Some things never change," Ved scoffed, eyeing Ram mistrustfully.

Ram sat up in his chair, feeling his strength slowly returning. "Have you two been saying anything I need to know?" he asked Ellie and Jack, trying to get a sense of what may have happened while he had been asleep.

"Not much – we've just been 'reconnecting' with Ved," Jack said.

Jack and Ellie hadn't told Ved of their flight from the city and escape from the invaders. Ved had always been a loose cannon. He was brilliant at computers and was highly intelligent but had been fiery and often reacted hastily, taking action first before thinking things through. Cloe had managed to slowly 'tame' him as they got to know each other more. But Jack and Ellie were unsure what to expect from Ved now.

He was so unlike his older brother, Jay, who was strategic, so cool and level-headed. Ved had never been a close friend or ally of the Mall Rats, except for Cloe of course. But had never been an enemy either. He had interacted with the Mall Rats often in the past, their lives overlapping with his during the Techno regime, but it was always more about serving his own purposes than their own.

Neither Ellie nor Jack had talked about Jay yet. They had no idea if Ved was aware of what had happened to his brother – and the fact that Jay had died. If it turned out he didn't know, they were each determined to tell him, carefully, of Jay's loss. Ved deserved the truth. But Ved hadn't asked anything about Jay yet – he seemed more intent on finding out why the three of them were there and was especially focused on his ex-mentor, Ram.

Ellie and Jack didn't know what Ved was doing in the abandoned, former Techno base where Ram had once lived. While Ram had been unconscious, they hadn't properly answered any of the questions Ved had asked them. They wanted to make sure they could first trust him. There was no sign of their Mall Rat companion Cloe, who Jack initially hoped might be with Ved. For all they knew, Ved could be connected to the invaders, even The Collective, somehow – or might be a volatile and unpredictable, potential danger to themselves in his own right.

"What are you doing here, Ved?" Ram wondered.

"We're doing our own thing, whatever we want."

"Who's *we*?" Jack enquired.

Ved explained – now that Ram was awake – that he founded his own tribe, The Virts, in the industrial factory that was once the Techno's base. Ved was their leader and they were comprised of a few renegade, former members of The Technos, as well as some inhabitants of Ram's old town, having been 'strays' out on the streets, who had barely managed to survive before Ved had taken them in.

Ved and his tribe had spent their days living in virtual reality worlds powered by some of the powerful computers The Technos had left behind. Having gutted the lower levels of the factory when they had relocated, making sure it appeared abandoned and worthless, Ram had secreted away some of his hardware in the upper levels of the building, leaving them secure – a backup – for the day he might ever need them or make his return to his former town. Ved was aware of Ram's plan and had taken the factory and its functioning computers and equipment for himself.

"It's really good to see you, Ved. I didn't expect to see you again," Ram said.

"What? – you thought I'd be *deleted*? Is that it? You gave that order for me to be sent away, didn't you?"

"Yeah. From what Mega was telling me, you were no longer loyal. You'd started to turn on me."

"Of course I had," Ved agreed, not disputing it. "You probably thought I'd be taken away – cast out, like the rest of the trash."

Ram shrugged. "Maybe. So, how'd you survive – and make it here?"

"That's none of your business. All that's in the past. What I want to know is – what are *you* doing here right now? We tracked your drone. That's a fancy piece of hardware. Where'd you get it?"

"I was feeling nostalgic," Ram replied, improvising. "I wanted to show these two lovebirds my old home, the place where The Technos all began. The three of us have become quite close, you see." Ram further explained that he had found the drone in Eagle Mountain and taken it for himself.

It all sounded a bit fanciful and Ram's cagey demeanour didn't help dispel Ved's suspicion that Ram was concocting a story - which is exactly what he was doing - to try and cover the real reasons why he was there, along with Jack and Ellie.

Ved didn't buy it. He knew Ram better than that.

"You expect me to believe that you have teamed up with these two – and are here for - a bit of a vacation?" Ved doubted. "What - is this some sort of ménage à trois the three of you've got going? You got a thing for nerds, blondie – is that it?"

"Blondie yourself," Ellie retorted. "You're more blonde than I am anyway. And you obviously must be very stupid or you wouldn't even ask such a question."

"I like a girl with attitude," Ved remarked, smiling at Ellie's rebellious spirit, a bit like his own. "But you better watch your mouth."

"And you'd better watch yours," Jack said, rising off his chair and standing up to defend Ellie, getting in between her and Ved.

"Or what?" Ved snapped.

"Or – or - one of us in this room might regret what happens," Jack said awkwardly.

"And who'd you think that would be?" Ved stated, powering up his stun gun, making it obvious Jack would likely end up on the losing end of any dispute.

"We're not your enemies," Ellie insisted. "There's no need for this. We're no threat to you. And neither's Ram."

"Thank you, Ellie," Ram said. "See? – I've changed."

"Then prove it. Why don't you tell me what you're doing here," Ved urged. "No tricks. No lies. Just the truth."

"Fine," Ellie agreed.

There was no getting away from it. They felt they couldn't keep the truth from Ved any longer and they would have to tell him why they had ended up in Ram's former town, appearing to Ved as if from nowhere. The more they kept things at bay from Ved, it would only encourage his suspicion that they were not to be trusted. If they revealed everything they knew, Ved would understand their reason for being there due to their escape from the invaders – and he might even help them in their time of need, Jack hoped. They had nothing to lose and could only gain by co-operating with Ved and his tribe, rather than trying to forever stall his questioning of them.

"Maybe you can tell us a few things in return," Ellie suggested.

"Like what?"

"Like, doesn't Cloe mean anything to you? Don't tell me you've forgotten about her."

Ved looked stunned by Ellie's words, pained at the mere mention of Cloe's name. "I haven't forgotten anything."

Ellie and Jack asked Ved what he knew about what had happened to Cloe. She was their missing friend and Jack felt particularly protective of Cloe, who was younger than him. He had known her since the very day Amber and the others had walked into the mall where he had lived, before the Mall Rats had even been formed.

Jack cared about her, as did all the others in the tribe, and had watched Cloe grow from a shy, vulnerable young girl into a more confident and even sometimes rebellious teen, who had fallen in love with Ved.

Ved explained that in his last days as a Techno, he had become concerned by Ram's erratic behaviour and willingness to achieve his own goals, even at the cost of ruining the lives of innocent others. That was never the Techno mission Ved and his brother, Jay, had signed up for when they first joined Ram.

Ved had done a deal with a slave trader, providing some stun weapons for his freedom. And it had been Ved's hope since then that he would cut all ties with his past life, except to hopefully track down Cloe eventually. Possibly even help many of the others who had been banished and transported by the Technos, including some of the Mall Rats among them.

However, Ved had been unable to discover Cloe's fate or whereabouts, as well as what had occurred to many of the prisoners who had been initially taken away. He believed they had been shipped offshore and had ended up in the possession of slave traders elsewhere, though he hadn't been able to find out exactly where.

He decided that the safest place to base himself was the former Techno headquarters where he used to live before Ram had permanently relocated from it in his invasion of the Mall Rats' city. Ved returned to the factory with some other Technos who had rebelled against Ram and together, they founded their own tribe, The Virts.

Using the powerful computers Ram had left behind at their old base, Ved had gone online on occasion, reaching out to other survivors of the new world in distant lands, seeing if there was any chance, even remote, that he could find out anything about Cloe, along with any other information which might be useful to help in this God-forsaken hell Ved's generation had inherited since the adults' demise.

Ved enquired if they knew how his brother was – and if Jay had ended up with Ebony or Amber, Ved having been aware that Jay felt attracted to them both the last time he had seen him in person. It was obvious to Ellie, Jack and Ram that Ved didn't appear to know that his brother was no longer alive.

They told Ved the truth. Jay had died a hero, trying to defend the mall against The Guardian and Eloise's Collective forces, giving his life to save the lives of others, including Amber, who he had been in love with. He had been buried back in their home city and was finally at peace.

"I'm so sorry, Ved," Jack said.

"We're all sorry," Ram agreed. "Especially me. Jay was a great guy. We accomplished so much together."

Ved had listened, taking it all in. He was angry, sad, feeling a mixture of emotions, his eyes filled with tears. He couldn't believe it. Though they had often clashed, Jay had always been someone Ved looked up to. He had seemed so capable, adaptable. He was strong-willed, spirited. And Ved felt like in this crazy world they were all living in that Jay was almost invulnerable and would live forever.

But now, he had gone. Ved was overwhelmed by the news. It was the worst thing and the last thing he would have ever expected to hear from them.

"If there's anything we can do…" Ellie said softly, going over to Ved, offering to give him a hug, to try and help take away the pain somehow, to give him her support.

Jack watched, slightly jealous, and Ram was intrigued as he had never seen Ved display much emotion before. It wasn't needed working with computers, which were always usually trustworthy, so much more reliable than humans in Ram's view. At least most of the time.

Ved quickly regained some of his composure but was still clearly upset to hear of his brother's passing. He shared Jay's tenacity and resilience and insisted that Jack, Ellie and Ram tell him more information, everything they knew, about those who were responsible for Jay's tragic death.

Honouring his request, they described to Ved all that they were aware of about The Collective. How Eloise, in alliance with The Guardian, had seized control over the city for a time, before being defeated by the Mall Rats, Jay losing his life in the process.

Ram revealed how he had been in contact with Kami, the mythical leader of The Collective, in the last days of the virus – and how he was *persona non grata*, a wanted man, as a result of defying The Collective's wishes when The Technos broke away and Ram had initially hoped to take over Eagle Mountain for himself. But ended up taking refuge in the small community of Liberty, with a huge price on his head.

Ved had heard rumours about the existence of The Collective from word of mouth in his time online but he didn't know the extent of their reach, power and activity.

Ved claimed he had certainly never had any contact or dealings, as far as he was aware, with anyone who was involved with The Collective. Whenever he had used Ram's old computers in the factory and gone online, he had always kept a low profile, being sure to mask his location through several layers of VPNs, encryption and secure protocols.

"We haven't bothered anyone else – and they haven't bothered us," Ved said. "But maybe all of that's about to change."

Ram was shocked when Ved expressed that he would make some initial approaches online to establish contact with The Collective.

"Are you completely out of your mind!?" Ram bellowed, upon hearing Ved's idea. "Why would you do such a thing?"

"For justice. You think I'm going to forget or forgive the things you did? And whatever happened to Jay? It's payback time, Ram."

If Ram hadn't have gone off on his extreme tangents during his reign over The Technos, Ved felt that Jay would still be alive. Ram had ruined everything. He was responsible for so much that had gone so wrong for so many. Because of him, Ved had lost not only his brother but the one girl he had ever truly cared about, Cloe.

"The Collective are welcome to take you," Ved threatened. "At least they can't be any worse than you. Maybe we should just tell them you're here, hand you in. I can't wait to see the look on your face the day they show up."

"You can't!" Ram said, panicked at the notion. "Try to think things through and be a bit more like your brother. Level-headed."

"Don't bring him into this!" Ved shouted.

"You can't just invite The Collective here!" Ellie implored, dreading the prospect. "You don't know what you're dealing with. None of us do."

"And what about us?" Jack said. "What have we ever done to you?"

"I don't owe you anything," Ved responded. "But from what you've told me – the Mall Rats mean something to The Collective…"

For Ved, it was simple. Jay would want Ved to live his life and to do what was important to him, as his brother had done in his own life. The Collective would no doubt give Ram the punishment he deserved.

And if they were as powerful and connected as he had been told they were meant to be, if he was able to trade over Jack and Ellie to them, The Collective might know information about some of the missing prisoners, some of whom could even be living in their lands. By exchanging two Mall Rats, Ved hoped he might get one back in return – Cloe. And receive a large bounty for his most valuable prisoner – Ram.

CHAPTER EIGHTEEN

Following the unexpected and joyful reunion with Tai San, Ryan and Alice, the Mall Rats eventually met The Selector, who arrived at the resort with a range of guards - along with a large retinue of servants and cooks laden with provisions. It was apparently to provide the 'guests' with a bountiful feast - a 'celebration'. A welcome to mark what would become a historic day.

The Mall Rats weren't quite sure what to expect when they met The Selector, given what Tai San, Alice and Ryan had revealed. But so far, he actually seemed quite charming in many ways when he initially arrived, complimenting them on finding the surveillance device originally discovered by Lex. Besides disabling the one found in Bray's room, the Mall Rats had checked and disabled other devices throughout the resort.

"I would expect nothing less," The Selector said. "Certainly not from Mall Rats. So, congratulations."

"Is that how you normally treat 'guests'?" Amber probed carefully. "By spying on them?"

"Not at all," The Selector replied. "The resort was once used as a medical facility and we wanted to monitor each patient, as well as hear what they were saying."

"Why – were they totally insane?" Alice scoffed, glaring at The Selector contemptuously. "Just like some others I've noticed around here?"

"Yes," The Selector replied matter-of-factly. "Totally insane. All sadly suffered extreme mental illnesses. And this was a holding facility prior to transporting them to the hospital we were building where they could have more intensive care."

That gave some of the Mall Rats a bit of reassurance with The Selector seemingly having some compassion, though they were still more than confused by The Selector's overly friendly demeanour. So far, they hadn't seen the other side - which had so stressed and tormented Tai San.

"What's your real set up here?" Bray had asked. "Are you part of a tribe?"

"In some ways," The Selector responded.

He was then met with an array of other questions and was evasive.

"If you don't mind, I'd prefer to answer any questions you might have on a tour I've arranged tomorrow. So that you can all see what we're trying to achieve. Believe me, you're in no danger. We just think we have very much in common and it might be in our best interests to form an alliance."

The Selector had even brought some cuddly toys, for Lottie and Brady to play with, along with a gaming system, for Sammy - but advised there would need to be some instruction on how to use it. So The Selector promised that he would personally arrange an expert from the technology team to spend time with Sammy.

The task at hand was to enjoy the banquet The Selector had arranged.

There was such a variety of food, the likes of which the Mall Rats hadn't experienced since the last days of the adults. There was every conceivable choice. With the focus more on vegetarianism and plant-based cuisine, Amber had noted, which confirmed Tai San's revelations that their 'host' seemed to be in tune with the natural world.

The impressive spread reminded Ryan of when he once dined with his parents at a top hotel buffet restaurant to celebrate his birthday. And the staff had almost thrown him out, given the amount that he had eaten.

The Mall Rats, without exception, were amazed by such an array of fresh produce – such a change from the tinned food and basic supplies they were more used to in their home city. The Selector had proudly announced that the agricultural unit had grown all of it and that it was totally organic, representing a gift from Mother Earth itself in return for all the good things The Creator had done for the world.

"This Creator – just exactly who is it? You?" Bray asked, mirroring the desire of all his fellow Mall Rats to find out more information.

The Selector became slightly agitated and breathed in slowly and exhaled, trying to remain calm, advising that he would prefer not to spoil the surprise all the guests would have when they would finally meet The Creator.

From the tone and slight vulnerability The Selector was displaying, the Mall Rats thought meeting The Creator wasn't some form of threat. But something The Selector seemed to sincerely hold in very high regard, almost reverence. And the thought of it seemed to overwhelm him somehow, resulting in him displaying nervous 'tics' as he told them that the Mall Rats' days of struggle were now over. They would be living in the land of plenty with the very real prospect of having a secure future. Just as long as they were under the care and protection of The Creator.

Amber was still somewhat reluctant to go along with The Selector's hospitality and had wondered what they were all supposed to be truly celebrating. What was the objective of it all? And how did the Mall Rats fit in? Whatever the plan, the Mall Rats clearly had some kind of status, currency, and were of value to The Selector in some way, somehow.

The Selector left them to enjoy their evening together. All the Mall Rats wondered if they would be free to talk and decided to still be careful of what they might say or do in case there were other devices like the surveillance ones which had been disabled.

Lex and Bray had doubted it though, having triple-checked, along with Alice and Ryan, areas of the resort. They even examined the toys The Selector had brought in case any devices had implants in them. But there was no sign.

Returning to the dining area, Lex speculated for a moment if the food could be poisoned or drugged. And if so, what a way to go it would be, Ryan had joked, to be taken out by a sumptuous buffet.

At least, it would be better than being hurt in other ways, he added, casting a glance at Salene. She wasn't sure if his comment really was aimed at her or was in fact born from an attempt at humour.

Bray pointed out that the food was there anyway and if they didn't use it, then it would go to waste. He was sure that it wasn't poisoned or drugged, given that he had offered some of the servants some helpings. They had prepared the banquet in the first place and seemed very appreciative to partake of any portions on offer.

This gave the Mall Rats a bit more confidence to enjoy the lavish feast and they all agreed that they may as well make the best of the situation, the first proper meal since they had been back at the mall.

They even invited the servants to join them. But sharing a portion was one thing. Joining the banquet, quite another, and the servants revealed that their duty was to serve.

Ryan was mostly quiet throughout. He sat at the furthest end of the banquet table away from Salene, who was beside May and clearly both enjoyed each other's company.

Lex had earlier tried to ease Ryan's obvious heartbreak, giving his best friend his full support and trying to cheer him up when they discussed the situation after a workout in the gym. Life could be cruel and unpredictable sometimes, Lex advised, but he just knew there would be someone special out there for Ryan – he deserved nothing less. Salene had to be literally crazy to not see the great qualities Ryan possessed, Lex insisted. Although he could see why she found May attractive, as indeed he had in the past.

Lex had always been Ryan's best and closest friend and had a way of understanding Ryan that nobody else did. The two of them had been through so much and usually shared many laughs as friends together.

Although Ryan appreciated Lex's words that night, it didn't help when he compared his own situation with Lex - who had seemingly got everything he ever wanted by reuniting with Tai San, whereas Ryan's dream of a life with Salene seemed finally over, and not by his choice. He wanted Salene to be happy – that had never changed. But he felt so lost and confused and didn't know what to do with himself now it seemed she wouldn't be a part of his future, certainly not romantically. Lex reminded Ryan that his first concern would be to ensure he has a future, given their current predicament.

After they had finished dining, the servants entered to clear the tables and were surprised when Amber and Trudy insisted the Mall Rats do most of the work, tidying up after themselves. Alice, May and Salene agreed, even Bray, who encouraged the servants to take as much food away with them as they could for their own personal use – there was more than enough left over for the Mall Rats.

The servants, however, were grateful for the offer but again refused. According to them, it was their honour to serve the Mall Rats as well as The Creator, none responding to the many probing questions the Mall Rats had as they tried to discover information. The servants refused to divulge any detail and went about their tasks in an almost robotized fashion. As if they could even be somehow brainwashed, Amber observed.

After the clean-up and the servants left, the Mall Rats returned to their rooms.

When May arrived a little later than Salene in their room, Salene was surprised to see May holding a bouquet of wild flowers.

"That's sweet. Are they for me?" she asked May.

"Not that you don't deserve them – but they're actually for me. Ryan picked them earlier in the day and just gave them to me before heading off to bed," May revealed. "I think he just wanted to show me that he's... well... 'cool' with everything."

"I feel so guilty," Salene said.

"Me too. He really is such a special guy. But you're special as well. And we've got to do what's right. For all of us," May tried to reassure Salene, as well as herself.

Salene nodded and sat on the edge of the bed, thinking about it all. May sat beside her and they kissed tentatively at first, then with increasing passion.

* * *

The following morning Commander Snake arrived with some guards, along with the medical unit, so that the Mall Rats could be microchipped. They had earlier assembled in the lobby and were waiting to be supposedly taken on the tour The Selector had advised would occur when he visited the night before.

"No way," Bray said, defiantly.

"Right," Lex agreed.

Amber, Tai San and the other Mall Rats encircled Sammy, Lottie and Brady, with Amber clinging to baby Jay while they all stole looks at the hypodermic needles the medical unit were unpacking while setting up other portable monitoring device equipment.

"I respect that," Snake said in admiration. "I can now see why you Mall Rats have something special. You really stick together, don't you?"

"Always," Amber replied.

The Selector arrived, having been summoned by Snake, who advised that the 'guests' were overly concerned about being microchipped.

"Understandable," The Selector said, with a slight tic. "If it's any comfort, I would like to reassure you that all in our society have biochips… including even myself. Along with The Creator. It's essential for your wellbeing and health."

The Selector instructed a medic to login to his own monitoring and he indicated various waveforms on the monitor displaying readings. Blood pressure. Pulse. Temperature. Liver function. Kidneys. Seemingly everything in his body.

"You'll note that my pulse rate and blood pressure seems to have been raised because it's stressing me to think of the consequences of you not being chipped. It could be a decision you might one day come to regret," he added in a menacing tone.

"And why would that be?" Bray asked cautiously, suspiciously.

"I would have thought that question was rhetorical," The Selector replied. "What would you prefer? A pathogen to find its way into your bloodstream? I am sure those who became extinct due to the pandemic would have much preferred to have had the biochips."

"Believe me," The Selector tried to reassure them. "It's quite painless and really essential for our own health and wellbeing," he reiterated.

"I wouldn't exactly call it painless," Alice scoffed.

The Selector mentioned that he was aware of Tai San, Alice and Ryan's distress and had referred that to the Surgeon General. Her team were now using a different anaesthetic mixed in the initial injection to allow the biochip to be inserted with greater ease. And less pain.

"We're constantly adapting and evolving," The Selector told the Mall Rats. "It's the philosophy we have been taught by The Creator. The last thing I – or we – would ever want was for Tai San and the others to have had any suffering of any kind."

"That's not what Tai San said," Lex commented, resentfully. She had relayed details to Lex, who had been furious, as she knew he would be. But she had made him promise that he wouldn't do anything that would get himself into trouble or risk endangering any of the others. Lex would have to buck the habit of a lifetime - and learn to control his temper. He vowed that he would wait for the right moment to get payback on The Selector for all the wrongs he had done to Tai San and no doubt many others.

Aware that he wasn't being too convincing, The Selector changed tack diplomatically.

"I realize this is all new to you. Perhaps we can delay the procedures until after your tour. And then you might come to realize the need to have them."

The Mall Rats exchanged cautious glances, wondering what it all meant and what their 'tour' might reveal.

* * *

The Mall Rats travelled again but in a bus this time compared to the driverless pods in which they were transported from the airstrip. The bus formed part of a convoy of military vehicles of guards who escorted the Mall Rats on the journey.

The Selector travelled in a driverless pod at the front of the convoy and the Mall Rats were aware that there were also small drones accompanying them as they sped through forests and began ascending a road leading up to the bordering mountains.

Before they left, The Selector explained that the heavy security presence was necessary for the Mall Rats' own protection. But also, that they were going into a highly classified area and The Selector himself, as well as their militia, needed to ensure that they themselves were not in any danger.

The region was overall safe but it was always possible that there could be nefarious forces, given the work which was being undertaken, resulting in rich and highly sought-after resources. Both natural. And human.

The Mall Rats speculated who any hostile forces might be and who The Selector was referring to. They had always wondered what had happened beyond their own city after the virus, who else might have survived in other regions. But they had never encountered any location such as the one in which the heavily guarded convoy was travelling.

The road passed the airstrip where they had arrived and the convoy turned off into a narrow and otherwise obscure side road cutting through the forest, travelling around winding corners, gradually ascending in altitude. The area was well-guarded through different check points - the convoy stopping, with the drones hovering above and guards in buildings scanning monitors displaying data, before advising that access was confirmed, waving the convoy on.

Wherever they were heading, the Mall Rats were starting to realize that this region wasn't only a classified area as The Selector advised. Whatever 'work' was occurring – it clearly was overly secretive and probably highly sought-after. All tensed at the prospects of what their tour might entail and what they might discover.

CHAPTER NINETEEN

When Ebony, Hawk and the other contestants had entered The Cube following the 'trial of life' involving the chickens, they had been allowed to take off their camera harnesses, which Ebony learned they had to wear only during the playing out of each particular feat they would be put through.

It didn't mean that they were no longer being watched, however, Ebony surmised. The Cube was wired up with several cameras throughout the building, in every room, Ebony spotting their lenses on the walls, in the ceilings of the cube shaped building in which Ebony and the contestants lived between each episode of the supposed game.

Ebony felt her chances of survival and doing well would be enhanced if she was able to ally herself with Hawk. He was resourceful and capable and she was determined to make an effort to bond with him and make amends for going against his wishes in the challenge with the chickens.

She explored the building, familiarizing herself with its surroundings. It was very basic, sparsely furnished and seemed to Ebony to have been built with some metallic-type elements, used either for heating the premises or for some reason to

221

keep it cold. She wondered if it was a derivative of solar panel utilization. She resolved probably not because the building seemed to be air conditioned and extremely cold.

Ebony found where Hawk's room was and made a deal with the contestant who had been staying in the room next door to Hawk's. His name was Orin and Ebony said that in exchange for his room, she would give him half her food rations every day for the next week if he gave it up to her so she could stay in it instead. Orin gladly accepted the deal, happy to move to another room. And Ebony got her place, roosting as close to Hawk as she could.

The contestants met in the communal dining area for a meal. Ebony had honoured her agreement, giving up half her food ration to Orin. But she resolved that it wouldn't be on a permanent basis, just temporary. She had no plans on staying a prisoner in this building, which felt more like a refrigeration unit.

The building was well guarded, and the contestants were served food by servants - who seemed cold and detached, almost robotized, and didn't interact in any way whatsoever.

Being the most recent newcomer reminded Ebony of how it felt on her first day in a new school, in many ways, when she was growing up. Now, she sussed each contestant out, aware that they were certainly not potential school friends. But competitors, central to her very survival.

Each contestant certainly seemed to have gotten to know each other well and had obviously been participating in this strange 'game' for some time.

Ebony watched them interact, passing the time through convivial banter. Some of them, male and female, had more of a personal chemistry than others. There was some flirting going on. Ebony wondered if it was genuine or more an effort by those involved to create alliances, maybe exchanging favours, even sexual, in hope of a more comfortable life, or to render some form of advantage in the next challenges they would have to go through.

Nova seemed like a sassy chick and was clearly capable, having finished runner up in the 'trial'. She was spending a disproportionate amount of time around Hawk, Ebony observed. She could pick up the 'signals', read the body language all too well - even if Hawk, who Ebony knew to be shy and reserved - seemed oblivious to Nova's efforts to woo the former Eco Tribe leader. Ebony found it amusing and endearing. Soon, Nova would get the hint, Ebony was sure, and realize Hawk's passions were more about nature than romantic conquests. He was more into trees and squirrels than the birds and the bees.

Nova's dominance of Hawk's time in the evening eventually became a distraction and source of irritation for Ebony, however. The longer she stayed around Hawk, the more difficult it made it for Ebony to interact with him herself, one on one.

She got around it and was able to make Nova leave Hawk's side by suggesting to Orin that Nova was actually interested in *him* – going as far to lie, saying that Nova told Ebony that she really fancied Orin. Ebony suggested that if Orin came on to Nova that he definitely wouldn't have to spend many more nights alone in the room he had given up.

Orin thanked Ebony for her help and set out on his own course to woo Nova, hovering around her like a moth to a flame. It wasn't long before Nova left the dining area, hoping to get as far away as possible from Orin. She even slapped Orin before she left to go to her room, making it clear to him in no doubt she wasn't returning his romantic overtones, feeling he was creepy and exceeding personal boundaries. She left the vicinity, leaving Orin totally confused by matters.

Ebony gave Orin a commiserating shrug. But was more interested in getting to work on Hawk herself.

As the night unfolded, Hawk was unwilling to talk to Ebony, despite her efforts to engineer conversation with him and make a connection. He was standoffish, aloof, and to Ebony, it was clear he was upset because of her actions at the challenge.

It was likely also that he had some lingering suspicions of her due to her past misdeeds in the city – which she had no doubt confirmed, rather than dispelled, due to doing things her way and not co-operating in following Hawk's suggestion in the trial. She would have to show Hawk that she was more than merely her bad reputation. And she felt she knew exactly how to do it.

She said she was truly sorry and asked for Hawk's forgiveness. She declared that she had merely panicked during the trial. If she could have lived it all over again, she would have done things Hawk's way and not taken the chicken's life. It was a mistake. And she promised she would learn, aware that Hawk and the Ecos were a peaceful tribe and that Hawk would view the killing of anything living to be sacrosanct to his inner beliefs.

Ebony's seemingly heartfelt and genuine apology got Hawk's attention and he listened as Ebony stated she had information about Amber, Trudy and the other Mall Rats - and wondered if she and Hawk could go somewhere in private. Away from the other contestants and hopefully, to anywhere in The Cube that wasn't under constant surveillance by the watching cameras, every moment of every day.

Hawk took the bait at Ebony's mention of the Mall Rats, his friends and allies, and he took Ebony to the bathroom on the ground floor. The toilet cubicles were the only place that apparently wasn't monitored – and to Ebony's bemusement, she stepped inside one of the cubicles, Hawk closing the door behind them.

"Well, this is cozy," Ebony said. There was hardly any room for the two of them in the toilet designed for one and it was a little awkward how close Hawk and she were together, in such tight physical proximity. "Mind if I take a seat?"

Ebony sat on the top of the toilet seat and kept her voice quiet, whispering as she conversed in case anyone else might overhear.

She explained what she had been through, as well as the others, since they had last encountered Hawk and the Ecos. She decided truth was the best currency and if she revealed nothing but the facts to Hawk, perhaps he would do the same to her in return. She relayed how she and the Mall Rats had initially fled from Mega's Technos, their first encounters with The Collective on the island they had ended up on after a period at sea... and their return to the city, as prisoners of Eloise and The Guardian's forces. The surprises and mysteries left behind by the adults they had been exposed to at Eagle Mountain... and the strange 'welcome' Ebony received at the airstrip prior to being transported to The Cube.

Hawk described how The Eco Tribe had fled deeper into the forest when they heard of the city being evacuated after Mega's fall from power. They had survived for months, living off the land, in harmony with nature, establishing a new camp. Then, one day, as if out of nowhere, the drones had appeared. They had been scouting the terrain north of the city where the Ecos had re-established themselves and discovered the Eco camp. Soon after, more drones arrived, the Eco tribe were captured and transported in much the same way as Ebony and the Mall Rats had seemingly experienced.

Hawk had been in The Cube for about a month, having previously been held in an abandoned town which had been used as a form of prison camp, a holding area.

Ebony asked more information about The Cube. Hawk revealed that as far as he could gather, everything the contestants were doing was being monitored. He had no idea who the audience were who viewed the episodes. But between each episode, the cameras recorded any and all activities that went on in the building housing the contestants. Arguments. Fights. Humour. Jealousy. Love affairs. Cheating. Co-operation. Even in the dark as night vision cameras observed every bedroom.

Hawk, Ebony and the ever-changing roster who lived in The Cube had no option but to play out all their day to day routines and the drama that unfolded, as well as participate in each episode, which was streamed weekly to its intended audience.

The Cube seemed to be an endless living experiment in addition to a bizarre form of entertainment. And it was more than just a game or experiment. Their very lives were at stake.

Since he had arrived, Hawk had been the most successful of the current crop of contestants. He had won four events, including the most recent 'trial', but had a long way to go before winning ten of them and thereby going before The Creator to hopefully gain his freedom. From what Hawk knew, very few participants ever survived long enough to win and show they were worthy of being released.

"Then that's all the more reason why you and I should team up," Ebony suggested. "We're from the same home town. And like they say – birds of a feather should stick together."

Ebony and Hawk froze as they heard others entering the bathroom. Somebody went into the toilet cubicle beside them.

Another suddenly knocked on the door to the cubicle where Ebony and Hawk had been in conversation.

"How long are you going to be?" Nova asked from the other side, desperate to use the facilities.

"Not long -," Hawk answered, his voice overlapping with Ebony's own reply, the two of them speaking simultaneously - "Just a minute," Ebony said, at the same time.

"What are you *doing* in there?" Nova asked, curious and sounding jealous at what she thought Hawk and Ebony could be getting up to.

"Just going about our business," Ebony replied. "I got stuck in this cubicle and Hawk leapt over to try and help with the lock, it seems to be jammed."

Ebony and Hawk couldn't help but smile to each other at their predicament, feeling awkward, the two of them in the cubicle, and how it must have seemed.

"So, what do you say? We look out for each other?" Ebony asked Hawk, her voice in an undertone.

Hawk looked at Ebony for a moment, thinking it over, contemplating her offer.

"Okay," Hawk whispered back, showing his agreement. "But I'll be keeping both my eyes on you."

"Like a hawk?" Ebony queried, a twinkle in her eye. "Then I hope you like what you see."

Nova bashed on the door, trying to hurry them up.

She watched as Hawk stepped out of the cubicle, looking embarrassed to be seen exiting with Ebony, closely behind.

"Sorry about the wait," Ebony said mischievously to Nova as she passed. "But sometimes you gotta do what you gotta do. Even if it does result in getting stuck."

Nova scowled at Ebony, envying the obvious connection she had with Hawk.

Ebony smiled, jubilant at having secured an alliance, and followed Hawk out of the bathroom, the two of them going their separate ways to their own rooms.

Maybe she would continue to align herself with him, Ebony thought. Equally, he might have to watch his back – Ebony had already considered taking him out as a threat, recognizing him as a genuine competitor to her own chances of doing well in the 'trials'. And she resolved if she was forced to take part in any games in The Cube, then she was determined she would win - and was intent to play by her own rules.

CHAPTER TWENTY

The Mall Rats were astonished by the size and scale of the community that the convoy had arrived at. From a distance, none of them – or anyone else for that matter - would have ever known it was even there due to it being so well camouflaged by the forest of trees all around the lower mountain ranges.

It appeared to be at first glance a vast military-style facility from the adult era, the convoy driving past several buildings of various sizes arranged in different blocks. Most of them were prefabricated, temporary type of structures that were still standing in the same place the adults must have left them. The largest buildings were permanent constructions, looking like they were made of concrete, standing several floors high, that were either administration or perhaps barracks of some kind.

In the far distance, mammoth superstructures were visible, reminiscent of the type that held rockets or missiles in place, which caused all the Mall Rats confusion, as well as concern, as they gazed through the bus windows.

Continuing on through the facility, the Mall Rats became more and more aware of a human presence seemingly going about their routine tasks, oblivious to the passing convoy of vehicles.

Dozens of females in various stages of pregnancy were walking to and from the different buildings. Medics in decontamination suits and masks arrived in futuristic pod vehicles transporting what appeared to be farm workers or slaves to a building which seemed to be covered by a mammoth plastic dome – as if some kind of isolation chamber.

Workers were emptying freshly harvested produce from a variety of trucks, passing containers of wheat from one to another in chain gangs, delivering supplies to one of the larger outbuildings.

An intimidating column of militia ran past, jogging as if in some form of official exercise, given that they were accompanied by a commander, barking orders.

The overriding impression all the Mall Rats had though was that without exception the human presence seemed to totally ignore the passing convoy, with the same detached, robotized, even brainwashed type of demeanour as the servants they had encountered back at the resort.

The convoy finally stopped besides the largest building the Mall Rats had seen so far in the facility. Where they disembarked, to be met by The Selector, who approached from his driverless pod and indicated the area. "Welcome to Eden," he said, greeting them proudly, enthusiastically.

"What – is this place?" Bray wondered, unsure what to make of it all, mirroring and voicing the sentiments shared by all the Mall Rats.

"Everything you see here is because of The Creator," The Selector replied.

He indicated further up the elevation of the mountain ranges where the Mall Rats could see a road, winding up the higher ridges towards the shadows of a mammoth, perfectly symmetrical structure, rectangular in shape, in the far distance, which seemed to be embedded in a range of rocks, protruding out above the long tree line.

"The Creator is up there, overseeing all that goes on here. And everyone. Probably watching your arrival even now. So, don't forget to smile," The Selector said, wryly.

"Is *Kami* The Creator?" Amber asked directly, recalling Ram's recollection of what he knew about The Collective. "And are all these people part of The Collective tribe?"

The Selector again reminded the Mall Rats that all would be revealed and the task at hand was an initial tour of the facility.

As he showed them around, The Selector revealed Project Eden was a highly-classified, military-scientific installation established by the adults long before the pandemic even reached its peak. Over the years, a number of experiments were conducted across a range of scientific disciplines mostly focused on the environment and changing ecosystems. As the virus progressed and raised its havoc around the world, the military nature and capability of the facility was strengthened with extra personnel and equipment being brought there. And Project Eden became an increasingly important element in the adults' plans to counteract the spread of the virus so that humanity would endure.

The Mall Rats, including even Tai San, asked a range of questions. She still seemed to be very cautious of The Selector but was now seeing a different side and he seemed to be almost like a totally different person to the creepy one she had been used to back in the resort.

There were so many questions which even The Selector had, he advised. Especially concerning the virus - as he didn't know if the virus was due to a natural pathogen or was indeed the result of possibly bacterial warfare. Even a genetically engineered experiment gone disastrously wrong.

He added that he personally had other theories, wondering if it had emanated due to global warming, with the planet seemingly dying. And he was aware of other theories that Project Eden was a staging post for evacuation to another planet, to facilitate the continuation of the human species which otherwise would become extinct.

What he did know and what had been confirmed by his specialist team in the scientific and educational departments was that Project Eden was part of a top-secret co-ordinated effort by the governments of the international community under the United Nations' control, chosen because of its remote position as a repository for a variety of resources, which the Mall Rats would discover in due course on their tour.

In this new world, Project Eden would be considered in a historical context because The Creator had been able to access the resources left behind, including powerful and prototype next generation technology.

Eagle Mountain was a similar type of facility although Eden – so named after the mountain which dominated the ranges where it was located - possessed far more resources than Eagle Mountain ever did, The Selector claimed, Eagle Mountain being a lesser scale facility, albeit still an important one. As far as he could gather, there were other similar, highly secret places such as Eagle Mountain – but certainly nothing existed like Project Eden.

In the town where The Selector had grown up, when the virus peaked and the last of the adults died out, The Creator had made all the difference, enabling The Selector to administer various tribes which might have otherwise been ripped apart by civil warfare due to the struggle to survive among the various groups which had formed in the early days, after the adults' demise.

It was all so familiar to the Mall Rats, reminding them of what had happened in their own city when the tribes were first formed in the post-virus incarnation of civilization. The Locos, under their talismanic leader, Zoot, had waged a war for control with their rivals, The Demon Dogs, as well as the Roosters.

The Mall Rats had once been a scattered group of individuals but had come together to survive – and ironically had been the group which prospered most in the end, the other tribes fading into disarray while the Mall Rats increased their own influence, trying to make a difference for the better in the lives of those who lived in their city.

"You are to be commended," The Selector said, in admiration. "You achieved much without the assistance of The Creator, whereas for us… we would have destroyed each other. But because of The Creator – we lived. And we thrived."

With the resources and knowledge they could access from Eden, as well as their own capability, The Creator encouraged The Selector to seek collaboration among all the tribes in existence within their region. A spirit of interdependence, co-operation rather than conflict. They were stronger together than apart.

"Perhaps had you lived in the town where I did, rather than your own, you might have joined us then in those early days and become one of us," The Selector said wistfully. "Or had the tribes in your city chosen to work together rather than fight one another - maybe you would have created your very own collective, just like we did."

"So, you are The Collective?" Amber asked.

"I didn't say that, Amber – you did. I can't confirm or deny anything. Only The Creator can."

* * *

The Selector began his tour in the large building which he described as being not only a hospital and medical facility but a decontamination unit. So, all had to wear gowns, masks, place protective coverings over their shoes and hair, to protect themselves as well as the inhabitants.

It was an impressive facility. Spotlessly clean, well presented, full of beds and equipment, in a sterile environment, in much the same original condition as it had must have presumably been in the adult era. The Selector showed them around the premises, escorted by Snake and his guards, all of whom wore decontamination and germ proof masks. So, clearly there was a concern that possibly traces of the virus were still present in the area, the Mall Rats speculated.

They entered into the main ward which contained several patients, each being treated for a variety of conditions. All patients wore surgical gowns and were convalescing, many with medical drips in their arms, or hooked up to other medical equipment.

The ward was well stocked with so much futuristic looking equipment, the patients clearly were being treated with the best possible care by the staff, themselves wearing protective decontamination suits, their faces masked.

"Let me introduce you to The Surgeon General," The Selector said, as the Mall Rats crossed to a female, who was examining the wave monitors of a patient who was hooked up to tubes and life-preserving equipment.

"Surgeon General, I'd like you to meet our 'guests' – the Mall Rats," The Selector said.

The Surgeon General was about the same age as the older Mall Rats who exchanged nods and smiles while The Selector enquired on the condition of the patient, who was apparently still unconscious having had a lung transplant operation which The Surgeon General had conducted herself.

It had been a busy morning in the operating theatre so far, The Surgeon General advised, as she led The Selector and the Mall Rats to visit other beds, indicating various patients and describing their conditions. One young girl was lucky to be an early recipient of one of the biochips as it had picked up something unusual in her system. A growth on the girl's skin that had been cut out before it could spread. Another patient also had a tumour removed from her neck.

Once again, the Mall Rats were aware that the patients and even the medical teams seemed to totally ignore the Mall Rats - as if they were robotized and seemed absolutely detached.

During the tour, The Surgeon General advised that she and her team had been checking the initial data feeds of the biochips of Alice, Tai San and Ryan which brought to her attention that all really did need to immediately change their diets. They were suffering vitamin deficiencies and were not getting the right nutrients. This was understandable given their recent plight. But The Surgeon General was concerned about the B12 levels of Alice which were far too low, including her Iron deficiencies. And without treatment, Alice might be on a pathway of potential nerve damage in the future and at the worst case, even damage to her internal organs.

"You're welcome to be checked in right now for further evaluation," The Surgeon General offered.

"Not right now, thanks," Alice responded, with a slight smile. "I'd... er... prefer to get a second opinion."

Her remark made all the other Mall Rats smile as well, even The Surgeon General and The Selector. "As you wish," he stated to Alice.

The Selector thanked The Surgeon General and her team for the amazing work they were doing and she expressed how she was looking forward to being of service to the Mall Rats in the future.

Their next stop was to visit another wing of the hospital but they were able to remove their masks and decontamination attire given that the area housed The Creator's Repopulation Programme and wasn't as vulnerable as the surgery unit.

According to The Creator's estimates, humanity had lost over 95% of its population, The Selector revealed, either from the initial virus itself that wiped out the adults or from the effects thereafter arising from the collapse of society and all its infrastructure.

The pandemic had just been one of many crises that they had survived, the Mall Rats knew too well. They had seen firsthand how people had suffered and lives had been lost without clean drinking water, enough food.

Without medical facilities, the Mall Rats' home city had been the victim of a number of other diseases that followed in the wake of the virus. And without the adult civilization and its structures, age old diseases that used to be contained had instead run rampant, many of the young survivors outliving the virus but not the side effects that arose after the demise of the adults.

To ensure humanity's continued existence, The Creator had highlighted how important it was for society to be repopulated.

The Selector took them to view a prenatal division of the birthing programme where the Mall Rats saw several teenage girls in differing stages of pregnancy. They were attending a class and were being instructed on what foods to eat, how much rest they needed to have, the importance of breast-feeding which would provide their babies the most natural form of immunization and overall, every element they would experience from one trimester of their pregnancy to another.

Amber and especially Trudy remembered what they had been through when they had been pregnant as they viewed the class.

Trudy had only been a very young teenage mother during the height of the virus when society was collapsing all around her. She had found it an anguishing experience, every day an unbearable, stressful ordeal.

Before the Mall Rats had even been formed, Bray had been the only one to stand by her side for a time, giving her his support, Trudy carrying his brother Zoot's child. Without him, she would have been completely by herself and doubted if she or her baby would have ever made it due to how vulnerable and lost she had been. The Mall Rats, of course, played their part too, providing much needed support once the tribe was formed.

Trudy had given Amber 'tips' on what it was like to become a mother when Amber became pregnant. And had been there at the birth, helping to deliver Amber's baby. Now, as a fellow mother, Amber was struck by the level of organization and the practical skills being shown to the mothers-to-be in the class and she echoed Trudy's sentiments, feeling that such a programme could only help both mother and child and how she would have benefited from it herself.

There was one thing Amber was uncertain of, however.

"Who – and where - are the fathers?" she asked. She hadn't seen any males at all at the class.

"There are none," The Selector answered, matter-of-factly. "Not for this class. They are part of our artificial insemination programme."

The Mall Rats exchanged discreet, uneasy glances.

"Come on, there's plenty more for you to see," The Selector promised.

The Mall Rats were taken to a different part of Eden where there were several, smaller, prefabricated buildings in the block. The Selector mentioned that each one was a classroom – part of the education system The Creator had put in place for the youngest members of The Collective.

Observing from the outside, the Mall Rats could see children, around five or six years old, sitting together at long tables in one of the classes, their backs turned to the windows. They were focusing on an older boy, their 'teacher', who was writing down on a whiteboard different things that began with the letter C - including cat, catch, clock and Creator.

Lottie, Sammy and even Brady seemed intrigued – but the young students once again seemed oblivious to the presence of the visitors who entered the classroom, listening and watching the routine day unfold.

"In our society, everyone will learn to read and write," The Selector advised. "The history of the adult world will be taught and preserved for generations to come."

But as well as mathematics and literacy, children would learn a range of practical life skills that would aid their survival in the new world. They would study hygiene and how to maintain all aspects of their health, to grow food, how to cook it, self-defense, exercise, develop trade skills and how to negotiate in the new economy that was being created.

All would be encouraged to participate in sports, even the arts, poetry, music, drama. But most of all, the new generation would be encouraged to have a sense of compassion and to always consider the greater good. The Creator had affirmed it was also essential for them to have an awareness of their environment and the importance of living in harmony with the natural world.

If it was all as The Selector was telling them, then it was impressive, to say the least. All the Mall Rats agreed.

The Selector took the Mall Rats to another block of larger buildings, some apparently off-limits due to highly classified research concerning the advanced technology and hardware at Project Eden. But in one laboratory they were allowed to view a team hard at work, taking apart some of the solar panels which were the source of energy and power to Eden.

Several drones were having maintenance done and being serviced in another warehouse. Jack, a self-proclaimed 'geek', would have loved it there if he could only see it, the Mall Rats all agreed, realizing Jack would have been in his element amongst such high-tech equipment.

In another facility, the Mall Rats were intrigued to see cryogenic hibernation chambers like the one Ram had used during his Techno era. These units were empty and were some of the same ones that had been in Eagle Mountain, The Selector remarked. They had been transported to Eden for study and analysis, because the chambers had once contained adults inside. It was The Creator's hope that by understanding the technology, there might even be a distant chance to one day revive some of the adults they might find from their states of hibernation in cryogenic sleep in one of the other military compounds – or even other areas - the adults had established elsewhere to try somehow to survive.

The Selector then took the Mall Rats to a large building housing an auditorium that must have been used for lectures or presentations in the adult era, the Mall Rats speculated.

They were quickly and quietly ushered into the back rows, so as not to disturb the proceedings going on below on the main stage in the centre.

A male teenager was in the middle of the stage and was being cross-examined by some form of judicial council sitting in large chairs on a dais, appearing to be overseeing matters. The Selector confirmed them to be judge and jury, with the male being the subject of the trial, having been accused of stealing some of the food he had harvested for his own selfish use.

"Everyone engaged in a crime is entitled to due process and to be represented so that both sides of the story can be fairly presented. A prosecution and defence," The Selector whispered to the Mall Rats, sitting beside him in the back row, looking down at the proceedings.

The Selector indicated for Amber and the others to follow him, leaving the trial to continue.

"As you have seen, some of the things the adults created – medicine, science, a justice system - are still of great use to us," The Selector explained. "We have retained what is of value – adapting it to improve it - and abandoned that which is no longer part of The Creator's purpose."

Society was like a person, The Selector described. According to The Creator, each individual could change the things they needed to change about their lives – learning new skills, adjusting their behaviour, gaining knowledge, improving themselves in whatever way they wanted. The traits of an individual's life that were already working to their optimal state didn't need to be changed.

The Creator's view was that society as a whole was ordered according to the same principles. Under The Creator's supervision, some elements of the adult legacy would be retained – such as an education system, a security force. But these would be adapted over time, constantly improving with every changing nuance and alteration, so the 'organism' of society could reach its full potential.

The visiting delegation then walked to another area in the north end of the vast facility, passing a range of various buildings where drones were arriving and leaving, seemingly surveillance or security details.

The Mall Rats were led to an area of bordering fields, acres and acres ablaze with the varying colours of an abundance of flowers. The scent was intoxicating, totally overwhelming. There was a pathway in one field leading to a temple, around which several people sat in deep concentration, meditation almost - ignoring the approaching party of the Mall Rats, their guards and The Selector, who confirmed that the building was indeed a place of worship - and the fields represented an area of peace and tranquility for anyone needing time out to tune in to the natural world or their inner spirituality.

Heading inside the huge temple, the Mall Rats' footsteps echoed in the cavernous building and without exception, each Mall Rat stopped walking, frozen in trepidation as they noticed an assembly, mostly prostrate, before huge photographs of Zoot above a dais.

"What do you think you're playing at?" Bray snapped at The Selector, angry at not only seeing photos of his brother being exploited in such a way but that The Selector somehow was using Zoot, displaying that there was indeed another side to The Selector and his charm and all they had witnessed so far on their tour.

The sentiments were shared by all the Mall Rats, who were now becoming tense as the assembly turned, gazing at the Mall Rats in utter adulation and disbelief.

"It's them!" a voice cried out.

"It's the divine child! And the Supreme Mother!" another yelled excitedly.

The worshippers all erupted, ululating and chanting, which caused Brady to start crying, burying her head and clinging to her mother.

"Zoot! Zoot! Zoot!" the worshippers chanted, working themselves into a frenzy before then repeating in unison, "Mall Rats! Mall Rats! Mall Rats!" Then "Lex! Lex! Lex!"

Lex stole a careful look at The Selector, who smiled coldly. "You're a legend, Lex," he said. "But there's nothing to fear. Without you, there would be no god Zoot after all now living in the heavens and in the hearts of all those we realize so fervently follow his legacy."

The Mall Rats were totally confused and panicked about what it all meant, uncertain and feeling awkward, seemingly the centre of it all, like living gods themselves, amongst the fanatical worshippers.

"What's going on?" Amber pleaded. "Tell us – please!"

"You have seen everything now," The Selector said, raising his voice above the frenzied chanting. "And you are now ready to meet The Creator!"

CHAPTER TWENTY-ONE

It had been some time since Ram had been separated from Jack and Ellie, Ved having kept him in solitary confinement in a different office room to the one Jack and Ellie were being held in, upstairs in the factory that was the old Techno base. It was ironic, Ram thought, reflecting back to his former days spent there - when he had reigned supreme as leader of The Technos, Ved doing his every bidding.

Now, he was totally at Ved's mercy and powerless. How the tables had turned. But if Ram sensed any opportunity, he would try and change the balance once more in his favour.

Ram's room had been constantly guarded throughout the night by two Virts, standing at the door in the corridor, and they had been replaced the following morning by two others, taking turns on duty.

Ram had barely slept, his mind racing, thinking through various ways he might be able to persuade Ved not to contact The Collective – or to find some way to make good his escape from his former base. He had been panicked at the thought of what The Collective might do to him should Ved arrange some deal where Ram would be handed over to them.

Ved was operating in a meticulous manner and had no doubt cross-referenced the answers Ram had given to his earlier questions with those by Jack and Ellie in their separate room, to check if there were any inconsistencies. After all, Ram had trained Ved well. Just like in software, Ram abided by the rule in life that the 'devil was in the detail' and his former apprentice would no doubt be doing the same, which was confirmed when Ved arrived and was shown into the room by the guards.

"You look almost as tired as I feel," Ved said, with a yawn.

He explained how he had been up most of the night, going online and making some initial enquiries to find out if he could open a dialogue with The Collective. He claimed he had managed to contact someone who called himself The Broker and he had confirmed that Ram indeed was a wanted man by The Collective, with a huge price on his head.

The Broker said he would be able to arrange a transaction but Ved had declined the offer at first, he revealed to Ram. His preference was to keep his location and identity anonymous. And his options open. For now. Ved was going to bide his time rather than rush into anything. He would liaise with The Collective on his own terms and negotiate only from a position of strength.

Ved wanted to first see if The Collective knew anything about Cloe, or the others who had disappeared, and to learn how far they would be willing to trade in terms of resources, as well as information, in return for his co-operation and the possible exchange of Ram and the two Mall Rats in his possession. It was like conducting an auction, Ved said, relaying his strategy. The longer he held out, the more likely The Collective were to raise the ante and give him more of what he wanted.

"And the longer you dangle the threat of The Collective above our heads," Ram speculated, "the more you think we'll give you whatever information you're after."

"Exactly," Ved said. "It's a win-win for me."

"That's very clever," Ram smiled, admiring Ved's playing one side against the other. "You were always promising, and I knew you had potential. You've done well, Ved. You'd already learned mastery of machines long ago and you're now learning mastery of people. But don't forget, humans aren't like computers and can never be trusted."

"That's a gross understatement and an ironic one, coming from you," Ved sneered.

"Then what is it you want? Why are you here? To gloat? Is that it?" Ram asked, carefully.

"I guess, in truth, I'm looking for some kind of sign. A sense of which way to go with all this."

"Meaning?"

"Jack and Ellie seemed to have gone through a lot with you, Ram. As well as the other Mall Rats. So, maybe you have changed."

"See? What have you been talking to them about then?"

"Don't get ahead of yourself, Ram," Ved sighed despondently. "They still seem to be wary of you but equally they wouldn't be involved if there was the danger of you getting up to your old tricks."

"Exactly," Ram replied, sensing a break in Ved's ice-cold demeanour.

Ved revealed how he had been trying to live a new life in relative contentment, having everything he needed there at the old Techno base to survive for many years, living with The Virts in perfect fantasies - in virtual reality worlds.

He didn't ever expect or want Ram or Ellie and Jack to show up on his doorstep. But had interfered with the drone Ram, Ellie and Jack had been flying – having tracked its approach to the town. And had hacked it, rerouting its destination, forcing it to come down nearer to the factory, so they could investigate why it was in the area.

Now Ram was here, along with Jack and Ellie, Ved didn't know exactly what to do with them, he confessed. He was in the odd and uncomfortable situation of not really having anyone he could talk to or get advice from concerning matters of great importance, rather than anything trivial. The other Virts were friends and fun to be with on a companionship level. But Ved no longer had anyone he could look up to, who he respected, to help him figure out what he should do. In the past, he would have talked things through with Jay. Cloe had also given him support and different perspectives. And in a previous chapter in his life, Ram himself would be the one Ved would have gone to in order to get the answers he needed or wisdom about whatever problems he was confronting.

And here he was, just like old times, explaining the troubles he had to overcome, to Ram once more. Ved was alone, he admitted, and facing a dilemma. There were three options – he could release them, let them stay with him – or proceed with his attempts to use Ram, Jack and Ellie as bargaining chips.

"I understand – maybe more than anyone," Ram said. "Being a leader isn't easy. Sometimes, it's difficult to know what to do. And even leaders make mistakes for all the best intentions. I know I certainly did," Ram said, emphasizing his last line, hoping somehow that it might lead to Ved being reassured.

"Now, this is something new. You're saying even a self-proclaimed genius like you, someone who demanded perfection of everyone else, could be fallible?" Ved asked, slightly amused.

"Yeah. I screwed up from time to time. I'm sorry about the things I did. Really. And I'm sorry about what happened to Jay. He was a good man. And I know the apple doesn't fall far from the tree. You always meant well, too."

Compared to the anger and resentment he had shown the day before when he had first re-encountered Ram and learned of his brother's passing, Ved was more calm and had been thinking things over, in a period of self-reflection.

"What would you do if you were me? If our situation was reversed?" Ved enquired.

"I'd be asking you the same question. Getting some advice. Trying to figure out what's the best thing to do. But know this - if you thought you'd seen it bad before when I was at my worst – and my low points – The Collective are another thing entirely. They're the greatest threat to us all. And they've got more power than anyone."

"Power? That's an interesting concept," Ved reflected, prior to standing up and crossing to the exit, knocking on the door, the Virts opening up from the other side.

"Thanks for the advice, Ram. You've helped me clarify my thinking. It won't hurt for me to have a little chat with The Collective. And who knows? Maybe they and I can come to some arrangement."

Ram glared at Ved, sensing he had been double-crossed, which caused Ved to smile menacingly.

"So interesting, isn't it? When the apprentice becomes the master!" Ved snapped, before slamming the door shut, leaving Ram clutching his head in his hands as he heard the door lock.

* * *

Ellie sat on the floor, leaning her head back against the wall of the office she was being kept in at the factory with Jack. She was restless – and furious – at being held captive by Ved.

Jack folded up another piece of paper, an old invoice from a folder left in one of the filing cabinets from the adult times. To pass the time – and in an attempt to take his mind off things and ease his nerves – he had been making paper airplanes and watching them glide across to the other side of the room.

"He shoots-" Jack said, taking aim at the wastepaper bin – and releasing it. "And he-" he watched as the paper plane took a nosedive, crashing headfirst in a heap on the floor in the middle of the office. "And he misses."

It was metaphorical of what they had experienced in recent days, Jack thought, since the city was invaded. Nothing seemed to be going right for them and everything felt like it was wrong, their experiences with Ved being the most recent difficulty life had thrown at them.

They just had to be patient and not give up hope, they knew. Jack and Ellie had a mostly sleepless night, discussing their plight, as well as thinking what might have happened to Lex and the Mall Rats who had been taken away.

"How are you two 'Rats' doing?" Ved asked, when he entered the office, the Virts guarding the door letting him in. "Can I get you a piece of cheese or whatever else it is Mall Rats like to eat?"

"Funny. How do you think we're doing?" Ellie scolded. "You have no right to keep us locked up in here."

"I know, I agree," Ved said. "And that's why I'm here. To talk. I'm not here for an argument and we don't need to have a falling out."

"It's a bit late for that, don't you think?" Ellie stated.

Ved told them he had been thinking overnight and that in recognizing the friendship they had both had with their fellow Mall Rat, Cloe – and how they had got on and co-operated with his brother against The Technos - that there was no need for them and him to be enemies.

He believed, after much reflection, that if anyone was to be given over to The Collective, then it would deservedly be Ram – and not the Mall Rats. Ved thought he would be able to get what he needed from The Collective – information about Cloe and technological resources – without necessarily having to give up Ellie and Jack in the bargain. If they would co-operate with him and give him the information he was after, he was thinking he would let them go on their way.

Specifically, Ved wanted more details on the invasion forces they had seen taking over their city, how many of their approximate number were at the airport where Jack and Ellie had fled from, with Ram, and whatever firepower and resources they seemed to have at their disposal. He wondered how many drones they had seen, what their capabilities appeared to be.

Ved was so curious about it all, he clarified, because if he did come to an agreement with The Collective, he planned to meet them back in the city that used to be home to the Mall Rats. His intention was to get the drone they had travelled in repaired and in working order and he would use that to transport Ram to The Collective, exchanging him over at the airport they had occupied. In the event of any double-cross by The Collective, Ved wanted to come up with a contingency strategy and make sure that he and the other Virts would be able to safely get away if they had to.

All Ellie and Jack had to do was answer his questions and then Ved was willing to set them free.

"So – what do you say?"

"I say – you can get stuffed," Ellie said.

"What Ellie means is-" Jack said, trying to diplomatically defuse matters, "… is that we need time to think about it."

"I mean exactly what I said," Ellie insisted. "You can get stuffed. If you're even contemplating doing some sort of a deal with whoever invaded the city, after what they did – then you're no better than they are."

Jack agreed with Ellie's stance though he stated it in a far less provocative manner. He said that Ved would be playing with fire if he tried to work out a trade with The Collective. After all, Jack reminded him, it was The Collective who were responsible for Jay's death. Had they not previously taken over the mall under Eloise and her Legion warriors, along with The Guardian and his Zootists, Jay would surely have still been alive.

"If you've still got a grudge against Ram – and I wouldn't blame you – you have to find a way to let go of it," Jack suggested. "Otherwise you're still living in the past. If you want revenge for what happened to Jay – you won't get it by handing Ram over. You should be trying to fight against The Collective, not collaborate with them."

Ellie agreed and reiterated that Ram had changed. Why else did Ved think that the two of them would have been with him? It was because they were desperate. The Collective was their common enemy. Ram wasn't the same Ram that Ved had known from his Techno days.

"Is he a saint? No," Ellie said. "Is Ram still a bit weird? Yes. Oh, yeah. But he also might be the best shot we have right now at standing up against The Collective. And you've got him locked away. You know what Ram's abilities are and what he's capable of."

"I do – why do you think I've got him locked up? He's dangerous."

Jack wondered if Ved had considered what Jay or Cloe would have wanted him to do. Did he think they would have been happy with the course of action he was considering pursuing?

"I came here for information from you. Don't try and turn it into some guilt trip," Ved said.

"Ram's not the only one who's changed, it seems," Ellie observed. "So have you. But for the worse. I never knew what Cloe saw in you in the first place – but even if you did manage to find her, she'd be ashamed of who you've become, and I bet she wouldn't want anything to do with you."

That stung Ved. He reeled at Ellie's barb.

"We'll see about that," Ved warned. "Don't get above yourselves and think you're indispensable. That you can say anything without there being consequences. I tried to be nice. At least *I* tried."

Ved said that once he had got the drone they had travelled in working again and back up in the air, he might just bring Ellie and Jack along with him for the ride in the event of any handing over of Ram to The Collective. They would be his insurance policy, extra bargaining chips. If he had to, he would be willing to give them up depending on the situation.

He wanted to see things for himself, he insisted, instead of relying on what Ram or Ellie and Jack told him about who The Collective were. He didn't know if they were the threat that the three of them were presenting The Collective to be.

He couldn't just let Ram leave and go on his way, just like that. For all Ved knew, Ram was potentially the biggest danger, as he had once been before. A likely menace in waiting to Ved and so many others, for all that Ellie and Jack were telling him Ram had changed. Ram might have tricked them into believing he was different, Ved claimed. Had they ever thought about that? Maybe the 'new Ram' was nothing but a pretense, a front, another of Ram's many tricks.

The only one who knew what Ram was truly after was Ram himself, Ved claimed. He knew enough about Ram to never forget it. Had Jack and Ellie considered *why* Ram was public enemy number one to The Collective?

Maybe it was with good reason, Ved proposed. Wasn't it at all possible, Ved wondered, that The Collective were actually a positive force for good? And that they were enemies of Ram because they knew too well that he was the reverse, a risk to society?

Ved didn't know why the city the Mall Rats lived in had been invaded – or why the rest of their tribe had been taken, from what Ellie and Jack had relayed to him.

In this mixed-up world they all inhabited, the one thing Ved had learned was that things were often not what they seemed at first. He wouldn't be hasty or impulsive anymore. He had once thought that Ram, through The Technos, would

251

be a benefit to the world but discovered in the end that Ram was the opposite. The others might think The Collective were a hostile threat now but maybe time would show that they were the opposite and perhaps the best thing that had ever happened to them.

He would discover for himself exactly who The Collective were and what their goals were – and the only way he could do that was by starting to open up a line of communication with them.

It was Ved's life to lead, not anyone else's. He would make up his own mind about The Collective and what to do with Ram, Jack and Ellie.

CHAPTER TWENTY-TWO

The heavily guarded convoy ascended up the winding road to the higher mountain ridges above.

Before departing on their journey, following the initial tour, The Selector said he could understand the confusion and unease about the religious zealots worshipping Zoot, reassuring the Mall Rats that The Creator would explain everything and then they might fully understand.

The convoy arrived at the mammoth, perfectly symmetrical shaped structure they had seen from the distance when they arrived in Eden, now way down below.

It was a huge structure, dwarfing the tree lines of tall pines beneath, and was shaped like an immense rectangle standing on its side. From the outside, it looked like it extended deep into the rocks, as if it had been wedged in by some giant, most of it appearing merged into the mountains itself, becoming one, the front section exposed and jutting out from the sides of the mountain ridges onto an elevated plateau. It seemed strangely out of place, an almost alien presence, contrasting with the natural world otherwise all around, as if nature and humanity had somehow collided in a profound way.

The superstructure was known as The Vault, The Selector advised. Its gigantic, metallic twin doors had a strong security presence on either side, protecting what was within.

The Selector led the Mall Rats inside and as they entered The Vault, all were astonished by the sheer scale of it, the structure containing a vast labyrinth of tunnels and corridors which ran deep inside, feeling as if they were going into the heart of the mountains.

In every corridor they passed were row upon row of shelves lining the walls, stacked from the floor to the ceiling. On each shelf were a myriad of assorted jars and containers of different sizes. They were each labelled and had a series of statistics printed on them, information about what they were storing.

The Vault was a remarkable feat, The Selector stated as he guided them through one corridor after another. It had originated in adult times as an international project involving over 180 countries and had been purpose-built to archive millions of seeds and samples representing plant species from all around the world. Some had nicknamed it *The Doomsday Vault* and it existed as a living museum, a depository which would enable plant species to be preserved and returned to the wild in future for cultivation in the event of any environmental cataclysm or ecological change which might threaten the extinction of the plants.

There were other vaults and 'seed banks' housing potentially endangered plant life from different countries, The Selector declared.

Under the guidance of The Creator, the agricultural team had used some of the seeds to repopulate the grain and wheat, contributing to the flourishing food production they had been able to establish in their lands, which had otherwise shown signs of becoming extinct following the demise of the adults.

The corridors of The Vault were cold, deliberately so, to assist the preservation of the seeds, along with all else The Vault housed – but as the assembly advanced, deeper into the maze of tunnels, the temperature began to noticeably increase, The Selector leading them to a residential quarters, which was once used by the adults who had lived within the complex before the virus.

When the community of Project Eden had taken over the region, they had been able to access highly classified levels within The Vault. In these lower levels near the accommodation unit, they had found advanced technology, computers and information left behind by the adults who inhabited the facility - which they had now harnessed for their own advantage to achieve The Creator's vision.

* * *

The Creator definitely had to be a person, most of the Mall Rats contemplated.

Recalling all Ram revealed and the Mall Rats' past visit to Eagle Mountain, Amber asked, "Does the *K.A.M.I* computer system figure in all this?"

"I'm sure The Creator will explain," The Selector replied.

If The Creator was based in the accommodation wing of The Vault the Mall Rats were now entering, whoever The Creator was then it most certainly wasn't a computer system but had to be human, judging by the furnishings.

It was sparse. The design was modern, functional, and minimalistic and all around the walls were banks of monitors displaying all kinds of animals and insects, plants and other items from the natural world.

It seemed like a relatively unassuming place for the enigmatic leader, who clearly had denied themselves any of the finer luxuries in life.

The Selector led the Mall Rats past more guards, standing either side of doors, deeper into the inner sanctum of The Creator.

They had entered into the prime living area, which again was sparsely furnished with just a couple of couches, a dining table, a few wooden chairs. Several paintings were on the walls, mostly displaying animals and various insects. The younger members of the Mall Rats stared in wonder at an illustration of the long extinct Dodo bird, an idealized painting of a plesiosaurus swimming in the oceans of the dinosaur age, an image of a buffalo herd on the plains.

The older Mall Rats were more interested in a black and white Victorian era photograph displaying the stern expression of Charles Darwin.

The inner sanctum was dimly lit, keeping any illumination at a minimal level as if conserving power.

Suddenly, a soft voice could be heard. "Welcome."

The Mall Rats tensed, sensing movement in the deep shadows.

Bray held his son in his arms and instinctively clutched him closer, shielding him protectively. Brady clung to Trudy. The Mall Rats relaxed a little when they finally saw the source of the voice, who indicated to The Selector. "That will be all for now, Selector."

The Selector nodded humbly, obediently, then left.

"Who are you?" Tai San asked cautiously.

"Are you *Kami*?" Amber asked.

"Yes," the voice replied. It belonged to a female, emerging from the shadows and squinting her eyes slightly, adjusting her vision to the still dimly-lit light. "I have been known as Kami. And many other names. To some, I am The Creator. To others, I am their leader. I was Camille to my mother. To my grandmother, I was simply 'Cami'."

Cami turned the lighting level up slightly through a control on the wall and stood, staring at the Mall Rats before her. Almost in awe.

Seeing her clearly for the first time, Cami was about the same age as the elder Mall Rats. Slight in stature, she wore glasses, the light partly reflecting off the lenses, and a simple white canvas linen dress extending to just above her knees, which looked like it was homemade rather than from a store in the adult times, the stitching and material uneven, not well-fitted. Her feet were uncovered, her legs bare, her arms exposed through her sleeveless dress. Around one of her ankles was a band into which leaves from different plants had been inserted by the stems, ranging from light to dark green.

The Mall Rats were struck by Cami's unusual hair. The colour seemed to interweave the entire colour spectrum, streaked almost like a rainbow, with loose curls hanging down over her shoulders and the side of her face. Small green leaves were woven together into a headpiece around the top of her head, with some feathers fastened into her hair at the back, along with a single pink and white rose.

Cami had no make-up on, wore no earrings, no jewelry but did have a rudimentary, homemade-looking necklace. Instead of conventional glistening charms or finer-grade metals, it was a simple wire through which some smaller, old computer parts had been threaded, a CPU dangling from the necklace, alongside pieces of memory chips. On her left shoulder, a small black tattoo silhouette of a full moon was visible, on her right shoulder, a contrasting shape representing the sun.

What was most striking though was that Cami had a condition known as heterochromia – where she had different coloured eyes. One was deep brown and the other appeared to be emerald green, her eyes intensely studying the Mall Rats as she slowly approached.

"What do you want with us?" Lex asked bluntly.

It was almost like Cami didn't hear the question, she was so absorbed, deeply focused, gazing intently at each Mall Rat, casting a slight smile and wave to the younger members of the party. Brady waved back shyly but Lottie and Sammy moved closer to Alice, feeling more secure under her protection.

"You're exactly as I pictured you to be," Cami said to them, reaching out, taking May and Salene by complete surprise, giving them a loving hug, followed by Trudy, Tai San, Alice, then Amber, all confused to be so embraced as if she was a long cherished, dear friend.

She knuckle-bumped Ryan, then Lex and Bray.

"We – we'd like some answers," Bray said, mystified, along with the others and unsure of what entirely was going on.

"Of course you would. That's what makes you who you are."

"So why have we been brought here?" Amber enquired. "What's all 'this' about?"

"It's all about you. All of you," Cami said, gazing fondly at all the Mall Rats. "Your combined traits and qualities have created something greater than any of you could have realized had you attempted to do so alone. You have adapted and evolved and achieved so much. You defeated The Chosen, you resisted The Technos. You tried to create a better, fairer future. And without ever knowing, you even created a legend. The legend of Zoot."

"Is that what this is about?" Trudy asked warily, clutching Brady to her, closer. After all she experienced with The Guardian, Trudy couldn't bear the thought of a twisted representation of Zoot playing a part in her life or that of her daughter again.

"I see before me Zoot's child," Cami said, giving another friendly smile to Brady. "And the mother of that child by her side. I see Zoot's brother" – she looked at Bray – "and his son - and the mother who gave birth to Zoot's nephew," Cami said, acknowledging Amber.

"I see the other members of the Mall Rats who have conquered so many challenges," Cami continued, as she glanced at May, Salene, Ryan, Tai San, and Alice, who scoffed.

"But the one person I don't see – is my sister, Ellie. Or her boyfriend, Jack."

"I am as disappointed as you, Alice, that they're not with us here today," Cami responded. "I can assure you."

"Well, I can assure you if anything happens to Ellie, then I'll personally break your pretty little face!"

"I'm sure you would," Cami replied. "I know how close you and Ellie have been. And I hope Ellie and Jack will be joining us all very soon."

"How? How do you know so much, Cami?" Amber asked.

"You're all legends in your own right. Especially you, Lex. The one who brought about the death of Zoot."

"It was an accident," Lex stated, defensively, aware that he could have a huge price on his head from any followers of Zoot if they discovered he was responsible for taking him out. "I didn't mean it to happen."

"But it did happen. Should Lex be punished? Put on trial for ending another life? Or celebrated? Because without that one deed, that act of creation, none of what followed would have ever happened. Centuries from now, should humanity live that long, your name, Lex, will be in the history books, along with the god Zoot – names which will live in perpetuity throughout the coming ages."

"We saw what was happening at your 'temple' – the worshippers," Bray commented disdainfully. "My brother was messed up. Lost. He wasn't some 'God'. You can't be saying that you honestly believe any of that stuff?"

"Of course not. But it has a power in it, nonetheless. And others do believe. You've seen it. If used properly, your brother's legacy can be the greatest that any of us could ever wish for. And can do so much good and make such a difference in this troubled world. Besides, everyone needs something – or someone – to believe in."

Ryan cast a glance at Salene, then considered Cami again, gripped, as were all the Mall Rats, by her rhetoric.

"There are many forms of belief, of course," Cami continued. "Religion, spirituality, the natural world, animal life, our fellow human species. Whatever can bring some meaning and purpose to our lives. So, your brother didn't die in vain, Bray. It can be a good thing, if used properly."

"Or the worst thing imaginable, if it's exploited. We've all seen what can happen," Bray replied.

"Then adapt and evolve. Mould it. Use it for something better. That's what we're doing here. From all that I know about you – and the actions you've done that speak for themselves – you Mall Rats and I... have so much in common. We are kindred spirits."

"Somehow, I don't think so," Tai San replied softly.

The Mall Rats listened as Cami declared her belief that there was a chance, if they worked together, that they could potentially save humanity from falling into a new and dangerous Dark Ages and instead of anarchy, create a new beginning, a society based on law, order and civilized principles.

Cami explained how she wanted to not only save lives – but to change life itself, to eliminate existential threats.

She believed that humanity had forgotten the importance of its close connection and co-existence with the natural world. The ecosystems, how all elements of the planet, including the human species, were interconnected and depended on each other.

The 'virus' itself that wiped out the adults was, Cami felt, a consequence of humanity's damage to its environment. She didn't believe any conspiracy theories, that there were other reasons for the demise of the adults, but did feel that the governments of the world at the time had not been entirely forthcoming with any exact detail. Which was understandable, so as not to cause mass panic when the young people were all evacuated.

Cami believed accelerated implications of global warming had released micro-organisms that had been buried away for millennia, underneath the ice. The 'virus' was a mutated version of one of these reawakened, long-dormant pathogens. The past had literally come back to haunt the present due to the permafrost and polar ice caps melting as a result of the damage the previous generations had done to the planet.

Tai San was intrigued by the theory, being the one Mall Rat especially in tune with the natural world and Mother Earth.

"How can you be so sure?" Tai San asked.

"I'm not entirely, I have to admit," Cami said. "But my thesis is not only borne from my own research but my late mother's."

Cami explained that her mother was a member of the scientific team who used to be based at The Vault. She was an evolutionary biologist and loved life – all living things. And was greatly respected throughout the world, even winning a Nobel Prize for her research.

She was one of the brightest minds and along with other key members of society, had been shortlisted, Cami believed, to go into hibernation and hopefully survive the pandemic in a secure and isolated area. It was all highly classified at the time and Cami's mother did not provide any great detail except to reassure a very distraught Cami during the height of the pandemic that her mother would always be there for her and that one day, they would meet again.

Cami was convinced that the reassurances weren't due to any abstract religious element, for all that her mother was certainly religious and believed in an afterlife. When Cami founded Project Eden with her chief administrator, The Selector, they had discovered cryogenic chambers deep within the lower levels of The Vault. But there was no sign that her mother was present. Causing Cami to suspect that if indeed she was shortlisted, then she could possibly be housed in other facilities, such as Eagle Mountain.

"Are you saying that there are actually adults still around? In this building?" Amber asked, as all the Mall Rats exchanged intrigued and uneasy glances.

"In a manner of speaking," Cami replied enthusiastically. "Would you all like to see a real living adult?"

* * *

Leaving the inner sanctum, Cami and the Mall Rats rejoined The Selector and all were escorted by a group of guards through a series of long, metallic tunnels, finally arriving at an area which, in addition to serving as a 'seed bank', housed a land-based 'Noah's Ark' containing a variety of endangered animal species, along with several types of fauna.

"What about the adults?" Bray pressed.

"Be patient," Cami replied. "You'll see one very soon."

The assembly entered into an area of The Vault which had been segmented into various sections. There was a myriad of fish of different sizes, cold and warm-water specimens, darting around their tanks in a large aquarium facility. Adjoining it was the Reptile House, an enclosed and humid, temperature-controlled structure housing several sealed units, each containing a multitude of lizards, chameleons and snakes, lazing under the heat lamps warming their homes.

The next section was designated by the signs on the walls as they passed into it, illustrating it to be the Entomology Department – an area holding burrows and dens, inside clear glass cases and units, of all kinds of insect life - the tiny creatures burrowing away and going about their routines, oblivious of the Mall Rats peeking through the glass into their worlds.

Above their heads, all the Mall Rats marveled as throngs and throngs of brightly coloured butterflies flew around.

Cami then took them to another zone, the signs displaying that it was a 'Special Creatures Section' – the atmosphere becoming damp, musty, condensation on the metallic walls.

"What the hell is that smell?" Lex said, disgusted by the odour. "And before anyone asks – it isn't me."

The Mall Rats braced themselves at the thought that the smell might emanate from decomposing bodies.

"It's the scent of an old friend," Cami replied, affectionately.

They soon discovered the 'adult' Cami had referred to earlier. But it was no human being she was showing them.

Standing by the barriers overlooking a large, muddy enclosure, Cami introduced them to Darwinia, the name given to an ancient Galapagos tortoise, who inched along the muddy terrain, as if in slow-motion.

Darwinia was the mascot that lived in The Vault with the adult scientists who had been stationed there and had actually belonged to Cami's mother. Darwinia was supposedly over 150 years old, Cami mentioned, once even owned by Cami's grandmother.

"With any luck, Darwinia might live another twenty-five to fifty years," Cami said. "Amazing to think she had lived before there was radio, television, air travel, nuclear power, the space age, computers – and yet she's even lived into the birth of the Internet. Can you image what life will be like in another 150 years from now, if each of us could live as long as she has? What world will Brady and baby Jay grow up into? How will life be for their children, and their grandchildren, decades from now? Will we all tear each other apart through infighting? Or will we adapt and evolve – and co-operate, learning to live together, to create a new world, one worthy of handing down to the children of the future?"

"Your vision is impressive, I'll grant you that," Amber said, amazed, as were all her fellow Mall Rats, at the scale and variety of the animal species they had seen, sensing Cami was genuine in her devotion to them.

"Why are you showing us all this?" Tai San asked.

"Hopefully you're not planning on putting us in your zoo," Lex said, drolly.

Cami ignored Lex's question and walked over to a large glass container on a shelf containing two reptiles, their backs ridged with little spiny crests – and she explained euphorically: "The mother tuatara has laid new eggs. It means everything we've done has been working. We've given life a chance to live on."

"Great," Lex said sarcastically. "Just what the world needs. More lizards."

"Not now, Lex – please," Amber scolded him, before turning back to consider Cami. "That's very good news – and we're all pleased. But I still don't understand what *we're* doing here. What exactly has this all got to do with us?"

Cami extended her hand, offering it, in invitation.

"I want you all to join us. To join The Selector and me. So that you can assist us with the vision I have. I am asking you – the Mall Rats – to become part of The Collective."

CHAPTER TWENTY-THREE

Ebony had been on a rollercoaster of emotions. If The Cube was meant to be a 'living experiment' as The Gamesmaster had called it for its audience, or whoever was actually watching, it was certainly a journey of self-discovery for all the contestants who were participating.

Ebony had encountered self-doubt, fear of failure, questioned her capabilities. Her confidence had been dented. She had always thought of herself, ever since the adults died, as a survivor, a warrior woman, someone who was ruthless and wouldn't let her emotions get in the way of what she was ever trying to achieve. Since she had been in The Cube, all kinds of emotions had flooded to the surface, forcing Ebony to, unusually for her, embark upon much self-reflection.

She had, she recognized, become paranoid about the other contestants. Not so much Hawk, to whom Ebony was still allied, but she wondered if The Selector had placed Ebony on the island deliberately as some kind of a set-up, to make sure she would fail. And fail spectacularly, on camera, in front of whatever audience was watching.

Ebony had initially sat on the bed in her room, and had smiled, waving occasionally into the cameras – but now she decided to ignore whoever was watching her. Possibly around the clock.

For the time being at least, Ebony decided to slightly alter her strategy, to try and mask any apparent vulnerability.

She hadn't done well so far in the series of 'trials of life' that had taken place. Any hopes of impressing, of storming to victory in one event after another, had been rocked by Ebony's poor performances. Even when she thought she did well – The Gamesmaster had judged Ebony to be in the very bottom half of the group of ten contestants. The chance of freedom by winning ten challenges seemed to be increasingly out of reach, slipping away, day by day.

She had wondered if the other competitors were in league with each other. Or had been given some kind of secret tips or advantages, to gain extra foresight or knowledge of what they needed to do in order to do well by The Gamesmaster before each trial had even begun. It couldn't be that Ebony, who had always had so much faith and confidence in her abilities, had suddenly become useless.

Hawk reassured her that from what he knew, The Gamesmaster had given no prior help to the others, certainly not to himself.

In Ebony's alliance with Hawk, they were able to co-operate and consult with each other during the different events but their performance would be marked as individuals, rather than a joint effort, by The Gamesmaster.

The same was true for the other competitors who had created alliances, such as Nova and Orin after Ebony ironically brought them together, Nova and Orin now becoming friends. Ebony would ultimately be on her own in each trial and couldn't rely on Hawk to 'carry her' by how he constantly excelled himself in the trials. Likewise Nova and Orin, along with the other contestants, would be judged independently, no matter what alliances manifested and evolved.

By her own tenacity and improvisation, Ebony had just managed to stay in the game. She had been through six 'trials of life' so far.

In one, the contestants were instructed to go out and search the island for guards who had been placed in hiding. The first contestant who managed to bring a warrior back to The Cube would win the round.

Hawk and Ebony had split up, each covering a part of the island to try and locate the camouflaged warriors. Unable to find any of the guards who were in hiding, instead of reconnecting with Hawk to revise their strategy, Ebony had cheated and brought back a guard who had been on duty around the perimeter of the island.

All across the lands, crowds had sat watching images on the agricultural buildings as Ebony had knocked the guard unconscious in that particular episode and literally dragged him to The Cube. She thought her inventive and unorthodox solution was proof of 'survival of the fittest' and would be bound to impress The Gamesmaster. But she was penalized, finishing second to last, and was warned not to attack any of the guards again who were keeping the island secure and contained or she would be disqualified and Discarded.

In another trial, the competitors had to solve a puzzle. Ebony had been desperate to finish first and raced ahead, following her intuition, whereas Hawk had taken his time, trying to work out the problem through logic. Ebony ignored his recommendations.

After all, it was totally illogical to Ebony that any elements she found from the natural world could ever match. But the trial was won by Nova, who Orin had helped complete the puzzle by matching up twigs on the ground with branches from a tree, placing them vertically into the ground - mirroring the shape of the perimeters of the bordering forest, along with the geography of where The Cube was located – with a small pile of twigs replicating the shape of The Cube residential and administrative building – perfectly.

Nova came first, Orin second, as they had worked together, Hawk third. And Ebony second to last, according to The Gamesmaster's assessment. She was fortunate not to be in total last place and only had survived due to some very rudimentary drawings she had carved out with a twig in the ground of the shape of The Cube.

It was a similar situation in another challenge where each contestant was required to build a shelter they were to stay the night in. Hawk constructed his own with ease, replicating a smaller version of one of the huts made of branches he had lived in at the Eco tribe's camp. He wasn't allowed to make Ebony's one for her but did his best to lead her, offering verbal assistance.

Ebony had been exasperated when her makeshift shelter collapsed in the night, forcing her to sleep outside, in the rain. Fortunately for her, another competitor had their shelter fail before her own one did and she didn't finish last but was placed eighth out of the ten. Hawk had won that round, demonstrating his survival skills and his affinity and understanding of the land, living in harmony with nature.

The Gamesmaster had advised in a separate trial that one of the ten pre-prepared meals that had been brought to The Cube was deliberately poisoned and whoever consumed it would be violently ill. It was a particularly cruel event, Ebony felt, and designed to test their ingenuity and patience, perhaps even trust, among other things, including their mental strength and stamina.

The contestants were all hungry and desperate to eat though they refrained from trying the meals for as long as possible. Nova had taken a little from each meal and left it outside to see if any of the birds would get sick from having sampled the meal – but there was no way of knowing because the birds flew away after eating their morsels and the impact of the food on them couldn't be tracked. Hawk wasn't allowed to forage for any berries or edible plants on the island, The Gamesmaster advised, and so had fasted, resisting the urge to eat even a mouthful.

It was like taking part in a lottery, a one in ten chance of getting a much-deserved meal or succumbing to poisoning. Maybe none of the meals were tainted and it was all a bluff, some of them wondered, a twisted check of resilience to observe how they reacted to a problem that might only be in their minds rather than being real.

In the end, Orin let hunger get the better of him. He picked one of the meals and seemed to be fine. Nova chose another plate. And then other contestants took the plunge, eating a meal, seemingly with no obvious side effects. With every plate selected, it increased the odds that one of the remaining meals would be the poisoned one.

Ebony followed Hawk's advice this time around and resisted the urge to eat though her body was craving the energy. Suddenly Orin became violently ill – and only then did the contestants discover The Gamesmaster had been serious with his threat.

Orin fell to the ground, gagging and struggling for air as the poison flowed through the blood in his body - before long, convulsing, almost as if in some anaphylaxis shock. Finally slipping into unconsciousness and dying.

"Oh, sad," The Gamesmaster said with a degree of manic intensity as he indicated Orin's corpse lying motionless on the ground. "What a pity. Orin was doing so well," The Gamesmaster continued, addressing the cameras before finally advising that the loser this week was Orin. So the viewers should look forward to welcoming a new contestant in the next episode while the remaining contestants were now safe to enjoy the remnants of the food. But all, including Ebony, picked carefully, unsure if there were other traces of poison.

The following day, the contestants dug a grave for Orin. Across the region, workers watched while they toiled in the fields. But no sound was transmitted or commentary by The Gamesmaster – as Orin was finally placed into the ground and then covered with earth, a white cross placed at the head of the grave.

After Orin's exit from The Cube, Ebony stayed awake most of the night, replaying her own performances in the different trials she had been in. She was analyzing what she had done wrong, anything she had done right, and trying to learn from any success she had witnessed that the other contestants had enjoyed.

She recalled some of the phrases The Gamesmaster had used during his running commentary. Each episode seemed to interweave a similar theme about testing the body, mind and spirit. And whether or not an individual's choices could ever be considered to be separate from the effects they would have on others.

The Gamesmaster had continually repeated that all the contestants, as any population, were interdependent and interconnected. The actions of one affected the lives of another. Even inaction could create a consequence for somebody else, compared to proactive action.

It finally dawned on Ebony. All this wasn't so much as purely examining or testing each individual on a manner of subjects such as morality, ideals, friendship, adaptability, survival skills or how one person affected the environment and vice versa, though these seemed to be important elements.

The greater emphasis was more that society as a whole could learn from what they were observing. The Gamesmaster had commented how each person was like a pebble in a communal pond – the contestants were a reflection of several different pebbles and were also pebbles themselves, mirroring back various ripples by their performance.

In assessing her own performance, Ebony concluded that she had always been trying to do well as an individual. She thought she might fare better if she tried to think of the others. Even if it was unnatural and superficial. She wouldn't reveal that, of course. But make it manifestly clear to The Gamesmaster that she intended to try a different approach in how she might respond to each trial. In an attempt to reassure The Gamesmaster, she revealed that she would be seeking new ideas and solutions that might bring benefits for others on the island, as well as society.

She was hopeful this apparent enlightenment might give her added kudos and advancement up the leaderboard as she certainly didn't want to join Orin, or stay on the island and in The Cube forever.

The following day, another contestant arrived to replace Orin. To Ebony's surprise and total dismay it was someone she knew. Though she had never been a friend, not even an acquaintance. It totally baffled Ebony where this new contestant had come from and more importantly, why she was there. It was Emma.

The last time she had seen Emma, she was being ushered away with The Guardian and Eloise, along with her little brother and sister, Shannon and Tiffany. Emma, along with the Zootists who were captured, hadn't been transported with Ebony and the Mall Rats after the city was invaded. And Ebony had never expected to see her ever again, let alone in The Cube.

Emma, with her blindness, was clearly panicked at her situation, being forced to go into The Cube, and was crying out desperately the names of her brother and sister, wondering where they were.

Ebony felt genuine pity for her. Though Emma had bonded with the Mall Rats, Bray especially, who had taken her under his protective wing in the past, Ebony had never really gotten to know Emma or even bothered to make an effort. She couldn't help but admire Emma's strength of character, however, and braveness in not giving up her love for her siblings. That was clear from what Ebony had witnessed back at the mall. Emma was certainly persistent and strong-willed and the fact that she had survived post the adults' demise without the support of conventional society and an infrastructure - was an achievement Ebony respected.

But there was no way she would ever be able to survive The Cube, Ebony knew. For some reason, Emma was being thrown right in the deep end, way out of her depth, which was callous even by Ebony's standards.

Emma stood, literally shaking, quivering in fear and distress, in a line along with the other contestants while The Gamesmaster explained the rules of their 'trial' for that particular episode.

Ebony stepped out of line and deliberately walked over to Emma, taking her by the hand, giving her a hug, telling her everything would be okay. The Gamesmaster, Hawk and the seven other competitors were taken aback by Ebony's move – as was Emma herself, who initially recoiled upon realizing she was with Ebony, of all people, recognizing her voice – but her apprehension of being around her was replaced by the surprise support and reassurance Ebony was giving her, something Emma desperately needed and was grateful to get, even if it was coming from Ebony, someone Emma had never particularly trusted and would never have counted on for support.

The aim of the challenge was to study the contestants' adaptability – with the age-old theme of 'survival of the fittest'. The contestants were expected to venture throughout the island and wouldn't be allowed back inside The Cube until one of them had experienced an encounter with a reptile species that was being introduced especially for the challenge. A snake with a highly toxic venom that had been let loose. They had to try and catch the snake – but would be severely penalized if they tried to injure or kill it, risking being Discarded.

The first person to discover the whereabouts would be declared the winner of the trial – though of course in doing so, they would risk being bitten by the snake. And if they were able to catch the snake, then they would receive extra points.

"Is it fair, Gamesmaster, for Emma to participate?" Ebony asked.

"Don't be selfish!" The Gamesmaster snapped. "Emma can't help it if she has an unfair advantage. Do you expect she should be – penalized?"

"I… don't understand," Ebony replied, in bewilderment.

"You will," The Gamesmaster said, placing his headset on and getting ready for the beginning of the episode while his camera crew converged.

The contestants wearily discussed tactics with those to whom they had allied. Some felt this trial was far too much of a dilemma and better not to try and win. It was almost better to finish second or third rather than get within one metre of the snake, let alone try and catch it for bonus points.

When the trial began, as the other competitors raced off and spread out around the island, Hawk stayed behind with Ebony outside the entrance to The Cube, the two of them determined to keep Emma company and make sure she was safe, in her vulnerable state.

Ebony sincerely didn't want to see Emma, who was already distraught, get bitten by some snake, if there even was one on the island.

She suspected it might even be a ruse to simply test them. But she wasn't about to take any chances. Or risk Emma taking any either.

Ebony's strategy was to blatantly display her new policy of showing her compassion and interest in the wellbeing of others.

To also portray innovation and resourcefulness, Ebony noticed a fellow contestant who was also lingering outside The Cube, wary and fearful to go off searching. Ebony lifted a branch, threw it and screamed out a warning, "It's there! Behind you!"

The contestant ran off hysterically, hearing the rustle when the branch landed.

The Gamesmaster couldn't help but smile as he addressed the camera and audience. "Nice! We all must be aware that the imagination can be so powerful whereby a simple tree branch can become a snake. And often a human can follow suit and also become a snake," he added, watching Ebony returning to Hawk and Emma.

The Gamesmaster followed, pursued by his camera unit, and continued with his commentary. "I'd like to introduce our latest contestant – Emma. Now, the one thing you will be aware of is that Emma is blind. She could never, of course, see a snake, no matter how close she got, and isn't handicapped by what she doesn't see, relying on her inner senses, which we all must do."

Hawk and Ebony exchanged a bewildered glance while Emma sat passively listening to The Gamesmaster continuing, addressing the cameras. "We'll return to Emma later to welcome her. Right now, let's see how our other contestants are doing," he said, rushing away with his camera unit towards the forest.

Hawk, himself, left - deciding it would be wise for him to at least try and participate. But Ebony decided for the time being at least that she would stay with Emma and take her chances, relying on her latest strategy which also gave her an opportunity to try and talk with Emma. But only on a superficial level, aware that anything they discussed might be overheard.

So, Ebony overplayed her insistence to Emma that she could trust her as she sat down on the grass clearing beside her. Once Emma was in a more secure area, Ebony would try and find out any information Emma might know from what she had been through before arriving at The Cube - which could be useful.

Until then, Ebony made a huge show of her attention, drying Emma's tears, giving her occasional hugs for some of the stationery cameras, as well as the one on Emma's chest which was no doubt also recording various images - as indeed was occurring with Ebony's camera herself.

Suddenly Emma flinched as she heard a long, hysterical, sustained scream. Not that far away, where Nova had encountered a snake among the leaves of the forest floor. But in so doing, was bitten.

She had accidentally stepped on the snake's head and though the snake appeared unharmed, The Gamesmaster declared into the camera that sadly it seemed as if they would be losing yet another contestant because Nova had well and truly lost this trial. And her life.

The cruelty was strangely in contrast shortly thereafter when The Gamesmaster's benevolent tone announced that due to her compassion and sense of collective awareness, Ebony was declared the winner of the trial for putting the interests of another ahead of her own. Emma had finished in second place for assessing her environment before venturing out. Hawk apparently had finished third for staying with Emma when she arrived.

As they went inside the building, Ebony carefully led Emma by her hands, feeling jubilant. Having her arrive was the best thing that had happened since Ebony herself had gotten there. She had finally won the victory she had been so eager to achieve and hoped she might now be able to turn the tide of fate to her advantage.

* * *

Emma and Ebony were excused burial duties due to Ebony's win. Hawk joined the other contestants, digging a plot for Nova, while inside the accommodation unit, Ebony led Emma to the bathroom so that they could speak more in private.

She told Emma that she would make sure Emma had a room close by, the other side of Ebony's own. And revealed that it was only safe to talk in the communal bathroom as far as any private matters were concerned because she was sure, as were all the contestants, that their every sound was being monitored, audibly, as well as their behaviour, visually.

Emma had never expected Ebony to have such a softer, generous side and expressed her gratitude. Ebony was more interested though in finding out any useful information and probed where Emma had been taken.

Emma explained that she and her siblings, Shannon and Tiffany, had been staying in some kind of town called The Void. She didn't know where The Guardian, Eloise and Zootists, along with the expectant mothers, had gone.

All she knew was that she, Shannon and Tiffany were apparently to stay temporarily in The Void, which was a holding community until whoever had abducted them decided their fate.

When Emma had been taken from The Void, she initially thought that she might face the prospect of living as a slave. No-one explained about The Cube, which Emma found to be a sinister place, as well as strange - from all Ebony had told her, as well as what Emma had experienced so far.

Ebony suspected that perhaps if the Mall Rats didn't co-operate, wherever they were, that Emma might be used somehow as leverage to try and influence Bray and the Mall Rats to co-operate. And she worried if this might somehow implicate her, due to her new and sudden alliance with Emma.

But her genuine compassion overruled her concern, for the time being. And she reassured Emma that as difficult a place as The Cube certainly was, there was no way she would be tortured or punished, and that Ebony would always try and protect her.

Ebony's concern that Emma was being used possibly as a human 'prop' and hostage, in the event their captors needed to exert pressure on Bray and the other Mall Rats, caused her a new dimension of anguish. Assuming, of course, there was credence in Ebony's theory because she could understand that Emma's presence on The Cube as a contestant certainly provided a different element of so called 'entertainment'.

If the Mall Rats were involved though, somehow, at some point, Ebony knew they weren't exactly the type to co-operate with their captors.

And Bray, no doubt, would always be a potential 'knight in shining armour' trying to come to Emma's rescue, given that she had been under his protective wing.

Ebony resolved that she would take it all one step at a time and alter her strategies accordingly.

CHAPTER TWENTY-FOUR

May and Salene considered whether or not they should resurrect their wedding plans and arrange a ceremony to officially join them together. On one hand, both felt it wasn't absolutely necessary to marry to enjoy a relationship as partners but equally May and Salene felt the need to officially exchange vows to commit to one another spiritually, as well as emotionally.

"As much as I would like to – I don't think the time is right," May had said to Salene, who agreed. Not solely for compassion for Ryan, who was still clearly hurt that there was no hope of reuniting with Salene - but there were more pressing matters at hand, with the prospect of the Mall Rats forming an alliance with Cami and her forces.

The Mall Rats had differing views on what The Creator suggested but all agreed that they should try and find out further information because it all seemed just too good to be true.

Lottie, Sammy and even little Brady were sold on the idea of joining The Collective. But the elder members of The Tribe were all aware that this was due to them viewing the animals and insects – finding Darwinia especially cute.

Sammy no doubt, the others had observed, seemed to find the girls attending The Collective school to be very cute as well and Lex thought the time might be fast approaching where he, Ryan and Bray would need to give Sammy an education. In the midst of puberty, Sammy would soon need to know more about the birds and the bees, which was natural. So he, for one, was in tune, albeit in a different dimension, to the natural world.

The older members of the Mall Rats were reunited in their resolve that there could be no further negotiations unless they were sure that The Collective weren't involved in any slave trading. Or that slaves featured in The Collective society. That had been such a dark stain in the history of previous generations of the adults which all - especially Tai San, Alice and Ryan after what they had experienced as slaves themselves - found to be totally abhorrent.

And they weren't entirely convinced by The Selector and Cami explaining that the people working in the fields that Tai San had seen during her journey to the *Lakeside Resort* were simply members of the agricultural unit. Certainly not slaves.

The Mall Rats discussed other options such as trying to return to their home city but didn't quite know how life would be, given that the Collective had invaded to expand their territory. Cami had reassured them, however, that it was an option for them if they wanted to take it because The Collective didn't 'own' the city as such and certainly not the mall. She was willing to consider agreeing to sharing various sectors.

It was unanimous that any decision would be deferred, which was the source of arguments between Amber and Bray especially.

Both, along with others in their tribe, had been genuinely impressed by the new society The Collective seemed to be building. Amber and Bray totally understood the need to have an education system, a medical infrastructure, militia, food and agriculture units, as well as a justice system where everyone had the right to due process and a fair trial.

Bray, however, was against a structured repopulation programme given what he had seen during his time when he was held captive by Eloise and her Zootist forces with sterile baby 'factories'.

Amber could see his point but had liked how young mothers were supported in Project Eden. Trudy was equally impressed, as were the rest of the tribe, and it was hard to think of a better way for a young mother to give birth than by what The Collective were doing, with both baby and mother being provided with the framework of care they needed.

Amber felt that this was no anarchic world where everyone was in it for themselves and was impressed by the well-organized and structured approach. Cami gave her deputy, The Selector, credit, being her core administrator.

It wasn't to say that Amber felt everything in Cami's world was perfect. It wasn't. Amber had her own concerns at the ethics and potential surveillance misuse, let alone the biochips, for all that they brought added health monitoring benefits.

She was unsettled by the odd behaviour of The Selector, as had been reported to her by Tai San, Ryan and Alice. Besides being a brilliant administrator, Cami explained, The Selector was overly pedantic at times, obsessive, even quirky and eccentric – but Cami just so admired his skills, which were essential to oversee all that needed to be done to build a better and more sustainable new world.

Amber had also made it clear to Cami, echoed by her fellow members of the tribe, how she objected to the way the Mall Rats had been taken by The Collective forces.

Cami explained that there was still much work which needed to be done. Areas refined, including in the militia. The Collective, after all, were not just a tribe in their own right but had alliances with other tribes such as The Privileged, even the

Zootists. And mirroring the work Cami's mother did in the old world, Cami's vision was to have a structure of alliances, a derivative of the United Nations which had been in place prior to the demise of the adults.

Cami regretted that The Technos had not agreed to work together.

"So, you know Ram?" Bray had asked carefully.

"I thought I did," Cami had replied, advising that she only knew The Techno leader from their connections in the past online and she had never even met Ram - but believed that The Technos could have been an interesting unit, bringing a sophisticated ability to adapt and mould all manner of areas of technology. Ram had initially committed to the notion of an alliance but had reneged.

Where the Legion forces who invaded the Mall Rats' home city under Commander Snake were concerned, they had been tasked with securing Eagle Mountain and the city, to safeguard it against potential future threats from outsiders. The Collective, through their intelligence network, were concerned that other rival alliance power blocks might be in existence in faraway lands. Other countries where survivors no doubt had their own vision of building a future in the aftermath of the adults' demise.

The Legion were young men and women of action, capable of highly-trained combat skills. But Cami would instruct The Selector to reprimand Commander Snake and his militia for any excess and unacceptable force he had used in The Collective's expansion into the Mall Rats' home city.

"Are you sure you don't mean invasion?" Lex had asked, coldly.

"No – expansion," Cami had reiterated. Her dream was to replicate the system she had established at Eden so it could be rolled out across all lands, eventually other countries.

"So, are you trying to take over the world?" May said disparagingly.

"No, just build a better one," Cami replied.

She added that The Selector, through his administration unit, was identifying potential infrastructures required to achieve the goal. And had already actioned through the network of The Collective to find Ram and the rest of the missing Mall Rats, such as Jack and Ellie, even investigate the whereabouts of those who had disappeared long before, such as Patsy and Paul. So that the Mall Rats could be reunited again.

The Mall Rats were encouraged by the news but all had reservations concerning the quasi-religious aspects embraced by The Collective surrounding Zoot and those most connected with him, which included his brother Bray, Zoot's daughter Brady, her mother Trudy, and Amber's son, who was Zoot's nephew - as well as Amber herself, being the mother of that child.

Cami said that she wanted the key Mall Rats, those like Amber, with a connection to Zoot, to 'spread the word' about Zoot among The Collective, to use The Guardian's 'teachings' as a positive, empowering belief system.

This was not the zealous 'Power and Chaos' that The Guardian had independently cultivated, demanding strict adherence, Cami assured all the Mall Rats. She believed there was a method to use the power of Zoot's legacy and name to instill humane and civilized values in an otherwise lost and frightened world which needed a belief system, some form of religion. Through a modified version of 'Zoot', Cami believed it would be possible to adapt and evolve to spread love, compassion, tolerance and co-operation. So that the once divisive and fear-inducing shadow Zoot cast could become a beneficial figurehead, a unifying force.

Amber agreed with Bray, who was against the current Zootist philosophy in The Collective homelands. But Amber accepted the logic of Cami's point that even if it wasn't Zoot – then it was likely that there would arise some other equivalent to a new religion in society, just as had occurred since humanity had begun.

In any event, as Cami made clear, whether Amber, Bray and the Mall Rats liked it or not, the Zootist movement *had* sprung up into existence and *was* something real to many followers. The word of the Zootist legend and the deeds of the Mall Rats had spread naturally far and wide across the lands. So it was all-powerful and needed to be restrained, kept under a tight grasp of leadership to ensure it remained a force for good rather than bad, something those more nefarious might seek to exploit.

Despite the Mall Rats' concerns, the Mall Rats felt on balance that they should at least give Cami and The Collective a chance, by meeting over a period of time to discuss all elements and observe in greater detail the various aspects of the society that had been put in place. If it turned out the Mall Rats and Collective were not in sync and any Mall Rat wanted to eventually leave and return to their former city, or anywhere else for that matter, then they would be able and free to do so, Cami had promised. Their fate was theirs to determine.

* * *

"How's my beautiful boy?" Amber said, giving her son a loving hug, taking him in her arms from Bray's own.

She had just returned to her room at the *Lakeside Resort* after her latest meeting with Cami at The Vault. Bray had been waiting behind, looking after baby Jay.

"He misses his Mommy," Bray said. "And I do, too."

"I've missed you both as well. But I feel we're accomplishing a lot."

"Are we?" Bray asked carefully.

"What's that supposed to mean?" Amber said, in concern as she considered Bray.

"I was meaning that I miss you. The old Amber, the one that is, who hadn't taken leave of her senses," Bray said.

"Please, Bray. Not now. Let's not argue."

"Why not? You worried I might upset things between you and your new best friend?"

"She's not my friend."

"Then what is she?"

"Someone trying to do the right thing. Just like I am."

Bray knew Amber was being sincere. And he loved her for it. He always had. She *was* trying to make the world a better place. He would never have a problem with her in that regard and only felt proud and believed in her vision. But he simply wasn't so sure about Cami and The Collective - and especially The Selector's motives. The Selector seemed, to Bray, to be a little too charming, manipulative.

But Bray's biggest concern was that the more he thought about it, the more he found the whole notion of the Zootist faith – 'religion' – 'philosophy' – whatever they wanted to call it – as an abomination. A denigration of who his brother really was. A fiction. A false depiction. It violated the truth and the reality of the life behind the brother and family that Bray had known, better than anyone. He was repulsed by Cami using his brother's legacy for her own purposes. However she justified it, claiming she was using it for 'good' – and The Collective weren't all bad, Bray had conceded that to Amber – he felt the whole idea of *encouraging* people to believe in Zoot was preposterous. He wanted nothing to do with it, of any kind.

Not only was he repulsed by the Zootist faith in principle, he was concerned that Cami would inadvertently and eventually open up a Pandora's Box, setting in motion forces that Bray doubted Cami and The Selector would be able to control. He had seen, firsthand, the zealotry of Zootists in the past. It had never been a force for good. It was tarnished and though he hated the fact, he believed his brother's legacy would always be a tainted one.

"You're being naïve, Amber. And you can't even see it."

"Am I? Aren't you the one being naïve? If you can't even keep an open mind?"

Bray repeated that he believed perpetrating the Zoot myth would only end up in haunting the future rather than brightening it, and he couldn't allow that to happen for the sake of Trudy, Brady, and their own son, baby Jay, let alone other members of the Mall Rats, as well as so many others throughout the lands.

"Okay. I take it back. You're not being naïve. But certainly cynical!" Amber said.

"Is that what you call it? I would call it realistic!" Bray said. "What kind of mother are you? That you could allow your son to be exposed and play a part of it all?"

Bray's words were like a blow to Amber's heart and she slapped his face, hard.

"How dare you say such a terrible thing!"

Baby Jay began to cry from the heated exchange between Amber and Bray, who glared at Amber, then left, slamming the door shut behind him.

Amber gathered her baby in her arms and slumped to the bed, sobbing, embracing her son tightly.

* * *

Trudy shared Bray's concerns about the threat of the Zootist faith The Collective were supporting and was unwilling to expose Brady or herself to any life where they were pressurized to be the centre of a Zootist universe that seemingly revolved around them. So, she had so far rejected Cami and The Selector's offers for her and Brady to make appearances in the temple at Eden and had remained at the *Lakeside Resort* every day.

This enabled her to also look after baby Jay, as well as Brady, Lottie and Sammy, while the Mall Rats negotiated with Cami and set about trying to find out more information regarding the society she so passionately was committed to building.

Alice, Ryan and Lex mostly stayed behind as well though, unwilling to leave Trudy alone, fearful of her security in the event that Cami and The Selector were not genuine.

But this concern evaporated with each passing day when their fellow Mall Rats returned to enthusiastically report back on what they had witnessed and discussed.

Cami certainly seemed to be genuine. Though the jury was still out regarding The Selector.

Bray and Amber's relationship remained tense, with more arguments about the merits of joining The Collective. Bray was especially struck at the irony that rather than an alliance with The Collective, it seemed to be tearing Amber and Bray apart. Amber tried to reassure Bray that this wasn't the case, and that she was becoming really inspired by Cami's vision. Bray, however, felt that it was more like she was becoming brainwashed, he had cautioned, which fuelled Amber's disdain of Bray's seemingly stubborn and obstinate stance.

Ryan joined the others on their visits and tours to Project Eden and had agreed to hold some self-defense courses at not only the school - but to train some recruits in the militia. He realized that he needed a new purpose in his life, something to focus on, to help him get over his rejection by Salene. He was happy that Salene had found someone special in May - for which he was genuinely glad – but it still left a void in his life that he needed to fill.

Salene and May themselves were becoming more and more involved in the education division at Eden, where they assisted teaching younger children how to read and write, as well as useful tips in life from their experiences.

Salene had always been a nurturing figure and was surprised how May was also starting to display those qualities, with the pupils responding in a very positive way.

Tai San, in turn, was confused on exactly how she felt while sitting on the bed in her room, waiting for Lex to arrive.

She couldn't reconcile her instincts. On one hand, she had found Cami to be a very impressive young woman, almost a kindred spirit, judging by Cami's connection with nature and all forms of life, including animal and plant, as well as human. This resonated with Tai San's own spirituality and elemental awareness.

The opposite side to this, however, were her concerns about The Selector. He was just so unlike Cami. Where Cami appeared sincere and genuine, The Selector still came across as anything but. From the moment Tai San had first met him.

How he could be involved with Cami, at such a high level in The Collective, was something Tai San couldn't understand. Did it mean Cami was insincere or suspect herself in some way? Were The Collective really a force for good, as Cami seemed to personify? Or was she right to feel uneasy, as embodied in the enigma that was The Selector? He was just plain creepy, in Tai San's view. And she recalled the mantra of her family in the old world that 'one is judged by the company one keeps'.

The other complication in life for Tai San was Lex. Since they had recently become a couple once again, their renewed relationship was under outside pressures.

Lex was facing distractions and possibly temptations every day that threatened to pull him away from Tai San. As he wanted to repeatedly visit The Privileged tribe. These would be testing times for him and for her, Tai San knew, and would prove the making - or the breaking – and ultimately confirm if there was to be a meaningful and continued relationship between them.

CHAPTER TWENTY-FIVE

"How was your day, beautiful?" Lex asked Tai San when he returned yet again from visiting The Privileged, giving her a hug in their room.

"Not as enjoyable for me as I'm sure your day was for you."

"Somehow that doesn't seem much like a compliment," Lex said, wryly. "What's the problem?"

"Why don't you tell me?" Tai San asked. "Why are you so interested in The Privileged?"

"Reconnaissance. Research. Speaking of which, what say we do a bit of 'research' ourselves before dinner?"

"Like what?" Tai San asked, confused.

"What do you think? You're pretty hot stuff. And so am I," Lex smouldered, kissing Tai San, who responded to his embrace and caresses.

She had spent most of her day so far with The Selector. He had arranged, in consultation with Cami, for her to visit the biosphere at Eden. It was a large geodesic glass dome structure and housed a myriad of plants inside its warm, hermetically-sealed atmosphere. It had been constructed by the adults as an adjunct in tandem with the 'seed bank' programme at Eden, a place for selected plants, mostly herbs, to thrive.

The Selector was aware of Tai San's interest and knowledge in plants and had accompanied her that day, as well as the three successive days previously. Ostensibly, he wanted to be with her to get Tai San's opinion on the biodome and see if she was interested in taking over the facility to run a herbalism programme there, to cultivate and expand the herbs so they could be used for homeopathic medicines and natural remedies, something Tai San was proficient in.

She still couldn't help but feel that he was enamoured with her, though he had been less blatantly creepy and attentive. But her antennae picked up that he was still absorbed in her.

Tai San had gone to the biodome to check it out and was curious about Cami's offer for her to lead a programme to see if it could contribute something useful to the lives of many through its rich variety of herb deposits. Both medicinally through homeopathic elements but also nutritionally.

But now, Tai San had The Selector on her mind and was clearly not in any mood for an encounter with Lex.

"What's with you?" he asked, aware that she was not responding to his embrace.

"I keep thinking about The Selector."

Lex leapt out of bed and immediately began to get dressed.

"What's wrong?" Tai San asked.

"What do you think? I'm not having you fantasizing, when we're getting it on!" Lex snapped angrily.

"I'm not fantasizing at all," Tai San said, laughing slightly at the absurdity of what Lex had said and the fact that his male ego was being bruised. "Believe me, there's no problem – just as long as you're not thinking about The Privileged, that is."

"Tai San – do you really think I enjoy going out there every day?" Lex responded.

"Don't you? Are you sure?" she asked, her eyes probing him, searchingly.

She advised that she was also finding it difficult to concentrate in any lovemaking because she could smell the scents of a mixture of sweet perfumes on Lex. He smelled as if he belonged in a florist shop, rather than a bed.

Lex explained that The Privileged had offered him some homemade aftershave lotion which he had tried.

"If it makes you feel any better, *they* can't keep their eyes off of me. But that doesn't mean to say that I can't keep my eyes off of them. Like I've said, I've just been doing some research. That's all."

"Into just exactly what?" Tai San asked.

"Defences… militia," Lex replied.

The Privileged lived further along the lake on the outskirts of Eden in what had once been an alpine accommodation block used by the adults who had worked at the facility around the time the pandemic was occurring. Now, most of the tribe spent their time outside, lounging in the sun on manicured lawns or exercising, fine-tuning their already honed and well-trimmed bodies.

They were all, without exception, physically attractive and represented the upper echelon of Collective society, enjoying the most comfortable of living conditions, and had a retinue of servants known as the Discards to look after their every need.

They were the pick of humanity, a selected few of near-perfect specimens who were not only amazing looking but had uncommon gifts or talents that gave them prominence over other members of the population. Some were gifted musicians, others were natural athletes, poets, writers, painters. Their role was to bring art and beauty to day to day life – as well as a status for others to strive for and be invited to belong to.

If someone showed enough loyalty to The Collective and worked hard, one day they could hope to be rewarded by being allowed to spend time temporarily in the company of The Privileged, perhaps a day or a week depending on what they had contributed to The Collective. It was a paradise-like environment, a refuge, a place of peace, a sanctuary within the environs of Eden.

The most loyal Collective members might even aspire, through their efforts in their day to day lives as medics or teachers or warriors, to be honoured by attaining permanent lifetime membership of The Privileged. Something that only a very special few would ever hope to receive in the future for exceptional service, even if they did not possess the natural attractiveness that would have otherwise already made them members.

Charismatic, beautiful, The Privileged were also in reality hedonistic and certainly narcissistic and self-absorbed. Their egos matched their seemingly perfect physiques, Lex thought, and had studied them posing while working out. Both male and female belonged to a militia section and Lex often had Ryan accompany him on his visits for security in case they 'turned'. All were more than capable of handling themselves in combat.

Many in The Privileged appeared to be well known individually by name by some of the younger members of The Collective who looked up to them, aspiring to be like their idols. It was like the perfect life but reserved especially for only the perfect few.

Lex was advised by The Selector that one day Lex might end up joining The Privileged. He might even usurp the enigmatic and mysterious leader of The Privileged known as Flame. He was apparently an accomplished musician, the ultimate guitar hero, a rock star god who lived mostly a reclusive existence high in the mountains, between making occasional personal appearances - and was adored and revered by all. But few were themselves privileged enough and worthy to cast their eyes on their ultimate idol.

The Selector reasoned that where Flame was only a rock star god – Lex had an exalted status which was god-like itself, having been the one who had been responsible for bringing the god Zoot into existence, having inadvertently created the whole phenomenon in the process. Lex would be revered. Not because The Privileged worshipped Zoot. Their only worship was to themselves, along with their idol, Flame. But they had recognized perfection in Lex's ability to kill. After all, he not only gave birth to Zoot – at the same time, he had 'killed a god'. And The Selector wanted him to educate the influential Privileged by revealing details more about his own life, to re-tell of the events leading up to when Zoot became immortal.

By acceding to The Selector's request to at least spend some time visiting The Privileged, Lex said he hoped to learn more about The Collective's defence capability and maybe he could 'influence the influencers' in The Privileged.

He had, in truth, felt like a kid in a candy shop, being surrounded by a bevy of beautiful people, male and female, fawning over him, attentive to his every word. It had been an exhilarating experience. The Privileged had laughed at his jokes, sat and listened - absorbed, as he told them about how Zoot had been despatched to the afterlife. He revealed to Tai San that he had embellished it all a little bit. He couldn't help himself and found it amusing, as well as mind-blowing, to be treated like a god himself.

Lex had shown his military prowess by teaching some street-fighting moves to the muscular Privileged males and warrior females, who were impressed. And Lex couldn't deny that some of the most beautiful female creatures he had ever seen had offered their bodies willingly for his gratification. All in The Privileged seemed to practice open relationships.

"I assume you mentioned the Mall Rats don't believe in the same philosophy?" Tai San asked.

"Of course," Lex replied.

Tai San believed him. Simply because she chose to do so, aware that Lex was clearly enjoying having his ego massaged and that it might be something he could so easily get used to, and eventually even become addicted to. Tai San wondered if The Selector had set things up to tempt Lex, to drive a wedge between him and Tai San.

"Don't you think you're the one with an ego problem?" Lex asked, amused at the thought. "What makes you so sure The Selector has any interest in you beyond being a Mall Rat?"

"Let's just call it feminine intuition," Tai San replied, confused how Lex could be so blind to the looks The Selector often gave, which were more than just leering from time to time. Tai San felt that The Selector's eyes were devouring her.

"There's only one girl for me, Tai San – and I'm looking at her, right now," Lex insisted, giving Tai San a kiss. "Why don't you come with me tomorrow and see for yourself what goes on and leave your herbs behind? I reckon The Privileged would be really impressed just to see you. And you'll see just how much they seem to adore me. They just can't seem to get enough of me."

"Well, someone's got to do it, I suppose, Lex," Tai San said. "And it may as well be you."

"I take it then that you'd prefer to spend more time with The Selector. Should I be jealous of him?"

"No," Tai San scoffed, in disdain. "Of course not."

"Then don't be jealous of The Privileged. None of them deserve me," he added, smiling mischievously.

"I hope you're joking, Lex," Tai San said. "And not getting a little too into yourself as those people seem to be in The Privileged?"

"Give me a break," Lex replied, sounding more convinced than he looked, which registered with Tai San, hoping that the adulation Lex seemed to be thriving on had no more repercussions than it just all going to his head. It would break her heart to lose him.

* * *

The Selector had arranged additional security during the time the Mall Rats spent on their tours and at Project Eden. And security had even been stepped up at the *Lakeside Resort* for the Mall Rats' safety, given that they were being more and more exposed and their profile was being raised. It wasn't just the conventional society within The Collective that caused The Selector concern …

… but the fanatical followers of Zoot, which reinforced Bray's view that the Mall Rats were making a huge mistake in participating in perpetrating the Zoot legend and the ensuing worship. Amber reluctantly agreed that perhaps she had become so blinded by all that was so good in Cami's vision that maybe she herself hadn't focused enough on the implications of the Zootists. And all that could be bad.

Trudy was relieved that Amber was now starting to see the wisdom in Bray's concern, which had always mirrored her own, and had been assigned a personal bodyguard by The Selector, who had followed her every move.

He was called Storm but Trudy felt like he was an unwelcome cloud that had descended, hanging over her life.

Storm was tall, powerfully built, strong-jawed and a young man of few words. He had been chosen apparently by The Selector himself to watch all the Mall Rats - but those especially with any link to Zoot. Above all, Trudy and Brady, whether Trudy wanted it or not, given that Brady was Zoot's child, and the legend of Trudy being the Supreme Mother had spread far and wide.

Storm deserved his moniker, The Selector had proudly mentioned, because he was a potent destructive force when he needed to be. And had been given the honour to guard Trudy and her daughter, day and night.

Storm not only possessed military prowess, The Selector claimed, but he was medically trained and could act as a first responder in the event Trudy or Brady or any other Mall Rat required immediate assistance. He was accomplished in all manner of areas – except not knowing when his presence was overly intrusive, Trudy thought.

She certainly wasn't against any extra security but found Storm's presence to be far too overwhelming and wondered in fact if he was there more to spy on her, for some reason.

He had often stood, silent and vigilant on duty, just watching Trudy and Brady at the resort. Even at night, Storm had stayed awake, outside their room. He was like a machine, requiring minimal sleep. He shadowed Trudy and Brady endlessly. Even at times throughout the resort whenever Brady and Trudy went to use the bathroom. Storm had waited outside the door. When they had gone to the dining area, Storm was only a few feet behind. If Trudy went outside to get some air or take Brady for a walk, Storm was not far away.

This simply fuelled Trudy's exasperation at him being forced into her previously private life, something that had been sacred to her, her day to day routine with Brady having been an inner sanctum. Even though he claimed not to want to interfere – Storm was intruding upon Trudy and Brady's existence by simply constantly being there. Although his supposed brief was to watch out for all the Mall Rats, especially those with any links to Zoot – his entire focus seemed more to be on Trudy and Brady.

Increasingly, his presence became irritating and unnecessary, in Trudy's view. It was like she was being haunted by him, as if he were a ghost. And she had tried everything she could to get him to leave her and her daughter alone. She asked politely, she had ordered him, she had even lost her temper, yelling at him at times. But Storm didn't waver. He simply listened to her insults, ignoring her pleas and requests – continuing to dutifully follow her everywhere like he was an unwanted but devoted pet.

Brady had initially been scared of Storm, who - by his size, compared to her, was an intimidating presence. And this hadn't helped endear him to Trudy.

After a while, however, Brady had found Storm's constant proximity a source of amusement. She had even instigated some games, playing hide and seek – or suddenly running off down the corridors of the resort – and each and every time, Storm had run off after her, Brady shrieking in delight, giggling at the absurdity of it all, having a giant companion around her and her mother.

Brady had even 'tested' Storm a few times, asking him to get her a glass of water or some more food in the communal dining area, Storm complying every time. The other Mall Rats were aware, as well as Trudy, that Brady was using Storm like some kind of servant and Amber agreed that it might be an idea to confront The Selector to instruct Storm to back off more and keep his distance.

Brady was also treating Storm like he was some kind of teddy bear, a plaything to her – and Trudy was concerned by the bond Brady was developing. Lottie and Sammy often participated in the games. Even May and Salene seemed to show signs of becoming familiar, believing that Storm seemed like a decent kind of guy. And both Lex and Ryan were warming to Storm, often comparing notes on various martial art moves and other tactics.

Bray noticed that as well as a bond with young Brady, Storm seemed to be developing closer relationships with each Mall Rat. Slowly. But surely. He was getting to know each member of the tribe. And yet was still a stranger – an outsider. And in reality, was violating their lives, intruding without being invited. Amber agreed with Bray that they themselves should try and keep their distance and keep an eye out if any Mall Rats were becoming overly familiar.

Amber and Bray trusted the Mall Rats, of course. That wasn't the issue. It was more that Storm seemed to have another agenda than simply being a personal bodyguard.

Trudy was back in her room after having gone to the dining area for an early dinner, hoping to get Brady to bed for an early night. She was sitting on the floor, her legs crossed, and had been playing catch with Brady, who was sitting on the couch - Storm having brought Brady a ball to play with in the morning. The first of many toys they were promised, on The Selector's instruction, to help keep Brady occupied and stimulated.

Trudy laughed, enjoying the moment with her daughter, Brady gently throwing the ball back to her mother - Trudy trying to keep her relatively calm and not too hyper before bed, just sharing a little fun and some one on one time with Brady prior to Trudy reading her a bedtime story.

Brady threw the ball again and Trudy mishandled it, the ball flying behind her, over her head. Brady ran after it, her little feet pitter-pattering on the carpet, chasing the ball rolling along the floor. Towards the doorway, where Storm stood, watching intently.

"I didn't invite you in!" Trudy snapped, frustrated by Storm's presence.

"You should be nice to Storm, Mommy," Brady said, as he threw the ball to her and she threw it back, both playing catch.

Trudy felt strangely humiliated. To be scolded by Brady. And it fuelled her simmering anger.

"Why don't you leave us alone!" Trudy cried out. "We didn't ask for you to be here. For any of this! Just - leave – us - alone!"

"I'm sorry – I can't," Storm replied. "I've got my orders."

Trudy couldn't take it anymore. She let out a howl of frustration, venting her feelings, lifted the ball and threw it across the room at him in a moment of rage, Storm catching it with ease.

"Get out!" Trudy implored him. "Please – get out!"

Brady began to cry, confused by what was going on, not liking seeing her mother in distress.

"Just this once – I'll give you some space to recover. Don't be upset – please," Storm said uneasily.

To Trudy's surprise, Storm defied his orders from The Selector – and had, for the first time ever, obeyed Trudy's instructions and stepped out, closing the door behind him. So, maybe he was human after all and had a shred of empathy and decency in him, Trudy hoped, beneath his disciplined, military manner.

"I'm so sorry I shouted," Trudy said to Brady, giving her a loving hug.

Trudy had felt that she was almost losing her mind with Storm's persistent presence – and had wondered if that was the real reason The Selector had put Storm on duty, to push Trudy to the limits, to stress her, to 'test' her in some way, to mess with her mind.

* * *

Later that evening, Amber awoke in her own room. It was pitch black, with only an almost imperceptible amount of light coming in from the moon reflecting on the lake outside the window.

She could hear her baby's soothing breathing in the bed next to her own and instinctively turning over, reached her arm out to touch Bray affectionately. The way things had been between them lately with their recent arguments, she wanted to kiss him lovingly, to feel his embrace.

"Are you awake?" she whispered.

But something was wrong. The space beside her was empty. "Bray?"

Panicked, she sat up in bed and turned on the side lamp, confirming there was no sign of Bray.

She leapt out of bed, rushing to the bathroom to see if he was there – it, too, was empty.

Amber then tried the door handle to the room, hoping to look out in the corridors in case Bray had gone for a walk or that she might find him perhaps in another part of the resort.

The door was locked from the outside and Amber couldn't get out.

But somehow, Bray had. It was like he hadn't just disappeared from the *Lakeside Resort*, but from the face of planet Earth.

CHAPTER TWENTY-SIX

Ram had stayed locked up in the room he was being kept in at the factory by Ved, allowed out only periodically for a few occasional toilet breaks or to stretch his legs by walking up and down the corridors of his old Techno base, always accompanied by some of the Virts, sometimes Ved himself.

It felt like he was a prisoner in what had once been his own home.

Ved had visited to keep him appraised of what he had been doing – claiming he had opened up an initial line of communication online with The Collective having been introduced to them via The Broker. Ved had let Ram know The Collective had responded favourably to Ved's contact with them and were promising him they would reward him with a lifetime's worth of food and technological resources if he was able to deliver Ram to them, as he said he could. His contacts at The Collective also assured Ved they were making enquiries throughout regions under The Collective jurisdiction to see if they could find out anything definitive about what had happened to Cloe.

Ved was pleased how things had gone, he advised Ram, and the positive overtures The Collective were making to him.

Ram insisted Ved had to be a fool to think he could trust them or ever do a deal. The Collective would be no doubt using their vast technological arsenal to try and track the real-life location of Ved every time he went online and reached out to them, Ram warned. It was only a matter of time before The Collective would be sure to descend upon Ram's former town in a display of force, taking over the factory, seizing Ram for themselves – and no doubt coercing Ellie, Jack, Ved and the rest of his Virts into a lifetime of slavery in servitude to Kami and The Collective's powerful block.

Ved was crazy to think he could negotiate with The Collective on equal terms – in this world without adults, might was right, Ram said – and the most mighty of them all that he was aware of were The Collective. They would crush Ved without a moment's hesitation and promise him the earth – without delivering it – if it would make it easier for them to get their way and get a hold of Ram.

Ved had fobbed off Ram's 'fear-mongering' he called it, certain that Ram was up to his old tricks again and trying to intimidate Ved into allowing him to go free due to the threat of The Collective.

And Ved was no fool. He had reassured Ram that each time he had gone online he had managed to keep his real-world location hidden behind several layers of encryption and false online addresses. The Collective would think he was somewhere else should they try and track him down in real life, not at the old Techno base.

Ved had learned from Ram and was keeping their location a well camouflaged secret safe from any prying eyes in case The Collective were double-crossing him. Ram should enjoy his 'freedom' at the factory, Ved teased, because it wouldn't be long before they would be on their way to exchange him to The

Collective at the city where Amber and the Mall Rats had lived, as well as Ram, now that the drone Ram had travelled in with Jack and Ellie was repaired and in functional flying order again.

With every day that passed, Ram was becoming increasingly concerned about his fate, searching every fibre of his being, calculating some move or strategy he could try to persuade Ved to drop his negotiations with The Collective – and even better, to completely release him. Yet Ved was stubborn and had grown in confidence to become very much his own man – he didn't listen to Ram anymore, as he had once done.

Ram sat up as the door to his room opened, one of the Virts bringing him his latest meal – a cold tin of spaghetti, way past its use by date. Ram glared disapprovingly but had no option but to eat what he was being given. It made him think that life wasn't as sweet and comfortable for Ved and The Virts as he was making it out to be. They were probably down to the last food stocks Ram had left at his old base. And that might have been one of the other reasons Ved was trying to barter with The Collective - to make sure they would bring extra supplies of food Ved could feed the Virts with in the event of any deal.

"Thanks for the food," Ram said, smiling in a friendly way to the Virt who had delivered the tawdry meal. His name was Giga – and Ram reached out, grabbing him by the arm as he turned to leave, "Hey – please, wait up for a sec."

"I'm not meant to talk to you," Giga said, giving Ram a cautious look.

"But you are – and there's no harm doing it. See? We're having a conversation," Ram said, smiling again.

"Ved warned us about you. My job is to deliver you your food and then get on my way. And that's exactly what I'm gonna do."

"By all means, feel free to do so," Ram said. "It's a shame though. I like you Giga. You're a smart guy, I can see that. I was hoping we could talk for a bit and I could pass over some of my skills and secrets to you, before I get taken out of here. Be a shame for them to go to waste."

"Nice try," Giga said. "Goodbye, Ram."

Giga turned and went toward the door.

"Imagine a self-sustaining virtual world never needing any reboots or patches. Like in the system I designed. Any inter-negative mega data bypasses fixed any glitches while the programme was running. I thought you might be interested," Ram called out, when Giga was almost fully out of the door.

Against his better instincts, what Ram said piqued Giga's curiosity. The Virts had spent much of their spare time living in computer fantasies, plugged in through virtual reality helmets into realistic programmes. It was an addictive and wonderful sensation, a passion for Giga and the other Virts. They always had to cut short their sessions to a few hours though.

The complex software could often be glitchy, the endless rendering spoiling the experiences for the users. And the systems had to be powered down to free up resources in the computers, which could too easily be taxed by powering the grunty realistic 360-degree graphics the virtual reality required. If there was a way to allow the programmes to continue running for longer – even in perpetuity, as Ram had alluded - then that would be something Giga would be interested to know and share with the other Virts.

"Can you – do such a thing?" Giga asked hesitantly, closing the door behind him as he considered Ram in awe. Aware of the former leader of The Technos and the reputation Ram had.

"I can do it – and so can you. Don't suppose Ved ever told you about my plans to live forever in reality space?"

He had. Giga knew of it. Ved had often spoke of Ram, his former mentor, and how Ram was a genius from whom Ved had learned so much.

"If I can pass on a little knowledge, it'll make me feel at least I did something worthwhile with my life – before The Collective get their collective hands on me."

Giga was sorely tempted – and caught in a conflict. He didn't want to go against Ved's wishes. But if Ram could show him a thing or two, it would be sure to impress Ved. Ram was a prisoner and wasn't going anywhere, in any event, and Giga felt he had nothing to lose and everything to gain if he gave Ram the opportunity to teach him some of his unique knowledge.

"What would you need in the form of hardware?" Giga asked tentatively.

Ram said if Giga could get him to a keyboard and a computer, he could sit back and watch while Ram typed in lines of code that would blow Giga's mind, let alone Ved's. A good leader never showed all his tricks, Ram claimed, and no doubt Ved hadn't relayed in turn everything he knew to Giga and the other Virts. If they knew as much as Ved did, there would be no need for Ved to be their leader anymore, Ram said. Leaders often held back certain knowledge so they could stay one step ahead of everyone else.

Giga told the two Virts at the door that he would be back in an hour, which is how long Ram thought they would need.

They walked down the corridor to another room, one where several of the powerful computers The Technos had left behind in the upper floors of the factory were located.

"Man, I've missed these babies," Ram said, gazing fondly at the computers that were once his playthings. Tilting his head from side to side to loosen up, Ram cracked his knuckles and began patting the computers warmly, affectionately, almost like they were his children, as he sat down at one of the computers, powering it up, Giga sitting beside him.

"It's amazing," Ram began, gently pressing the keys while the computer booted into life. "One keyboard is it all it takes – and with a few instructions-"

Ram suddenly picked up the keyboard and smashed it on the side of Giga's head. Giga, totally caught by surprise, almost fell off his seat. Ram then grabbed the large widescreen monitor, bringing it down on Giga, who this time dropped to the floor, unconscious.

"Like I said. A leader doesn't show someone all their tricks."

Ram grabbed a set of keys from Giga's pockets and rushed to the door. He wasn't done yet and there was no way he was going to allow Ved to hand him over to The Collective.

* * *

Two storeys up from where Ram been held, Ved walked down the corridor to the office where Jack and Ellie had been kept prisoner. He was intensely focused, reflecting on matters.

The contact he had made online with The Collective hadn't been going as he had hoped in recent days. Despite his requests for information about Cloe and a detailed list of the precise equipment and food he could expect from entering into a deal, The Collective hadn't been forthcoming with anything specific. Instead, when Ved had been online, his chats with whoever was at the other end of The Collective had become progressively laboured and didn't seem to be going anywhere.

Ved got the feeling that they were stalling somehow, deliberately keeping him online for as long as possible. It was taking too long to get the answers to his questions. They were meant to be living in the age of instant communication but often his point of contact would take a few minutes before replying to Ved's messages. Even when he complained to the intermediary known as The Broker.

This had set alarm bells ringing in Ved's mind. He felt something was wrong – and was concerned that the longer he stayed online, there was a likelihood The Collective might indeed be able to trace his real-world location, getting through the layers of proxies he had been hoping to conceal his actual position.

Ved wished he could get his brother's advice, and imagining what Jay would have said, was of the view that he would advise him to pull out of the negotiations immediately. To change his strategy. From the way they were conducting themselves, Ved just sensed The Collective were biding their time, setting up some sort of trap, saying one thing but doing another. Ved knew enough about bad faith from all the time he had spent with Ram during Ram's Techno heyday.

"What do you want now?" Ellie wondered, giving Ved a disdainful look as he entered the room where she and Jack were being held.

"Nothing. There's been a change of plan," Ved advised.

"Which is?" Jack questioned.

"You're free to go," Ved said.

"You're kidding. Are you trolling us?" Ellie asked.

"No, seriously. I really mean it. You can go on your way, if you want to. Or you can stay here with us. Whatever makes you happy."

Ellie and Jack exchanged unsure glances with each other but Ved seemed genuine enough.

They asked him why there had been a change – and Ved told them about his doubts about The Collective from his interaction with them over the past few days.

But it wasn't just how The Collective had been. Jack and Ellie had managed to persuade him, he conceded, that he had been going about things the wrong way. Even if The Collective had shown they were being sincere and trustworthy, Ved no longer wanted to hand them over. He wasn't so sure about Ram though.

Ved said he had searched his soul for the right thing to do – and felt that the approach and outlook Jack and Ellie had, which is one the Mall Rats had as a whole, Ved knew, from his dealings with them earlier when they had all lived in the same city during Ram's Techno reign, was the right way to go. Cloe had also tried to show Ved in the past there was another way to live life – and he had finally accepted that the Mall Rat way of thinking and philosophy in life had some merit. But his ideology, he knew, would always revolve around technology.

Ved explained that he missed his brother deeply. He wished he could wind the clock back and spend more time with him. He only had one brother but didn't regret the hours he had instead devoted in days gone by to computers and other pursuits. Because Jay had been equally fascinated with technology and computers at that time. And they shared their passion, every single detail they were discovering. Even if they were not necessarily together.

He had been struck, he confessed, by something Ellie had said to him recently when he had visited her and Jack, about knowing the pain of what it was like to be separated from a sibling – and every day without Alice clearly caused Ellie anguish.

Jay may have gone but Ved could keep his spirit alive, Ellie had suggested, by never forgetting who he was and what he believed in. Ved would always have his brother in his life as long as he remembered Jay and what he stood for. He may not be able to spend more time with Jay in person – but Ved could do the next best thing, which was to honour Jay's wishes and safeguard what was important to him. He could look out for Amber and the Mall Rats, to whom Jay had gravitated to in his life – and by ensuring they were okay, Ved would be keeping his brother's wishes alive, and in so doing, Jay would be with him forever.

"I've got no beef with the Mall Rats," Ved admitted. "And this Broker I've been dealing with - he seems to be really well connected and might be able to help not just me. But you, Ellie, especially."

"How?" Ellie said.

"I'll let you know once I've checked out a few things," Ved replied.

Since he had been the leader of The Virts, Ved had been forced to shoulder more responsibility. That was precisely one of the key reasons he had been motivated to try and seek some deal from The Collective. So he could provide for his own tribe. They were running out of food, fresh drinking water. It was only a matter of time before the life he enjoyed with The Virts would be over.

And Ram was certainly a valuable trading commodity, which Ved couldn't ignore.

"Jay used to say that I shouldn't rely on him – or that someone else would always do what needed to be done for me. I should have listened to him. Then I might have been able to decide the best thing to do myself."

"We all learn things," said Ellie. "Alice and I certainly never always saw things eye to eye."

"That's the thing with hindsight," Jack agreed. "You only know what the right thing to do is after it's happened. We can learn from the past. But we can't re-live it. Unless, that is, you know anybody who's invented a time machine."

"Who knows? From the technology The Collective seem to have, according to The Broker, it might not be long before they do," Ved reflected.

Jack and Ellie smiled at the comment but then exchanged incredulous glances, realizing that Ved was not joking.

Sensing an opportunity to persuade Ved to let Ram also go free, Jack said, "If there's anyone with a brain to invent a time machine, then he's sitting in this very building. Sometimes

Ram can be a real ass – but overall, he can be a big asset to us as well."

"Who needs The Collective or this Broker you keep mentioning when we can have our own tribal alliance," Ellie joked. "We'd have to think of a good name though. The *Mall Rat-Virts-and ex-Technos* just doesn't sound right. We'd need something catchy."

"We need Ram," Ved said, and Ellie and Jack followed him, happy at the supposed turnaround in his attitude and behaviour.

He was a chip off the old block after all, Jack thought, and really was Jay's little brother. Jay would be proud Ved was doing the right thing, Jack was certain.

The two Virts who had been guarding the room where Ram was being kept were now running towards Ved, Ellie and Jack.

"Ram's gone!" one of the Virts shouted.

Giga had regained consciousness and had alerted the guards, who had searched throughout the factory and there was no sign of Ram anywhere at his former Techno base.

"If he's gone out into the town – it could be like finding a needle in a haystack," Jack pointed out. "We might never find him."

"If I know Ram – I bet there's one place he could have gone," Ved said.

It was somewhere Ved had once visited in the virtual world when he had entered a virtual reality fantasy Ram had designed, recreating the house where he had grown up. But this time, Ved, along with Jack and Ellie, would be going there for real.

* * *

Far above the town and away from the factory, Ram noticed a drone scouting the area.

The Collective must have been trying to track down Ved's location every time he had contacted them online, confirming

Ram's unease that with their sophisticated technology and team of hackers, it was only a matter of time before The Collective were able to approximate the town where Ved had been communicating with them from, even though they didn't have a fix yet on the precise co-ordinates.

Ram made his way furtively as the drone flew past overhead. He realized the drone wouldn't have enough charge in its batteries to stay out for too long. And no doubt would be accompanied by other drones on a reconnaissance mission collecting data, looking out for any heat signatures with its infrared cameras which would be analyzed by The Collective, intending to create a perimeter net around the town that would enable them to find and catch Kami's long-term rival and antagonist – Ram.

The drone returned in a zigzag motion, causing Ram to dive for cover and leap into a trash bin, burying himself beneath the filth piled up within, resisting the acrid smell, the phobias about germs resurfacing, as he hoped the layers of rubbish would conceal his position, keeping him hidden from the prying lenses of the drone.

This was only the first drone, Ram knew, and wouldn't be the last. He cringed at the thought that The Collective were mobilized, looking for him - and would soon close in.

CHAPTER TWENTY-SEVEN

Amber couldn't believe that Bray was gone – and irrationally it felt all the more worse because she blamed herself in part for his disappearance. If only she hadn't been so trusting, so sure that Cami and The Collective were a positive force for good in this world. She should have paid attention to Bray's suspicions that all was not well with The Collective.

Instead, she chose to believe perhaps what she wanted to believe. She was so passionate about making the world a better place, helping the lives of others – that she realized to herself she might have seen in The Collective something that was never really even there. So intent was she on doing right, she might have overlooked the things that were wrong. But Bray hadn't.

He had warned about the dangers of the Zootist faith and now was possibly taken by some zealot of the ideology given that Bray was Zoot's brother and held a twisted status and value.

All the Mall Rats were deeply concerned and rallied around Amber to give their support with Lex, Ryan and Alice searching the grounds, fearing that perhaps Bray had wandered away.

And might have even tripped and fallen into the water if he had strolled on one of the jetties.

Storm had advised that according to the security log of all the guards that they had seen Bray in the grounds at 3.08 A.M. in the morning, shortly after Storm himself noticed Bray in the corridor passing Trudy's room, apparently en route to grab something to eat in the dining area because he was restless and couldn't sleep.

Amber insisted that the Mall Rats would refrain from visiting Eden and indeed anywhere else until Bray was found safe and well, demanding The Selector meet the Mall Rats because they deserved an explanation how Bray could have gone missing from a seemingly secure and well-guarded facility.

The Selector struggled with his nervous 'tics' as he examined security footage Storm had showed, displaying an image of Bray who indeed had been recorded in the grounds by the lake. But he disappeared from frame and for some reason wasn't picked up by the next security camera, which scanned the ensuing section.

"It doesn't make any sense," The Selector said. "It's as if he has totally evaporated into thin air."

"He can't have disappeared – he has to be somewhere!" Amber snapped, trying to control her emotions and sense of rising panic.

"Perhaps, had you all agreed to have the biochips implanted, then we could have tracked him," The Selector sneered, taking clear delight that in this instance the Mall Rats had been hoist with their own petard.

Ryan lunged at The Selector and had to be restrained by Lex.

"Easy, Ryan. That's not going to help," Lex said.

"Especially to any of you," The Selector insisted. "There's no need to resort to violence. Otherwise we can't guarantee your safety. And I won't be held responsible for any retaliation."

"What you said about those biochips – that was so insensitive," Trudy exclaimed.

"You can see how difficult this is for Amber. For all of us," Salene added.

"Of course I can. I totally understand. And I want you to know that we've sent out our finest dogs and trackers, along with a fleet of drones. We'll find him, wherever he is."

"I hope so," May said, taking baby Jay from Amber's arms, who was crying and making it difficult for Amber to concentrate and think clearly.

Amber didn't believe The Selector was being sincere in his concern. He certainly seemed to be troubled. But she felt – as did all the Mall Rats – that he was giving a slant on matters, even placing the blame for what happened on Bray, suggesting that maybe Bray had left on his own accord.

"And why would he do that?" Amber said angrily.

"The course of true love never runs smooth," The Selector said wryly, casting a discreet glance at Tai San who was standing close to Lex. "Have you both been having any 'problems' of late?" The Selector continued, probing. Lex and Tai San didn't answer and The Selector considered Amber. "What about you, Amber – and Bray?"

Amber wondered if somehow the Mall Rats were still under surveillance and checked if The Selector had reactivated the monitoring of the *Lakeside Resort*. The Selector advised that this hadn't occurred and that he simply had examined the security log and couldn't help but notice on the data file that Storm and the guards had recorded that they had overheard some arguments of late emanating from Bray and Amber's room.

"So, you ARE still 'listening'?" Salene said disdainfully.

"The guards wouldn't be doing their jobs unless they did. How else could they protect you if something untoward had happened and you were screaming for help?"

"It didn't exactly 'help' Bray though, did it, pal?" Lex said.

"I don't recall any references to the security detail hearing any screaming from Bray. But I'll check with Storm and take another look at the overnight log," The Selector replied sarcastically, knowing full well that Bray disappeared amidst no noise whatsoever.

Lottie and Sammy were becoming distraught overhearing it all and were struggling to reconcile the gravity of Bray missing with The Selector's overly friendly but clearly insincere demeanour.

Amber demanded a face to face meeting with Cami. The Selector advised that there was no need for them to travel to Eden because The Creator had been informed that Bray was missing and wanted to visit the *Lakeside Resort*. An unprecedented situation given that The Creator was reclusive, seldom venturing into the outside world, choosing to spend her time in her inner sanctum carrying out her research.

* * *

Cami's procession arrived at the *Lakeside Resort* in the late afternoon, the alpine background a silhouette cast in the sun's golden light, the lake perfectly still, barely even a breeze, as if nature herself was appearing at its very best and most scenic, heralding the arrival of The Creator.

The Selector said it was an honour for the Mall Rats that she was choosing to visit from her exalted position high in the mountains overlooking her world and symbolized the respect she had for them, by her visiting them as opposed to them coming to see her at Project Eden.

A convoy of vehicles pulled into the driveway by the resort entrance. Mostly electric driverless pods. Cami disembarked, surrounded by a retinue of servants who arranged themselves in a V-shaped split of two welcoming lines, making a gap through which Cami, herself, and the elite guards who escorted her, could pass.

An advanced party under instructions given by The Selector had already cleaned up the resort pending Cami's arrival, making it utterly spotless, free of even a single speck of dust. But Cami was wearing a germ-protective mask when she arrived as a precaution.

"I personally checked all areas, doing random samples inside and outside the grounds, making sure everything is perfect for you, Creator. And safe." The Selector said. "My staff's monitoring can find no evidence at all of any bacteria which might harm you," The Selector added, indicating an array of waveforms on various equipment.

Cami nodded gratefully and removed her mask as she entered through the swing doors, followed by her retinue of guards and servants.

There were three Mall Rats in particular who Cami wanted to see. She was going to grant an audience to all of the Mall Rats, of course, but wanted especially to meet Amber, Trudy and Lex, given their connection to Zoot.

It was as if they were having a royal visit, Amber felt, the formalities reminding her of ceremonies with dignitaries in the adult times she had seen on the news.

"I am so sorry to hear about Bray," Cami said. "It must be awful for you all. Please rest assured that we'll do everything we can to return him. Perhaps we can all spend some time together to discuss any concerns you all might have throughout dinner. But I'd be grateful if I could have some time with Amber, Trudy and Lex. Starting with you first, Amber?"

"Of course," Amber replied.

On The Selector's prompting, the servants made themselves scarce and waited in the lobby. The other Mall Rats dispersed as well.

The only people left in the lounge area were The Creator's personal guards, who stationed themselves at various exit and entry points.

A few minutes of silence passed between them, Amber wondering what Cami wanted to say to her.

Cami was barefoot and wore the same type of patchwork linen dress as every time Amber had seen her before. Her hair was adorned with a circle of green leaves, like a crown. A mixture of twigs, flowers and different shades of green leaves were inserted in bands around her ankles. She carried a single white rose in one hand and sniffed the scent appreciatively several times since she had arrived. And Amber felt a sense of calm in Cami's demeanour and serenity. She looked like a dryad, a wood fairy from a children's book - a living embodiment of Mother Nature.

"This rose could have been extinct. Had it not adapted and evolved from the work we carried out in the laboratories," Cami finally said, while staring at the flower closely, feeling its petals with her finger, breathing in deeply through her nose, savouring the smell of the scent. She was contemplating its contours, rubbing the stalk with her thumb, lost in her own private reverie as she continued.

"I don't know if you have ever followed his writings but Charles Darwin said it is not the strongest or the most intelligent who survive – but the ones who are the most adaptable," Cami said, gazing thoughtfully at the flower, twirling it in her fingers. "Are you going to be adaptable, Amber?"

"That depends on what has happened to Bray. And if he returns."

"Of course, I understand. But I wasn't just referring to Bray. How can I best describe what I mean?" Cami pondered, then once again indicated the rose. "First, we need to be aware of a flower – and if so, then we will also be aware of a tree – then a forest – then it's the world itself. If we can live in harmony with

318

nature, not treat it with disdain but respect. Then there is hope for the human species if we can realize that we're not the only living things on this planet. Hopefully - future generations might not replicate what has gone before."

She passed the rose to Amber, who took it and smelt the scent. "Thank you. It's beautiful."

"The human species can also be beautiful, Amber," Cami replied. "If it can only learn to adapt and evolve."

"Possibly," Amber said introspectively, slightly preoccupied, still thinking about Bray - which registered with Cami.

"Tell me about the love you feel for Bray," Cami said, explaining that she had personally never experienced love for a man before – and wondered what it was like, how it felt, the real feelings, not those from romantic stories she had read in her repository of books. But real love. "How would you define it?"

"That's a difficult question," Amber pondered. "Without love, I think possibly everything else is irrelevant."

"Nature?" Cami probed.

"In some ways," Amber said. "I think having someone - or perhaps even something to love - is essential to existence. Otherwise, there is no meaning to it all and life itself might simply become dysfunctional."

"That's interesting," Cami said. "I've always thought that the definition of love is where someone's happiness might be central to one's own happiness. If the person one loves isn't happy, then obviously how could anyone be happy too?"

"Exactly," Amber agreed. "That's an interesting definition as well."

"What I'm most interested in though is - do you think it's possible for love to adapt and evolve? To go through the same process as nature?"

"I don't quite understand," Amber said.

"Let me put this a different way. Your love… Bray… Do you think you could exist without him?"

Amber exchanged a long glance with Cami, wondering where her line of questioning was going. "Are you suggesting that Bray might not return?" Amber said, horrified at the prospect.

"No, not at all. I'm just interested… Did you love your parents?" Cami clarified.

"Very much so," Amber replied.

"But you've adapted and evolved in this new world we're all trying to create."

"I think that's a different comparison though."

"I was just wondering. Because I don't think I loved my mother. I admired her. And the work she carried out. But I didn't love her as such. In fact, we rarely spent much time together."

"What about your father?" Amber asked.

"I didn't know him very well either. He was a 'test tube'," Cami replied matter-of-factly.

"I'm… sorry."

"Don't be. I'm not. Science gave me life. And it has also given me the ability to love all living species in the natural world. So I am researching more about the human condition."

* * *

Trudy paced up and down in her room, trying to keep her composure, waiting to be 'summoned' for her audience with Cami.

She determined that she wasn't going to wait and be kept on call and decided to join Storm, who had taken Brady outside to play catch with the ball – along with Sammy and Lottie but also Storm's little sister, whom he had received permission to visit, and had just recently arrived.

Storm had apparently said he thought it might help Trudy if Brady had some friends to play with. But Trudy suspected that in reality Storm perhaps wanted his sister to catch a glimpse of The Creator, Cami herself, whom very few had ever seen.

From feeling Storm was an unwanted presence in their lives, a nuisance, who represented intrusion, Trudy's outlook was slowing turning. She had discovered Storm was kind, gentle and had an honourable, almost noble quality about him.

He had revealed how he had become streamed into the militia after his own town had been taken over by The Collective and seemed a little more 'human' when Trudy overheard him speaking of his younger sister, Charlotte, who was thirteen years his junior, the result of a second marriage his mother had entered into after his parents divorced. Brady reminded him of his little sister. Who was now seven years old.

When their town had been invaded by The Collective, Charlotte was entered into The Collective's educational programme – and ironically, Trudy knew, that she was being raised to believe in the Zootist faith, taught to hold Brady and Trudy in positions of esteem, reverence.

Intrigued by his own personal view, Trudy had one day asked him how he felt about Zoot. And was surprised to discover that he didn't believe in it or sanction it. But had clearly confided in Trudy because the revelation could have endangered his standing and also Charlotte, who was living in one of the dormitories in Eden.

When Trudy and the others had been brought to their lands, The Selector personally assigned Storm to become Trudy's bodyguard, being aware of Storm's affinity and care for younger children from the way he had devoted himself to protecting his younger sister, visiting her regularly from his barracks when he was not on duty.

* * *

Lex pulled on the oars of the rowing boat he was in, taking it further out to the lake, as Cami has requested him to. It was just the two of them in the boat, the oars leaving imprints in the surface of the water as Lex rowed.

All around them was nothing but nature. Peaceful, serene. The sound of the oars swooshing through the water rhythmically. A few birds flew overhead, passing by, taking a curious look at the little boat disturbing their natural habitat by its presence. Lounging in the back of the boat, almost flat on her back, Cami stared up at the birds as they soared above against the golden sky, a palette of warm colours, the late afternoon sun not having long before it set.

Cami was utterly relaxed and in a reverie, enjoying every moment of her boat ride with Lex. She had dipped her hands in the water and was waving them gently, as if paddling along, accompanying Lex's languid strokes. She looked ecstatic, joyously contented – Lex stealing looks at The Collective leader, wondering what on earth she was thinking about – and why she had asked Lex to row her out into the lake so she could talk with him.

About a hundred metres away, following behind, keeping their distance so as not to get too close and interrupt Cami and Lex's journey together, several boats maintained their formation, the guards on board peering through binoculars at The Creator and the Mall Rat with her, their boat engines idling, ready to drive the throttle forward if they needed to get to The Creator quickly.

"It's beautiful, isn't it?" Cami said to Lex, suddenly speaking to him for the first time since they had left the shoreline. "To think that life would have begun in a place somewhere like this, so many millennia ago. And now here we are, just you and I. Humanity has conquered and taken over this planet. Do you think we can save it?"

Lex continued rowing for a moment, unsure, before answering. "Only if we survive ourselves."

"From what I know of you, Lex – you're certainly a 'survivor'," Cami said, her voice soft and sensuous almost, so relaxed was she in the boat, waving her hand through the water once more.

Lex elaborated that he thought it would take a lot more than The Collective to save the world. Or Lex. And Cami. He was uncertain how he should behave in her company and how he would respond. But decided just to be honest. He had nothing to hide.

Cami suddenly jumped overboard and disappeared beneath the surface, the boat rocking back and forth, side to side, from the momentum of her sudden movement – Lex was totally surprised – and froze in confusion and concern.

"What the hell are you doing?" he called out to her, searching the water, his eyes rapidly scanning around the boat for any sign of her. "Cami!?"

There was nothing. She had been gone for a few seconds.

"I don't know why I get myself into these things," Lex grumbled to himself, and dove into the water, searching for her.

About a minute later, Lex breached the surface - Cami in his arms, the two of them gasping for breath, clutching the side of the boat, their chests heaving, feeling the fresh mountain air in their lungs.

With a mighty effort, Lex pushed Cami, shoving her up and back into the boat before clambering in himself.

Cami was laughing, finding delight in what had just happened, almost amused by Lex's actions and the bemused look on his face. She motioned to the security detail that she was fine, indicating that all was well.

"What was all that about?" Lex questioned, spluttering, still getting his breath back. "Why'd you do that?"

"I needed to check…" Cami said, breathing deeply from being submerged, pausing as she spoke, "… You're not only a survivor, Lex… but you killed Zoot by your actions… I needed to see if you had the same capacity to cherish life – and if you would save me."

"You could have just asked," Lex said, flabbergasted by her.

"Not that I might need to be saved," Cami said. "I was raised swimming with dolphins. I'm more than capable of getting back to the shore. I appreciated the opportunity to have a chat."

"A test more like?" Lex asked, intrigued by it all.

Cami smiled slightly, then dove into the water and swam towards the shore while Lex pulled on the oars, the boat following in pursuit.

* * *

While Ryan waited to be summoned for his audience with Cami, he took time to have a workout in the gym with Salene, who stated that she didn't trust Cami and suspected for sure that The Selector had something to do with Bray's disappearance. Both resolved that if The Collective's forces couldn't shed any light on the mystery, then they would set up a plan to try and find him again themselves.

Tai San was lost in meditation doing a series of Tai Chi moves while she watched Lex row to the shore and Cami being greeted by servants as she climbed out of the water, the servants wrapping her with towels and blankets.

Trudy was watching Alice play with Storm and Sammy, Lottie, Brady and Storm's little sister, Charlotte. It was a game of hide and seek.

Amber had returned to her room to relieve May, who was looking after baby Jay.

All the Mall Rats were concerned when Salene and Ryan arrived, advising that they had been trying to track down Alice

324

to see what she thought the merits might be of them having a contingent plan to send out another search party of their own, rather than rely on Cami's militia to track Bray down.

But so far, there was no sign of Alice anywhere and she, as with Bray, had seemingly disappeared.

"It doesn't make any sense. She was here just a minute ago. I saw her with my own eyes," Trudy said.

"Maybe she's still hiding and is waiting to be found," Ryan pondered reflectively.

"Since I've known you, Ryan, you've said a lot of dumb things. But that's gotta take the top spot," Lex snapped impatiently.

"If you don't mind me saying, Sir, I think Mister Ryan is just trying to help," Storm said.

"And you can just shut it!" Lex said, glaring at Storm.

"Back off, Lex. Storm's only trying to help as well," Trudy protested.

"What are you defending him for? He's not even a Mall Rat!" Lex scoffed. "Unless you two have got a 'thing' going. Is that it?"

"Don't be ridiculous. How can you suggest such a thing!?" Trudy exclaimed.

"Right. And you should try and calm down, Lex," May said in an attempt to defuse the situation. "Arguing between ourselves isn't going to help matters."

"Right! You shouldn't yell at my big brother!" Charlotte said angrily.

"Apologise to Mister Lex, Charlotte. That's disrespectful," Storm scolded his little sister and she sighed.

"I'm sorry, Sir."

"The name's Lex."

"Sorry, Sir Lex," Charlotte said softly, innocently.

"Have you been giving that kid some lessons?" Lex asked Ryan, then turned back to Charlotte. "I told you. My name's Lex. Not Sir Lex. Or Sir. Just Lex."

"My little sister's apologized, Sir. And I hope you'll not only accept it. But respect it. But if not, we can always meet, off the grid, and sort it all out," Storm said. There was a utility of restrained emotion and motion, a force which registered with Trudy and she now realized that Storm was aptly named as he stood, controlling his obvious simmering anger.

"I might just take you up on that, pal, if you give me any more hassle," Lex said, squaring up to Storm.

Amber appeared in the lobby with baby Jay in her arms. "What's all this I hear about Alice disappearing!?"

* * *

The Selector was furious and scolded Commander Snake, standing before him, in The Selector's private quarters at the lodge. "She couldn't just 'vanish'," The Selector snapped irritably and again was struggling to contain his nervous 'tics'.

"I just don't understand it, Sir," Snake replied. "Our security detail at the resort is the very best. It's impossible for anyone to have gotten through."

"So, what are you suggesting, Snake? That the Mall Rat just decided to walk off? And join Bray? Is that what you think?" he scoffed.

Snake sighed, not entirely sure what he did think, while The Selector breathed slowly, in through his nose and out through his mouth, trying somehow to calm himself and control his nervous tics. And he clearly was becoming paranoid, as well as panicked.

"Those Mall Rats… I wonder if they're 'rats' and we can trust them? Maybe they're playing games with us. Trying to test us, just as we are them."

"I honestly don't know, Sir," Snake said, stealing wary looks as The Selector gazed around suspiciously, as if checking if someone, somewhere was watching him.

"I can trust you, Snake – can't I?" he asked.

"Of course, Sir," Snake replied. "There is really no need to ask."

"But I did ask! And I demand to know!" The Selector erupted, in total fury.

"Like I said, Sir, all my team – we have your back. We always have. Always will."

"Good. Good. Essential that we have each other's backs in this God-forsaken world, Snake. If we don't look out for each other, then no one else will."

Snake nodded in agreement and watched The Selector, who was becoming more agitated, lost in his thoughts, as he reflected introspectively.

"Something's wrong. I just know it. If our team weren't responsible for those 'rats' going missing - and Alice and Bray aren't involved in some conspiracy themselves – then we might have a 'rat' within, Snake. We might have someone trying to undermine us. And bring us down."

* * *

The Selector was unaware that his concerns were prophetic and his destiny was about to change, precipitated by an event in The Cube.

Each contestant had been instructed to hold a rope at which some rocks had been placed on the other end, in proportion to each of the contestant's body weight, so that one contestant wasn't disadvantaged compared to another, with them all having to endure the same relative burden.

The aim of the 'trial', according to The Gamesmaster, was to test the human spirit. It wasn't a battle of strength but a contest of wills, to see how long each of them would last before they gave up and dropped the rope, unable to hold onto their encumbrance any longer. It was truly a question of mind over matter, The Gamesmaster had emphasized into the cameras.

Across the lands, the vast audience watched The Cube as it was projected onto buildings.

And to everyone's surprise – especially her own – Emma had finished triumphant. With her blindness, she was able to compete equally with the other contestants and had displayed tremendous willpower and inner resolve to hold on to her own weight far longer than anyone else. The endeavour had exhausted her and she had collapsed shortly afterwards, riven by cramps.

Ebony had finished second, Hawk third. Emma's effort had impressed both of them, Ebony especially, who was really coming to admire Emma's spirit and no longer perceived her as a vulnerable girl - but someone with great resolve who deserved respect.

In the 'final' test of the episode The Gamesmaster advised that one of the guards, Wolf, lived by a strict code and never lied. Whereas another guard, Dog, was known to lie. On occasion. The aim of the last game was to check each contestant's powers of observation, senses, and mental agility.

There were two paths at the end of which one path held a basket full of food which the winner could enjoy as well as winning the 'test'. Wolf said that the basket was at the end of path one. Dog said it was actually at the end of path two. So the contestants were unanimous that the basket of food would be at the end of path one. Because Wolf said it was and never lied. And Dog said it was pathway two and if he is lying, then clearly it would be pathway one.

The Gamesmaster reminded the contestants though that Dog only lies on occasion. The contestants didn't think it would make any difference if Wolf never lied because he had stated the basket was at the end of pathway one.

Emma though was the sole contestant who felt that it all depended upon how they introduced themselves in the first place. Wolf introduced himself as Wolf and Dog as Dog, which meant that he was actually Dog. Otherwise if he was lying he would have introduced himself as Wolf.

The other contestants including Ebony cringed, realizing that they hadn't paid particular attention to who was speaking. Ebony believed it shouldn't make any difference just as long as Wolf introduced himself because he never lied. Emma though clearly had her own view given that it was important to determine when Dog might be lying, which he does on occasion. Because he might have introduced himself as Wolf.

"Can I ask Wolf and Dog a question?" she asked.

"Be my guest," The Gamesmaster replied.

"Wolf – did you change the sign of pathway one to pathway two?"

"I did," Wolf replied.

"What about you, Dog – did you change the sign?"

"I did," Dog replied.

"Then this time you're lying and not telling the truth, Dog, otherwise you would have said you didn't if you were telling the truth. This means then that before you were lying otherwise you would have said the pathway was one given that in actual fact the food must be in pathway two."

"So you think it's pathway two then, Emma?" The Gamesmaster said.

"Yes. Otherwise Dog should have said no that he hadn't changed the sign which meant that he did."

"But only if he was lying, which he only does on occasion," The Gamesmaster replied, clearly getting as confused as all the contestants along with Wolf and Dog.

Emma was positive with her reasoning and especially that she distinctly heard Dog first time around introducing himself as Dog but second time around had introduced himself as

Wolf. So was lying either first or second time around and telling the truth on the other occasion. Which was central to linking when Wolf was speaking.

The Gamesmaster addressed the audience, gazing intently into the cameras reminding all who were watching that things aren't always what someone sees or what even anyone else says, but in this case, Emma was relying on her highly developed sense of recall of what she had heard but not seen evoking a way of thinking through mental reasoning. And was declared the winner of the test.

At the end of the game, The Gamesmaster had a discreet word with Ebony and asked her to make sure that she and Emma stayed behind, rather than join their fellow contestants in The Cube living quarters for dinner.

"Why?" Ebony asked.

Normally so cool, composed and confident, there had been a change in The Gamesmaster's demeanour, which hadn't gone unnoticed by Ebony. He seemed nervous, unsettled, worried almost. Preoccupied.

"There's no time for any questions," he said carefully. "Just follow me."

He led them through the darkness to the shore of the lake and instructed Ebony to use one of the security jet skis to take Emma and her further down the lake, the far south end where they would be met by others who would then brief them.

"What's going on?" Ebony asked, unsettled herself and wondering if this all might be some kind of test, even part of the game and if Wolf and Dog were participating. The Gamesmaster was preoccupied, revealing that his instructions involved a different source and unbelievably, it seemed that The Gamesmaster was giving Ebony and Emma an opportunity to escape. If that indeed was the case, however slim and unpredictable, Ebony was going to take it.

She caught the keys The Gamesmaster tossed her and sat on the jet ski, while he helped Emma, who sat behind Ebony.

"You'd better hold on tight," Ebony said.

Emma wrapped her arms around Ebony's waist.

"I can give you ten minutes. But no more. Then I'll have to alert the guards that you've escaped."

"Is this some kind of a joke?" Ebony asked, still unable to comprehend what was occurring.

"It won't be if you're caught. You'd better get a move on," The Gamesmaster said uneasily. And he watched as Ebony started the engine of the jet ski, which sped away - and then returned towards the main administration building and living quarters of The Cube.

Emma clung desperately to Ebony as they sped along, the jet ski hurling into the air occasionally due to the high speed they were travelling.

"Where are we going!?" Emma shouted over the engine noise.

"I have no idea!" Ebony yelled back. "Now keep quiet and let me concentrate. I can hardly see where we're going in this darkness!"

"Tell me about it," Emma replied dryly, which caused Ebony to smile, despite herself, as the jet ski sped through the darkness of night towards its destination – wherever that destination might be.

CHAPTER TWENTY-EIGHT

The Broker stood on the quayside in an area nearby the docks at which Tai San had arrived. He was watching grain, rice and pallets of fresh water being loaded into the hold of a ship.

Nearby, there were some people fishing off the jetty. All looked ravaged, malnourished and defeated. Others were scavenging for fish in stacked bins, fighting gulls shrieking in frenzy, some attacking their competitors to grab remnants of any scraps of food.

A trader looking down at heel himself arrived on a rusty bicycle, seemingly from a bygone age.

"You're late," The Broker said, disdainfully.

"It seems there's a bit of a problem," the trader replied uneasily.

"What kind of a 'problem'!?"

"I've just checked in The Void and there's no sign of the 'cargo'," the trader replied.

"Then that really is a problem, isn't it? For you," The Broker said, menacingly.

"Give me a break. Times are hard. It's not my fault. I must have been double-crossed."

"That's not my problem. It looks as if I'll be keeping my deposit then, if you're unable to deliver. The deal's off."

* * *

A short distance away, further along the dockside, Bray walked through a busy marketplace. He was wearing a hoodie which had been given to him so that he could mask his appearance and remain as disguised as he could be.

Since he had been snatched while having a stroll in the early hours of the morning at the *Lakeside Resort*, Bray had been plunged from the material comforts of life and delivered into a hell hole.

The Void, as he had discovered it was called, fully deserved its name. It was a place devoid of any resemblance of civilization – a lawless, anarchic and wild shanty town. A slum where those who had been put in it had been left to be forgotten.

Besides being a refuge of the lost, the unwanted, those who society had given up on, The Void also housed transients and traders. There was a cacophony of noise from peddlers trying to sell their wares - which ranged from goats, cattle, chickens, clothes and animal skins. All around, beggars pleaded for scraps of food. Other inhabitants were given fruit in return for performing. There were surreal tumblers, fire eaters, and acrobats and Bray was concerned if he might encounter the infamous Top Hat and his crazed Tribe Circus, who were once a nightmarish adversary.

On the night he was seized, Bray had almost successfully resisted being taken but had soon been overwhelmed by a group of renegade warriors who had bound his legs and arms, prior to throwing him in the back of a decaying military vehicle.

Underneath the flapping canvas, throughout the long journey as the mountains and lakes disappeared in the alpine area, Bray was aware that the vehicle was seemingly travelling in the middle of nowhere.

The terrain of the well-tended agricultural crops of The Collective soon gave way to a dusty, desert-like region, the soil barren, devoid of plants, even without grass, a lifeless area, a bleak wasteland.

They had driven for hours, passing road signs from the adult days warning of contamination, bio-hazards, finally announcing that anyone on the journey was now leaving a restricted sector. Soon after, Bray finally fell asleep, wakening in the early morning as the vehicle arrived in the docklands area.

The Void was segmented by high wire fencing and curiously watchtowers which were now abandoned. Bray eventually became aware that the community originated as a holding area of quarantine during the height of the pandemic and evolved into the slum it was today.

Some of the inhabitants lived in stacked cargo containers, or in warehouses and stores long-ago since looted and now covered in graffiti. Others were clearly homeless and lived on the street with nothing but their ragged clothes and cardboard box blankets - and an array of meagre personal items which they guarded as if valuable jewels.

Bray had originally been held in a warehouse, apparently waiting to be traded and 'transported'. But he was surprised by a guard who had released him, mentioning that he was part of the resistance and that Bray had to travel to a safehouse, *The Mermaid's Booty*. Bray had enquired just exactly what the guard was resisting, only to be advised that it would be well and truly apparent during his journey through The Void.

And his journey so far was worse than anything Bray had ever witnessed. It was a living hell. The collapse of humanity. He pitied those poor residents who had been quarantined in the past but now the stench in the air was nauseating from a lack of sewage and it was like God had forsaken this place, doomed it to judgement, afflicted it with a plague that had ripped the heart and life out of any form of decency, let alone a society.

There was pestilence everywhere, the victims covered in welts, sores, had to have all kinds of diseases, Bray thought, likely to be infectious too. Some coughed uncontrollably. He wished he could so something for them but he simply could not. Bray promised himself that if he could find someone, anyone, in The Void who might be able to help these people, or provide any medical supplies, he would return to them to try and improve their situation. Otherwise, many of them were slipping away, some willingly it seemed, wanting it to be all over, heading into death's door as a welcome escape.

Having cautiously made his way through the marketplace, Bray arrived at a building which was a hub of activity - but rather than inhabitants domiciled in The Void, seemed to be frequented by more of a transient population – including the crews of some ships who were visiting temporarily. Though quite why anyone would want to visit, Bray didn't understand – but soon would when he walked into *The Mermaid's Booty* which resonated with life from those inside the bar who were talking, drinking, gambling. And intriguingly, Bray could hear music, the sounds of perfect harmonies, *a cappella* singing which was strangely familiar although Bray couldn't quite recall why.

Stepping past towering bouncers who guarded the door and must have been expecting Bray from the ease in which they allowed him in, Bray surveyed customers gathered at the bar, knocking back their drinks, bantering with each other.

The singing was coming from a trio Bray finally recognized. And he almost did a double-take upon seeing them, standing on top of a small stage, kicking their legs like they were can-can girls while they sung and entertained the raucous crowd. They were Lips, Teeth and Dimples – and were from Bray's home city originally. They had always been eccentric, unstable even, a musically-obsessed group that had caused problems for the Mall Rats in the past and were no friends of Bray's.

They seemed to act and look even more bizarre now, their faces caked in grotesque make-up like a cruel caricature portrait of the *avant garde* but punctuated now by the absurd, their make-up smeared, almost cartoon-like.

Bray dipped his head, trying to avoid eye contact with them, hoping to blend in with the others as he made his way to the bar to get a much-needed drink, as well as to try and meet the contact he was advised would provide further instructions.

Lips, Teeth and Dimples spotted Bray, however, from their vantage on the stage above the crowd and began to point at him, calling his name.

"Fancy that – a Mall Rat – here today – we can see Bray."

They weren't speaking as such nor rapping but had interwoven Bray's name into the lyrics of the song they were singing.

So much for his hopes of going about unnoticed – but the other attendees in the tavern paid scant attention to his presence being highlighted by the singers. Apart from a few occasional looks at him, Bray was ignored by most of the denizens who were more interested in their drinks and their conversation.

"Hey, honey – you want a good time?" a female in her late teens standing at the bar, asked Bray.

She had a spluttering cough and Bray felt sorry for her, her skin a yellowing pallor, some sores around her cracked lips. She was obviously exchanging her body for food and drink to survive.

"I'm fine – thanks anyway."

The prostitute sneered, then slinked away while Bray got the attention of the barkeeper, an assertive and confident person – and one he also recognized. It was Roanne. He was aware she had run her own brothel, long ago, in his own city - Salene having fallen into Roanne's debt, accidentally ensnared when she was particularly vulnerable and at a low ebb. Like Lips, Teeth and Dimples - Roanne, too, was far from home and had ended up in The Void, like Bray – though with her entrepreneurial ways, she seemed in a position of influence in comparison to others Bray had encountered.

"Well, well," Roanne said. "I heard rumours the Mall Rats were around – but I didn't expect any of 'em to show up here. If you don't fancy one of my girls – you look like you could fancy a drink. But only the first one's on the house. After that, you gotta pay up and trade. Or else you get out."

Bray asked for the largest drink she had by size – much to her amusement. He wasn't after alcohol but just as much liquid as he could get, clean water even. Roanne gave him a bottle of ginger beer – from her special reserves.

"What are you doing here, Mall Rat?" Roanne asked, as Bray took some welcome sips from his drink.

"I'm supposed to meet up with someone," Bray replied, enigmatically.

"Well, you look out for yourself. Not everyone here are fans of the Mall Rats. You've made yourself some enemies over the years."

A little while later, an acrobat had wanted another drink but had been refused because last orders had already been taken.

The acrobat grabbed a bottle of brandy, took a swig and had breathed 'fire', the flame setting another drunken customer's hair alight.

"Put that out – and get him out!" Roanne yelled, as her bouncers and some of her close 'girls' threw items of clothing on the customer's head, denying oxygen to the flames while the bouncers dragged the protesting and drunk acrobat out.

Lips, Teeth and Dimples looked on in absolute fascination and started to laugh manically prior to proceeding doing backwards somersaults themselves while continuing singing as they disappeared through the doors.

"The bar's shut – everybody out!" Roanne said. But added in an undertone, "Just stay where you are, Bray."

Mumbling and voicing their discontentment, the clientele of the bar began to slowly make their way to the exit door and Roanne said, for dramatic effect - "You too, Mall Rat," apparently urging him to leave. "This isn't a charity – you want to sleep here, you pay for one of the girls or the rooms – or you don't stay at all."

She shook her head discreetly, indicating she wasn't meaning what she was saying and Bray waited, while protesting.

"I really appreciate you giving away my identity," he said sarcastically.

"Don't worry. It isn't a problem," Roanne replied, then added in an undertone, "You won't be here for long. But we don't want anyone to know that. For the time being, at least, trust me. It's in your interests for all our 'citizens' in The Void to think you've relocated and are now living here."

* * *

When the bouncers had locked the doors, Roanne led Bray into a living area of the bordello inhabited by 'her girls'. And to Bray's surprise, he had come face to face with Alice, Tiffany and Shannon, who had been staying in Roanne's private quarters.

"What are you doing here?" Bray asked, unable to believe what he was seeing.

"Well, certainly not 'working'," Alice required. "Though there's plenty of me to go around," she added, wryly.

Tiffany and Shannon gave Bray a huge hug, as did Alice. Then Roanne took the children away to pick something for them to eat, leaving Bray and Alice to catch up with one another.

Alice revealed that her journey was very similar to Bray's and brought him up to date on The Creator's 'royal visit'. She reassured him that all the Mall Rats were otherwise safe, which brought a great sense of relief to Bray, knowing that especially Amber and his young son were fine.

On the day that she was seized, Alice advised that she had checked the lakeside again while waiting for her audience with Cami and had noticed a mug Bray had used for drinking coffee. He confirmed he had a bite to eat, then took a stroll in the grounds of the resort, sipping on his coffee while enjoying the brisk night mountain air. Alice was about to tell the others but had been seized by guards and taken to a military vehicle under the control of a different group she had never experienced before, who seemed to be a bit renegade.

She, too, had been in a 'holding area' and had been released by the resistance, a part of which Roanne was also a member. And their network didn't just operate in The Void but had been extending because there had been a lot of rumours that The Creator was unaware of the true existence of the new society under The Collective banner – such as The Privileged, their servants The Discards, the slave population who toiled in the agricultural sector. As far as Alice could gather from what Roanne had said, The Creator was certainly unaware of the slum areas in The Void and the elicit trading on the dockside which consistently went on.

Bray was keen to know more about it when Roanne returned, having assured him and Alice that Shannon and Tiffany would be safe and that all of them would be departing The Void in the early hours of the morning. She just had to double-check various arrangements.

CHAPTER TWENTY-NINE

Ram was home. In the house that he had grown up in. A place full of many memories. The building he had been in when the whole adult world had come tumbling down around him. The house where he had established The Technos. And it felt fitting that if his time was finally running out, that he would meet his end at the house where his new life after the virus had begun. There was something almost poetic to it, he thought. But Ram had long resolved that his time wouldn't run out - yet.

After a stressful ordeal going through the abandoned streets of his old town, evading the drones flying overhead, Ram had finally made it to the house. *#60 Warren Road.* He didn't think he would have ever been back there – and never wanted to go back, always determined to go forward in life, to look to the future.

But since he was on the run from Ved – and trying to keep out of sight of the drones hunting the town, the house had beckoned to him in the recesses of his mind as the natural place to go, a sanctuary, like it had been since childhood when he had first started to become obsessed with computers and had played online gaming, eventually becoming a bit of a celebrity in the online world for his prowess and constant status as being top of the leaderboard.

He had only ever really had one competitor, as such – being Kami. Who was also proficient in gaming and computers.

The house had long ago been looted, vandalized, like all the other houses seemed to be in his street. The garden was overgrown. The swing Ram used to sit on as a little boy was nearly covered, obscured by the tall grass and looming weeds, only the top metal frame standing out above.

Ram felt strangely calm, a sense of peace, as he sat at the desk in the bedroom that used to be his. The gaming and technology posters that were on the walls were yellowing from the exposure to the sun blazing in the window, peeling off, fading. There was dust everywhere, the room stank of stale air.

But still, despite the passage of time and the decay it had suffered, it was *his* Room. In his parents' house. It was home.

He closed his eyes, leaning back in the chair at his old desk, the office-style chair creaking under his weight. He could picture his former life clearly and imagined his parents being in the house, how it used to be. He could almost hear the sound of the television coming from downstairs in his head, where his father had sat watching the news. It brought back his mother's voice, he could hear her clearly, calling to Ram from the kitchen below that his dinner was ready, like she once had. Ram could smell her homemade cooking, almost taste it.

Being in the house conjured up so many memories. It all felt so real. And Ram wondered if his recollections were real or if they stemmed from visits he had made in the virtual reality space he had designed and utilized.

Reality space was always a welcome escape but now it seemed to conflict with his recollections of boyhood. As powerful as computers and graphics were, the human mind was still eminently more capable and vivid in its recall, in the fantasies it could come up with. But equally, Ram's world of computers still seemed to dominate his entire being.

From outside, far in the distance, Ram could hear the current, very real noise of the drones buzzing around the town. There were more of them now, Ram having counted at least twenty, each scouting over various areas, searching for him, he expected, The Collective utilizing some of their high-tech resources in an effort to locate him. Ved must have let his guard slip, given away their real-world location, alerting The Collective that there *was* someone in the town, instead of it being deserted. And that someone was Ram, Ellie and Jack.

Standing on top of the desk, Ram reached up, removing the surround leading into the attic and climbed up inside, where he beamed, noticing his 'box of toys', action figures from his youth that he had kept. They were underneath a tattered duvet. And underneath the toys in the box, buried out of sight, was what Ram was looking for in the event he ever needed it. And he needed it now, more than ever.

It was his old laptop, from the days before he had left the house to base himself in the factory that The Technos had lived in. And he hoped that there was still power in the auxiliary emergency backup which he had arranged in the event that he ever needed it.

The street had been cabled and Ram bypassed the old system which he thought was decrepit, for all the adults at the time felt that it was next generation. But Ram was always frustrated by the bandwidth and in the midst of the pandemic had implemented various bypass systems through the fibre optic cables which had run underground and he was able to hook into his Techno base.

"I've missed you," Ram said to it, caressing the laptop affectionately with his fingers. "Let's just hope you still can get some juice."

He plugged a cable into the side, opened the lid and to his relief was able to power the laptop on. It still wouldn't have much charge, the battery having lost its cycles due to inactivity, Ram thought. But if he could get enough power, even for a few seconds, he might be able to copy over the files he needed onto one of the miniature drives that were also in his hidden 'toy box', concealed under the piles of action figures.

* * *

On the journey to Ram's house from the factory, Ved's search party, which included Jack and Ellie, had several panicked, close encounters with the drones flying overhead. They had nearly been spotted several times. Ved had thought to shoot the drones down with his stun gun but had been warned against doing so by Jack who thought if he did, Ved would only alert The Collective that someone *was* in the town - if the drones fell under attack and began dropping out of the sky. It was better to leave the drones alone, Jack suggested, and hope they left them alone, thinking that the town was uninhabited after all.

Ved, Jack and Ellie continued furtively, trying to stay out of sight – but suddenly all the drones started to zigzag, almost out of control. Like they were possessed. Hurling high into the sky, then speeding down towards the ground before receding away at speed.

Rather than being possessed, if Ellie didn't know better, she would swear that the drones were actually UFOs and not of this world.

* * *

Ram, in his attic, typed feverishly - then suddenly froze – hearing movement, someone else in the house coming upstairs.

"Ram? Are you there?" Jack's voice called out.

Ram didn't answer, trying to be invisible, keeping as quiet as possible.

"There's no-one here," Jack said, peering into the bedroom.

"What about the attic?" Ellie said, noticing the entrance cover had been open on one side.

Jack hoisted himself up from the desk he stood on, peeked his head in and noticed Ram, who faked a slight smile.

"Any sign of him?" Ved called up from downstairs.

"Please – don't give me away," Ram urged, whispering his request.

Ellie climbed on the desk to join Jack and both elevated themselves higher, into the attic, trying to reassure Ram that Ved was on his side. But Ram scoffed, advising that it wasn't what he had been given to believe, having successfully hacked not only the drones searching the town and finally disabling them - but he had made initial inroads into a network derived from Kami's main system. "Our friend, Ved, has been a very naughty boy," Ram advised.

* * *

Ram, Ellie and Jack travelled with Ved back to the Technos base. Ved was totally overwhelmed by what Ram had discovered. He advised that he had been in touch with The Broker online, hacking into Ved's own account.

"Impossible," Ved said, defensively.

"Well, it wasn't for me," Ram said. "I got in and you'd better not use your personal terminal again because I've inflicted a virus which is pretty malicious."

Ved finally owned up that he did have a plan in mind whereby he had hoped to trade Ram for Bray and Alice. As angry as Ellie and Jack were, they were also strangely grateful at Ved's hairbrained scheme because he had been trying to deliver Alice back to Ellie - he was touched by all that they had discussed. And was doing it for Jay – as a homage to his late brother, who would have approved of the two loving sisters being reunited.

He quickly realized though that Jay would have totally disapproved of trying to use Ram as a bargaining tool. Also, Bray, who didn't deserve to be treated as a commodity even if he was Zoot's brother and seemed as if he had a large price on his head for any bounty hunters.

"I bet not as high as mine," Ram reflected, with a degree of pride.

"You're something else, Ram," Jack said, amazed at Ram's ego - as was Ellie, even Ved.

Ram pointed to his head and said it wasn't a question of being egotistical but simply that he had a plan in mind. If it worked, he'd be a hero. But if it failed, then his value would rise dramatically. Along with probably Ellie, Jack and Ved's.

"Thank you very much," Ellie said. "Don't involve Jack and me in anything."

"I reckon it's our only chance," Ram stated.

"What have you got in mind?" Ved asked, in growing curiosity.

Ram said it would be too complicated to explain in any great detail. But he was sure that Ellie, Jack and Ved would geek out. And that he needed their assistance. The only place capable of mounting his plan was his old Techno base.

Jack, Ellie and Ved realized that they probably had no choice and travelled with Ram back to the industrial complex where Ram said they didn't have much time and that he needed all the help he could get in setting up.

He opened a small unit in the warehouse area, pressed a switch, and a screen descended, covering the entirety of one wall. Ved was amazed and had never known it was there before. Ram then assembled a long set of tables, assisted by Ellie, Jack and Ved, on a raised dais in front of the screen and said that he needed some laptops with a bit more grunt, capable of doing what he had in mind.

Ram then proceeded to adapt the software, keying in codes - realizing that each computer needed to be upgraded - and relied on his expertise from designing a digital version of whatever he wanted in the virtual world during his reign over The Technos.

Jack, Ellie and Ved watched, astonished, as Ram worked feverishly, manically. All being very literate technologically, they understood some of what Ram was doing but certainly not the software he was writing, with codes buried deep within the recesses of only Ram's mind.

"I'll tell you what," Ram said enthusiastically. "Why don't you get the rest of your Virts here and I'll give them a masterclass in the world of technology and what it's really capable of. And I'm not just talking about gaming or reality space. But something a little more mind-blowing, shall we say?"

Ved rounded up The Virts, who grouped together on chairs behind the raised dais, and watched Ved, Jack and Ellie - either side of Ram, who tilted his head from side to side, preparing for whatever he had in mind, cracking his knuckles.

"Now, just follow my instructions through each phase and then we'll get along just fine," Ram said. "And you'd better hold onto your hats – and keyboards. We're in for an awesome ride!"

He laughed almost manically as he typed in data on his own keyboard before exclaiming, in mounting excitement – "Good!... Good!... Now, Ved, Ellie and Jack – now that I'm in, I want you all to use this password: b@n@na$9894230.monk#y$419355. jungl82943&.concrete428932.eag!emounta!n."

Ved, Ellie and Jack typed the data into their computers, trying somehow to keep up with the information they were given.

"Everyone in?" Ram asked.

Jack and Ved confirmed that they seemed to be, but Ellie was having difficulty.

Ram leaned to his side, glancing at the screen, at the digital stars disguising the letters and numbers and noticed that there was one missing – '42832.eag!emounta!n'. I think you've missed out the 9 at the end - so strike the last four numbers and type in again 428932.eag!emounta!n."

Ellie did as instructed, then nodded, confirming that she had also been able to login.

Jack stole an incredulous look at Ram. "How the hell did you remember all that?"

"Let me take a minute and run my disc data manager in my brain. Then I'll be able to confirm that my memory functions are operating efficiently and effectively," Ram replied, laughing intently at his own joke.

Suddenly, the ominous visual of the colossus *K.A.M.I* computer in Eagle Mountain filled the entire screen on the wall ahead of them, with an intrusive, ominous presence – its 'eyes' emitting piercing beams of green light, seemingly bearing into not only everyone present – but into the depths of their very souls.

"IDENTIFY YOURSELF," the Eagle Mountain *K.A.M.I* said.

"It's Ram," Ram replied.

"AND WHAT ABOUT THE OTHERS?" the *K.A.M.I* Eagle Mountain computer probed.

Ram's expression clouded and he typed in more data on his keyboard feverishly. "You can't actually see us, can you *K.A.M.I?*" he asked.

"NOT NOW," the *K.A.M.I* Eagle Mountain system said softly, the voice echoing around the cavernous industrial warehouse. "BECAUSE YOU HAVE DISABLED MY SYSTEMS."

"Sorry about that," Ram replied, winking at Ved, Ellie and Jack, who gazed open-mouthed, as did the audience of Virts, totally geeking out on what they were witnessing.

"I need to check out the systems in your sister, *K.A.M.I*," Ram said. "You can log off and relax. Because I want to connect with the main prototype. The *K.A.M.I* system located – where is it - in Project Eden?"

"ACCESS DENIED. ACCESS DENIED. ACCESS DENIED," the *K.A.M.I* Eagle Mountain system repeated, over and over again.

"Yeah, right! That's what you think," Ram responded. But there was no disdain in the tone, only a manic excitement as he yelled, "Just like the old days, eh, Ved, boyo? Stand by Ellie and Jack. It's time to unleash the dogs of war!"

He typed in a growing frenzy on the keyboard, laughing hysterically, like some arch-villain, a madman, intent on destroying not only the world but the galaxies, let alone the entire universe.

CHAPTER THIRTY

From the haunted and anxious expression on The Selector's face, it was apparent he hadn't arrived at the *Lakeside Resort* to bring good news. Amber had initially dreaded that he was going to tell them something untoward had happened to Bray and Alice but was still nevertheless deeply concerned by what The Selector was revealing, causing him to have difficulty controlling his nervous tics.

"This is a dark day in our history," The Selector said, meeting all the Mall Rats in the main lounge. "Our hallowed and revered Creator has been struck down by a vicious illness. She wants to see you, Amber, and Tai San before her time on this Earth runs out."

"What do you mean 'runs out'?" Amber said, mirroring what all the Mall Rats were feeling. "She appeared totally fine when she visited."

"Indeed. Certainly not now. And I wonder - why?" The Selector asked inquisitively, suspiciously.

"What's that supposed to mean?" Trudy asked.

The Selector explained that The Creator had faced a rapid decline in her health when she had returned to The Vault. And he was there to personally escort Amber and Tai San to see her. Immediately.

"In the meantime, as Deputy of The Collective I will be the temporary Leader. So I suggest you follow my instructions. And my first order, pending a formal enquiry – is to place you, Lex, on house arrest."

"What? That's outrageous! I haven't done anything!" Lex shouted.

"Then you have nothing to fear," The Selector said. "But I know our Supreme Council will want some answers if The Creator dies as to why you took her out on the lake alone. Some might wonder if you had tried to drown her. Or even if she picked up some bacteria in the water."

"That was her idea to take a boat trip – not mine!"

"I'm not here to adjudicate on any evidence, Lex. That is the duty of the Supreme Council. My priority right now is to insist that The Creator's wishes are carried out. Especially if it is indeed her last wishes," he added, his voice cracking slightly with emotion,

* * *

Amber and Tai San were escorted through all security check points at Project Eden and raced down the long, metallic corridors of The Vault, accompanied by The Selector and the inner sanctum guards, the group walking briskly at pace, breaking out into a run at times, to quickly get to The Collective leader.

Tai San and Amber had both been shocked that the reason for Cami's sudden illness levied by The Selector had been aimed at Lex and knew it was a false claim. There had either been a genuine misunderstanding or it was a deliberate charge looking to pin the blame on him, for whatever reason. If someone was hoping to frame Lex for any tragedy that might occur if anything did indeed happen to Cami, then both Tai San and

Amber knew that all the Mall Rats would do everything in their power to prevent Lex from becoming a scapegoat in some future hearing of the Supreme Council.

They also didn't trust The Selector in the slightest – and his seemingly self-proclaimed reluctance to take over the leadership of The Collective in light of what was happening. The thought of that situation evoked nothing but dread.

Tai San, Amber and The Selector rushed into the inner sanctum of The Creator while the guards stood either side of the huge doors.

Cami was laying stretched out on a bed, the Surgeon General and her medic team attending their leader, checking monitors on various machines displaying Cami's vital signs.

"What's happened!?" Amber said.

"It's difficult to know. So far, we have been unable to identify a specific diagnosis," the Surgeon General advised.

Cami was murmuring in pain, her body dripping wet with perspiration, beads of sweat on her brow, the medics gently patting it with a facecloth.

"She's got a fever, her temperature's sky high," the Surgeon General said, looking at the monitors of the medical equipment. "I can't understand why the computer monitoring system is not picking anything up. I think it's possibly a virulent strain of staphylococcus that's invaded her system, hopefully not her blood stream. It's like she is being poisoned somehow."

The Surgeon General explained that Cami had been given medication to try and stabilize her but so far there hadn't been any improvement in Cami's health – but the opposite, a complete decline.

Suddenly, the inner sanctum was placed in total darkness, followed by a pulsing alarm and red-flashing warning lights, along with a voice belonging to an adult female.

"RED ALERT. ALL FORMS OF LIFE FORCE D-Y-I-N-G."

The voice lowered in tone and pitch to a deep voice as if the occupant of the voice was also dying.

Auxiliary emergency lighting was automatically activated, casting looming, eerie shadows and illuminating The Selector, the Surgeon General and her medics, and Amber and Tai San, who gazed around, in mounting panic.

"That voice. Who is it!?" Amber said. "More importantly – where's it coming from?"

"ACCESS DENIED. ACCESS DENIED. ACCESS DENIED. MALICIOUS VIRUS QUARANTINED. LIFE SYSTEMS ATTEMPTING TO BE RESTORED," the voice boomed again through a range of security speakers in the ceiling. The pulsing red lights suddenly stopped, as did the alarm. The auxiliary light faded, replaced by the normal lighting systems coming on again.

The Surgeon General gazed at the blips on the medical monitors. "That's interesting," she said. "The vital signs are stabilizing."

"What is this? Are you saying the computer monitoring systems had something to do with it?" The Selector asked, in a mixture of confusion and concern.

"It certainly seems that way," the Surgeon General reflected, as confused as all the others who were present.

"It must be overriding our normal online systems, monitoring The Creator's personal microchip," the Surgeon General surmised.

"You're not seriously suggesting that a computer has been trying to harm Cami?" Amber probed.

The Selector gazed suspiciously at the Surgeon General. Tai San's antennae picked up that he was communicating something unsaid when the Surgeon General replied, overly casually:-

"Could be… could be. I think it might be wise for our technology teams to investigate. I'll go and brief them, shall I, Selector?"

"Urgently," The Selector instructed.

The Surgeon General, followed by her medic team, left and Cami spoke softly, regaining consciousness and recognizing Amber and Tai San.

"Amber… Tai San… How good of you to visit."

Their presence gave Cami renewed energy, determination. She asked if The Selector would take Tai San to the biodome to obtain some herbs which she believed might help make her feel better. And it would give Cami some time to speak with Amber – alone.

The Selector was reluctant to agree to the request, preferring that The Creator rest and conserve her energy. Cami reassured The Selector that she was fine.

Though he was opposed, The Selector obsequiously bowed his head in a display of respect and left Amber alone in the room, indicating for Tai San to follow him.

* * *

Tai San focused on the multitude of herb varieties growing inside the vast glass panels of the biodome. Eden was aptly named – every time Tai San had visited the dome, it felt like she was in some garden of Eden, lush with plant life, a self-contained world of natural wonders, a peaceful and quiet environment protecting the plants within from the chaos and uncertainty of the outside world inside the mammoth, hermetically-sealed dome.

There was little time to enjoy being around the plant life, however. Tai San's mission there was urgent. She was looking for specific herbs and hoped she would be able to get them in time to help the dire situation with Cami's health.

Cami clearly knew the benefits of homeopathic medicine, Tai San thought, as she gathered up a range of various herbs and spices and plants because Tai San had been raised to practice alternative medicine rather than conventional.

She had already retrieved some large amounts of Coneflower, Goldenseal, Ginseng and Ginger – and although Cami hadn't requested, Tai San thought she should pick some Elderflower.

The Selector had been by her side constantly since he escorted her to the biodome.

As Tai San gathered her supplies, The Selector seemed more interested in discussing the future he envisaged after Cami's death, with him taking over her place as permanent leader.

He hoped Tai San would have a part in that future – and be by his side. Perhaps to head research into plant life, herbs, spices, medicine - anything she wanted. It was apparent to Tai San, not that she needed further convincing, that The Selector was still personally enamoured of her – which was bordering on an obsessional level.

It had been a deeply unpleasant experience for Tai San. She hated having him around, the insincere flattery and compliments he was paying her, especially when his 'former' leader, as he intimated, was on her deathbed.

The Selector seemed to have everything worked out. A plan of some kind, which involved Tai San. He hinted that if Tai San felt Lex still had a place in her heart – he hoped she would come to accept The Selector, as she did Lex, in the future.

Tai San had no option but to listen to The Selector, to have him follow her, like a moth to a flame, wherever she went in the biodome while she collected the herbs and spices. He certainly admired her skills.

The Selector's 'skills', however, were more to do with manipulation and treachery, Tai San thought, faking a smile at him as he complimented her on how beautiful her eyes were, the latest of many praises he had accorded her. She didn't want to encourage his advances or lead him on – or let him know, of course, what she was truly thinking. But she didn't want to totally alienate him at this vulnerable state in time.

"That's kind of you to say," Tai San replied, at his compliment.

She turned to pick more Elderflower, then advised that she was ready to leave. "I've finally been able to get everything that I need," she advised.

"So have I," The Selector informed her – and leaned in, to give Tai San a kiss.

She recoiled, and The Selector's charm was suddenly replaced by an ice-cold smile. "Do you not find me – attractive?"

"I'm in a relationship with Lex," Tai San replied, not knowing what else to say - with the truth being that rather than attractive, the only thing he evoked in her was repulsion.

"Tai San, you are not only a beautiful woman but a spiritual one. And a clever one as well. And I would hate if anything ever happened to you or Lex. So a piece of advice:- whenever you're making any decisions, just make sure they're not ones you might one day come to regret."

He smiled benevolently, Tai San aware of the veiled threat.

The Selector drew her closer again and feeling totally repulsed, like she was going to be sick, Tai San accepted the kiss, trying somehow not to vomit into The Selector's mouth.

"You don't know how long I've been wanting to do that," The Selector said, releasing Tai San from his embrace.

"We need to get back to Cami immediately," Tai San urged.

The Selector moved forward, as if he was going to embrace and kiss her again.

The lights flickered, the electricity surging once more – and the biodome was plunged into darkness.

When the auxiliary lighting went on less than a minute later, The Selector was enraged. There was no sign of Tai San anywhere. She had gone.

* * *

Amber tenderly wiped Cami's brow with the cloth she had just rinsed in cold water, hoping to lower the high temperature that Cami was affected by.

She was joined by Tai San, who had returned from the biodome and was now preparing a selection of herbs and plants, grinding them in a bowl to a pulp, to produce liquid.

Tai San worked quickly, suspecting that before long The Selector would return, and she hoped that The Creator might be the one giving instructions to the guards waiting outside the entrance doors, rather than anyone taking orders from The Selector - if indeed they were all in the midst of a nefarious coup.

The Creator of The Collective was conscious, mostly, but seemed to be passing in and out of it often, sometimes lying still, almost silent – making Amber and Tai San fear the worst, that she might have slipped from this world.

Tai San couldn't say for sure if any of the computer monitoring systems had anything to do with it as the Surgeon General had implied earlier. Tai San suspected that a possible cause could have something to do with the Elderberries she had observed in the containers in the inner sanctum. They were exquisite but needed to be cooked. If eaten raw, then they were highly dangerous and could poison the system.

Amber felt she and Tai San needed to give Cami hope. Something to live for. The belief that she could survive her illness and fully recover.

While Tai San had been away in the biodome, in an attempt to make sure Cami remained awake, Amber had engaged her in conversation, asking Cami questions about her past. She had spoken affectionately of her mother and the work she had done as an evolutionary biologist at The Vault, helping to conserve the rare and endangered species which had been brought there, not only the plants but the many forms of animal life.

Amber probed more about what Cami had revealed regarding not being close to her mother. Cami had advised that her mother was often away due to work commitments or attending lectures at conferences around the world. Cami would often be left on her own, under the care of her nanny, and absorbed herself in reading a range of literature, studying her mother's selection of books and research – many of which dealt with themes of evolution.

But it wasn't all scholarly pursuits. Cami's other passion she had developed was online gaming – and it offered a chance to interact and meet interesting people from all over the world. Being mostly introverted and reclusive, Cami never had any friends as such and she had often found the world of technology and computers to be a refuge.

Being online provided her with a way to interact with others. She had found it fascinating hearing different opinions to her own, learning about the lives of others and viewing it as a living experiment, a form of sociology almost, as she got a sense of the 'culture' of those she interacted with – what they believed in, how they filled their days, what their existence meant to them.

Tai San crossed to the bed with a small spoon.

"Let's try and get her to sit up and sip on this," Tai San said, indicating the liquid concoction she had ground in the bowl.

Amber gently aided Cami, fluffing the pillows behind her back. "There we go," Amber said, gently. "Now please try and take a few sips of this. Tai San has prepared it and we think it might help you feel better."

Cami sipped but winced occasionally in distress, her body fighting whatever illness was within.

"Try and take some more, Cami," Tai San said. "I'm sure it will help make you feel better."

"We're both here with you," Amber continued. "Try and take as much as you can and think about how you'd like life to be, fifty years from now. Imagine you're telling us about your life then – and all the things that you had done."

Cami continued sipping on the medicine and although her voice was still weak, she spoke, letting Amber and Tai San know how she wished to fall in love – and had never really thought about it so far ahead. But if she could, she hoped to be a mother, even a grandmother, and to have helped rebuild not only society but make her mark on it. And that maybe she, Tai San and Amber would have become firm friends by then, growing old, becoming the first of the next generation of adults who had survived the previous generation who had all perished before.

Amber and Tai San were encouraged by what they were hearing. Not solely Cami's dreams but the fact that she was remaining conscious.

Cami's illness brought back painful memories of those who had perished during the height of the pandemic, when they would never wake, their ravaged bodies giving up not long after they lost the spirit and will to live on.

Amber agreed with Tai San's hypothesis that spiritually - the power of the mind was so very important whereby the human condition relies on the need to have something to live for.

"We can make it happen, together," Amber encouraged, while Cami sipped more of the liquid Tai San was offering from the spoon.

"After all, if you keep that dream to yourself, it might forever stay a dream," Tai San added. "But if you share it with others, they can help you make that dream become a reality."

Unbeknownst to Amber and Tai San – they were being observed from several angles, all at once, by surveillance cameras, not required for security but the source of live feeds which were being monitored several levels down, in the depths of The Vault, in the very lowest level in a highly-classified area that The Collective leader was the only human in this generation to know about it – and of what was located inside the secured section.

The live feeds were linked into a highly powerful system with an ability to process trillions of calculations per second, built of the most advanced prototype components humanity had constructed before the collapse of its civilization, powered by its own energy source – the sound and images that had been digitized and input into its vast memory banks had been quickly processed and assimilated by the network of central processing units that formed the hardware and system which hosted the artificial intelligence of the *K.A.M.I* supercomputer.

It was the original prototype to its sister, housed in Eagle Mountain, and yet another one in Arthurs Air Force Base. But at the height of the pandemic, it had been upgraded. And eventually after the demise of the adults, Cami had adapted some of the software herself.

It had been nicknamed after the little girl who was the child of the mother who had played an initial part in its development, applying biological principles and evolutionary theory to the self-aware software so it would have the ability to learn, to adapt and evolve – and in so doing, given life, in digital form, to the *Knowledge Artificial Machine Intelligence* mainframe computer that controlled every aspect of The Vault and Eden's infrastructure.

The human Cami had grown up into a capable and confident teenager – she had worked closely with the supercomputer that bore the moniker of her name, getting its advice, channeling its resources, the digital *K.A.M.I* system having been pivotal in the success of The Collective, being shaped in its development and education, learning from The Collective leader. It, too, in tandem with its human companion, *K.A.M.I*, had adapted and evolved, developing an identity of its own, an awareness.

And it had paid attention to the advice Tai San and Amber had been giving its grievously ill 'friend'. The only companion the *K.A.M.I* system had ever known since the adults perished.

Now, the system was concerned what might occur if the human Cami might die. And it was running programmes, believing that the sister *K.A.M.I* in Eagle Mountain was a threat, trying to attack not only the human Cami but the *K.A.M.I* system itself. And it knew exactly what to do.

As Tai San gave Cami the last of the herbal juice, all three froze at the sudden intrusion of the alarm again. The inner sanctum fell into darkness. Amber, Tai San and Cami were illuminated by a pulsing light as they listened to the computer *K.A.M.I* system's voice booming through the speakers – again, the voice phased slightly now, but still very clearly a female adult's voice:-

"PREPARE TO EVACUATE. PREPARE TO EVACUATE. PREPARE TO EVACUATE. ALL DEFENCE SYSTEMS ACTIVE."

The guards each side of the front entrance doors leapt as a mammoth metal door within the ceiling hurled down, with a gigantic thud, the metallic noise echoing around and around the inner sanctum.

"What was that!?" Amber asked, panic-stricken, gazing around the semi-darkness and blocking her ears slightly, as were Tai San and Cami, at the deafening pulsating alarm, which was becoming louder and louder.

"We seem to be at the highest security threat level," Cami said, weakly. "Which means that the highest form of defence mechanisms will have been activated. Including the backup security doors to The Vault. Fortunately, no one will ever be able to get in. But there is a great danger, that unfortunately we might never equally be able to get out."

Tai San, Cami and Amber exchanged terrified glances at the prospect that they were now seemingly entombed, cut off from the world, possibly forever.

CHAPTER THIRTY-ONE

Ebony was glad when darkness fell. She was taking cover in bushes bordering the deserted, bleak highway. Emma was asleep.

Ebony had earlier recommended that they stay hidden until nightfall and speculated with Emma, wondering if they had indeed been set up by The Gamesmaster, suspecting that their current plight was yet another test. So far, they hadn't encountered any sign of another human being since arriving at the far end of the lake, where they were to have been met by someone, according to The Gamesmaster, to provide further instruction.

When the dawn had broken, Ebony noticed a figure in the distance and asked Emma to stay put, under cover, while she investigated to check if the figure was the planned contact.

But it had become apparent when the figure became more visible, as Ebony approached, that the figure was a farm worker, probably a slave, toiling the land, as the sun rose.

What disturbed Ebony was that in noticing her, he seemed in utter shock when he recognized her, treating her like some kind of superstar.

"Is it really you? Ebony – from The Cube!?" the farm worker asked.

Ebony wasn't going to confirm or deny for fear of giving any information away. She did enquire tentatively, "Are you 'my contact' who I'm supposed to meet?"

"I don't know what you mean," the farm worker replied, with a sudden sense of unease.

"Ever heard of The Gamesmaster?" Ebony asked.

"Please. I beg you. If you're looking for a contestant - I don't want any part of it!" the farm worker screamed, in total fear as he ran as far away as could in utter distress.

Ebony watched him recede into the distance, then returned to where Emma was in hiding and recommended that they stay undercover for the rest of the day and then travel under the cover of night.

The problem though was which way to go. They agreed that they only had four options: being north, south, east, west.

Suddenly, Ebony and Emma were both bathed in the glare of the headlights from an approaching vehicle and recoiled, moving deeper into the bushes. To their relief, the vehicle sped past. It was a military vehicle, a large truck which suddenly screeched to a skidding stop and reversed at high speed.

"Let's get out of here! They don't look too friendly!" Ebony whispered in an undertone to Emma and led her further into the bush before being easily and quickly seized by four guards, who brought them to the back of the vehicle.

Ebony climbed in, assisting Emma, and was stunned to discover Bray, Alice, Tiffany and Shannon were also in the back.

Tiffany and Shannon rushed to give their sister a huge hug while Bray tried somehow to reassure her.

"It's alright, Emma. It's alright. You're totally safe," Bray said.

Ebony gazed in utter disbelief and confusion, struggling to reconcile what she was seeing with her very own eyes.

"I never thought I'd see you again, Ebony," Alice said exuberantly.

"That makes two of us," Ebony replied, steadying herself as the vehicle sped away. "What the hell's going on!?"

* * *

"We've got to get you out of here," Ryan said to Lex.

They were in the main lounge at the *Lakeside Resort* with Salene and Trudy.

May was in Amber's room, keeping an eye on baby Jay, who was fast asleep. She was also watching Sammy, Lottie and Brady, who had been brought to the room, and had been reading the younger Mall Rats stories.

"You've always been there for me, Lex. And if anyone wants to lay a finger on you, then they'll have to get past me first," Ryan said.

"The way The Selector was speaking, I think it might be more than a finger Lex can expect," Trudy said.

"Well, he'll soon discover where he can shove his finger and anything else. No way I'm being set up. Appreciate the support, Ryan. I owe you one."

"I hope Amber and Tai San are alright," Salene said, uneasily and suddenly cried out as the resort was plunged into total darkness.

"What's happening!?" Trudy yelled.

"That's what I'd like to know. Something's going down, you can bet on it!" Lex exclaimed.

The emergency auxiliary lighting cast a dim glow, outlining Storm, arriving with his security detail. "Everybody okay?" he asked.

The Mall Rats advised that they were all fine but were becoming increasingly concerned when Storm informed them that all the water, for some reason, had been switched off, the electricity grid seemed to have been compromised, and the plumbing was out, as well as his communication devices, which illustrated there were some problems with their computer network.

Trudy was keen to go and check on May and the children, as indeed were Salene, Ryan and Lex.

Storm tried to reassure them that it was probably just a glitch and nothing to worry about.

"I wouldn't be too sure about that," Lex stated, noting beams of light cutting a path through the darkness and the glass entrance doors to the resort as a militia truck screeched to a stop in the driveway.

Then all the Mall Rats stared open-mouthed as Bray, Alice, Ebony, Shannon and Tiffany led Emma through the doors, followed by guards.

Lex and Ryan immediately leapt into action with the security detail already at the resort but Storm ordered his team to stand down, that no action was needed. For the time being, at least.

* * *

The streets in Eden were crowded. Ever since the first power outage, the inhabitants who lived there had been anxious and unsettled at the disruption that had descended upon their lives.

Now, there was no electricity at all and like the problems at the *Lakeside Resort*, there was no water or plumbing or Internet or communication systems.

Throughout the lands, the surviving generations since the adults' demise no longer lived in a digital world but mostly an analogue one. Some were fortunate to enjoy modern conveniences such as all at Eden, thanks to an ability to have hooked into the once highly-classified UNANET system - which had been discovered to have remained in existence in the event of any post-apocalyptic event, arranged initially at a tense time in the history of the Cold War, many years before the virus descended. Other survivors and many tribes across all the lands lived an almost primitive existence reminiscent of the Dark Ages.

Now Eden had, for some reason, been plunged into total darkness, barring a few battery-powered flashlights that some of the guards were wielding to guide people and which were used by medics in the hospital so they could illuminate their way as they evacuated the patients and young mothers-to-be from the buildings where they had been in their care.

There had never been anything like it in Eden - for so long a place of order, stability, routine, efficiency. The community had mysteriously been struck down, its interconnected infrastructure under siege, grinding the apparatus of so much of what the residents depended on to a halt.

A collective feeling of panic, uncertainty prevailed. Rumours were circulating. Suspicious talk of a coup taking place or that Eden was under assault from outside forces, the first stage in an inevitable invasion by rival power blocks. Others felt that they could have displeased or offended Zoot – brought upon his wrath, the mighty spirit of Zoot punishing them somehow – and that this could only be the start of a new divinely-interventioned apocalypse, heralding the end of their days.

Further down the lake, The Selector hid in his lodge and was struggling to control his nervous tics, breathing in through his nose and out through his mouth to try and somehow calm himself.

He was expecting a coup but not exactly unfolding in such a way and he couldn't grasp who might be responsible. Or why it was all occurring.

* * *

Unknown to all in the faraway lands of Eden – Ram inadvertently had a hand in it. Though he wasn't quite totally responsible and didn't even know so at that time.

All he was aware of so far was that he had successfully managed to hack into the Eagle Mountain *K.A.M.I* system, giving him a pathway to evading firewalls protecting the main colossus *K.A.M.I* system at Eden where he was now attempting to attack various programmes, shutting them down, going directly into the core operating system, altering lines of code, breaking the software apart and the infrastructure systems that were dependent upon it, from working.

"How are we doing?" Jack asked.

"I'll let you know when I've figured it out myself," Ram said absently.

"Is there anything we can do to help?" Ellie asked.

"If I can't work it out - then you've got no chance."

"No need to be like that," Jack said, coming to Ellie's defence. But she shook her head slightly, indicating for Jack not to pursue it, aware that Ram was not only preoccupied but seemed agitated, not quite believing what he was seeing on his computer screen. The images also visible on the mammoth screen covering the entire wall - which had elicited a gasp of surprise from The Virts sitting behind Ellie, Jack, Ram and Ved on the main dais.

"What's all that stuff?" Jack said, confused.

"Software data. What do you think it is!?" Ram snapped, irritably before glaring at Ved. "Do you know anything about this?"

Ved was eagerly casting his eyes across the complex lettering and numbers filling the wall on the screen and clearly was struggling to assimilate it.

"No! I haven't got a clue!" Ved said.

Ram typed in more details on his keyboard and gazed at the text on his screen and covering the entire wall, yelling panicked instructions:- "Ellie – I need an urgent firewall in subsection 31A. Move it, move it! Jack – you'd better take a look at ports 14 to 28 and get a few firewalls in there, too! As quick as you can, Jack! Ved, check out the interpositive and internegative bisections bordering the mega data in article 2."

"Is everything… alright, Ram?" Ellie asked nervously, aware that Ram was becoming increasingly alarmed, almost terror-stricken.

And suddenly, footage of Ram appeared on the screen. Ram, in days gone by, trapped in his virtual reality wheelchair on the garbage dump, thrusting his hands in the air, drool spewing from his mouth, and screaming in pure disbelief, "This isn't reality space – this is R-E-A-L!!!"

"What the hell's going on?" Ved yelled, fearfully.

"What do you think!? We've been hacked!"

"By who!?" Jack asked, in utter anguish. "It can't be the *K.A.M.I* system in Eagle Mountain because I've set up a firewall – unless you made a mistake with the codes?"

"No, no mistake, Jack! The hack isn't from Eagle Mountain! I reckon it's coming from its sister, the *K.A.M.I* prototype in Project Eden!" Ram said, unable to believe his own thought process.

"So, what does it all mean?" Jack asked, in mounting panic.

"That *K.A.M.I* prototype not only has artificial intelligence. But it's self-aware. It seems to be not only attacking the system in Eagle Mountain but it's now ripping apart all my personal hard drives. We're going to have to shut down because I reckon we've got a hell of a virus inflicted on all our core systems!"

* * *

Back on the streets of Eden, the inhabitants were still out in force, many now carrying flaming torches to help them see in the darkness. All screamed out in unison as a voice suddenly boomed through the community loudspeakers. Again, the voice was soft, soothing, that of an adult female.

"THIS IS *K.A.M.I*," the voice said, the tone slightly phased, digitized. "I – THE CREATOR – AM ILL. A COUP HAS BEEN INSTIGATED AGAINST ME. AND I NEED YOUR HELP IN MY TIME OF NEED. IF I DO NOT SURVIVE THE ACTIONS OF MY USURPER, WE WILL NOT ADAPT AND EVOLVE."

Suddenly the voice stopped, replaced with the frenzied shouting of Zoot: "*Rise up!! Take control!!!!!*"

The crowds gazed around, confused, and cast glances up at the heavens where the voice seemed to originate from, reverberating and echoing all around.

The crowd recoiled, totally panic-stricken, as images of Zoot appeared on the walls of the many buildings, images derived from Ram's reality space programmes of Zoot - seemingly resurrected, screaming manically, arms aloft: "*Power and Chaos! Power and Chaos! Power and Chaos!*"

* * *

Back in Ram's old Techno headquarters, Ram, Ellie, Jack and Ved, along with the Virt spectators, stared open-mouthed at the same images on the screen of Zoot, imploring all to rise up and take control, to inflict Power and Chaos.

"Did you do that?" Jack screamed, above the noise.

"You don't understand it, do you?" Ram said, almost unable to believe it himself. "I think we've not just unleashed the dogs of war – but our friend, the *K.A.M.I* system in Eagle Mountain, seems to be in a battle with the prototype colossus *K.A.M.I* system in Project Eden."

"Are you saying the computers are fighting each other!?" Ellie asked, panic-stricken.

"Not just each other – but us as well. All my drives… they're being used against us," Ram said, clutching his head with his hands. "Oh God – what have I done!?"

* * *

In the inner sanctum of The Vault, sealed off from the inhabitants at Eden, Cami led Amber and Tai San into the lower levels, Cami inserting codes to enable them to proceed through the semi-darkness, the three of them illuminated in the glow of a pulsing red light.

Finally, reaching the lowest level, Cami led Tai San and Amber into a cavernous area.

"Hello, *K.A.M.I*," Cami said, calmly to the mainframe colossus system, its infrastructure towering way above Tai San, Amber and the human Cami, its lights blinking, hard drives whirring, its bank of monitors showing various images, such as the evacuations occurring all over the world at the height of the pandemic and news anchors of broadcasters of the time stating that "*Authorities are appealing for calm throughout the evacuation process.*"

Other monitors displayed the enigmatic Area 51, the source of so many conspiracy theories in the old world. Another monitor, pictures of empty, ghostly streets - a patrol vehicle, its windows darkened, advising any stragglers still in their homes, through its loudspeaker on top of the vehicle, that "*Code 1, civil isolation was now in effect.*"

On another monitor, much to Tai San and Amber's great concern, an image showing a range of surface to air missiles from the adult days - with data appearing on the monitor confirming that nuclear warheads were on standby. And requesting verification with everything being on high alert - simply requiring the final instruction, that the system was locked and loaded, ready to go.

"Is that image on that monitor what I think it is!?" Amber asked, uneasily.

"Don't worry. It's from the old world and obsolete. *K.A.M.I*'s just cleaning out its files, indexing and self-regulating."

"WHAT ARE YOU DOING HERE, CHILD? YOU SHOULD BE IN BED," *K.A.M.I* reprimanded.

Cami was still weak from her illness but the remedy Tai San had offered was already showing positive results and that she was alert – though slightly embarrassed. "That's my mother's voice. I programmed it myself. So you'll have to excuse *K.A.M.I.* It seems a bit confused right now."

All the images on the monitors implanted into the mammoth superstructure of the colossal mainframe computer disappeared and were replaced by a satellite orbiting the earth.

Each monitor emitted sounds of a variety of voices overlapping in various languages through which Amber and Tai San recognized the English element, "ATTENTION. THIS IS A PRE-RECORDED MESSAGE. IF YOU ARE LISTENING TO THIS, THE ONLY HOPE FOR HUMANITY LIES WITH YOU. WHOEVER YOU ARE."

Amber and Tai San gazed dumbfounded, recalling the mysterious time they first visited Eagle Mountain. They had only been on the upper levels at that point and had no idea even that the Eagle Mountain *K.A.M.I* computer system had ever existed. Jack, though, in the upper level had managed to log on to the computer grid accessed to a signal from a satellite circling Earth.

They had never been able to find the significance of the message. And didn't know exactly what it all meant right now. But the satellite images they were watching and the message they were listening to - the very same one they had heard so long before at Eagle Mountain - seemed to be almost like a talisman, which had led them not only to Eden but the human Cami, the very Creator herself.

* * *

A crowd of fanatical Zoot followers carrying flaming torches arrived outside the *Lakeside Resort* chanting, "Power and Chaos! Power and Chaos! Power and Chaos!"

Inside, the doors had been barred and were guarded by Storm and his detail. Lex, Ryan, Alice and Ebony were with them, ready to fight shoulder to shoulder, which would be a challenging task because they were so outnumbered by the crowd growing in size, it seemed, with each passing second.

Salene and May had locked themselves in a room to safeguard baby Jay, Brady, Lottie, Sammy, Emma, Shannon and Tiffany.

Bray led Trudy through a maintenance hatch and both moved stealthily across the rooftop towards the entrance.

They were both noticed by the crowd and some members pointed ecstatically, "It's the brother of Zoot, Bray! And The Supreme Mother!"

Bray asked, "Are you sure you're up to this, Trudy?"

Trudy nodded, braced herself and stood by Bray on the rooftop as they began addressing the assembly below, who all fell silent in reverence.

But none had ever expected what they were about to hear.

"I'm not going to tell you what you should do," Trudy began, searching for the right words. "And each of you must decide for yourself. But please listen to me. To who exactly I am. I am like you. Each and every one of you. I was a scared teenager who lived through the world crumbling, seeing the people I loved – die – and there was nothing I could do about it. All I could do was try and live – to survive. And in so doing, a lot of rumours and false things have been said about me – and my tribe. We're not special or different. Zoot wasn't some god. And my daughter is a beautiful, innocent, little girl. Neither she or I can perform any 'miracles'. And never should be worshipped. I could be any one of you – standing out there – if fate had turned out differently. And any of you could have been me. I'm not a Supreme Mother. I'm a mother. I'm not connected with any divine magic or mystical powers. I'm me. I'm normal. I'm another human being who just wants to get through each day and try and make tomorrow a little bit better than the day before."

The crowd listened attentively, some seeming as if they might accept what Trudy was saying – but others were clearly unconvinced. One shouted out, "Are you being pressurized to say this, Supreme Mother?" the voice yelled.

"No! No one's pressurizing Trudy whatsoever. And I'm not being pressured as well," Bray called out. "Yes, it's true that I am the brother of Zoot. And I loved him. But he and I… we just had a different ideology. Zoot was a proud warrior and a legend to many. But to me, somehow in this world we've all inherited, he was – and always will be – my brother. Sadly, just someone troubled, who lost their way."

* * *

Back in The Technos' quarters, Ellie, Jack, Ram and Ved - along with the Virt spectators - watched a series of visuals on the screen along the wall, differing images which seemed to be fragmenting and increasing. Images of planets, polar ice caps melting, plague and famine, in barren lands, politicians in the old-world making speeches, Zoot, Ram in his virtual reality paradise.

"Do you reckon those computers are still fighting?" Jack asked, gazing intently at the mammoth screen. "And if so – who's winning?"

"Certainly not us," Ram said.

"What do we do now?" Ellie asked, in growing panic.

Ram tilted his head from side to side, cracked his knuckles, shook his arms slightly and started to type fervently. "We've gotta get back in 'the game'."

"How?" Ved asked, incredulously.

The images on the screen across the wall disappeared and Ram laughed enthusiastically, whooping it up.

"Ellie, Jack and Ved – you'd better listen carefully to all my instructions. It's - game on!"

* * *

The crowd outside the *Lakeside Resort*, along with Bray and Trudy, gazed dumbfoundedly at a series of drones approaching at tremendous speed, zigzagging as if out of control and swooping low over the assembly.

"It's a sign from the Mighty One! He must be avenged!" a voice yelled.

Most of the crowd though were dispersing, some clearly accepting what Trudy and Bray had said and now, mostly concerned about the out of control drones, began to flee, while a few remaining pointed at Lex through the locked glass window doors.

"It's him! He's the one responsible for killing our God, Zoot!"

With the crush, the crowd were able to enter the lobby area and hand to hand combat occurred, with Alice knocking several of the attacking crowd out with single blows. Ebony was equally effective, like the streetfighter she was. So, too, were Ryan and Lex, disposing of opponents amidst a spectacle of swirling, mixed martial arts, kicks.

Trudy returned to watch over the children in her room, giving Salene, May and Bray the chance to enter into the battle, fighting alongside Lex, Ryan, Alice, Ebony, Storm and his guards.

In the midst of battle, each side ducked for cover as an out of control drone sped into the lobby, zigzagging as if attacking anyone left standing, prior to smashing totally out of control through a back window, crash-landing and descending into the lake.

With the superior fighting skills of the Mall Rats and Storm and the guards, the battle ended in no time at all after it began, with the crowd dispersing - Storm, the guards, Alice, May, Salene, Bray, Lex, Ryan and Ebony regained their breath, all exhausted, and exchanged high-fives.

* * *

On the ground level in the inner sanctum, Cami sat at a table typing data into a keyboard, advising Tai San and Amber that some unknown force seemed to have tried to hack the main *K.A.M.I* system. And had succeeded. But now, she had matters under control.

Tai San and Amber exchanged knowing glances, suspecting who might possibly be responsible.

* * *

On the streets of Eden, calmness began to descend as the main lights were switched back on, as were normal supplies of water, plumbing and communication.

Bray and Lex arrived shortly thereafter in a driverless pod vehicle, accompanied by a few of Storm's guards. Storm himself, along with Ebony, Alice and Ryan, were left behind to help guard their fellow Mall Rats and friends in the event of something untoward occurring again.

* * *

Bray and Lex raced to the inner sanctum just as the mammoth security doors slid upwards. But they were stopped by the guards either side of the doors from entering.

"It's alright," Cami said, appearing at the doorway with Amber and Tai San, who rushed into Bray and Lex's arms.

"Thank goodness you're okay!" Amber said, as she tried to contain emotion, hugging Bray tightly.

"We've got a lot to catch up on," Bray said. "What's been going on here?"

"Any sign of The Selector?" Tai San asked, uneasily, as she gripped tightly in her embrace of Lex.

"Not as far as I know," Lex reassured her. "Take it easy. Everything's okay. It's all over."

"But I think it's not the end," Cami replied. "It's only just begun…"

EPILOGUE

The Creator was no more – but Cami lived on.

She had managed to survive the serious infection that she had been deliberately infected with. Tai San's herbal medicine had helped stem the spread. Cami was impressed by Tai San's knowledge of the natural world and alternative medicine, as indeed was the Surgeon General and her team of medics.

Their monitoring system was in total disarray due to Ram inadvertently hacking the *K.A.M.I* system at Eden which checked the health of The Collective, including Cami, and a range of other important elements of society.

The Selector and those loyal to him had been prevented in their bid from toppling Cami and seizing power.

The Selector was arrested, along with the last vestige of Collective renegade warriors who were obedient to him – and their group was transported to the island in the lake where The Cube was located, The Selector's own creation, isolated as it was and well-guarded, becoming his prison pending the future trial that would occur.

He was charged with not solely the attempted murder of Cami but a range of other indignities and crimes he had committed during his position of influence in The Collective, all of which Cami herself had been completely unaware of.

Ironically, he himself was to be the victim of an attempted coup by the resistance, led by his perceived loyal follower, Commander Snake.

The Mall Rats worked with Cami and The Collective on a temporary basis in the aftermath of the attempted coup, feeling that Cami needed assistance to stabilize the society and restructure and rebuild.

The Collective had so much potential for doing good and there needed to be a transition period to assess what would be the best future for all who lived under its auspices previously. History was full of fragmentation and dissension resulting from factions and groups jostling for authority if there was a sudden vacuum following a coup, while The Collective was being rehabilitated. So the Mall Rats felt they had no option but to accept Cami's request for them to work alongside her in the short-term as caretakers in charge.

Cami blamed herself in part for her plight believing that she had been foolish and too trusting to have delegated so much power allowing, inadvertently, The Selector to have brought so much discontent and suffering to so many. Cami genuinely wanted to learn, to improve – to adapt and evolve – and she realized this was something she wouldn't be able to do on her own.

Working with Cami and her Supreme Council, the Mall Rats helped draft a Bill of Rights to facilitate a New Collective who could maintain communication with one another and form a commonwealth of tribes who would establish trade and co-operation, as well as a security alliance, to aid each other and to shape a new world from the ashes of the old.

Those who preferred to stay behind in Eden and live among the new, revitalized – and changed – Collective would have the right to do so. They would hold regular elections, to be monitored by an independent committee, and vote for representatives who would govern them in their own form of parliamentary democracy. Never again would so much power be controlled by one or two individuals, as it had been with The Selector administrating matters.

There would be religious freedoms. A central Zootist faith would certainly never again be encouraged or promoted by the Collective authorities – and Bray was insistent that the truth of his brother be publicly known, hoping it would dispel the myths and legend of Zoot that had otherwise built up and indeed been spread previously by The Collective propaganda.

Those, however, who wanted to believe in any religion would have the right to do so. But all on the Supreme Council had yet to reconcile within the constitution the definition of freedoms within the new laws if they denied the right of any zealots who worshipped Zoot. They would have to ensure it didn't infringe on the lives and freedoms of others, of course, but for true freedom and a society of toleration, there needed to be the right for every person to pursue whatever religion they wanted to follow, just as long as it wasn't unlawful.

The Void was also abolished from existence by the new laws and its inhabitants were to be rehabilitated. Cami was stunned to discover that it had even existed in the first place.

The Broker was arrested and was to be put on trial, given the nefarious activities he had undertaken throughout his trading. And all slaves were set free. Cami had fully sanctioned the agricultural unit in her regime but was totally unaware that the workers were treated in such a repugnant manner.

The new 'blueprint' that had been drafted at Eden was something Amber wanted to roll out and bring back with her when she eventually returned to their home city.

The New Collective of tribes within the constitution would investigate and share access to any knowledge uncovered from the adults' scientific and military bases, such as Arthurs

Air Force Base and Eagle Mountain. It was hoped that any technological resources could be adapted and 'datamined' to help create the foundations for the new civilization all hoped would arise in the aftermath of the adults' demise.

There was so much advanced and powerful technology that could aid the new world in the bases, which Cami had already adapted and utilized. Highly developed drones, automated vehicles, equipment to harvest sustainable renewable energy sources with efficient solar and wind powered batteries, seed banks to restore agriculture and food production, vast quantities of stockpiled medicines that the adults had put away in The Vault, reserves of fuel to power the internal combustion engines of the still functional vehicles from the adult times, which were slowly being phased out, replaced with other forms of energy.

These were all important legacies from the adult era which could help propel future innovation and improve the quality of life for so many - when the world otherwise seemed like it could so easily tip into a primitive, anarchic, new Dark Ages.

There was also the possibility that there could be more secret scientific-military installations around the region and possibly – probably more like – around the world which had been implemented in the old world by the previous generation and their desperate attempts in their last days to create a shelter for themselves, their precious material resources, and to assist a new generation who might survive in the event the previous one did not.

The Collective, Cami revealed, had just been one substantial power block. Some of her scouts and explorers who had adventured out beyond their boundaries into other regions hadn't actually come back – but those who did reported that there were other powerful entities who had risen up from the ruins of the adult world. The Western Alliance, the Eastern

Kingdom – these were growing and supposedly powerful, with ambitions to expand. And one day might invade.

Amber was aware of the quotation from the acclaimed scientist Albert Einstein in the previous generations mentioning that if there ever was a Third World War, then the weapons used in any potential Fourth World War would be sticks and stones, implying a totally apocalyptic situation.

All the Mall Rats, as well as Cami and her Collective, were aware of the need for a united security force with the ability to defend themselves in the event of any future attack or conflict from any dangerous 'megatribe' associations that might be already in existence.

The Mall Rats hoped it would never come to that – how cruel the irony would be if having survived the virus and all the devastating consequences that flowed in the wake of it, if the young people who continued to live in the world without adults didn't become adults themselves due to wiping each other out in a massive, future conflict aiming at paradoxically ensuring their survival.

Jack and Ellie – along with Ram and Ved – travelled to Eden, joining the Mall Rats in the aftermath of the attempted coup.

Ellie was thrilled to be reunited with her beloved sister, Alice.

Amber was sympathetic to Ved and agreed with Bray that they would have to watch over Jay's younger brother not solely as a homage to Jay but because it was the right thing to do. Bray agreed with the sentiment of it but his motive was a little more pragmatic and practical, as he saw it, because he didn't quite trust Ved.

Ram and Cami had communicated online so often in the old world that Ram was stunned to come face to face with The Creator, the leader of The Collective he so feared - given that he was no longer *persona non grata* as a result of him breaking a deal by invading the Mall Rats' home city due to the importance of Eagle Mountain.

Cami seemed totally unlike her online personality. And certainly meeting her in the flesh was a total contradiction to what Ram perceived her to be. He wasn't prepared for such a slight, awkward, slightly shy and introverted person who clearly, from all she was trying to achieve, would never harm anything living – even a fly.

At a celebration party held at the *Lakeside Resort* following the coup, all were aware how engrossed Ram and Cami had been. Ram was especially interested in the technology of the cryogenic chambers, ostensibly a key factor he once thought fuelled The Collective's interests in Eagle Mountain.

He was totally unaware that Cami believed there was a chance that her mother had been shortlisted during the demise of the adults to be amongst the gifted and important adults who had been placed in the chambers.

Cami confirmed that a Collective advance party had been responsible for removing the bodies of the adults who were deceased due to the breakdown of the Eagle Mountain *K.A.M.I* system. The adults had now been given a respectful burial back at Eden and Cami was determined that she would never give up on her search of finding her mother, sure that there was a chance that she might be in a cryogenic chamber somehow, somewhere.

Some of the Mall Rats speculated if Cami might have finally found the true love of her life in the form of Ram. But their connection was purely down to their computer and technological prowess, both respecting each other's vast abilities and knowledge.

Cami actually seemed to be more interested in Ryan, as indeed he was with her. They danced together at the celebrations but were both awkward and shy, so it was early days.

Ryan was keen though to stay at Eden with Alice, who was considering working in the new regime in the agricultural unit with Hawk. Amber was overjoyed to be reunited with the ex-member of the Eco tribe and knew that he would be perfect, bringing much skill and dedication to his role.

Lex was amused that Ryan suddenly wanted to turn his hand at 'gardening', having never shown any interest in the natural world before. Ryan revealed that he finally understood why Tai San was so in tune with Mother Nature, let alone how her skills and abilities and knowledge of herbs and spices brought with it so much exciting information, especially medicinally.

Others thought that the match between Ryan and Cami could be interesting. It wasn't a question of brain and brawn but both could be good for each other, Ryan learning from Cami's high intellect and Cami responding to Ryan's innate gentleness and purity of spirit. So both could be equally strong and good for each other in very profound ways.

May and Salene certainly hoped Ryan would find another love and were considering utilizing the celebrations of the failed coup as a platform for their wedding but decided against it, partly out of respect for Ryan, but also because they didn't want to distract from the jubilant atmosphere as the Mall Rats and The Collective 'partied', celebrating their victory.

A simmering romance which was very apparent, however, was that Trudy and Storm were clearly attracted to each other from the way they were dancing closely and holding each other tightly on the dance floor. It was also early days but Trudy confided to Amber that she felt that she might have found 'her man' in Storm. He, along with his superior, Commander Snake, had been central within the resistance who were planning on taking down The Selector when the time was right. And Trudy was hopeful that Storm and his sister, Charlotte, might consider returning with the Mall Rats to their home city.

Emma, Tiffany and Shannon had determined, however, that they would prefer to stay at Eden and the Mall Rats thought that was a good decision given the infrastructure already in place in the educational system and also that Emma's disabilities would be best served with the support systems in place.

Ebony didn't believe Emma had much disability, however, and felt protective and close to Emma and now her siblings. She was undecided whether or not she would stay at Eden or return to their home city.

Jack and Ellie preferred that Ebony would return so at least it would be a case of 'better the devil you know'. They were never convinced that Ebony had truly changed and wanted to work with the Mall Rats - and didn't exactly trust her.

But they now believed that Ram could be fully trusted, having seen how he had helped them since the invasion. They were especially overwhelmed by his considerable knowledge in technology, mind-blown in fact by the 'mega game' they had experienced at the old Techno base. It wasn't just a question of them 'geeking out' but clearly Ram could be an asset to the tribe and any efforts of interweaving technology.

There was concern within the New Collective concerning The Guardian and Eloise - and the tribe of Zootists who were living in the northern provinces.

Eloise, who was cunning and intelligent, had originally been recruited by The Selector from the ranks of The Privileged tribe, of which she used to be a former member. This was a natural fit for them with her beautiful looks and sharp mind – and the plan, according to Cami, had been that The Selector had apparently recruited Eloise to use her charisma and leadership qualities to act as a foil, a controlling and regulating influence on The Guardian's own undoubted abilities as an orator and proponent of the Zootist faith. Eloise would be the leader, of course, with The Guardian a figurehead, an archbishop to his fellow believers.

Cami pondered on how Eloise, The Guardian and the Zootists would feature in the future – and if at all within The Collective. Probably not.

There were other Mall Rats, of course, still missing. And no news of them had surfaced to date. But the search would go on in the future to try and discover their fate.

Soon, peace and order would be restored at Eden with new laws and institutions of the New Collective to be set up under Cami's leadership – leaving only one thing more for the Mall Rats to do next.

And that was to go back home.

HOME

It was where they belonged. And it felt so good to be back.

Amber walked along the waterfront, the waves in the harbour lapping gently, the gentle breeze and warm sun providing a sense of calm and peace, a relaxing and pleasant atmosphere – the perfect weather conditions mirroring a perfect, potential, pivotal time.

She was walking with Bray, by her side. He was carrying their son, the two of them reminiscing on all the many things they had been through since the last days of the adults. They remembered the first time they had met, at the mall. The first kiss they shared. The pain of loss Bray had felt when he thought Amber had died and been taken from him. Their reunion when he found, to his joy, that Amber still lived. The day Amber discovered she was pregnant with their child. The agonizing moment she thought she would have to raise that child alone after Bray had been taken from her following the invasion of the city by Ram and his Technos.

Like the tide, their lives had ebbed and flowed. They had been apart, fate often stepping in to separate them – but by their own endeavours and in 'never giving up or giving in', they had always found a way to return to each other and be together.

After all they had experienced with Cami, The Selector and The Collective – and with the establishment of the New Collective that succeeded the old, and the commonwealth of independent tribes – Amber was feeling positive about the future for her, Bray, their son and so many others in society.

They had come so close, all of them, so many times to face the prospect of their lives turning into a nightmare, of literally losing everything they held dear and watching their society collapse and implode around them into an endless circle of decay, violence and anarchy.

But by their hard work, perseverance – and in always never losing sight of their dreams – and what could be - they had clung to their visions of the future through thick and thin – and by clinging to each other, supporting each other, no matter how hard life got, they had held on and lived to see the beginnings of the future they so wished to bring into being.

Cami was right – everyone needed something to believe in. Something to give them hope. Purpose. Meaning. A direction in their lives. Without that, they would be lost. Vulnerable. Their lives out of balance, living day to day without going forward due to the absence of any goal.

All the Mall Rats, as well as Bray and Amber, more than ever before, still had a sense of purpose. And Bray and Amber realized the importance of their future dreams as they walked along the beach, the seagulls flying overhead, watching them in great fascination.

All important to Bray and Amber was that they and the Mall Rats always kept their dreams alive.

* * *

Back in Eagle Mountain, the *K.A.M.I* computer in the cavernous vault in the lower levels of the scientific facility suddenly sprung to life, lights twinkling in the darkness, as a voice boomed through its audible facilities. The voice of its sister *K.A.M.I* prototype, located in the lower levels of Project Eden.

"THIS IS THE CREATOR. ADAPT. EVOLVE. DEFEAT. SURVIVE," the voice said. It was a familiar voice. The voice of Cami's mother…

Keeping The Dream Alive

by

Raymond Thompson.

The fascinating inside story about the making of the cult television series, The Tribe.

An intriguing memoir charting the life and times of how someone growing up on the wrong side of the tracks in a very poor working class environment in post-War Britain was able to journey to the glittering arena of Hollywood, providing an inspirational insight into how the one most likely to fail at school due to a special need battled and succeeded against all the odds to travel the world, founding and overseeing a prolific international independent television production company.

With humorous insight into the fertile imagination of a writer's mind, the book explores life away from the red carpet in the global world of motion pictures and television - and reveals the unique story of how the cult series 'The Tribe' came into being. Along with a personal quest to exist and survive amidst the ups and downs and pressures of a long and successful career as a writer/producer, culminating in being appointed an Adjunct Professor and featuring in the New Years Honours List, recognized by Her Majesty Queen Elizabeth II for services to television.

The Tribe: A New Dawn

by

A.J. Penn

Following the many challenges in the best selling novel, 'The Tribe: A New World', the Mall Rats find themselves faced with an even greater struggle as they try to unravel the many unexplained mysteries they now encounter - in the equivalent of Season 7 in the continuing saga.

What was the real mission of the United Nations survival fleet? Who is the enigmatic leader of the Collective? What really did occur at Arthurs Air Force Base? Is there something more sinister to the secrets revealed on the paradise island where they are now stranded?

Forced to resolve the agonizing conflict in their personal lives, the Mall Rats must also decide which path to take and whether or not to confront the ghosts of their past in their battle to survive against an ominous adversary. With the very real threat of human existence becoming extinct, can they endure against all odds to secure a future and the promise of a better tomorrow? Or will they suffer the same fate as the adults who had gone before and perish?

The tribe must fight not only for their lives but face their greatest fears to prevent the new world plunging further into darkness - and ensure hope prevails in a new dawn. And that they keep their dream alive.

The Tribe: A New World

by

A.J. Penn

The official story continues in this novel, set immediately after the conclusion of season 5 of The Tribe television series, with The Tribe: A New World effectively becoming Season 6 in the continuing saga.

Forced to flee the city in their homeland - along with abandoning their dream of building a better world from the ashes of the old - the Mall Rats embark upon a perilous journey of discovery into the unknown.

Cast adrift, few could have foreseen the dangers that lay in store. What is the secret surrounding the Jzhao Li? Will they unravel the mysteries of The Collective? Let alone overcome the many challenges and obstacles they encounter as they battle the forces of mother nature, unexpected adversaries, and at times, even themselves? Above all, can they build a new world in their own images - by keeping their dream alive?

The Tribe: Birth Of The Mall Rats

by

Harry Duffin

The Birth of The Mall Rats is the first story in a compelling series of novelizations of the global cult television phenomenon, The Tribe.

The world began without the human race. Now, after a mysterious pandemic decimates the entire adult population, it looks as if it will end exactly the same way. Unless the young survivors – who band together in warring Tribes – overcome the power struggles, dangers and unexpected challenges in a lawless dystopian society to unite and build a new world from the ashes of the old.

Creating a new world in their own image – whatever that image might be…

FOR MORE INFORMATION

Please visit the official website

www.tribeworld.com

"Like"
on
facebook.com/thetribeofficial

twitter.com/thetribeseries

instagram.com/thetribetvseries

youtube.com/thetribetvseries

The Tribe:
(R)Evolution

A.J. PENN

CUMULUS PUBLISHING LIMITED

CPSIA information can be obtained
at www.ICGtesting.com
Printed in the USA
LVHW090218040321
680556LV00009B/33

9 780473 501259